THE BIG BAD WOLF BOOK 4

DEATH TOLL

13 PITCH BLACK CATS

PROLOGUE.

YOU CAN'T OUTRUN DEATH

Terrin placed his hands on his temples and rubbed them in a vain attempt to wake himself up and stave off his growing headache.

Last night, goblins had performed the world's most horridly coordinated raid. They'd been barely armed, they didn't have anything to carry their loot, and they looked far too exhausted to be raiding. They didn't even seem all that interested in attacking the keep. Killing them had been more of a chore than a matter of national security.

Regardless of his feelings on the matter, Terrin was sent to interrogate their one prisoner. She was feisty, even for a goblin. The other guards had probably used more rope than needed to restrain her, but after she bit Nicholas, all niceties were forgotten.

"Three years, that's all I signed up for," Terrin said to himself as he stood outside the room where they'd stashed the goblin. He didn't bother stifling his yawn. "I'm gonna have to take a nap later." It was time to go to work. The goblin wasn't going to interrogate herself.

He took a deep breath and straightened himself. He didn't want the goblin to know that he was tired and had been woken up far too early.

He grabbed the lantern by the door and walked in.

The first thing he noticed was the rancid smell of feces. The second thing he noticed was the grayish-green-skinned creature hissing at him in the corner.

Terrin stood in the doorway, questioning all of his life choices up to this point. Deciding insubordination wasn't something he wanted on his record one season before his tour of duty was up, he strode in but left the door open. He wanted all the fresh air he could get.

The goblin in the corner continued to hiss at him like an animal, not at all like the supposedly sentient humanoid she was said to be. She was short—maybe thirty-five inches tall. The other guards had wrapped much of her body in coarse rope, but from what Terrin could see, she was far too thin to be considered healthy. Her face was slightly round and would have been cute on a little girl if it weren't for the line of tiny, sharp needles in her mouth.

Terrin reflexively touched the arming sword at his hip to reassure himself he wasn't defenseless. With his confidence bolstered, he placed the lamp on the hook just inside the door before standing in the center of the room.

He crossed his arms and stared down at the goblin. "So, are you going to be cooperative, or are you going to make things difficult for yourself?"

"What I do is no longer meaningful." The goblin's shrill voice grated in Terrin's ears. He held back a twitch as the goblin continued to speak. "You call us raiders, but you do not understand."

"Of course we don't understand. That was the worst-executed raid in the history of raids." Terrin's quip earned him another hiss from the goblin. "So, if it's that big of a deal, how about you enlighten me?"

"Why should I?" The goblin lowered her tone. "You are all going to die. All you have done is saved him the trouble of hunting us down. He is still coming for us. Now he will come for you."

Terrin raised an eyebrow. "Who's coming? Who's chasing you?"

The goblin grinned. "Death."

The man rolled his eyes. "Can you be a little more specific? Who's coming to kill you?"

"Death," the goblin repeated.

Sighing, Terrin turned to walk away. "Here I thought you were gonna be cooperative, but if you're going to be cryptic, we'll see how cryptic you'll be after staying here in the dark, alone in your own filth for a day or two. Let's see if that loosens your tongue."

"You think you are safe here?"

Terrin turned back to face the goblin. "Are you threatening us?"

The goblin's grin widened. "I am not the one who threatens you. It is him."

"Who's him?"

"Death."

Terrin rubbed the side of his face with a groan. "And we're back where we started."

"You think your stone walls will stop him?" the goblin continued. "You will not stop him. He will kill everyone. He killed all the goblins, and now they serve him."

"What did you just say?" Terrin hoped he didn't hear her correctly.

The goblin's voice dropped terrifyingly low. "You will die, and your corpse will only add to his army. Death comes for you, and there is no stopping him. I will die happily knowing that you will all die before me."

The color drained from his face.

Without a second thought, Terrin left the creature in her corner and sprinted for his sergeant's office. While running through the fort towards the barracks, a voice called out to the panicking guard.

"Oi! Where are you running to?" the shortest human in the fort, Nicholas, called out to Terrin. "Where's the fire?"

Nicholas was quite short. He was so short that he was often teased for being half-dwarf. No record of such a person existed since if a dwarf had a child with another race, the child would be the same race as the mother. A fact Terrin only knew because his cousin was a dwarf.

Terrin held up his bandaged hand as he ran towards his friend. "It's worse." Terrin stopped. "I need you to send a message to the king. And I need you to do it now. If that goblin isn't lying, then this is bad. I've got to tell the sergeant."

Nicholas grabbed Terrin. "How about you start by telling me what needs to go in the message and why it's so important? Also, why do you care what that filth says? Of course it's lying."

Terrin shook his head. "No, she didn't look like lying was even an option. She was all too happy to tell me."

Nicholas held out his hand. "So…"

"Right." Terrin took a deep breath. "It's a necromancer. She said he's headed this way. And he already has an army of goblin undead."

Nicholas stiffened. "Go, before you do anything else. I'll get that message sent immediately. No, wait. We need to burn the bodies right now."

Terrin pointed to the pile of goblin bodies the other guards had stacked outside, near the fort's entrance. "Go then. Take whoever you run into."

Nicholas nodded as he sprinted towards the nearest oil lamp. Terrin returned to his previous mission of finding the sergeant. But just as he reached the barracks door, there was a series of shouts from the watchtowers. Terrin turned to look at the guard calling from his wooden post.

"Goblins!" An elven scout pointed in the direction the goblins always came from. "That isn't a raid; it's an army."

"She was right," Terrin whispered to himself. "We are going to die."

As per protocol, the warning bells sounded, attempting to rouse whichever poor souls had tried to go back to sleep after the night's previous disturbance.

The door next to Terrin opened as he stared at the bells tilting from side to side. He jumped as the sergeant nearly knocked him over.

"Terrin?" The massive sergeant grabbed Terrin's shoulders as soon as they collided. And as soon as the guard had his feet firmly planted under him, Terrin lifted his head towards the sergeant's. "Situation report, soldier."

"Sergeant Sadon, sir, we have a problem." Terrin saluted the superior officer. "It's…"

"Goblin army approaching," the call interrupted Terrin.

"Actually, sir, it's worse." Terrin slumped his shoulders.

Sargent Sadon raised an eyebrow. "How does it get worse than an army of goblins?"

Terrin chuckled. "An army of undead goblins led by a necromancer." He chuckled again.

Sadon grabbed the soldier's shoulders and shook him once he noticed the guard's stare was emptying. "Get ahold of yourself, soldier." He shook him harder after he got no response. "Snap out of it." The guard's eyes moved to look into his superior's. "Are you sure? How do you know?"

"The goblin said so." Terrin's voice was still distant. "The one you ordered me to question. Yeah, that's the one. She said it was Death that chased them. She said that Death was coming for us. And that we were going to die and add to his army. She was right. We're all going to..."

His words died in his throat as a pair of screams came from the gate.

Nicholas tumbled through the gate with a goblin whose entrails were dragging behind her. She'd bitten into his shoulder. The man punched her in the face with his bandaged hand. Another goblin jumped from behind and tackled the two. The three hit the ground, and the new addition took her arm and held Nicholas's head back as she bit down on the other shoulder.

Nicholas's screams grew as a third goblin piled on top and started slashing at his flesh with her meager claws. Nicholas kicked and tried pushing the goblins off him, but his screams died off as a fourth goblin zombie jumped onto the pile.

The guards drew their weapons to save their comrade, but as they got closer, Nicholas grew weaker and eventually stopped moving.

Sadon shouted orders and pointed towards the gate as he drew his sword.

Terrin stared at the undead ripping his friend apart. He had seen his share of bloody combat, but seeing the dead kill his closest friend shattered something inside him. He couldn't look away or move to help.

As he stood there and watched, more zombies flooded into the fort.

Guards filed out of the barracks and didn't bother helping Terrin after they knocked him to the ground. He just sat up and watched the scene play out before him.

The soldiers attacked the zombies, but the zombies didn't bother defending themselves. They took the attacks without concern as they clamored for the living. Swords hacked at limbs and beheaded the goblins—it was one of the few ways to kill the undead permanently.

The undead pressed on, swarming the knights one by one. Biting, clawing, and tearing. It didn't matter how the soldiers defended themselves, the zombies overwhelmed and slaughtered them.

Terrin remained seated on the ground, watching the carnage. He stared at his dead friend's pale face. The look of fear and pain burned itself into the guard's mind. But when Nicholas's jaw twitched, Terrin's first thought was to wonder whether his friend was truly dead.

Nicholas stumbled to his feet. His body moved in jerky movements at first, but they quickly became more fluid and natural. When he turned to look at Terrin, the living guard saw no recognition in his friend's eyes. They just stared ahead, empty.

Terrin watched Nicholas walk towards him and pick up a discarded sword from another fallen soldier. Every instinct in his being told him to run away, but he couldn't. His muscles tightened as his friend approached him slowly. More of the fallen soldiers of the fort stood up and grabbed their weapons before turning on their comrades.

Nicholas stopped right in front of Terrin and lifted the bloody sword. Terrin shook as he stared at his friend, unable to draw his own weapon. When the sword finally dropped, Terrin rolled to the side. The blade buried itself into the ground as Terrin scrambled to his feet.

Nicholas pulled the blade from the ground and swung it towards Terrin. Terrin stepped backwards, and the blade missed disemboweling him by inches.

Terrin gave his friend one last look before he turned towards the gate and ran. He could see more of his friends fighting and dying, only to stand again and join the invaders. But only one thought remained in the soldier's mind.

He needed to run.

Maybe if he could make it somewhere and warn the kingdom, they could end this nightmare.

The man ran past everyone, dodging through the ever-growing enemy numbers, and ran out the gate. He didn't look back; he couldn't. He ran, and he continued to run. Step after step, the sounds of battle died down. He didn't dare slow down in case one of them was following him.

Terrin ran until he heard the distinct sounds of hooves galloping towards him. Hope swelled even more as he thought that someone else had survived and grabbed a horse on the way out. He slowed down and turned to hail the rider.

He shouldn't have.

The rider wasn't anyone from the fort. They weren't a man or woman. A black horse with smoke coming from its hooves galloped far faster than any horse Terrin knew. Atop the mount sat a suit of plate armor, almost as dark as the horse. But one detail about the armor told a story nobody wished to hear.

There was no head.

Where the head should have been, a red, bloody stump stood out against the black plate armor around it. In the creature's hand was a scythe made of bones. The blade was easily as long as the rider's arm, protruding from the mouth of a skull that sat at the end of a spine. Something radiated from the evil weapon, something Terrin couldn't see but could feel from afar.

All rationality left Terrin's mind as he turned and ran until something hit him in the back. He didn't fall to the ground. But when he tried to run, he couldn't move. His legs felt like they weren't there.

Terrin looked down and saw the weapon's spine coming out of his stomach and holding him up, its tip buried in the ground. Pain flooded his mind moments before his screaming started. He grabbed the weapon, attempting to pull it from himself. As he did, he could feel his strength deteriorating rapidly. It wasn't until he heard hooves clopping next to him that he finally looked away from the weapon that hurt so much.

The headless creature dismounted and stood over the poor

soldier. Even without a head, it was taller than most humans. Each step the rider took unnaturally crunched the ground underneath.

It grabbed Terrin by the front of his gambeson and lifted him up.

"You will not escape me." A deep voice echoed from the headless creature. "I am inevitable. All will fall before me, for I am Death."

Every word the creature said to Terrin flooded through his mind. He now knew he was wrong. It wasn't a necromancer; it was something far worse.

Death grabbed his weapon with one hand and pulled it through Terrin. Half of Terrin's body exploded in a shower of blood as the other half held his legs to his torso.

Terrin's vision quickly disappeared as he barely screamed before his life ended.

1

SIBLING SPAT

There are some days when no amount of violence is sufficient to placate my insatiable rage, and today was one of those days.

I paced back and forth in the living room, begging some idiot to knock on the front door so I could rip them apart. I wasn't allowed outside right now because I didn't trust myself, especially if I saw Victor.

Lexia cried in her room, continuing her daily streak of breaking down in tears over her decision. My recent comments might not have helped in that regard. An empty feeling in my gut and my instincts clawing at the back of my mind made thinking nearly impossible—something I was desperately trying to do.

How do I say I'm sorry for the fifth time this week? At some point, she isn't going to believe those words. I know what I said was mean, and I meant it, but I didn't mean to say it so harshly.

I grabbed my head and growled. It took a lot of willpower to keep myself from raking my claws across my face out of guilt. That, and the nearly irresistible urge to find Victor and beg him to impregnate me, were mentally pulling me apart.

This is just another part of being a woman beastkin. Lexia is going through the same thing. There's no reason to bite her head off. She's doing this of her own volition. All she wants to do is help.

I stopped pacing, but my tail flicked behind me. I took a deep breath. Slowly, I moped to my sister's room. Her wailing had been easy to hear throughout the house before, but she had mellowed to a quiet sobbing. When I entered the room, I stared at my twin sister.

The light from the window glistened off her silver fur as she lifted her head from the pillow she held. She stared at me with shimmering blue eyes. Tears soaked the fur on her face, but her beauty wasn't marred in the slightest as she sniffled.

I watched her two triangle-shaped ears flatten as her expression turned aggressive. She growled at me as she bared her human-looking teeth. After a few moments of me just staring at her, she threw the pillow away, stood on her digitigrade feet, and coated her arms, hands, and claws in ice.

"I'm..." I started to apologize.

Lexia's tail stopped for a moment before she pounced at me. I sidestepped her easily, moved behind her, and pushed her to the ground—all before she'd realized I moved.

I may have screwed up. But I don't deserve to be attacked. I'm going to have to beat some sense into you, aren't I?

I jumped on her back and growled, baring my wolf-like teeth next to her ear.

Lexia growled, turning her head. Her body glowed from the magic she channeled. A pillar of ice erupted from the ground by her outstretched arm and slammed into my side.

Her attack pinned me against the wall. I clawed at the icy pillar as Lexia stood up. Her tail flicked behind her as she walked around her creation towards me. I started slamming my hands into the ice, and cracks appeared. Each time I hit the ice, more cracks appeared, and the previous ones grew.

After the fifth time I struck the pillar, ice encapsulated my hands, binding them to the block.

I pulled hard and shattered the ice, and I saw Lexia stumble backwards like someone had punched her in the face.

Seeing her magic aura dissipate, I channeled my magic to break off the piece of ice holding me against the wall. Lexia's eyes went wide as I threw the block of ice towards her. She ducked the projectile, but she didn't avoid me. I tackled her and pinned her to the ground again.

This time I noticed her using magic, so I lifted her off the ground and threw her against a wall. She bounced off the wall and somehow stayed on her feet. I growled and pounced on her.

Lexia turned and dove for the open door. I dug my claws into the wood floor and followed her. My sister dropped to all fours and ran out of the room.

When I left the room, I halted, a sphere of ice missing my face by inches. I turned and glared at Lexia. She stared at me, holding another ice ball. My vision turned red as I growled.

My sister backpedaled as she launched her icy projectiles, only to create more before sending them towards my face. I dodged each one as they flew towards me, but Lexia used them to keep me from sprinting towards her and ending it. There was eventually enough space for me to close the gap to where she couldn't use her magic to throw them at me.

I took the opening, and Lexia attempted to strike me in the gut with her knee. My hand caught her attack while the other slammed into her chest. She dropped to her knees as she gasped for air. I grabbed her throat and bared my fangs.

The front door opened, and I barely had a moment to recognize who walked in. My vision returned to normal as I saw my mother, Nora Stormleaf.

"Enough!" Mom's voice shook the world.

I grabbed my ears and fell to my knees. Lexia did the same.

Mom stomped her way over to us and grabbed a cheek in each hand. "You two will stop it this instant. Am I clear?"

The two of us whimpered as the elven woman who'd adopted us curbed all aggression.

"Yes, Mom." Lexia's voice was weak, but she sounded like she had mostly regained her breath.

Mom turned and glared at me.

"Yes, Mom," I mimicked my sister.

Our adoptive mother released us and put her hands on her hips, taking a step back. "You are going to tell me what this is about. And this had better be good."

Lexia and I rubbed our cheeks as we flinched away from the woman who sent both our instincts into flight mode.

Sit." Mom pointed to the couch.

We're in so much trouble.

We slinked to the couch, sitting as far away from each other as possible.

"She started it," Lexia said as she pointed a finger at me.

I flattened my ears and pointed back. "But you started the fight."

"Knock it off!" Mom's tone left the two of us cowering. She sighed as she sat in a chair across from us. "Now, I know you're both in heat right now, but you need to stop acting like children and start at the beginning."

I picked at my claws as I stared at the suddenly very interesting groove I'd gouged into the floor earlier this week. Lexia stayed silent as well.

There's no way I'm getting out of this without a punishment. Maybe if I don't talk, Mom will just give up and drop it.

"Neither one of you wants to talk? Fine, you want to act like children, I'll treat you like children." I heard Mom stand up. "Lexia, go to your room."

Great, there goes that plan.

I turned and saw Lexia walk towards her room with her head down and her tail wrapped around her leg.

Mom stepped in front of me with her arms crossed. My instincts screamed at me to run, but I knew better.

I'm in trouble, and running will only make things worse.

"You can start at any time," Mom said.

I wrapped my tail around my waist and held it tight. "You don't know what it's like. All of my emotions are just so... so much."

Mom sat on the couch next to me. "I've dealt with your mating season for three years now. And this is the first time I'm dealing with hers. While I don't know what it feels like, I know that this is different. You and your sister were fighting, again. Why?"

I stared straight ahead. "I just wanted to apologize."

"For?" Mom leaned forward to look me in the eye.

I closed my eyes. "For calling Gifford weak. And for saying that if she can't handle it, she should just forget about helping me." *And now for the part she's really ticked off about.* "Then I said something about how she'll never be ready to join me on missions for The Maidens at this rate."

"Lucia." Mom sounded disappointed, and when I opened my eyes, I could see the disappointment too. "Your sister cares for you. I know you know that. She wants to help. Are you upset that she joined The Maidens too? Do you not want her help?"

I ducked my head further into my shoulders. "No."

"And your sister could have run to Gifford at any time, gotten pregnant, and ended this. But she hasn't." Mom put a hand on my chin and turned my head to face her. "And why is that?"

"Because she heard about the demon king's impending arrival and wants to help. And she agrees that if she's pregnant or caring for pups, she won't be able to." *It really is all my fault.*

"Nobody is making her do this. Try to be supportive of her." She pulled me close and wrapped an arm around my shoulders. "I know you want to protect your sister. But maybe to protect her, you should let her help you more. She's shown great progress in her magic over these last eight weeks. I'd say she's one of the more powerful combat mages in the city now. You can't do everything on your own. One day, you will need her help. Remember all those things you told Aurtour about Evalana during the tournament five years ago?"

I flinched. "You just had to bring that up, didn't you?"

"Is it getting my point across?"

I sighed. "Yes."

"Are you going to behave?"

"Yes, Mom."

Mom stood up. "How much longer is this going to be?"

I curled my tail around me as I held it close. "Tomorrow should be the last day."

"Come on, get up." She held out a hand for me to grab. I looked at her, confused. "Aren't you going to apologize?"

13

I grabbed her hand and rolled off the couch to my feet. Mom gave me a smile before she turned and led me towards Lexia's room. My padded feet didn't make any sound, but Mom's boots announced our coming as we walked through the hall littered with spheres of hail.

Mom waved her hand and opened the door before we arrived. Lexia was sitting on the edge of the bed, digging her toe claws into the floor. She looked up at us when we entered.

Mom extended an arm towards Lexia. "Well, Lucia? Aren't you going to say something?"

I scratched my toe claws across the floor. "Sorry, sis."

"I'm sorry too," Lexia replied sorrowfully. "I didn't mean to attack you. It was just that I was so angry about the things you said. I couldn't stop myself."

I chuckled. "Yeah, I know what that's like."

Lexia wrapped her arms around her gut. "It's this mating season. Our emotions, our everything, is just more intense."

"I know exactly how you feel," I said reflexively.

A chuckle escaped my sister. "Yeah, I know you know."

Mom gave me a slight shove towards my sister. "Now that mess is dealt with…" I turned to see her with her arms crossed. "You two are going to clean this mess up while I go and make lunch. The longer you take to clean, the more your meat is going to cook."

Lexia shot to her feet. "Yes, Mom. Right away, Mom."

"Anything but that," I said as I held out my hands.

Mom smiled. "Then get to work." She turned and left.

The moment I heard Mom's footsteps enter the kitchen, I turned to face my sister. "Let's hurry."

Lexia nodded and immediately started channeling her magic to lift the pillar she'd created off the floor and shape it into a sphere. I ran out of the room into the hallway and collected the spheres, using my magic to consolidate them into one with a handle. After we collected all the ice, we stared at each other.

"What do we do with them?" Lexia asked. "Throw them outside?"

I shrugged. "Sure."

We went to the window in her room and shaped the ice to fit through before dumping it to melt in the warm air. While we stared absently at the chunks of ice, Lexia placed a hand on my shoulder.

"Are we good?" she asked.

"Yeah, we're good." I gave her a smile. "This has been rough for both of us. Let's just get through tomorrow without saying or doing anything stupid."

"It's not like you really hurt me." Lexia smiled back. *Oh, really?* I poked her in the stomach. She doubled over, clutching the spot I'd touched. "Okay, maybe you got one good hit in. But you have to admit, I made you work for it."

I nodded. "You did."

She gave me a knowing grin as she leaned forward. "Does that mean I'm better at fighting than you thought? I told you, I'm ready for missions. Captain Aenwyn thinks so too."

"Maybe I just want to keep my happy family together." I let my ears droop slightly. "Sorry, sis, again. These last dozen weeks since you followed me here and let Mom adopt you have been like nothing I've ever had. All my life, I've had no one around who knows what it's like. But that's not true anymore. You're here, and all I want is for you to stay safe." I gave my sister a hug as she straightened up. "Why do we keep fighting with each other? You've always been the more sensible of the two of us. Me? I'm... I am..."

Lexia chuckled. "Because my sis is an emotionally unstable ball of uncontrollable rage." She gave me a mischievous smile and a wink. "Maybe I have a little of that rage in me too."

"Okay, that's fair," I said, nodding. "But enough fooling around. Let's make sure Mom doesn't cook the meat too much longer."

We laughed as we headed for the kitchen.

Lexia looked at me from the corner of her eye and hummed.

"What?" I asked.

She smiled and put her hands behind her head. "You're more relaxed now. Maybe you've been penned in here too long."

I paused for a moment. *Huh, she's right. I know Captain Aenwyn told me to take some time off, but that might have been the wrong move.*

I'll need to talk to her to see if I can get a quick mission. Something to do and maybe take my sister along. I smiled. *Yeah, that sounds way better than sitting at home.*

2

SOME PEOPLE'S KIDS

"Are you two feeling better?" Mom asked as she placed a pair of cups in front of Lexia and me.

Lexia and I sat at the table for breakfast, mirroring each other. We rested our heads on our arms as we leaned on the table. Yesterday, we'd locked ourselves in our respective rooms, not leaving unless it was to eat or use the bathroom. And after two weeks of everything running on eleven, we were too tired to move now.

Breakfast helped. Mom gave me an uncooked liver and Lexia lightly cooked sausages and eggs. *She can have the eggs.*

"A bit," Lexia said, not lifting her head off the table.

"Not really." I buried my face in my arms. "I kinda want to spend the day alone."

Mom started scratching my back. "Ah, sweetie, you don't want to go out and hunt, or maybe go and see Evalana while she's visiting?"

"I sorta want to meet Evalana." Lexia took a drink. "Why haven't we heard anything about her being here?"

Mom grinned mischievously. "I've kept it quiet. Given Evalana's condition, it was best if Lucia wasn't so aggressive."

I slammed my cup onto the table. Thankfully, I didn't hit it too hard and break either the cup or the table. "Her condition? What happened?" I jumped up and grabbed Mom's shoulders. "Tell me what's wrong with my friend."

She just grabbed my wrists and patted them. "It's alright. She's in a little pain, but that's expected. There's nothing wrong. But she is a little pregnant. So she can't move too much before she exhausts herself. You need to behave yourself."

I performed an exaggerated pout. "Fine. I'll behave."

"I guess that's all the progress I'll get out of you today, isn't it?" Mom slumped her shoulders. "Are you still wanting to stay home and not go anywhere? We can go see her tomorrow, if that's the case."

Lexia waved her hand. "Nah, she can just take a nap and she'll be ready to go in no time."

"What about you?" I pointed to my sister. "You're just as tired as I am. I'll recover faster. You shouldn't feel obligated to follow me around."

Lexia smiled. "I'll be fine. It's so nice of you to care. But that nap sounds nice." She started staring wistfully at the ceiling.

"Go take a nap, girls. We can visit her for lunch." Mom grabbed the empty cups and waved her hands towards the bedrooms. "I'll let Evalana know your plans while I'm in town."

Lexia turned to Mom and wagged her tail. "What are you going to do today? I didn't know you had a job today. Can I come with?"

Mom flicked her wrist, and the cups glided towards the sink. "What happened to that nap, young lady?"

"But I like watching you use magic. You can do so much." Lexia bounced from one foot to the other. "Watching you use earth magic to help with the gate repairs was amazing."

I couldn't hold back a smile as my sister gushed over our mother's control of magic.

Mom couldn't either. "I know you love to watch me use magic, honey. But I don't think Boris and Brann would like it if I brought you two along."

"And why would I be coming along?" I asked.

Mom gave me a sidelong smirk. "Because if you learned that I took your sister to hunt rats and didn't take you, I would never hear the end of it."

My mother, the most powerful mage in the kingdom, is reduced to hunting rats in a local tavern's cellar. Yes, it's the largest and most prestigious tavern, but even still, that's a little demeaning. It makes sense for Lexia and me since we love hunting things—I'm way better at it than her—but the most important question is... "Why wouldn't they like it if we came?"

Mom turned to face me, crossed her arms, and glared. "Because the last time I took you, you ate the rats in the middle of the dining room on the way out."

I shrugged. "They make a great snack. And I worked up an appetite catching them."

Mom's glare darkened. "You offered a woman a half-eaten rat."

"She wouldn't stop staring at me. Maybe she wanted to try it."

"She fainted."

"So?"

"You know better, and the fact that you laughed the entire way out the door proved you did," Mom said through her clenched teeth.

I gave Mom a sheepish grin. "It was kinda funny."

Lexia snorted as she tried to cover her laughter. When Mom glared at her, too, she copied my grin. "It was."

Mom dropped her arms and rolled her eyes. "Kids."

I scurried up to my mother and hugged her. "But we're your kids, and you love us."

Lexia joined in. "And we love you too."

"You're right," Mom said as she hugged us close. "But I know when you're manipulating me," she whispered in our ears.

"Is it working?" I asked in the same whisper while wagging my tail.

I could see the internal struggle on her face. She wanted to say "no," but our combined cuteness was too much for her to deny us outright.

"Yes." Our mother squeezed us tighter. "But not as much as you want it to," she quickly added.

"I think I'll check up on Fina later today too," I said as we broke up the family hug. "She's probably feeling pretty down."

"Absolutely." Mom shoved us towards the bedrooms.

As if on cue, Lexia yawned. "Yeah, I think I'll take that nap now. Sis's probably already feeling better." She headed towards her bedroom. "I'm a bit jealous of her recovery aptitude."

"Coming from the one who learned how to read in one day." I tapped my chin. "You know what? You're right. I am feeling better. I guess I don't need that nap."

"Alright, you two." Mom stepped in between the two of us. "You're each special in your own way. Even as twins, you both excel in areas the other doesn't." She turned and pointed at me. "If you're feeling better, why don't you go see Fina now? I'm sure she really wants someone to talk to right now."

"Tell her 'hi' for me, would you?" Lexia called as she resumed her march to her bed.

"I will." I waved my hand. "Sleep tight. We'll get you for lunch. Evalana will definitely treat us to something special."

I grabbed my blue magical cloak that was decorated with yellow snowflakes embroidered on the edges. I held it out and hummed.

Mom wrapped the cloak around my shoulders and tied the strings. "Okay, sweetie. Just take it easy today. If you decide you want to go hunting, take your sister. I don't care if she's still sleeping. Don't go into the forest alone."

"Why?"

"This last week there were rumors of an orc warband." Mom frowned. "The worst part is, nobody's been able to catch them. They move too quickly and intelligently. Something's not right about them."

"Then I would be the best one to track them down and catch them." *I haven't had a mission since I got back from the one to the Wild Kingdom. I've been itching to stretch my legs.* "But how do they know it's orcs? Has anyone been attacked?"

Mom shook her head. "No, some trackers found marks from their sleighs. How they got this far in again, I don't know. But it feels like that time when you showed up." I laughed. She stuck a finger in my face. "Don't get any ideas. I can see it in your eyes. You want to go find them. Don't, not unless Captain Aenwyn gives you the mission and you don't go alone." It suddenly became harder to breathe. "Promise me."

I stared at the finger inches from my nose. "I promise that I won't hunt the orcs unless Captain Aenwyn gives me the mission and I don't go alone." *Now I have something I can do, but I'll have to wait.*

The dark, foreboding feeling vanished immediately as my mother stood up straight and smiled. "Now be a good girl and go have fun cheering up your friend." Mom scratched the top of my head for a few moments before turning for the door.

I listened to the rhythmic sounds of my mother's footsteps as they steadily grew more distant. *This family is one I wouldn't trade for anything in this world. When it was just Mom and me, I thought it was great. Finding Lexia, however unlikely it was, has made our little family so much more... complete. Yeah, that's a good word, complete.*

After I walked out the back door and took a deep breath of the fresh air, I looked to my left and saw Lexia's window. *Even though Lexia and I had more than a reasonable amount of arguments over the last two weeks, it wasn't all our fault. Our biology has just made us more intense. We love each other, and we were never in danger of hurting each other too badly. If I were ever in trouble, there's nobody I would want at my back more than Lexia.*

I looked out at the field of potatoes still yet to be harvested. Our house sat on the edge of the farmland of a lovely family. They were nice to me since I was free pest control. *Normally, I charge for that kinda service.* The breeze ruffled the green leaves of the potatoes. *If I didn't know any better, I'd say this is as peaceful as things can get.*

I shook my head and walked towards the field. *That couldn't be further from the truth. The demon king is coming, and he has sins working on manipulating mortals to bring him to this world. I don't know what his plan is when he gets here, other than that it's supposed to be bad. At least that's what The Voice said when it sent me here.*

There was an unusual scent in the field as I walked around. It didn't smell like the usual small pests that hid and foraged in the crops. *Whatever it is, it can wait. Fina has probably been pretty lonely for the last two weeks. That's another reason to like Bosco and his wife, Lentilee. Taking in*

Fina like they did was strangely nice. Most humans would've let her wander around homeless. They gave her a job, food, and housing. She's basically a farmhand. It was to last only until she got her feet under her, but since their kids left home, they need the help. So I don't think Fina is going to leave them anytime soon. Besides, she seems pretty happy working for them.

I wrapped my hand around my wrist. A silver bracelet roughly an inch wide hugged my arm. *Victor... I'm so thankful you understand. We can't have kids, not while there's such an enormous threat looming over the world. I guess that's why you went and joined The Brilliant Crusade. And you needed a job. It was the only thing Allen could do to help you out. You and Gifford will one day be knights worthy of joining the fight. But until then, wait for us.*

I couldn't help but laugh. *We're one big family of knights. Mom was a knight for Excelsior. Then Lexia joined me in The Maidens. And both our mates joined The Brilliant Crusade. Fina might be the only normal one of us. She just wanted something quiet and peaceful.*

I stepped up to our neighbor's door and gave it a knock. The door opened and revealed a human woman. She was short, with curly black hair reaching her shoulders. Her heavily tanned skin was only outshined by her brown eyes, which looked like they would like nothing more than to go to sleep.

Her face held plenty of wrinkles, but her expression softened as she craned her head to look me in the eye.

"I didn't expect to see you today," Lentilee said. Her voice, while normally high-pitched, sounded as tired as her eyes looked. "But I'm glad you're here. Your friend..." She turned back to look inside. "She's a bit out of it. You told us what to expect, and she told us what to expect, but this isn't something I can't handle."

"What's wrong?" I pushed past her. "Where is she?"

"Hey. Watch where you're walking, girl." Lentilee stomped behind me. "But if you must know, she's been locked in her room all day, weeping." Her footsteps died down. "She won't come out for food. She's not talking to us. If it weren't for her sobbing, I'd question if she were still alive."

I glared at the woman. "You have locks on your doors?"

"No," a voice from another room called out. Heavier footsteps followed the voice, and another human joined us. "She blocked her door and window. The lady wants to be left alone."

Bosco looked old, and I imagined he felt old, as his shoulders were perpetually slumped forwards. His black hair had long since turned gray, almost matching his pale blue eyes. He looked like a worn piece of leather that had been left out in the sun without being properly treated.

"Crying alone in a room like that ain't healthy, you know that." Lentilee jabbed her finger through the air at her husband. "We can't just leave the poor girl like that."

The man pointed behind him with his thumb. "If you think you can help her, by all means, do."

Lentilee grabbed the edge of my cloak. "There's some food on the table for her. Some bread and butter with some fruit and a few pieces of fat that she likes."

Not a bad breakfast. "Fine, but I'm going to suggest you leave. She might want a bit more privacy."

Bosco flinched and paused for a moment. "Bah, whatever. I've planned to check the back fields, anyway." He grabbed his wife's shoulder as he walked by. "That, and we need to make sure we don't have any uninvited guests in the barn."

I stood and waited until the pair left the building before heading to where Bosco pointed. Everything was silent, but there was only one door closed. After I gave it a gentle rap, there was the sound of something being dragged across the floor.

When the sound stopped, the door opened. "I heard you," Fina said softly.

I stared at the lynx beastkin woman, and my heart pulled me towards her. She didn't look at anything but the floor in front of her feet as she held her wrist. A copper band similar to my silver band clutched to her arm—the symbol of her mourning her mate.

Poor Fina.

I extended a hand to the woman. "Do you want to talk about it?"

Fina didn't respond with words. She just jumped forward and wrapped her arms around me. I barely had the time to move my arms over her head as she clung to me. Her tears and sobbing spoke volumes. So I let her cry. There wasn't a reason to stop her. I embraced her and held her.

"It hurts." Fina then immediately fell into another bout of more sobbing. I took her words as progress of her working through her grief.

I closed my eyes. "I can only imagine."

After Silver died, I was a bit of a mess. He was someone I could call a friend, but he wasn't my mate. Fina lost her mate last year during the fire season. I never asked how; just asking her when was painful enough for her. And this was her first mating season without him. Every year, she'll be reminded of his death and how she won't be able to move on.

I rubbed her back with one hand and ran my other hand through her red hair. She slowly quieted down. After wiping her face on her arm, she straightened up and looked me in the eye.

"Sorry, but thank you," Fina said. She wrapped her tail around her waist as her stomach growled. "Um, food?"

I smiled. "Yes, Lentilee left you some."

Extending an arm towards the scent of food, I led Fina to the table. Her steps seemed a bit shaky. I noticed her leaning on me as she walked. It wasn't much to help hold her up, but I gladly did it.

She's just as fatigued as Lexia and me, maybe more so. She probably spent the morning crying. Actually, how much of the last two weeks has she spent crying? Like us, she probably didn't get out much. We helped around the house sometimes, but we never left.

Fina practically climbed into the chair with how slowly she was moving. I grabbed a chair and sat next to her, keeping a hand on her back while she ate. She saved the fat for last.

Fina has willpower that I don't.

After the last piece of fat entered her mouth, she almost looked content. Her eyelids drooped a bit, but that was likely because she was ready for a nap.

I watched Fina lick her fingers clean with her eyes closed. And while I was scratching her back, it felt like she was purring.

That's adorable. But any port in a storm. Maybe I'll stay with her while she naps.

Fina turned towards me after she finished cleaning her claws. "Can you stay? I need a nap."

It was hard not to smile at the woman. *Maybe if I smile enough, she will too.* "Of course. I help."

Fina flicked her ears to the side as she quickly snapped to look at the table. I thought I saw just the slightest hint of a smile.

"You help," she said in a whisper so quiet I barely heard her.

While we walked back to her room she wasn't leaning on me as much, but she never let go. I sat on the edge of her bed, and she curled up into a tight ball around her pillow. *Wow, she's flexible.* Even though there was a twelve-inch height difference between us, our tails were the same length. Her longer tail was an oddity for a lynx, but it seemed to suit her just fine.

Fina curled her tail around her legs to cover her face.

Her cuteness is irresistible.

I didn't move and watched her until I heard her breathing change into the rhythmic cadence of sleep. The more I watched her, the more my eyes felt heavy.

It wouldn't hurt to take a nap here. Lexia's taking one too.

Gently, I laid down on the bed next to the lynxkin. I didn't want to wake her, and I don't think I did. She stirred for a moment, nudging closer to me, and started purring, but her heart rate didn't change.

I closed my eyes and let myself drift to sleep.

A sinister laugh woke me up.

3

DISSENT AMONGST THE RANKS

I shot up, and Fina leaped out of the bed, her fur puffing out in every direction. After scrambling out of the bed, I watched Fina. Her eyes darted everywhere as her ears swiveled constantly.

The haunting laughter rang out again. *Why does that sound so familiar?*

Fina hunched over and extended her claws. I followed her lead. *It sounded like it came from outside. If Fina is expecting a fight, then I better be too.* I let my vision slip into my focused state. My vision turning red was almost comforting.

A third chilling giggling teased my ears. I was able to pinpoint it on the other side of the house. When I turned to look at Fina, she nodded. So I took the lead and headed towards her window.

We climbed out and crouched low. There was nobody around to see, but I heard footsteps heading towards us. Without looking at Fina, I waved my hand to tell her to get lower. Then it sounded like there was a flapping of wings.

"I know you're there, my pet," a husky feminine voice called out.

No way! I know that voice. She was dead, or close to it, wasn't she?

To spite me, the sin of lust flapped into view. But she didn't look like how I remembered her. *I know my memory isn't like my sister's, but it isn't that bad.*

The demon leaned forward, still flapping her wings. "Now I know what you're thinking, and the answer is yes. While I've learned something incredible, there were some—how should I say this—aesthetic alterations." She straightened up and waved her hands at her new cherry-red skin. There still wasn't an inch of cloth covering anything, exposing her to everyone. Her hooves were also a strange sight.

I created a spiked ball of ice and threw it at the demon's wing. She flicked her wrist, and a wave of water washed over the projectile and carried it away. There was a distinct scent of salt in the air.

The demoness pouted. "That wasn't friendly. I came here to chat, and you throw things at me."

I growled. "If you come down here, I will politely tear you apart limb from limb until you're nothing more than a pile of dismembered limbs that nobody will be able to put together."

She laughed. "I may have taken that rider's power, but I didn't inherit his stupidity. I'm not going anywhere near you."

"You want something," Fina called out from behind me.

The sin of lust grinned at us. "Ah, finally. Someone who uses her head for more than just wanton acts of visceral carnage. Although, even I can admire such acts." She gave me a wink. "But right now, I need you to do something for me."

I created two spiked ice projectiles and threw them one after another. The demon sighed and flapped her wings hard. My makeshift missiles flew harmlessly under her as she flew higher in the air.

"And why would I ever do anything for you?" *Come on. Why can't I hit her? Hold still.*

"This interests you too. But if you don't want to hear it..." The sin of lust shrugged and closed her eyes.

I created another spike and prepared to throw it, but Fina grabbed my arm.

She shook her head. "No good. If she wanted to hurt us, she would have done so as we napped."

"You really should listen to her. She uses her head." The demon pointed at Fina. "But back to business. There's another rider."

My vision returned to normal. "What? How?"

The demoness pinched the bridge of her nose. "Did you really think that Greed would put all her eggs in one basket? No, she had Envy working in another part of the continent. Envy summoned the Rider of Death. And he's headed this way."

"How do you know?" Fina asked.

"I'm bringing him here." The demon's nonchalant tone worried me. "I know something that I shouldn't. And the other riders won't take kindly to that. So they're drawn to kill me. But I want you to kill them first, or at least try to. Just like you did the Rider of Pain. He was delicious, by the way."

"He... He was dead." I turned to face Fina. "Wasn't he?"

I turned to face the demon when she started laughing. "Oh, my sweet, dear little pet. You have so much to learn." The demon wiped a tear from her eye before continuing. "An attack like the one your sister pulled off would certainly destroy a sin. But to kill a rider, you can't leave the body. You need to destroy them utterly."

"Thanks for telling me how to kill you and all your little friends." *Now just get down here so I can tear you apart.*

The succubus smirked before chuckling. "Knowing won't make it any easier. Also, I'm not friendly with them anymore. To them, I'm nothing more than an abomination that needs eliminating."

"Why tell us? Why now?" Fina tried to pull me back but couldn't.

The flying demon looked almost bored. "This might sound odd to you, but I don't want to die. Yes, if I die here, I'll return to the demon realm, but that is a fate worse than death. Here, I stand a chance to live."

There's something not right here. "But what's your goal? If you simply wanted to live, you wouldn't be acting like you want something more from us. You would just keep running away or hide." *I doubt she'll just answer me outright. She's been rather dodgy this entire time.*

"I want to kill the demon king," the demoness said with a straight face.

I shook my head. "You... what?"

Lust crossed her arms as she continued to hover. "You heard me."

I did, but I don't believe it. "Why?" *That's mine and Daric's job. I don't get it.*

"I've had the taste of true power, and now I simply want more." She turned her head and waved a hand. "My plan is to absorb the power from all four riders and challenge the demon king while he's in this world. Where our power would be the most equal."

Fina and I couldn't help but stare at the blatant declaration of a potential takeover.

The demon floated towards the ground. "Now you're wondering, why am I telling you this?" She didn't touch the ground, but she was close. "Because the enemy of my enemy is supposed to be my friend." She grimaced for a moment before forcing a smile again. "But seeing you so on edge makes me believe you're not my friend, but I'm not your biggest threat. And we might be able to work out an arrangement where both parties benefit."

I badly wanted to shove Fina back and charge Lust. My instincts were on the fence about it too. They really wanted to tear that smug look off her face, but something about her new form left me feeling cautious, more so now that she was closer to the ground.

I can't believe the words that are about to come out of my mouth. "What kinda deal?"

The demon's tail flicked behind her as her grin grew wide. She extended a hand. "So the big bad wolf can negotiate. I..."

"I haven't agreed to anything yet!" I snapped.

She recoiled her arm and stood silently for a moment. After she resumed her usual posture, she nodded. "You're right, you haven't agreed—yet." There was something about the way she said that last word that caused my fur to stand up. "I have no interest in this world. While having my pets here has been fun in the past, I don't want to limit myself. The demon king is obsessed with this world, but I can't figure out why."

It was hard not to interrupt her again after hearing about multiple worlds. *Does that mean there's a way to get to them? Can I go back to*

Earth? I shook my head. *Stop it, Lucia. Now isn't the time. Concentrate on the extra-powerful demon in front of you.*

"The deal is simple: help me become the new demon queen, and I'll leave your world in peace for as long as I reign." The demon's wing flapped hard, causing her to take to the sky again. "I don't expect an answer right now, but know that I'll be watching. You're going to help me one way or another. So why not get something out of it?"

"What's the big deal with this Death guy anyway?" My question caused the sin of lust to pause. "What does one demon, even if he's a rider, hope to do against an entire kingdom?"

The demoness grinned. "Because his two goals are to kill me and finish summoning the demon king." She pointed to herself with a slight bow while still hovering. "He's already gotten a huge head start by nearly wiping out the goblins. But the most dangerous thing about him is his ever-growing, limitless army of undead."

"He has an army?" I asked.

"Now do you see, my pet? I'm not your biggest threat." The demoness relaxed. "All this wasted animosity could be better spent on the Rider of Death. The enemy of my enemy is my friend, is it not?"

You will never be my friend! I created another ice spike and hurled it at her as hard as I could. She twisted and dodged it easily. The demon laughed as she turned invisible and hid the sound of her wings flapping.

I turned to look at Fina. "How am I going to explain this to Mom?"

4

OLD AND NEW FACES

I waved a hand towards my home. "Mom's going to want to hear about this. If you're there, you can help me explain everything."

Fina nodded. "It felt wrong. She looked wrong."

I nodded my head slightly. "Yeah. But maybe Mom will be able to help explain some of it. Or we might need to talk to Anna." I scratched the back of my head as I went home. "Do we need to make a deal with the devil to save the world? It'll be impossible to hunt her down. Also, the demon king sounds really powerful if she needs the power of the four riders to consider challenging him."

"Is it right to fight evil with evil?" Fina asked as she followed me.

"I don't know." My head started hurting. "We really should talk with my mom. If we tell Evalana, can the kingdom help?" I shook my head. "I'm getting distracted again."

We walked to my home together. *I hope Evalana didn't have to do anything today. She'll be able to take care of it after lunch.* My stomach grumbled. *Evalana will try to treat us to a super special, succulent lunch.*

I groaned. *Why is it that food always distracts me? Oh, right, I eat as much as two people. Feeding me would be impossible with a normal job where I didn't go hunting.*

Lexia was brushing her fur in the living room as a fire burned in the fireplace. When she noticed Fina and me walking in, she bolted to her feet and ran to hug the lynx beastkin. Seeing the mash of brown-and-silver fur, I didn't want to feel left out and joined in.

After we hugged for a bit, Lexia examined Fina. "How are you feeling?"

Fina's tail swayed behind her as she smiled lightly. "Better after a nap with Lucia."

Lexia turned to me and smirked. "So you did need a nap after all."

I shrugged. "So?"

Lexia rolled her eyes before turning her attention back to Fina. "Did my sis invite you for lunch?"

"No. We spoke to the demoness," Fina answered in an emotionless tone.

My sister's eyes went wide as she flinched backwards. Her tail whipped back and forth in tandem with her head. "She's here? Where? Why?"

I held out my arms. "Relax. It's okay, she wasn't interested in you. It was more like she wanted me to do something for her."

Lexia's head snapped to face me. "You didn't agree, right? You didn't. Never do it." I could see her hands shaking and her claws extending as shuffled her feet.

"I didn't agree to anything. Honestly, the things she told us were difficult to believe."

"But she had no reason to lie," Fina added.

I waved a hand towards my friend. "Yeah, but I can't help thinking she's not telling us everything. But what, I couldn't tell you."

Lexia rubbed her eyes with her palms. "Your life is way too complicated for a fifteen-year-old."

I slumped. "Tell me about it."

We heard the sound of footsteps approaching. "It sounds like Mom's home already," Lexia said as she turned to look out the window. "Is it really that late? Did I sleep that much?"

"My stomach says it is." I gave my sister a pat on the back. "But it's nice to hear you slept well. I'm going to grab my gambeson."

I shuddered after mentioning my gambeson. While I was on vacation and after hearing the entire story of my adventure in the Wild Kingdom, Mom demanded that I get some armor. And after trying practically every armor under the sun, the gambeson unfortunately was the most comfortable for me.

She also made me promise that if I ever went out on a mission, I would take it with me, and, more annoyingly, wear it. *After seeing the sin of lust, the orcs in the area sound dangerous. After lunch and talking with Evalana about getting a message to her brother about the Rider of Death, I want to ask Captain Aenwyn if I can help hunt them. She'll probably make me prove that I'm still in good condition. So I'd better come prepared for some sparring.*

Mom's footsteps ended in her usual rapid triple step before she entered. Lexia filled Mom in on why Fina was there. As expected, Mom didn't stay calm.

"Lucia, where are you?" Mom's shout was on the cusp of hurting my ears.

I flicked my ears back. "I'm right here. Everything is fine, mostly."

She looked at my hand. "What are you grabbing that for? Wasn't the plan to have lunch?" Her eyes went wide before she pointed a finger at me. "You aren't going after that demon. No. Even if your captain mobilizes her entire company."

I shook my head. "I doubt that will be enough to kill her anymore. She's more..." Fina's face didn't help me find the words I wanted to use. "She's not just more powerful. Before, she didn't seem to be the one in charge. Now she has a mission of her own, and she's fighting for her survival. Almost like she's cornered herself. And a cornered animal is the most dangerous animal."

Mom crossed her arms. "So you think she's more dangerous, and that's why you're not going after her? But if you're right, she'll need to be dealt with. It won't be easy or simple."

I turned and looked at the ground while scratching at it with my toe claws. "About that..." The room went silent. I could distinctly pick out the sounds of everyone's heartbeats. Mine was the fastest. "She wants to help kill the demon king."

"She does," Fina said to break the silence.

"That's..." Mom's voice trailed off.

"Hard to believe? Yeah, I know." I wrapped my tail around my waist. "Regardless of what we want to do about her, we have another, more immediate danger coming."

"You're just full of good news today," Mom said.

Trust me, I enjoy this as much as you do.

"But it's something Evalana is going to need to hear. So will the king." I hugged the gambeson tightly. *This thing's going to see a lot of use in the near future, isn't it?*

Mom sighed. "Because Fina was there, she's going to help fill in the details. Am I right?" I nodded. "I'm sure Evalana will be fine with one more for lunch. She already ordered extra food because of you. Come on, let's go. She's already said that she's plenty hungry." As we filed out of the house, Mom grabbed my shoulder. "So much for a quiet life, huh?"

I didn't answer and shrugged her hand off. My claws itched as I led the way towards the gates. Fina kept pace with me, and with how much she'd not moved recently, she enjoyed the chance to at least jog.

The guards gave us a worried look as I stormed past. After I entered the city, I realized that I didn't know where we were meeting Evalana for lunch. When Mom caught up, she waved for me to follow. So I did.

Mom led the three of us through the streets until we reached a rather extensive building in the wealthy part of town. All the windows held solid panes of glass. White-washed stone walls loomed over us for three stories. A pair of massive oak doors marked the entrance, with a sign above them saying, "The Silken Clouds."

I glared at Mom as Lexia grabbed my hand.

"She said we'll have a private room." Mom tapped my nose before I could say anything. "So don't throw a fit. We all know how much you don't like crowds."

I closed my eyes and tried to visualize a peaceful waterfall. There was a tingling sensation in my hand that held Lexia's. My arm felt cooler, and I could feel ice wrapping around it. I smiled at my sister as she cooled me down, and Fina grabbed my other hand. I turned and saw her staring at the door. She also looked like she was shivering.

The people walking around started watching us as we stood

outside the tavern. I squeezed Lexia's hand. When she turned towards me, I nudged my head towards Fina. With one look, Lexia released my hand and went to wrap an arm around the lynxkin's shoulders. Fina's shaking stopped immediately.

Mom opened the door once all three of us looked at it. *We're quite the sight, aren't we? I loathe crowds, Fina's scared of them, and Lexia needs to balance both of us.*

The cacophony of sounds that assaulted my ears once Mom opened the door nearly turned my vision red. As soon as we walked in, the elven hostess's eyes went wide before she ran towards the tables and bar, whispering to everyone to keep it down.

I guess having a reputation for violence can be nice. We stood and watched as, table by table, voices quieted down after most of them checked the door to see if the elven woman was telling the truth. Even the trio of musicians lowered the volume at which they played.

After the volume of the dining room was reduced to an almost acceptable level, the elf returned to greet us. She tried to hold back her heavy breathing. She was just below average height with an average build and face, but her hair was anything but average. Shiny red locks woven into an intricate braid danced behind her and reached just behind her knees.

That looks like a nightmare to care for.

The lady stood in front of Mom. "Sorry about that. My name is Yaprenzal. The dining room is nearly full, and the bar is full." Yaprenzal extended an arm towards the stairway. "Would you like one of our more private rooms? I promise they will be more quiet for you and your, um..."—she looked at us from the corner of her eye— "entourage."

Lexia and I both started growling. The elf squeaked and jumped backwards.

"My daughters and I are here to join Princess Evalana."

The elf shrank as Mom glared at her as she stood between us and the elf. "I'm so sorry. I didn't know you were Nora Stormleaf. Please forgive me. Please save me," Yaprenzal rambled as she lowered her head and raised her hands.

"Save you?" My growl silenced the room. Nobody even moved.

Lexia scraped her toe claws into the wood floor. "You don't deserve to be saved."

"Girls," Mom snapped as she held up a hand to us. "I suggest you treat beastkin with respect in the future. My daughters, while lovely and loyal, are short-tempered."

The elven hostess didn't lift her head. "You're right; I'm so sorry."

"Just take us to Evalana." I tapped my toe claw on the ground. The sound echoed through the still silent room.

"Yes, ma'am." The elf didn't lift her head as she headed to the stairway. "Right this way, ladies."

Just before I went up the stairs, I felt like someone was staring at me. I turned to see the human bartender glaring at me with one hand below the counter.

If you want to die that badly, bring it on. I bared my fangs for a moment before turning to follow the others up the stairs. The bartender didn't move. *I guess that'll save me some hassle explaining why I tore up a human in the middle of a tavern.*

Our guide led us to the second floor and towards the far end. She opened the door to reveal a table loaded with candles, empty plates, and utensils for seven people. All the chairs had cutouts for a tail. *She thought about that detail. This is why I like Evalana.*

Evalana sat in the corner of the room with all the curtains closed next to an out-of-place stone.

She wore a leaf-green silk dress. Its delicate, loosely tied fabric covered her bulging stomach. A wide red ribbon wrapped fairly low around her waist, below her pregnant stomach as if it were trying to hold up the baby. Below the ribbon, the green dress opened up to the left and revealed another dress below, a yellow one. The front of the bottom dress danced above the ground in the front, as the back continued to flow behind her and ended in a broad tip. One arm was covered in a long sleeve that opened up at the elbow, while the other sleeve ended abruptly just past the shoulder.

Standing next to her, glowing with magic, was another woman whom I'd never seen before. She was a human who looked about the same height as Evalana, but older. There were minute signs of wrinkles developing on her brow and cheeks. She was slightly heavyset, with a round face. With short, curly brown hair and brown eyes, she looked normal—until you saw her right arm. A spiral of music notes tattooed on her skin started from her shoulder and traveled down, ending on the back of her hand.

Daric was sitting at the table, looking bored. His auburn hair was shorter than when I last saw him. His squarish face lit up when I walked into the room. He stood up and punched his fist in the air.

"Finally!" he nearly shouted. "She's here. Time to eat."

A human male who looked like he was in the middle of pacing stopped midstride and glanced at Daric before turning his attention to us. When his eyes landed on me, his body went rigid.

Ah, Mr. Prissy-Pants, or Dante, as the rest of the world knows him.

The pudgy man—who had early onset male pattern baldness—stared at me like so many deer had done before. My instincts tugged at me to chase him down. I could see Lexia wanted to as well. His actions even earned Fina's attention. With three beastkin watching him, Dante backpedaled until his back hit the wall.

I leaned forward and let go of Fina as my tail went still.

"Lucia!" Evalana's delightfully cheery voice called out to me. She started moving to get out of her chair. With only one arm and being more than "a little" pregnant, Evalana struggled to stand up, so the other lady stepped up and helped her. "Thanks, Gwen."

"You should keep still." The older woman's voice was strangely similar to Mom's.

Evalana waved at the woman. "Stop worrying. Lucia's my friend. And what kind of friend would I be if I didn't give her a hug?" She placed her hand on the underside of her belly. "Besides, I've sat around plenty today. My butt's getting sore."

I turned to Mom. "She looks more than a little pregnant."

Mom just gave me a wink.

I rolled my eyes as I lost interest in hunting Dante. There was an odd scent in the air, and it got stronger the closer Evalana got.

She waddled towards me with the fussy old lady behind her. Evalana stretched her arm out wide and wrapped it around me while I leaned forward to make things easier for her. *Don't hug too hard. Easy on the touches.* I hugged her as gingerly as I could. It almost felt like I didn't touch her, just in case she would shatter like a fragile clay cup.

"Wow, you're about to pop, aren't you?" I couldn't stop staring at the round bulge of flesh covering the soon-to-be-born child.

Daric laughed. "Yeah, she is." He started walking around the table. "Everyone kept telling her that coming here right now was a bad idea. And for the last five days, I've heard every complaint a pregnant woman can have."

"Let's put a massive baby in you and see how you feel!" Evalana snapped.

I flinched away from the hormonal woman. But the more I looked at her, the more I saw my future—a future that terrified me.

This is what you want? I asked my instincts. As expected, there wasn't an answer.

Daric stopped moving and held up his arms. "Sorry. But even you have to admit that your baby is due any day now."

"They better be." Evalana grabbed a chair at the table and sat down. She rubbed her belly while staring at it. "I don't know how much longer I can take this. Just walking across the room is exhausting." She looked up at Lexia and Fina. "Who are you two?"

"Oh, that's right. I didn't tell you," Daric said.

"One arm. Are you Evalana?" Lexia asked as she sniffed the air. "You smell weird."

I elbowed my sister. "That wasn't very nice, sis." She glared at me, rubbing her arm. "Yes, this is Evalana. And what you're probably smelling is Mr. Prissy-Pants." I pointed with my thumb towards the coward hugging the wall with his back. "Or more formally known as Dante." I turned to see Dante puff out his cheeks, but he wilted under my look.

"I wish you wouldn't call me that." His voice was high enough to make me question if he was old enough to get Evalana pregnant. He rubbed his hands together, making them look like a ball of tasty sausages.

I slammed my eyes shut. "Stop that!" Everyone jumped. I pointed a claw at Dante. "Stop acting so scared. You're driving me crazy. Standing there like cowering prey is making me want to hunt you."

Lexia hopped next to me and stared at Dante. "Can I join?"

"Girls." There was a tingling sensation across my torso. I could feel Mom attempting to hold me back with her magic. "Stop that."

"But we weren't going to hurt him, just hunt him," Lexia whined. "Even Fina wants to. Look." She pointed a finger at the lynx beastkin. Everyone turned to look at her, and she wrapped her arms and tail around her waist before nodding slightly. "See."

I closed my eyes. "Lexia, hunting people might be normal in the Wild Kingdom, but it's not here."

Mom groaned. "I guess I have to say it now. Dante, grow a backbone." She stepped in between us and him. "Your actions have roused three beastkins' desire to hunt. If you're going to keep acting like this, it would be best if you leave."

Dante's eyes darted between the three of us. He started shaking and swallowed visibly. "I think... three?" The cowardly human couldn't stop wringing his hands together as he watched us. Sweat dripped from his brow. "Maybe, maybe it's best if I find someplace else to eat."

Mom waved for us to head towards the table, away from the door. Dante walked out of the room without removing his back from the wall. He closed the door behind himself and, by the sounds of his footsteps, ran down the stairs.

I shook my head. *Every time I see him, it's so hard see him as anything other than prey. My instincts keep pushing that thought into my head.*

"I don't know what you see in him," I said as I sat at the table. "How does someone so scared of anything that isn't his own shadow survive this long? I've eaten rats who faced their imminent demise with more courage than him. How can your parents be okay with him?"

"You could try to be a little nicer to him." Evalana drummed her fingers on the table. "He's unbelievably smart and kind. Yeah, even I will admit he's a colossal coward. But not everyone needs to be as brave as you." She glared at me. "And my parents don't dictate *every* aspect of my life. I'm free to love whomever I want."

"I have to insist that those three identify themselves." Gwen pointed towards me, my sister, and my friend.

Lexia flattened her ears and growled subtly.

Mom placed a hand on her shoulder. "This is Lexia, my second daughter." She extended a hand towards Fina. "This is Fina, an immigrant from the Wild Kingdom." Then she extended her hand towards me. "You should be familiar with my first daughter, Lucia Silverbreeze."

I glared at the older woman. At the mention of my last name, it looked like she flinched ever so slightly. If I hadn't watched her as closely as I did, I would never have seen it.

"My apologies," Gwen said with a stony face.

Finally you show me some respect.

"I'm gonna go get the food," Daric blurted as he dashed for the door. His exit was a little more dignified than Dante's, but not by much.

You do that. At least you can make yourself useful. We were back to stewing in the silence and tension as everyone picked a seat. The three of us beastkin sat on the far side of the table, away from Gwen and Evalana. We sat so that Daric and Mom would be the buffer between the grumpy woman and us.

"Lucia is my friend." Evalana's voice broke the silence. "This is Gwen, my midwife, whom my mother picked out for me." She clenched her jaw. "And she's just as much of a mother hen."

"So, Lucia, do you want to talk now or wait until there's food?" Mom asked me.

I kept glaring at Gwen. *Something about her is annoying me.* "I'll wait until there's food. Hopefully, eating will calm me down."

At least Daric did his job and returned with four people in tow. They placed platters on the table. I wasn't interested in most of it once I saw the platter of whole chickens. My mouth turned into a waterfall of drool.

Business will have to wait. Besides, bad news always goes over better with a full stomach, right?

5

BREAKING THE ICE AND MORE

I stared at the plate full of bones. Three nearly complete chicken skeletons piled on top of one another, and I felt bloated.

I can't believe I ate three of them. Although Lexia and Fina weren't much better. A perfectly cleaned chicken carcass sat on Fina's plate while she licked her claws. Lexia had eaten an entire chicken and half a plate of purplish-brown fruits. Her eyes drooped and she had to catch her head from falling forward.

Daric somehow had gotten it in his mind that he needed to keep up with me. That was a mistake. Three-quarters of his chicken sat eaten while the remaining drumstick taunted him. He looked a little green around the edges as he stared at the ceiling, breathing slowly.

"Sorry again about the cooked meat," Evalana said. She'd eaten a larger meal than I thought she was capable of, but I guessed that came with eating for two. *If I eat like I do now, what will happen if I get pregnant?* "But the smell of raw meat has been too repulsive. It has been for the last sixteen weeks."

I waved my hand. "Don't worry." A belch escaped and filled my nose with the aftertaste of chicken. "It wasn't all that bad." I pointed to the remains on my plate. "See. If I didn't like it, would I have eaten all this?"

Evalana giggled. "I guess not. Still, I know how much you like your meat raw."

Gwen stared at my plate. "She ate three," she whispered to herself.

"Where does she put it?" Daric closed his mouth and looked like he held back a burp. Although, by the look in his eye and his hand covering his mouth, it wasn't just a burp.

Mom propped her head on a hand as she leaned on the table. "Don't get her started."

Fina stopped licking her claws and placed them in her lap before turning to look at Evalana. "Sorry for not being invited. But it was good."

Evalana, using her earth manipulation magic, waved her artificial arm made of a smooth black rock. She smiled at the lynxkin. "Nonsense. If Lucia invited you, consider yourself invited."

Fina curled her tail around herself and bowed her head. "Thank you."

Lexia gave me a look, and I knew what she wanted me to do. I took a deep breath and closed my eyes as I prepared to end the camaraderie.

"We need to talk," I said as calmly as I could.

"This can't be good."

I glared at Daric for his comment. "You're lucky that I need you to hear this." Daric tilted his head. I returned my attention to Evalana, who wasn't smiling anymore.

I told them about my entire encounter with the sin of lust. Fina helped fill in the details. To his credit, Daric didn't say a word. He sat there quietly. Evalana asked a few questions, more for clarification than anything. After I told them about everything, ending with the deal that she offered me, everyone stared at the table, contemplating.

Daric spoke first. "That's easy. Don't agree."

"Under most conditions, I would agree with you," I said. "But what she said about the demon king has me more worried than ever."

"Also, how do we know she won't go back on her word?" Evalana had placed her prosthetic arm on the table, but she continued to fidget with the fingers. "If we didn't already have enough problems, I would say we hunt her down and kill her."

Mom turned to look at the princess. "Problems? What else is going on?"

Gwen placed a hand on Evalana's shoulder. "Now isn't the time to worry about things. Too much stress is bad for the child."

"But I can't just sit by with this kind of important knowledge." Evalana brushed Gwen's hand off. "I'll need to send this information to my brother. We need to defend the border cities as soon as possible and find out where this Rider of Death is coming from."

Lexia lifted her hand. "When we saw Greed in town talking to the man named Tobey, she said that Envy had completed her mission with the goblins. Like she told Lucia, that had been her mission: to summon the rider."

I turned to Mom and shrugged. "The rider is coming for the sin. It doesn't makes sense."

Mom crossed her arms and stared at the table again. "It doesn't. What does this all mean? Is there something we need to know about the Rider of Death? You said just before the fight with the Rider of Pain, the angel told you a little about the rider, right?"

Lexia nodded. "That's right."

"So, where do we get an angel?" Daric asked. "Can we ask Anna again?"

"Maybe." I shrugged. "We've kinda been in seclusion for the last two weeks."

"I heard," Evalana said. "Your mom filled me in. I was going to ask you to help us with another problem. But her and your captain told me you were unavailable until further notice."

I scratched the back of my head as I turned away. "Yeah. I had some things to work out, and then I went into heat." After I realized what I'd said, I clamped my hands over my mouth.

"Is that where you've been?" Daric slapped his hands on the table. "I missed it?"

I bared my fangs and growled at the man. "One more word about that, and I will castrate you. You don't need those to be my moral compass. It might help you—one less distraction to worry about."

Daric tried to disappear into his chair.

"Do you have a death wish, cousin?" Evalana asked. She shook her head. "Please forget my cousin's lack of tact. But we have a more local problem, one that can't wait either."

"Is this about the orcs?" I folded my arms on the table.

"I take it you've heard the rumors, then?" Evalana relaxed slightly. "Unfortunately, things are far worse than they appear."

Mom looked worried. "There have been attacks?"

Evalana slumped in her chair. "Three of them. Two on trade caravans, and one on a collection of farmhouses."

"Why didn't you tell me?" Daric asked in a soft voice.

"Because I knew you'd run off looking for them like the five previous companies we sent." Evalana raised her voice. "They all came back empty-handed. They couldn't find them. But from what their trackers said, there are at least sixty of them. That many will only cause more problems."

I flattened my ears. "And you want me to find them, isn't that right?"

Evalana rubbed the stump of her missing arm. "Yes. You're the best tracker we have."

Daric stood up, knocking his chair back. "I'm going with you!"

"That's fine, but I need someone else's permission first. Now sit back down." I pointed at Daric and he returned to his seat. I leaned my head on the back of my chair. "And sixty orcs? You're going to need an army. Preferably a mobile one."

"We have the army organized. The Maidens, Golden Guards, and The Breakers will follow you and help deal with them." Evalana lurched forward as she placed her hand on her stomach. "Oh, someone's awake."

"You talked to Captain Aenwyn already?" I asked. "Didn't she tell you about me? I'm not allowed to take a mission without her approval."

Evalana tapped her chin. "She didn't. But you brought a gambeson. What's your plan with it? Are you going to see her after this?"

I shrugged. "Yeah."

"I'm surprised you own a gambeson, especially after the fuss you made during the tournament." Evalana gave me a mischievous smile. "Can your ice magic cool you down enough?"

Daric looked at me, scratching his head. "If you owned armor, why didn't you wear it when you went with us?"

"It's because she hates it," Lexia blurted out before I could say anything. "It's way too hot for any beastkin to wear. I don't know how you do it."

I turned to look at Mom. "Part of our agreement with me wearing it on missions was that we would enchant it to make it more tolerable for me. What happened to that?"

Mom's jaw stiffened. "I've sent a letter to an acquaintance who is far more capable with enchanting than me. He said he would travel this way as soon as he was able. And just so you know, you'll need to pay him. He won't do it for free."

I waved my hand as I shook my hand. "I've got some money saved up. And if I do this mission quickly, I'll have some more. It should be enough."

"I guess you'll see." Mom's tone worried me.

"Oh." Evalana nearly doubled over. Her prosthetic arm floated to fill the spot where it belonged as she grabbed the table. "I'm sorry, but someone just kicked something they weren't supposed to."

She slowly stood up, but when she went to take a step, she froze. There was an odd, almost sweet yet acrid scent that caused me to flinch and wrinkle my nose. Fina and Lexia did the same.

"Uh..." Evalana stared into space and then down towards her feet. "I think my water just broke."

Gwen stood up and wrapped her arm around Evalana. "We need to get you to a bed. I think your child is more than awake. They're on their way."

Lexia shot up. "Oh, oh, is she having her babies now?"

"I'm out," Daric said as he headed for the door.

I chuckled. "You don't want to help?"

He turned, leaned back, and stared at me with wide eyes. "Absolutely not. That's something for you four *women* to handle. Especially the one who was specifically hired to help with this." He turned and shook his head as he walked out the door. "Not me. Nope. I'll do you a favor and let your husband know, cousin."

Lexia jumped up and down. "I wanna help. Please, can I?"

"Yes, you can help." Gwen started leading Evalana towards the door. "An extra pair of hands will be useful."

"Are any of the rooms on this floor for rent?" I asked.

"We have a room on the third floor." Evalana wrapped her real arm over Gwen's shoulder as she caressed her belly with her other arm. "But that sounds like a really long walk right now."

"Just bear with it," Gwen said in the softest tone I'd heard from her yet. "This will take a while."

I stood up and shook my head. "Move; I'll get her."

Gwen glared at me. "I've got her."

I pulled her off Evalana and shoved her backwards. "You'll take too long. Besides, she's not that heavy." I scooped her up into my arms. "Princess."

"Knight," Evalana said as she held on to me. "I know full well that I'm huge. You're just that strong. But since you're offering..."

"Put her down this instant, you ruffian!" Gwen barked behind me. I turned and growled at her with bared fangs. "Did you just growl at me? You—"

Mom ran up and raised her arms. "Don't. Not now."

Fina and Lexia stood next to me. "She doesn't like you," Lexia said in a low, threatening tone.

"Play nice." Evalana flicked my nose. "She's not used to your direct approach."

I flattened my ears. "Fine, for now." As I headed towards the door, my tail flicked back and forth. "You're taking this rather well. I'd probably be a horrible mess at this point."

"I'm deflecting." Evalana smiled. "For the last hundred days, I've had everything that's about to happen drilled into me to the point I just want this over. I know that this is only the beginning and that what's coming later is where I need to worry. So I'm trying to save my energy for that."

Right. Princess. She has quite the doting parents after all. One hundred days? That sounds awful. I'd want it over too if I had to hear the same information that many times.

"Just let her go." I heard my mother's voice behind me. "She's direct, but she cares for her friend. Don't worry, she's in safe hands."

There was some incoherent mumbling from Gwen as I headed for the stairs. Evalana gave me directions to their room. I placed her on the large, fluffy bed with an unnecessary number of blankets and pillows. Everyone followed behind me. Gwen went to direct Mom and Lexia.

Fina pulled me to the side. "Can I go?" She avoided looking at me.

"Do you need me to take you to the gates?" *This situation is making her anxious.*

Fina shook her head. "I want to see Melody."

A smile spread across my face. *It's been a while since I've seen her too.* "Come on, let's go." I turned to look at my mother. "I'm going to take Fina to the orphanage and head over to talk with Captain Aenwyn."

Mom smiled. "Go ahead. This will take a while." She placed a stack of sheets next to the bed just as Dante burst into the room. "We'll be here if you want to stop by afterwards."

"I just want to talk to Aenwyn. I'll be back shortly after." I waved to Mom and Lexia.

Dante slid to a stop and grabbed his wife's hand.

Evalana groaned for a moment as she sat up. "So that's a bit more than someone moving."

"You can do it, love." Dante brushed the golden hair from Evalana's face.

Fina followed me as we headed for the orphanage. The mass of people in the street didn't help Fina's nerves. I held her hand as I pushed people aside and made my way through.

We made it just outside the familiar brick building. *Oh, the memories.* Fina took off for the door, a smile spreading across her face. *She's off to help.*

I followed in after her.

6

I HELP

The familiar scent of the orphanage greeted us as Fina and I stepped inside. It hadn't changed much over the years—it was the same cozy atmosphere that I'd called home years ago.

Fina's eyes darted around, and her ears twitched as she took in the surroundings.

"They're in the courtyard." I nodded as I heard the kids laughing.

The laughter must have reached Fina. Her ears perked up, and she tugged at my sleeve. We headed through the entryway and through the double doors into the courtyard where the kids were no doubt playing.

As we entered the courtyard, a flood of familiar scents assaulted my nose. *Her garden still smells the same despite her not being here.* The garden Molly worked on daily had fallen into less-than-perfect care. None of the kids currently here had the same gardening aptitude as she did.

But I did notice Molly's favorite plant, felonweed, still lining the front of the garden. The black stems were full of sharp barbs that, if one wasn't careful, would get stuck and have to be pulled out. The flowers were blooming a bright yellow with their petals folded outwards, similar to a rose but more angular.

A group of four kids, ranging in age and appearance, lined up to watch two other kids. The two were playing tag. The kid-friendly version of sparring halted once Fina stood with her arms out wide.

"Fina!" all six kids shouted as they turned to run towards her.

Melody, watching over the kids, smiled as she saw them tackle the overwhelmed lynxkin. "It's been a while since I've seen you, Lucia."

I scratched at the back of my head. "Yeah, I know. Don't take it personally. I was just going through some tough times."

Melody walked over and put her arm on my shoulder. "I understand. Nora explained the whole situation to me." A smile crept across her face. "And Fina stopping by, I'm guessing that means her mating season is over."

Fina shifted in the pile of hugs. "I help," she said with a small smile.

Melody chuckled. "You do."

The kids held her tighter. "We missed you, Fina!" A small human girl with bright blue eyes and red pigtails, whom I recognized as Tilly, nuzzled Fina's left arm. "You're back."

I ruffled Tilly's hair and grinned. "Hello, Tilly. Are you the one who's been causing trouble around here?" I glanced at the others with a playful smirk.

"She has," Emma said as she stroked Fina's fluffy tail. The elven girl's brown hair was her pride and joy. *I don't know how Fina can stand someone touching her tail like that. That would drive me nuts.*

Wyat, a human boy and the youngest at five, tried pulling Fina to her feet. "Let's play. We can start over, and you can join us for tag."

Tyon, the oldest at eleven, stood up and grabbed Wyat's head. "Why, so you can lose again? Or do you want to go against Fina because you know she'll take it easy on you?"

Wyat stomped his foot and glared at the older boy.

I stepped in between the two. "Alright, you two, save it."

They instantly stepped back and turned away from me. "Sorry," they spat.

Melody scowled. "Always the charmer you are. Growl at the kids once, and they fear you for the rest of their lives." She ushered the two boys back towards the area they were using for tag. "You really need to work on that temper in front of the kids."

All the other kids stopped hugging Fina and stared at me. I sighed. "Trust me, I know." I extended a hand to Fina. "It wasn't my intent to sound that angry. I wanted to make sure Fina and the others weren't going to get hurt in their fighting."

Tyon rubbed the toe of his boot on the ground. Another boy jumped up and grabbed my hand. "They didn't mean anything by it. Those two are always like that."

"Brason, there's a fine line between rivalry and bullying." Melody pointed a finger at the boy, grabbing my hand. "And Tyon was dangerously close to crossing it. While Lucia was right to step in..."

"Lucia is a good friend." Fina stood up and walked next to me. "She won't hurt kids."

"I know, Fina," Melody said with a slump of her shoulders. "It's just that her approach could have been softer." She walked up to Fina and brushed her hair over her shoulder. "Why don't you take the kids and play with them? They've been asking when you'd come back."

"Yay!" all the kids shouted together.

She hadn't said yes yet. But we all know she can't refuse to play with the kids. I smiled at Fina. "You can't refuse now."

Wide-eyed and smiling, Fina tapped her chest with her fist. "I play."

Melody nodded towards the double doors back inside. "I have something I could use your help with, if you don't mind."

I left Fina and the kids to frolic and followed Melody back inside. *Fina probably missed the kids as much as they missed her.*

As Melody and I reentered the main building of the orphanage, the atmosphere shifted from the lively courtyard to a quieter, more serene space despite my ability to still hear the kids cheering outside. The scent of well-worn books tickled my nose.

Melody led me into the classroom filled with shelves of books, and in the center, there was a heavy wooden table covered in papers and writing materials. Many of the pages had the children's attempts at learning to write on them.

Melody pointed to the bookcases. "Do you mind helping me

move some of these shelves around? I've been wanting to reorganize this room for weeks, but the furniture is too heavy for me and I've been busier without Fina's help."

I grinned. "Of course. Just tell me where you want them." I looked at them closer. There was a noticeable bowing as the shelves held up the plethora of books left behind by Mom after she moved out with me because she adopted me. There was some rule that whoever was running the orphanage couldn't have kids of their own. It had been explained to me once, but the reason never really stuck. *Besides, Melody is quite happy running the place now.*

As I began lifting the furniture, I could hear the wood groaning in protest. "Uh, Melody, do you want me to try and replace the shelves that look like they're going to give out?"

She shook her head. "That won't be necessary. Someone else is coming by tomorrow. They were going to help move them, but since you're here, I thought you'd help so they could concentrate on fixing them. And it'd give us a chance to talk."

I hefted the bookcase. "Yes, it isn't heavy, but could you tell me where you want it? It feels like you're taking advantage of the situation a bit."

"And what if I am?" Melody giggled and pointed to the opposite side of the room. I arched an eyebrow. "Just place it over here, please. Do you remember the first time you played tag?"

I sighed as I set the bookshelf against the wall. "How could I forget?" I placed my hand on my neck. "Back then, I truly wasn't in control. I would've hurt someone. I was about to."

Melody placed a hand on my shoulder. "That's right. But do you see how far you've come? Do you see how your actions have made a difference?"

A tear formed in the corner of my eye. "A lot has changed since then. I'm not the same, mostly."

"Nor should you be." Melody turned me to face her. "You've done great things. And I have no doubt you'll do even greater things. All I ask is to remember where you came from and those who are there now."

"And speaking of where I came from, I just wanted to say thank you for letting Fina help you and be with the kids." My tail flicked behind me as I headed towards the other bookcase. "It means a lot to her."

Melody smiled warmly. "You were a big part of this orphanage. It wasn't just about giving you a place to stay; it was about finding families. That was because of you. You showed Nora a new way of thinking. That's how you found your family. The reason it took so long was that while Nora was selfish and kept you to herself, nobody understood you like we did."

I gave her a wry smile. "As the first beastkin to live in this city, let alone an orphan, being misunderstood was only the beginning."

"And Fina... she found a purpose here. She loves helping out with the kids." Melody pointed from one bookcase to the spot next to the first one I'd moved. "I see that as good for her and for Aquittemia, even all of Rophmna. If people can see that beastkin such as Fina are out there, we can help demystify beastkin to the population. And educating the children is the strongest way to bring about that kind of change."

My smile turned genuine. "She has a gentle way about her. She's who everyone should see beastkin as, not me." I lifted another bookcase to move it.

"Being a beastkin does not dictate who you are." Melody moved out of the way. "I know you know that. Nora made sure you learned that lesson. You are Lucia Silverbreeze, knight of The Maidens, with a doting mother and an overprotective sister." She winked. "Nora's told me some stories."

I rolled my eyes as I set the bookcase down. I gave Melody a smile. "You've become just as motherly as Nora. If you find yourself in the same place as her, it's alright to find someone else to run the orphanage. You can have the family you deserve too."

Melody laughed. "That's sweet of you to be thinking of me." She shook her head. "But no, the most fulfilling part of this job is seeing the kids walk up to their new parents. Speaking of which, with Fina keeping the kids busy, I can go check up on a couple who were asking questions about Emma."

I nodded. "Do you want me to just keep lining these along this wall?" Melody nodded. "Why?"

She pointed to the wall. "This room has always been a bit boring. I thought since Junara has the painting aptitude, this wall could be turned into a mural. You know, liven the place up."

I crossed my arms and tried to picture the wall covered in a painting. I tapped my chin with my finger. "Will that really help the kids not get bored while in here? It might work on Fina while she's still learning to read and write."

"I have faith it will." Melody smiled as she walked over to the table that replaced the individual desks. "Wyat put in a lot more effort whenever he saw Fina practicing. Maybe since she's back he'll put in more effort again."

I shrugged. "What can I say other than she helps?" A lump formed in my throat. "Thank you, Melody. For everything. You will always have a special place in my heart."

Melody enveloped me in a warm hug. As we pulled away, a tear glistened in the corner of her eye. "You help too." She gave her best Fina impression. We both sputtered into a fit of laughter. "The world will always be better with you in it, Lucia. Take care of yourself as you take care of your family."

I gave Melody another squeeze. "You're part of that family too. If you need anything, no matter how small, just find me. I'll do whatever I can."

"Thanks." Melody wiped a tear from her eye. "I know that means a lot coming from you. If you want to stay after you finish and play with the kids, you're welcome to."

I licked my lips. "That sounds tempting, but I've got to go see my captain after this."

"Okay," Melody said as she headed for the door. She paused and turned. "Tomorrow, then?"

I smiled. "We'll see. If not, as soon as I have free time."

I waved Melody goodbye and finished moving the bookcases to make room for the mural. Afterwards, I said goodbye to the kids and Fina before leaving. I strode through the city, everything feeling a bit lighter, and navigated myself to my next order of business at Aenwyn's office.

WHAT IS IN A NAME

I walked into the office but didn't find Captain Aenwyn. *Now that I think about it, there wasn't anyone walking around the halls.* I closed the door behind me as I left and started searching through the headquarters. I eventually heard something coming from the training rooms.

Since Evalana said that The Maidens were assigned to take on the orcs, the captain probably wants to make sure everyone's good to go. Even still, I doubt she'll take everyone. I haven't seen Zenny since before I left for the Wild Kingdom. Maybe I should find her and talk to her soon. But how is that going to go? Maybe I should do it later.

Attempting to avoid my encounter with Zenny, I walked towards the strength-training rooms. When I walked in, anyone who wasn't in the middle of an exercise stopped and looked at me.

Nope.

Without looking at the crowd for the captain, I backed out of the room and hid around a corner.

"You alright?" a smooth and light voice asked. A girl with teal-blue hair poked her head around the corner.

She was thin but athletic and stood about sixty-six inches tall. Her short hair was a bit messy, as some of it stuck to her face courtesy of the layer of sweat that I could see and smell. Her ears poked out through her hair, marking her as an elf.

"Not really," I said as I tried to relax by visualizing a waterfall. As the woman kept standing next to me, my instincts urged me to keep her out of arm's reach. "There were too many people for me. But I've never seen you before. Who are you?"

Her childishly round face frowned. "Are you always this rude?"

"What she meant to say was that usually, you offer your name before asking for someone else's." I heard her voice, but her lips didn't move.

A copy of the woman next to me walked out from behind her. My eyes darted between the identical pair.

"Hello, my name is Escaeris Teal Aqua." The second woman extended a hand towards the ruder of the two. "This is my sister, Elasha Teal Aqua."

Oh, twins. Cute.

I straightened myself. "Lucia Silverbreeze."

Elasha crossed her arms and raised an eyebrow.

Escaeris smiled. "A title. Interesting." She tapped a finger on her chin as she looked upwards. "I didn't realize they would give titles to foreigners. Maybe that means I can get one, too."

While the twins looked identical, their stances were as different as they could get. Elasha never took her green eyes off me, especially my hands. Escaeris moved like nothing bothered her and she didn't have a care in the world. What was even more odd was that my instincts drew my attention more towards Escaeris. They wanted me to avoid her.

"You have three names already. Why do you need another? Why do you have three in the first place?" *I've heard some elves have three names, but I never remembered to ask why that is. I keep getting distracted.*

Elasha clicked her tongue. "No surprise that a stupid beastkin doesn't comprehend Osarin naming practices."

I growled and leaned forward as I flexed my claws.

Escaeris pulled her sister back with one arm and stepped between us. "No. Remember what they told us when we joined?"

Elasha opened her mouth but closed it without saying anything.

"Don't antagonize the carnivore beastkin." Escaeris pointed back at me. "Look at her teeth. She's the carnivore."

The technical term is primal, but as long as you get the point.

Elasha swatted her sister's arm as she threw her arms up and turned around. "Bah, why do I care? If you want to play nice with her, knock yourself out. Just don't bring her home."

Escaeris sighed after her sister walked back into the room. "I really wish she didn't expect me to pull her out of every fire," she whispered.

I leaned back and crossed my arms. "Then don't."

She turned and tilted her head.

I wiggled my ears.

"Of course you heard me. Sorry. I didn't mean to say that out loud." She slumped her shoulders. "But I can't do that. She's the only family I have left."

Now I can't help but feel a little sorry for this sister. She's nicer. They kinda remind me of how Lexia and I act. "What happened?"

"Sorry, but we've just met. I'm not talking to you about that." She smiled in an almost childishly innocent way. "But I will answer your other question. Osarin citizens have three names."

She held up her hands, palms up, and they glowed with magic. I instinctively tensed but relaxed as soon as soft blue lights appeared. They were shaped into odd symbols above her hands.

"This is my name." She moved her right hand over the right-most collection of symbols.

I took a closer look at the lights. "Uh, they're backwards."

Her cheeks flushed pink as her eyes went wide. "Oops," she giggled. With a wave of her hand, the letters rotated. "Is that better?"

"Yes."

"Now, as I was saying." She moved her right hand over the left word. "This is my given name. The one my parents gave me at birth." She moved her hand to hover over the middle name. "All elves have hair. In Osarin, we distinguish everyone by their hair color. That's where the middle name comes from." She then hovered her hand over the last name. "This is my clan name. There are—were—fourteen clans. All clan names are based on gemstones. Ours was the Aquamarine. Thus, Aqua is our clan name."

"That's a lot." *Is her clan gone? I guess that would be something you wouldn't want to talk to strangers about. What about Dinar?* "Didn't you say all elves have hair?"

She nodded. "I did."

"But I've seen a few bald elves in this kingdom."

Escaeris's eyebrows scrunched at my statement. "That's..."—she paused—"complicated." I tilted my head in response. "They must have been exiles. It's the harshest punishment one can earn."

Dinar an exile? She said she was an assassin. "That doesn't sound like the worst thing. They could have been executed instead."

A tear manifested in the corner of Escaeris's eye. "I don't expect you to understand." She turned to follow her sister. "I guess I'll see you around."

I shrugged. "It's likely." *Wait, wasn't I looking for Captain Aenwyn?* "Wait. Do you know where the captain is? I need to talk to her."

"Sparring field," Escaeris said without stopping.

One day I should find Dinar and ask her if she's really doing okay. She seemed well-adjusted. I would never have guessed she was exiled from her home. And I'll just pretend the announcer from the tournament didn't exist.

With nothing left to do, I headed towards the back door of the headquarters and the sparring field. "The sparring field" wasn't really a good name for it since it looked more like a covered outdoor park. But "field" rolled off the tongue better, so everyone called it that.

When I walked outside, there were three people standing in the center of the octagonal area.

I recognized two of the three people on the platform. Captain Aenwyn stood in the center of the three. Over the last season, she'd let her hair grow out until she could put it into a ponytail that tickled the nape of her neck. Her soft face held a slight frown. She wore her uniform—a steel breastplate and a white quilted gambeson skirt down to her shins.

To her left was, unfortunately for me, Zenny. She stared at me while pouting with the angriest face I had ever seen on her. Her azure eyes burned a hole through me. Zenny kept her blonde hair was much shorter; it barely went past her ears. She had an average build with a deceptively large bust but thin hips. The tap of her boot rang in my ears.

Why does today have to be so complicated? I should've appologized to her for all the work I caused her while I was training. Now I have to deal with having stayed away from Zenny before I left for the Wild Kingdom. And having avoided her since I returned probably hasn't helped my situation either.

"It took you long enough to show up. Having second thoughts?" Captain Aenwyn's voice echoed throughout the area. "At least you came prepared." She nodded to the third woman, who I recognized as being part of The Maidens, but I couldn't remember her name. "Go and get them for me, please."

I glanced at my gambeson in my hand and shrugged. "I wish wearing this thing was the most difficult part of my life right now."

Aenwyn placed a hand on Zenny's wrist. "You'll talk with her after. Don't worry, I'll leave her with the capability to talk when I'm done with her." She gave the human girl a wink.

Zenny didn't say anything. She simply walked to the side, where a couple of benches sat alongside some of the metal practice weapons.

"What do you mean? You can't possibly be thinking of sparring with me by yourself, can you?" I stared at the blonde elf. "I've never seen you fight before."

"That's right, you haven't." The grin on her face caused me to tuck my tail around my leg. She held out her hand towards the wooden practice weapons and curled her fingers. "But I need the exercise."

A wooden staff lifted itself off the rack and floated through the air towards her. She grabbed it the moment it was within her reach, tossed it to her other hand, and repeated the motion. A second staff floated towards her.

"Go on. Put your gambeson on and step up." Captain Aenwyn grabbed the second staff and stood with one in each hand.

"Um, you know I don't fight with weapons, right?" I asked as I pulled the cloth armor over my head while walking towards the platform.

The captain laughed. "Yes, I do. Both of these are for me."

I stopped at the edge of the platform. My captain held one staff with two hands in a stance I'd seen many of the others practice when holding a spear. The other staff floated over her shoulder, and it looked like she was aiming the tip at me.

Her title is Glimmerstance. That means she's done something to earn it. This won't be easy.

"After this, though, I have something important to talk to you about," I said as I coated my forearms and the backs of my hands with ice.

She nodded. "Understood. Now stay on your feet as long as you can."

I stepped onto the platform.

8

HAZING

Aenwyn let me take three steps into the arena before she leaned forward and charged, her floating imitation spear hovering over her shoulder.

I waited for her to strike first. *My objective should be to strip her of her weapons. After I do that, she'll be defenseless—and offenseless.*

I dropped my right foot back as I lifted my hands.

While I'd thought she would stop and stab at me from as far as her reach would allow, she didn't. Instead, she lowered her shoulder and attempted to drive it into my chest. I dug my toe claws into the ground and caught her.

Okay, that was too easy.

The floating staff cracked me on the head. I reflexively let go of her pauldrons and covered my head. Then Aenwyn turned and swung the staff in her hands at my knee.

After I felt the impact of the strike, I knew what she had attempted to do. It didn't work because my claws held my leg in place.

The captain looked at my knee disapprovingly.

"Ow," I said with as little emotion as possible. It was impossible to hold back a growl for what she did.

She looked up at me, and for the briefest moment there was a hint of fear in her eyes. She hopped out of my reach just before my claws slashed her face.

"This is a sparring match, remember." Aenwyn started pacing to her right while keeping the tip of her staff aimed at me.

"That hurt!" I lunged for her as my vision turned red.

As my vision shifted, my focus increased. Every step my opponent took echoed in my ears. I saw every breath that flared her nostrils, the folds in her gambeson quilt, and the vulnerable gaps in her armor. I could smell the sweat dotting her forehead and the pine perfume she was so fond of. Each detail practically glowed as I reached out for her.

She swung her staff from right to left to deflect my hand. I stepped to my right as I pulled my hand back. The staff over her shoulder flew for my face. I batted it away, then grabbed it.

With the weapon in my right hand, I swung it at Aenwyn's face. She ducked the blow and thrust the staff in her hands towards my gut. I caught that one with my empty hand. A toothy grin spread across my face as I felt her tug at the weapon. She wasn't nearly as strong as me, and I dug my claws into the wood for good measure.

I lifted the staff in my right hand before swinging as hard as I could down. Aenwyn relinquished her weapon and rolled to the side. An ear-piercing crack stung my ears as the staff hit the ground and splintered.

With a growl, I tossed the splintered stick out of the arena. Captain Aenwyn didn't take her eyes off me as she stayed in a low, three-point stance. She lifted her other hand and made a pulling motion.

As I stepped towards the elf, something hit me in the back, causing me to stumble forwards.

I growled as I blocked out the pain and threw the staff in my hand at my opponent. She lifted a hand and stopped the stick from hitting her before she grabbed it. I swiped my right hand at her face. With a quick turn of her wrist, Aenwyn spun the staff so that it caught my arm and deflected my attack enough for her to duck under it.

With Aenwyn leaning forward, I lifted my left claw into an uppercut slash for the opening in her elbow. She twisted away from me as she swung her staff out, hitting me in the stomach. But before she could pull her weapon back, I grabbed ahold of it with one hand and slammed my other hand into the middle of it, snapping it in half.

Aenwyn took a step back and held out her left hand. Something hit me in the back again. I turned to see who kept hitting me and saw a floating staff fly past me. When I turned back around, I had enough time to catch Aenwyn's downward strike with the ice on my forearm.

I swung my arm around, grabbed the pole, and snapped that one in half. Then I threw both pieces of broken quarterstaffs at the captain. She sidestepped one and batted the other with her broken stick. When she raised her arm again, I assumed she was going to pull another weapon towards her.

I sprinted forward as fast as I could.

She tried to dive away, but my claws caught the inside of her pauldrons and twisted her landing.

After sliding to a stop, I pounced towards Captain Aenwyn as she landed gracelessly on her back. She lifted her legs to catch me. Both of her boots collided with my gut, and I could feel her beginning to carry my momentum over her. I grabbed her legs just past the knee.

The elf's eyes went wide as I growled and squeezed. "Waterfalls!"

Everything came to a jarring halt after she screamed my code word. I shook my head and released the prone woman as I took a step back. My vision returned to normal while our company's leader got to her feet. I noticed she was trying to hold back her breathing.

Sweat poured from her brow as she gave up trying to look tough. *I'm guessing using magic really took it out of her.*

"You did a lot better than I thought you would," she said, after taking a moment to steady her breathing.

I rubbed the top of my head. "That really hurt, you know."

"You were the one who left yourself open." Aenwyn took a deep breath. "Besides, I wanted to see you angry."

"Why?"

She pointed to the doors and stepped off the platform. "To see if you were ready for this next part."

What?

I turned and saw two people walking through the doors—a pair of familiar teal-haired elves.

You've got to be kidding me.

"So, what did you need us for, Captain?" Elasha asked.

Captain Aenwyn took her gloves off and set them on a table towards the back of the sparring field. "It's time to see what you two are capable of." She turned and faced us. "The two of you are going to spar against Lucia."

Escaeris looked at her sister. "You want to go first, or shall I?"

"No, you two will face her together," Aenwyn interrupted.

Escaeris blinked several times as she shook her head. "That's not fair. She doesn't stand a chance."

Who doesn't stand a chance? I flicked my tail back and forth. "It's you who doesn't stand a chance."

Elasha stepped up. "You know what? I think it's time I showed you why elves will always be superior to everyone else."

My vision subtly shifted to a reddish hue. "Since I've eaten elves, I'm higher on the food chain."

The sisters froze and stared at each other.

"Both of you, stop that!" Aenwyn shouted. "This is a test of skill, not a place to settle grudges. Lucia, no blood or breaking anything. Escaeris, same thing. And Elasha, no magic."

I flexed my claws as I reinforced the ice on my forearms. "I'll do what I can." *But I'm not promising anything.*

Elasha crossed her arms and stared at Aenwyn, who I could hear removing parts of her armor. "Why can't I use magic?"

"I said so." Aenwyn's voice felt like I was listening to Mom and another one of her lectures. "Fire magic is never allowed during a sparring match."

The elf rolled her eyes as she dropped her arms and headed to the wooden practice weapons. "Whatever."

"Do you want to grab me a staff while you're over there?" Escaeris asked her sister.

The annoying sister gave a thumbs-up as she approached a rack of wooden longswords. She headed back with a sword in one hand and the only remaining staff.

I kicked the remnants of my fight with Aenwyn out of the arena. The sisters stepped onto the platform, weapons at the ready.

I dropped into a low four-point stance. *The sword sister needs to go first. My instincts are still warning me about the one with the staff.*

I pulled myself forward and charged the two. As soon as I did, Elasha charged ahead of her sister.

"Don't." Escaeris raised her arm to reach for her sister, but she was already out of her reach.

Elasha lifted her sword over her head and swung downwards. I rose to stand on two legs as I weaved around the attack. The elf turned her head to follow me while twisting her upper body and trying to swing her sword at me. But her attack failed the moment my hand caught hers.

I effortlessly ripped the wooden sword from her as I grabbed her shirt. Her fear and sweat mixed into an intoxicating scent that urged me to rip her throat out with my teeth. After I threw the weapon behind me, I pulled her close and opened my jaw wide as her face came closer.

She tried to push me away, but with a little more effort, she was in a prime throat-biting position. Elasha started screaming and squirming, doing anything she could to delay the inevitable.

Snap! I slammed my jaw shut.

There was a moment of silence as a quiet whimper escaped the proud elf. My teeth were inches from the soft, deliciously sweet flesh of her cheek.

Escaeris resumed her charge. Hearing her footsteps, I threw Elasha behind me. She screamed as she tumbled away.

"Claws off my sister!" Escaeris swung her staff from left to right.

I blocked with the ice covering my arm. The tip of the staff snapped and broke where it collided with me. The piece of wood flew off harmlessly.

The elf stared, shocked.

It felt like my bones were vibrating.

"Ow." I didn't hide the fact that it really hurt. I recoiled and cradled my arm, hoping the tingling sensation would go away.

"How did you do that?" Ecaeris asked, her shock still obvious.

I shook my forearm. "I was about to ask you the same thing."

The elf didn't answer me. She narrowed her eyes as she planted her feet firmly, one slightly behind her, and held her weapon out. There wasn't any sign of innocence in her eyes anymore. It was replaced by what looked like fear.

My instincts jumped at the sight. Suddenly, she wasn't as frightening anymore. So I made the first move to grab her weapon. *I'm still not allowed to hurt her... much.*

Escaeris stepped back and swung her weapon horizontally. I pulled back just enough so the attack would miss. As the staff passed in front of me, I surged forward and grabbed it with my hand. But when I pulled, it didn't move, and neither did the elf holding it. She didn't pull back; instead, she raised her leg and kicked me in the side.

My vision lurched as I hurled myself towards the ground. I rolled to my feet and grabbed my side where she'd kicked me.

I know this feeling. That wasn't a regular kick. Someone her size shouldn't be able to hit that hard. She has the physical aptitude. That's what my instincts were warning me about.

The elf didn't chase me. She just stood there. I heard her sister groaning as she marched up with her wooden sword in hand.

"Elasha, stand down." Aenwyn's voice cut through the air. "She's already beaten you."

She slumped her shoulders as she turned. "But, but..."

"Go," Escaeris said without taking her eyes off me. "You don't stand a chance against me, and she's just as strong as me. Maybe a little stronger."

Elasha turned her head towards me. "No way."

I stood up. The pain in my arm and side was quickly becoming tolerable. *She figured it out that quickly too.* I shrugged. "So what if I am?"

Escaeris tightened the grip on her weapon. "That means I need to take this more seriously."

"Fine, so will I."

Escaeris's eyes widened as I dropped to all fours and charged her. Everything slowed down as my claws tore through the wooden platform. Escaeris swung her staff low, but I jumped over the attack and tackled her.

We rolled to a stop with me pinning her shoulders and her staff out to her left. She punched my ribs with her right hand, and we started rolling again. Again, we ended with me on top. This time, I held her shirt and slammed her to the ground. She grunted as her back almost bounced.

Escaeris scowled as she focused on me. I bared my fangs. The elf rolled again after she punched me in the face. My vision swam from the blow and the spinning. When everything stopped, I felt pressure against my neck and someone sitting on top of me.

"Give up." Escaeris leaned further on my neck.

I tensed the muscles in my neck to keep her from choking me. She only tried harder. I grinned. She didn't have a staff in her hands.

The elf paused. "Why are you smiling?"

"Because you've lost." My rumbling growl caused her to shake.

She shook her head. "But I've got you pinned."

"I'm still armed."

That was the only warning I gave her as I stabbed her sides with my claws. Escaeris screamed as she arched her back.

I pulled out one hand and grabbed her throat, then reversed our positions.

She glared at me. Her eyes felt so full of hate. "No. I won't lose. I can't lose," she said in a strained voice.

My vision turned darker. *If you won't give up, I'll make you.*

I lifted her off the ground as she tried to grab my wrist. She couldn't get a good hold on the ice covering my forearms. As she flailed, I drove her back to the ground. She didn't stop. So I did it again. And again. And again. Each time, I put more power behind my arm.

She just wouldn't lose consciousness. I don't know how, but she never hit her head once. She just kept glaring at me and grabbing my arm. But I noticed her eyelids starting to droop.

"Waterfalls!" Aenwyn's voice cut through everything. "Lucia, I order you to stand down. Don't make me do this."

I released the elf, who immediately started coughing as air entered her lungs. When I turned, I saw Zenny attempting to hold back a screaming teal-haired elf as Aenwyn held a bow with an arrow pulled back and aimed at me.

Not again. I was getting carried away again. But it didn't feel like it.

I held up a hand and shook my head as I headed for the edge of the training field.

Aenwyn better have a good reason to have pitted me against Escaeris.

9

LIFE ON THE EVE OF DEATH

I heard the creak of the bow relaxing as the captain lowered her weapon, but I needed to focus on the waterfalls in my mind. Which wasn't easy with Elasha screaming.

"Calm down, Elasha," Aenwyn said. "Your sister's fine."

Zenny was losing her grip as Elasha kept pushing her arms. "You hurt my sister."

I covered my ears. "Nothing serious. She'll be fine."

Escaeris sat up and looked at her hands. "How could I lose? That shouldn't be possible. I tried." Her shoulders sagged, and it seemed like she wasn't looking at her hands, but past them.

Now I get it.

I walked over to help Escaeris to her feet. When I stood over the elf, I extended a hand to her.

"No!" Elasha finally pushed Zenny away. Zenny tripped and landed on her butt. "Stay away from her, you animal."

My vision burst with red as I prepared to kill Elasha. But as I went to move, a wooden stick struck Elasha in the back of the head. She went limp, and Zenny moved to catch her so her head didn't hit the ground.

I tensed my jaw as I watched Zenny inspect the place Aenwyn had struck.

"She's just unconscious. There's no bleeding." Zenny rolled the teal-haired elf onto her back and stood up.

Aenwyn eyed me as I kept flexing my claws. But I knew the look she gave me. I needed to calm down. I used my magic to remove the ice armor around my forearms and crushed each bracer into dust. My claws still itched, but I could at least get my vision back to normal.

"What happened?" Escaeris stared at her unconscious sister.

"She said something I told you two never to say," Aenwyn answered. "Lucia and all beastkin are not mindless animals. They are people just like you and me. And if I didn't knock her out, Lucia wouldn't have been as forgiving."

"Oh." Her green eyes looked duller.

"Come on," I said as I held out a hand for Escaeris to grab. "Stand up."

She took it, and I pulled her to her feet. "What was this about? Why did I lose?"

I sighed. "I can answer that for you." There was a tightness in my chest. "Since you have the physical aptitude, all your life you've been stronger than everyone around you, right?" She nodded. "How old are you?"

"Twenty-four."

Still pretty young, especially for an elf. "It's hard to believe, but there's always someone stronger, more powerful, faster, smarter, or whatever, than you." I shuddered as I remembered the feeling of almost drowning while fighting the original Rider of Pain. "It was a lesson I had to learn too. I learned it the hard way and recently."

I turned to see Zenny quickly look away from me as she grabbed her elbow. "Is that why you were gone for the ice season? And why you've been avoiding me these past few weeks?"

"Yeah." I scratched the back of my head as I stared at my feet. "That and I've been in heat. I haven't exactly been in a sound emotional state lately." I turned to the elf. "Be grateful that Captain Aenwyn saw you needed this lesson and gave it to you in probably the safest way possible."

"That was safe?" Escaeris placed a hand where my claws had dug into her.

Aenwyn stepped towards her. "Well, maybe not the best, given Lucia's mental state. But you and your sister were way too eager to join us to kill the orcs. You aren't ready yet."

"A friend of mine was killed, another almost killed, I almost died, and someone I was traveling with was permanently crippled when we took on something far more powerful than us." At my words, Escaeris's face lost its color. "Imagine if, while fighting the orcs, who could overpower you, they killed your sister. What if they cut off one of your limbs? A friend of mine lost her arm years ago during a demon attack. The risk of injury is real, and sometimes those injuries can affect the rest of your life."

"If it's so dangerous, why do you do it?" Escaeris turned to me, a tear rolling down her cheek.

I swallowed hard. "Because this world is under attack. I won't ignore it anymore. Because if I want to save my friends and my family, I have to fight." I felt a tingle down my spine. "No matter the danger, I will protect my pack."

Aenwyn grabbed Escaeris's shoulder with one hand and her chin with the other. "Everyone has a reason to fight. If you don't know yours, I suggest you find it, or find something else to spend your life on."

Escaeris sniffled. "Can I have time to think about it?"

Aenwyn smiled as she let the woman go. "Take all the time you need. And please, make sure your sister understands, too."

"Speaking of which..." I pointed to the still-motionless elf on the ground. "You're sure she's going to be okay?"

Zenny nodded. "Yes. You're not the only one who can heal quickly."

I narrowed my gaze at my captain. "Wait. She has the recovery aptitude?" Aenwyn nodded. "Did you really find a pair of twins with both of my aptitudes?"

Aenwyn smiled as she shrugged. "It's kind of funny if you think about it."

I turned to Zenny. "What are the chances of that?"

Zenny's eyes darted around as she took a half-step back. "I, uh, don't know. Really, really, really small?"

"You have two aptitudes? Physical and recovery?" Escaeris's jaw slowly descended to the ground.

I rolled my eyes. "Yes, get over it."

"We really should get her to a bed, at least." Zenny knelt down and attempted to lift Elasha.

Escaeris moved to help but ended up just taking over and lifting her sister into a princess carry. Zenny tucked the helpless elf's arms in and positioned her head so it wouldn't flop around.

"I'll place her on an empty bunk." Escaeris turned to the captain. "If that's alright with you."

Aenwyn waved her hand. "You're both still a part of this company. We're here to help you with anything you need."

The teal-haired elf bowed her head slightly. "Thank you." Escaeris carried her sister back inside. Zenny and Aenwyn continued to stand next to me.

"You wanted to talk?" Aenwyn asked in a low voice.

"So did I," Zenny said afterwards.

I slumped my shoulders. "Yeah." I started scratching the tips of my claws together. "It's about what happened while I was in the Wild Kingdom."

Aenwyn crossed her arms. "Well?"

It's not going to hurt anything if Zenny's here. "Here's the short version." I took a deep breath. "Fina and I were woken up by the sin of lust, who wasn't just the sin of lust anymore. She said she absorbed the powers of the Rider of Pain, or at least, that's what it sounded like. Then she said there's another rider, and he's coming for her. She wants me to kill him so she can take his power too, and then wanted me to make a deal with her. She wants to absorb all the riders and take on the demon king so she can become the queen and rule the demon realm, but she wants my help for some reason because she's afraid that, because she knows something, all the other demons are going to kill her. She proposed a deal that if I helped her, she wouldn't bother this world as long as she was queen."

I panted slightly, finally finishing my rant.

Zenny and Aenwyn had the same blank look on their faces as they blinked several times. I flicked my tail back and forth in the silence. *Did I overload their minds?*

"Wow. That—" Aenwyn shook her head. "That was a lot. Are you sure that was the short version?"

"Did you forget anything?" Zenny asked emotionlessly.

I scratched at the back of my head. "It doesn't feel like it. Sorry, I guess the full version just spilled out."

"I don't like it." Aenwyn shook her head. "But we can't stay here and do nothing."

I shrugged. "I've already told Evalana about it. She said she'd send a message to the king."

The elf captain pinched the bridge of her nose. "Unfortunately, we have to do something about the orcs first." Aenwyn paced in front of the door for a few minutes before she spoke up again. "I'll go talk to Evalana about the message. We'll need to make sure it's safe for her to send it."

"Okay," I said, not really sure what else to say. "But what do you need me to do?"

"Lucia, come back tomorrow with your sister," Aenwyn said as she headed for the door. "We're going to need to deal with the orcs so we can concentrate on that rider as soon as possible."

After Aenwyn left, I turned to Zenny. "Do you want to help deliver a baby?"

Zenny's eyes went wide. "Evalana's having her child now? I'd love to help."

I scowled. "How did you know I was talking about Evalana?"

Zenny clapped her hands and had a dreamy look in her eye. "Because she sent me a letter when she found out. I was going to ask if you wanted come with me to see her, but you instead went on a mission to the Wild Kingdom." Then she crossed her arms and pouted.

"You knew?" I threw my hands in the air as I headed for the door. "Of course you knew." I stormed out, slamming the door behind me.

Zenny followed me while attempting and failing to hide her giggling. The streets were even more packed as people bumped shoulders, although everyone knew not to get close to me. Zenny followed in my wake through the crowded streets.

After I finally walked into the tavern, I headed towards Evalana's room where I heard screaming.

That's Evalana. She was going into labor earlier today. Hopefully she—

I opened the door to the room and was met with the sight of Evalana in the final stages of labor. Dante's hand was in hers. Both of their faces were contorted with pain. Gwen crouched between Evalana's legs, holding her hands out. The scent of blood and other fluids hit me like a wall.

All rational thought left my brain as I stared at the sight.

Evalana's eyes were closed. Sweat soaked her forehead; her hair stuck to her face as she took each labored breath. She clutched Dante's hand tightly. Her knuckles were white as she squeezed. Dante squirmed next to her. The pain on his face was clear, as his eyes were glued to his hand. He whimpered, wiping the sweat from his forehead with his sleeve.

Zenny pushed past me and ran in to help. Strangely, two people weren't in the room as I expected—Mom and Lexia. But I couldn't take my eyes off Evalana as she leaned back against a pile of pillows supporting her.

"Give me one more big push. I see the head. They're almost out." Gwen crowded in closer to Evalana. "Keep pushing and don't stop."

"I—" Evalana gasped as she panted. "I'm too tired."

My vision swayed as the scent of blood pulled my instincts to find it and hunt. Rationality slowly dripped in as I did everything to fight back the urge. I knew the source of the blood and forced myself to suppress my instincts.

Evalana took a few deep breaths as she leaned forward and screamed. Dante stood up and screamed along with her, his hand still held hostage by his wife.

My ears immediately flattened as I flinched backwards. I closed my eyes and stumbled out of the room.

Evalana's screams burned in my ears as they slowly turned to grunts. But as they died down, another sound rose up to replace them.

It was crying, specifically a baby crying. It sounded almost like it was a wet cry, like the sound fought through a liquid to reach the air.

That sound was much easier to handle than Evalana's screams.

"I don't know who you are, but thank you for helping clean her." Gwen huddled with Evalana over a table with towels and a small bucket of water behind her.

"My name's Zenny," Zenny said as she stood next to Gwen. "My mother taught me how to be a doctor. And I've done this a couple of times with her, so I know what to do."

The crying ended as the small purple baby sat on Evalana's naked chest, but I walked back in and the scent of blood was even stronger than before.

No, I need to stop. I used my magic to cover my nose in ice so I couldn't smell. *Much better.*

With my instincts under control, I walked in to check on Evalana. She was a mess and the sheets she sat in were soaked in blood. At some point she'd released Dante's hand, and he fled back, cradling it as he continued to whimper. Evalana lay on the pile of pillows, breathing raggedly with her eyes closed.

"How do you feel?" *My voice sounds kinda funny with my nose plugged.* "You doing alright?"

Evalana continued lying with her eyes closed. "Awful. Is it over?" Her voice was weak and scratchy.

Zenny grabbed a small cup and brought it over to me. "Please, fill it with ice water." I used my magic to fill it. Zenny then walked over to the exhausted woman. "Here, have a drink. It should help."

Evalana didn't lift her hand to grab the cup. So Zenny gently placed it against her lips, and she puckered as if she was ready to drink. Zenny carefully tilted the cup, slowly pouring water into her mouth, pausing often to give her the chance to swallow.

She opened her eyes, only slightly, but that was an improvement. "Thanks, but did you have to make it so cold?"

I chuckled. "Sorry." I pointed to myself. "Ice magic user here. I'm unable to gauge what's cold since I handle it really well."

Evalana turned to look down at her daughter.

"Congratulations, it's a healthy baby girl." Gwen quivered as she gave Evalana a wide smile, placing a hand on the baby's back.

"She's so beautiful," Evalana whispered. She caressed the baby's head. "Seeing her, feeling her like this, makes the entire experience is worth it. The pain, the weeks of uncomfortableness, all of it was worth it just to see her face."

She looks so happy. Still, that looked terrifying and painful. Maybe it will feel different when it's one of mine. Maybe that's something to look forward to once I save the world. Speaking of which...

"I hate to ruin this moment, but where are my mother and sister?" I asked as I looked around outside the room.

10

PROMISES, PREPARATIONS, AND PERILS

Dante stepped up to Evalana as Gwen finished cleaning the child. "The wolf girl couldn't stand the noise and asked Nora to take her somewhere else."

I turned to Gwen. "Do you know where they went?"

Gwen shook her head. "I was concentrating on more important matters, so no."

Fine, be that way. I rolled my eyes and turned to leave. But as I did, I heard the slightest cooing.

"Sounds like someone's ready for her first meal." Gwen's tone shifted to an almost playful one.

I stood in the doorway and watched as Gwen pulled down the front of Evalana's dress and positioned the child over a breast. The subtle sounds of the child nursing and the smile on Evalana's face left a tingling sensation in my heart.

"Hey, Zenny." Zenny looked at me as I called her. "Take care of her. Don't worry, I promise to keep this city safe."

I left the room and closed the door behind me. *Why did I say it like that? What is this feeling? It's like I have to protect her and the baby. Great, now I'm committed.* I used my magic to clear the ice from my nose and took a deep breath. *Now I just need to find Lexia and Mom.*

As I walked down the hall, a door opened up, and out walked my mother and sister. Mom turned and looked at me. "Are you feeling alright?"

I perked my ears up. "What makes you think something's wrong?"

She pointed to my tail. I didn't realize how it nearly brushed the ground. *Oh.*

"You want to talk about it?" Lexia stepped up next to me and wrapped her arm around my shoulder.

I looked at my claws. "If I knew what I wanted to say or talk about, then yeah."

Lexia nodded slightly. "That's fair." Suddenly she jumped forwards and spun on one foot to end with a clawed finger pointed at me. "What you need is a distraction."

I couldn't suppress a chuckle.

Mom crossed her arms and tapped a foot. "How did it go with Captain Aenwyn?"

I shrugged and headed for the stairs. "We had a sparring match."

Mom waved her hand, and I walked into a wall of hardened air. I could have easily destroyed it with my strength, but I knew what it meant. *She wants to continue talking. I'm not allowed to deflect this one.*

She extended her hand invitingly towards me. "And..."

"I won, but she got me a few times." I started pacing back and forth from wall to wall. "Afterwards, she had me spar with a couple of newbies. They were twins, actually. The two of them each have one of my aptitudes."

Lexia giggled. "Did you meet your match?"

I shook my head slightly. "No. The one with recovery was practically useless, and I took her out instantly. The one with the physical aptitude put up a lot more of a fight. She got me good a few times."

"Is everything alright? Nothing too badly hurt, I assume." Mom eyed me from head to toe.

I waved my hand. "I'm fine. Nothing was bothering me by the time I walked back here with Zenny."

"Oh, Zenny's here?" Mom's voice perked up. "She wanted to see Evalana's baby."

"Yeah, she's been helping Gwen clean her too." The memory of seeing Evalana lying there with her baby pushed a smile onto my face.

"Did you talk to Captain Aenwyn about the demon and rider?" Lexia asked as she flicked her tail behind her.

I scratched the back of my head. "Yeah. And we have to report for a mission tomorrow." Lexia arched an eyebrow. "She wants both of us to help deal with the orcs as soon as possible. So first thing in the morning we're to show up to headquarters."

Lexia straightened her back. "Okay."

"Well, that means you two better rest up." Mom waved her hand towards the stairs. "Let's make sure you've packed before you go to bed tonight. Did your captain tell you how much to pack?"

I lifted a finger and opened my mouth for a moment before deflating. "I didn't ask."

It sounded like someone was headed up the stairs, and when I turned towards the sound, Aenwyn strode up the stairs. *Sometimes it feels like my life is a little too coincidental.*

"Ah, wonderful to see you, Nora." Aenwyn held out her arms as she approached.

"It's nice to see my daughter hasn't roughed you up too much." Mom hugged the elf captain.

As they separated, Aenwyn chuckled. "So I take she told you already?"

Mom nodded. "Yeah, but she seems to have forgotten to ask about some details."

Aenwyn gave me a wink. "It's partially my fault." She reached into her cloak and pulled a roll of paper out. "Here are the details for the girls. I'm sure you'll get them packed accordingly."

Mom took the roll of paper and nodded.

More sounds of someone walking caught my attention. This time, it was Zenny heading our way. "Hi, Captain." She gave a slight wave to the elven captain. "You said you wanted to talk to Evalana about the rider. Is that why you're here?"

"It is," Aenwyn said.

Zenny shook her head as she waved her hand. "She's sleeping right now, her and the baby both. I suggest you leave her be for now. She just had a baby, after all. It took a lot out of her."

Aenwyn gave a knowing smile. "It does. I'll talk to her in the morning. Hopefully, she'll be awake." She lifted an arm out. "Here, I'll take you home."

Lexia watched the human girl. "So, I take it you're Zenny. You're kinda cute."

Zenny's eyes went wide as her head darted back and forth between Lexia and me. "Uh, yes. But who are you? You look like Lucia, but I can see your teeth are different."

Lexia glared at me. "You didn't introduce me, your sister?" She stomped her foot and placed her hands on her hips.

I held my hands up. "Sorry, I got a little distracted." Lexia kept glaring but relaxed some. "Sorry. Zenny"—I pointed towards my sister —"this is my twin sister, Lexia. I met her while I was on my mission with Daric."

Zenny examined Lexia without moving more than her eyes. "I would like to talk to you later." She held out a hand for Lexia to shake. "It's nice meeting you, Lexia." When she turned back to me, the glare in her eyes told me I was in a lot hotter water than I'd realized. "You're going to tell me everything one of these days."

Lexia pouted. "If you're my sister's best friend, we can at least be friends." My sister moved Zenny's hand out of the way as she scooped her up for a hug. "Let's be friends too."

Zenny grabbed onto Lexia more in a panic than wanting to hug my sister. "Oh." Her voice shook. "Yeah, that, uh, sounds nice."

She's going to take some time to warm up to my sister. But if anyone will get her to open up, Lexia's the one to do it.

Lexia let Zenny go and smiled as her tail wagged energetically. "We can go do things after we get back from the mission."

Zenny returned the smile. "I would like that."

Slowly, and sadly, we went our separate ways as Aenwyn walked with Zenny to her home while me and my family walked to ours.

As we walked home, I couldn't help but feel a sense of unease. I watched Lexia chatter excitedly about the new baby, her eyes shining with wonder and longing. She bounced around us while she gestured animatedly and talked. I wanted to feel that same excitement, but all I felt was a knot in my stomach. My shoulders ached from tension as my hands clenched into fists.

I glanced over at our adopted mother and saw the familiar look of concern etched on her face. She must have noticed my emotions as we walked. She placed her arm around my shoulders, and her hand rubbed soothing circles on my upper arm.

"I can see you're thrilled, dear." Mom's voice seemed a little distant. "Honestly, I don't think I've ever seen anyone be this excited about someone else giving birth. Especially after you asked to leave because you couldn't watch her be in so much pain."

Lexia stopped in the middle of her prancing and looked disappointed. "Do all humans suffer while giving birth like that? It sounded like it was killing her."

Mom removed her arm from me. "Yes. It's the same for elves." She tilted her head slightly. "Why? Is it different for beastkin?"

Please say yes. Even after hearing what Evalana said, I don't know if I want to go through with it. Although, my body seems to want to do everything it can to make sure I do. Thanks, biology.

"Yes," Lexia said in a disbelieving tone. "There's hardly any pain. Some women have described it as uncomfortable, not painful. But it usually takes an entire day, sometimes longer."

I blinked at her nonchalant tone. "A whole day? Longer?"

Lexia's eyes shifted from me to Mom and back to me. "Oh right, you weren't raised around your kind. Sometimes it's easy to overlook that fact." *Thanks, sis.* "We normally have twins, so of course it will take longer."

"Well, that would change things." Mom put a finger to her chin. "How many times have you watched another woman give birth in the Wild Kingdom?"

Lexia shrugged. "Five times." She clapped her hands together and looked up at the sky with a dreamy look in her eyes. "I can't wait until it's my turn to have children. I'm sure Mom will make a fantastic grandmother." Her eyes fell on me. "And I'm sure someone else is eager to have her own, isn't she?"

A tingle traveled down my spine and all the way through my tail when I saw the grin on her face.

Mom nervously chuckled as she rubbed the back of her neck. "I don't know; I just got my second daughter. And she's already talking about making me a grandmother? Isn't this moving things a little too quickly?"

I grabbed my elbow and looked at the ground.

I wish I could tell Lexia that I'm not ready for all of this. I'm not ready to have children or even think about becoming a mother. It's all too much, too soon. The words stuck in my throat.

I felt Nora's arm around my shoulders as she pulled me close. "It's okay, honey. You don't have to worry about it right now. You're still young and have plenty of time to wait until you're ready."

Am I that easy to read?

I nodded, but the knot of anxiety didn't loosen. My head was low, and I dragged my steps. We continued on our way home. *I know I'll have to decide eventually, but the thought of it fills me with dread. Will I be good enough? Can I make the world safe enough so that my kids can grow up without worrying?*

As we passed through the gate, I couldn't help but feel trapped, like I was being pulled in a direction I didn't want to go. *I want to be like Lexia, excited and ready for the future, but I'm just not there yet. I'm not sure if I ever will be. Maybe having a job to do will distract me.*

We packed for the two days that we expected to be gone, and Lexia and I practiced our magic with Mom for a bit before bed. But even as I froze my waterbed, I couldn't sleep and stared at the ceiling, hoping that eventually I would be too tired to stay awake.

Something about the events of the day left me unable to relax. My mind kept running away with every worst-case scenario. At one point, I felt extremely guilty that Victor might be upset with me since I was afraid to give him the children he undoubtedly wanted.

Every depressing thought hammered into my mind, leaving me a weeping mess, unable to comfort myself. *I can't do this by myself anymore. I promised that if I needed help, I would ask Mom or Lexia for it. Since we have a mission in the morning, Lexia needs the sleep. I'll ask Mom for advice. Maybe she can help.*

I got out of bed and headed towards my mother's room. My padded feet never made a sound while I walked, so when I heard something walking as I moved through the house, I grew curious.

Whatever it was sounded heavy and outside. I headed to the living room window and saw a little orange light in the night. It was moving through the field and growing larger.

When I looked more closely, my vision turned red as a memory I had thought long-buried resurfaced. One of my first memories of this world spurred my instincts to fuel my rage.

I stalked through the house to wake my family. I entered my mom's room first, since she was the closest, and gently nudged her awake.

She sat up. "Lucia? What—"

Before she could say another word, I put my hand on her mouth. "Orcs are coming this way," I whispered.

11

NIGHT RAID

Mom nodded and pointed to Lexia's room. "I'll get your sister. You go out and pick off any of the ones who are too far separated from the others. But stay safe until we come out and help you."

"What's the plan after that?" I whispered as I headed to the door.

Mom put on her boots and a heavy cloak. "Your sister and I will create enough distractions and openings for you to pick your targets one at a time."

A knot in my stomach grew. "Will you make sure Lexia is safe?"

"They won't touch her." Mom's steely voice dispelled my anxiety.

I quickly made my way out the front door since I saw the orcs coming towards the back of the house. My heart pounded in my chest. I couldn't suppress the thrill building in the back of my mind as I set out to hunt the unsuspecting orcs.

The night air enveloped me, but my keen eyes easily picked out the shapes of the orcs through the moonlight. They were heavily armed and armored. But unfortunately for them, I knew they were coming.

With my magic, I covered my torso and arms with the densest ice I could make, providing myself with some protection. I crept over and hid in some bushes as I looked for my first target.

They weren't as spread out as much as I'd have liked, and the crops in the field weren't tall enough to hide me and my silver fur. I studied their movements while I waited for Mom and Lexia, and I noticed an orc on the end was coming closer to me and would eventually be near enough to ambush.

I waited until one was close enough for me to practically taste his stench before I struck. I darted forward, my claws and teeth bared. The satisfying crunch of bone reverberated through my jaw as I sank my teeth into the neck of the first orc. They stumbled to the ground, gurgling through the blood.

It tasted oily with a bitter aftertaste.

Yuck. I guess orcs are off the menu. Whatever. One down, eight to go.

My sister and mother exploded from the back door with a massive gust of wind. Lexia launched an icy spear at the closest orc. The creature flew backwards as the ice pierced through his chest.

Nora, on the other hand, kept the wind blowing as she spun her arms around, the air following. The remaining seven orcs fell to the ground, the torches they had snuffing out as they hit the dirt.

I dropped to all fours to keep myself from getting blown away. Dirt and debris added to the disorienting situation.

There was another orc on the ground who was trying to roll to his feet, and I took my chance. I thrust my claws into his neck and pulled them through. The orc spun away as my claws got a little stuck on its spine.

There was a loud rumble that I heard and felt in my feet just as the wind died down. Two orcs suddenly became airborne, and a large pillar of earth stood where they'd been on the ground. They were heading in my direction, their arms and legs flailing as they fell.

I reached up and grabbed a leg before slamming it down in front of me.

A satisfyingly wet crunch sounded as the orc's screaming sharply ended.

I stepped on the other one's throat and sliced it open with a flick of my toe claws.

Lexia had two orcs running towards her. She pushed her arms forward. A wall of ice manifested and hammered into the closest one's knees. The second one didn't trip on my sister's wall; instead, he hurdled it. After stumbling for a couple of steps, the orc resumed its charge.

I immediately dropped to all fours and sprinted towards the orc. Lexia jumped backwards and pointed a finger at the orc. A crystalline beam shot out from her finger and struck the creature in the shoulder. Ice encased its shoulder as it grunted and recoiled from the magic.

The orc stomped its foot and howled at my sister.

Oh no you don't.

My vision turned red as I pounced. My claws dug into the orc's shoulder and neck as we tumbled to the ground. There was a satisfying snap as I continued rolling and flipped the orc over my head.

I ended in a three-point stance, looking for another victim.

I heard the stomping of boots to my left, and I turned to see an orc raising a club over its head. It swung the wooden weapon down at my head, but I raised an arm and blocked it with my ice-covered forearm. The impact vibrated through my arm, but despite the pain, I held the weapon at bay.

The orc snarled in my face before roaring a heinous sound that threatened to make my ears bleed.

If your voice didn't scare everyone away, your breath would certainly do the trick. What crawled in there and died?

I stabbed my claws through its bottom jaw, silencing the worst sound I'd ever heard in my entire life. As the orc's eyes went wide, I pulled its jaw away, and it dropped into the club. The orc tripped backwards, clutching at its gaping wound, pathetically attempting to stanch the bleeding.

The remaining three orcs exchanged glances before turning and running. My instincts kicked in and demanded I hunt them down like so many prey before them. Before I could move to the closest one, the ground opened up, and the orc dropped until only his head was above the ground before it closed around him.

"Go, get the last two!" Mom shouted as she pointed. "Leave this one for questioning."

Did Mom just tell me to hunt them down? Best mother ever!

I sprinted towards the next closest orc and pounced. He didn't stand a chance as my jaws severed its spine in one quick movement.

As I spat out the bone and terrible-tasting flesh, Lexia came from behind me and pounced on the other orc and bit down on its neck, exactly like I had.

Well done, sis. You've been paying attention and practicing.

Lexia spat the bone and flesh out as she stood up. "Yuck." She shook her head. "Do they taste that bad for you, too?"

I relaxed and let my vision return to normal. "Yeah, they do."

Mom grimaced as we walked towards her. She stood next to the orc's head sticking out of the ground. It was almost comical to see the head swivel and snarl.

"Watching you two do that is disturbing," Mom said as she shuddered.

I turned to Lexia. "Why didn't you use your ice magic to kill him?"

My sister shrugged. "I sort of felt compelled to pounce on him like prey. You know how it is."

I nodded. *She's got me there.* "So why are we keeping this... guy?" I looked down at the head. The orc looked masculine enough, and as I looked at the other orc corpses, they all looked male. "What do you want to ask him?"

Mom crossed her arms and stared down at the head. "Why are you here? What did you hope to accomplish? How many more of you are there?"

The orc laughed. I wished he hadn't. It sounded like nails on a chalkboard. "You all would have made excellent broodmothers. Our children would have been mighty." Lexia and I both shuddered at the mention of broodmothers. Then I stared, wishing he had stopped talking. "There are too many of us. You think you're mighty? You think you can take us all? Ha!"

I flattened my ears and turned to leave. "Can we just kill him already? His voice is getting on my nerves."

The talking head growled at me, and I couldn't help but growl back. The useless head paused his growling only grate at my ears with his awful voice. "I've never seen a dog like you move that fast or throw an orc like that. You will definitely birth many chieftains."

Dog! My vision exploded with red as I snarled and extended my claws.

"You won't touch her!" Lexia's shout froze the air. Even I could feel the drop in temperature.

"And you, dog, we will get many shamans from you." The orc grinned before snapping his head back and howling with laughter.

His laughter was drowned out by the feral snarl that came from my sister. Before I could run over and stomp on his puny head, the air turned frigid, even for me. Then the orc's head stopped moving as ice encased it. And then I stomped on it, and it shattered into countless tiny crystals.

I stared at the stump. It was still for a moment until a couple of squirts of blood erupted from it. I turned and walked towards my sister, who was still growling at the orc's remains. My vision returned to normal as I turned her head to focus on me.

Her voice cracked. "They won't take you away again. I won't let them."

I hugged my sister. "I'll never let them touch you so long as I live."

I could feel the magic from my sister slowly fading as the air returned to normal. When I looked around, everything within three arcs of us was frozen solid. The crops were likely ruined by my sister's rage.

She remembers what happened the day I "died," the day I was sent here. It seems she hasn't gotten over it.

"It's fine, sis; I'm here to stay," I whispered as I rubbed her back.

There was a crunch of ice, and we turned to see what had made the sound.

Mom was stepping on the ice, out from a small section that was never frozen.

"While I'm impressed at such a display of power, please be careful not to harm friends, family, and allies with your magic." Mom surveyed the area. "Please remember, even though you two want to look after each other so much, I'm here too. You are my daughters and mean an awful lot to me. If you think I'll let anything happen to you, it will be over my dead body." Her flat and even tone brought a smile to my face, and when I glanced at Lexia, I saw she had one too.

"Sorry about that." Lexia pointed to the still-bleeding, headless corpse. "He just—just got me so angry. I couldn't help myself."

Mom looked at the orc who'd so foolishly taunted us. "It's fine. He wasn't giving us much else." She looked towards our neighbors. "But it looks like we weren't the only ones attacked tonight."

She pointed to each side of her. In both directions, there was an orange glow and a pillar of smoke.

Isn't one of those directions where Bosco's and Lentilee's house is? "Fina!" I shouted as I took off towards the house.

I heard as I sprinted on all fours, "Go with your sister. I'll make sure the others are safe."

The world blurred around me as I traveled through the farmlands. A sense of dread ballooned in my gut as I saw more evidence of the orcs' brutal attack. Fields littered with the corpses of slaughtered livestock and trampled crops, the once-lush fields reduced to nothing but mud and destruction, the ground scarred with deep grooves.

As I rushed to Fina's home, I could see the smoke rising in the distance. My heart raced faster the closer I got.

I arrived at Bosco and Lentilee's home, my heart pounding in my chest. The sight before me was devastating—flames engulfed the house, and smoke billowed into the night sky. I couldn't get close due to my pyrophobia, but I could see that there was no hope for the building.

The intense heat from the fire started melting the ice on my chest and arms, soaking my clothes and fur. I had to look away. And then I saw her—Lentilee—sitting on the ground away from the burning house. She was crying, huddled over her husband's lifeless body. I ran towards her.

I kneeled down beside her, barely able to hold any semblance of control. "What happened?" I asked her, my voice choked.

Lentilee cried as she held her husband's head. Her clothes were torn, and her hair was matted with blood. I could see that she was badly injured. Her leg was bent at an unnatural angle, and there was a huge gash in her side.

I rushed to stem the bleeding with my ice magic, but the burning building made it impossible to freeze what little moisture there was in the air.

She looked up at me with tears in her eyes and said, "They killed my Bosco. And they got me too." Bosco's gut looked like something had pierced through it. "I'm not going to make it through the night. They took everything from me. My home, my husband, our farm, everything."

"But where's Fina?" I grabbed her and held her up.

Her voice was weak and raspy. "They took her."

Her words stopped my heart.

They took her? No. I felt a wave of guilt and anger wash over me. *She's my friend. She's a part of my pack. Now she's in the hands of those monsters. They touched the wrong person.*

"I'll do everything in my power to bring her back," I told Lentilee, clenching my teeth.

"Promise me," she said, her hand reaching out to grasp mine. "Promise me that you'll make them pay for what they've done. My husband and I... we didn't deserve this."

I looked into her eyes, seeing the pain and fear. I knew that I couldn't let her die like this, but there was only one thing I could do.

"I promise," I said, squeezing her hand. "I'll make them pay. They will suffer."

Lentilee gave a small nod and closed her eyes, her hand going limp in mine. She was dead, and my heart ached. *She wasn't a bad person, and neither was Bosco. They didn't deserve to die.* I stood up and turned to search for the orc's trail.

"I promise, I'll save Fina," I said to myself, gritting my teeth. "And I'll make them pay for what they did. I will tear them to pieces."

12

ACTION PLAN

I heard someone wheezing nearby. When I turned to look, Lexia was on all fours, gasping for air.

"You... run... too... fast," she said, inhaling between each word.

"Sorry." I offered a hand to my sister. "Let's get you back home." *I'm already on edge; the fire is triggering my pyrophobia, and the thought of Fina being taken is too much. I can't wait another second.*

Lexia lifted her head, and horror replaced her exhaustion. "What happened? Are those..." She took my hand, and I pulled her to her feet.

I turned her away before she could finish her question. "Yes, Bosco and Lentilee are dead. The orcs killed them."

"Fina?" Lexia sounded like she struggled to say her name, tears welling up in her eyes.

I closed my eyes and gritted my teeth. "They took her." I could feel my sister about to explode with a response. "And I will get her back."

"I'll go with you," Lexia said, her voice shaking.

I shook my head. "Not this time. You'll only slow me down. I can run faster and longer, and I require less time to recover. It will be nothing for me to catch up with them."

She grabbed my shoulders. "But it will be just you against who knows how many. Evalana said they estimated there were at least sixty. What if there are far more than that? Even you couldn't take that many on by yourself."

I looked away. *I hadn't thought about that. Getting Fina back was the only thing I could think of.* "Maybe you're right." My sister's eyes lit up. "But my point still stands, and I can't leave her alone like this."

Lexia curled her tail around her waist. "Then what do we do?"

"That's a good question," I said before I took her home.

What do I do? If I can pick them off one by one, then it won't be a problem. But based on the conversation we had with the one orc, they sound intelligent, or at least intelligent enough to plan.

Lexia looked to be just as lost in thought as I was as we walked together. *There has to be something. If I start taking them out one by one, they'll likely figure it out and work in tighter groups. And if the opportunity presents itself where I can get Fina out safely, we can run away together. She's the only one I know who's faster than me.*

We made it back home without saying another word. Neither one of us had a working plan. I looked around and didn't see any signs of Mom either. But it wasn't long before I heard footsteps heading our way. Lexia and I immediately tensed up, ready to take on any orcs who stayed behind.

But when Mom walked around the bushes, we relaxed. She gave us a worried look before sighing. "You two are too worked up. But what happened? Are Bosco, Lentilee, and Fina safe?"

"It's bad," Lexia started, her voice shaking with anger. "Bosco and Lentilee, the orcs killed them. Lucia told me what happened. She also said Fina was taken by the orcs. And now she wants to go after her, alone. But I can't let her do that. It's too dangerous." Lexia's eyes were filled with a mix of anger and concern. "You have to tell her she can't go."

Mom turned to look at me. "Are you going?"

"Fina's been captured," I said, my voice breaking. "I need to go after her." *I can't get Fina out of my mind.* "I need to leave now. Every second I waste here is another second Fina is suffering."

Lexia grabbed my hand and pulled it to her chest. "I know that, but it's not safe for you to go alone. What if there's a whole army of orcs waiting for you?"

I pulled my hand away. "You know how strong I am. I can handle myself, and I need to get Fina back."

Mom stepped in between us. "Girls, calm down. Arguing won't solve anything." She glared at each of us in turn. "We need to think of a plan."

I huffed as I crossed my arms. "There's nothing to think about. I need to go."

Lexia stomped her foot. "But Mom's right. We need to make sure we have a plan and backup. What if you get captured or hurt? How will we find you? You need to think about this."

Mom hummed for a moment. "Lucia, go ahead and leave a trail for the rest to follow. Lexia, go gather the needed reinforcements, including Captain Aenwyn. You'll all follow Lucia's trail and confront the orcs together."

I nodded and said, "Fine. But I'm leaving now."

Lexia's voice rose. "No way, I'm going with you."

Mom raised her voice. "Girls, stop." She turned to look at me. "Lucia, you need to be careful and not take unnecessary risks." Mom then turned and pointed a finger at my sister. "Lexia, you need to trust that your sister can handle herself. Now go. Hurry up and gather The Maidens and the other knights. Both of you need to listen to each other and work together."

We both looked at our mother, then at each other. I let out a sigh. "Okay. I'll be careful. And Lexia, don't be late."

Lexia nodded. "I won't. We'll get Fina back together."

I turned to leave, but a hand grabbed my shoulder. It was Mom's.

"You aren't planning to go after the orcs in your nightdress, are you?" Mom asked in an almost relaxed tone.

I looked down and chuckled. "That's fair."

She turned me around. "Let's get you cleaned up somewhat."

I watched her fill with magic, and a bubble of water condensed and floated to cover my hands. The blood and dirt in my claws and fur floated away before the bubble moved to my face. I could feel the water pulling at the fur around my mouth, cleaning up the blood from the orcs I'd bitten.

Mom waved her hand, and the ball of dirty water flew out the nearest window before it popped.

"There, at least you look a little better." Mom gave me a slight smile. "Now put on some real clothes and grab your gambeson. I'll get you a small pack with some food for you and a waterskin."

My eye twitched at the mention of my gambeson.

Mom stood up. "This is a mission. Treat it like one. You promised."

I closed my eyes and took a deep breath before turning and heading to my room. I put on a simple shirt and skirt before I added my gambeson to my attire. As I walked out of my room, tying the strings around my neck, Mom was wrapping some jerky in a thick paper sheet.

I didn't know where she'd gotten it, but she had a pack that was quite small. It barely held the waterskin and food.

"You need to travel light. If you can't catch them in a day, you'll need food to have the energy to fight." Mom handed me the bag she packed. "This should last you for a day or two if you ration it."

"Thanks, Mom." I pulled the straps over my shoulders and tied an extra string between them to try to limit their movement as much as possible. "I'll be careful."

She smiled. "I know I don't need to tell you this, but I'll say it anyway. Take care of yourself. Not just for you, but for me and your sister too."

I looked down at the ground, away from my mother. *She's right. I should take their feelings into account more. Stop being impulsive, Lucia. I'm not alone anymore. Lexia, Mom, Victor, Evalana, Zenny, and even Daric. They're all a part of my life now. How would they feel if I died? I've already died once, and I never gave any thought to who I left behind. All because I have no memory of anyone I left behind.*

I gave Mom a smirk as Lexia walked into the room. "You know, it would be much easier for me if I learned things the first time."

Lexia glanced at Mom before turning to me. "Sis, I love you. You know that."

"I do," I started. "There is nothing I want more than to help you raise your kids with Gifford." Lexia's lip quivered. "I have a family. I want to keep it. Fina needs my help. She might not be part of our family, but she feels like it. I'm sorry for how I was acting."

Lexia slumped her shoulders and walked up to me. "I get it. It's the same for me. You're my super-strong, brave, impulsive, and hard-headed sister. I love that about you."

I giggled. "And you're my super smart, powerful, caring, and blunt sister." I snatched her up in a tight hug.

"Take care. We'll be there as soon as we can," Lexia whispered in my ear.

I let her go and turned to Mom. "I'll see you when you catch up."

She shook her head. "No, I'm not coming. There are still burning buildings. I put out one fire. Now I need to make sure the others are put out and take care of Bosco and Lentilee. And after that, I'll do what I can to help with the rider."

"Oh." *I had forgotten about that. One of these days I need to not get so easily distracted.*

Mom pushed me towards the door. "The orcs will probably head north, back to their territory. If the rider is coming from the goblin deserts, then he will come from the south."

I hugged my mother. "I'll be there as soon as I can. With Lexia, Fina, and the rest of the knights."

As I walked out the door, Mom called out, "Be careful if you see that demon again. It sounds like she has a personal vendetta against you."

I waved back and headed back towards Bosco and Lentilee's home. *That will be the best place to start. There should be tracks to follow, especially if they're carrying loot and prisoners. But Mom just reminded me about the sin of lust. Is she really the sin of lust anymore? Is she considered the new Rider of Pain? It doesn't matter. She's a demon and up to no good.*

I reached the remains of the burning building, which wasn't burning much anymore. It wasn't much more than a smoldering pile of charcoal and ash. Unfortunately for me, the smell of ash and burned wood was so heavy in the air I could taste it. And it was awful.

Finding the orcs' tracks was effortless since they trampled through everything. *I need to get that demon out of my head. I'm about to hunt down at least sixty orcs, minus the nine we killed, and save Fina. There's no room for error.*

13

LEXIA'S DETERMINATION

My sister's counting on me. I can't let Lucia down. I ran towards the town, my heart pounding in my chest. I could see the gates ahead. *Good, I'm almost there.*

But as I got closer, I realized something was off. The gates were closed, and soldiers were stationed inside. I dug my toe claws in to stop myself, panting and confused.

The solid steel bars, each as thick as my wrist and crisscrossed, taunted me with a clear view of where I needed to go. Two human guards stood on the other side of the gate. Each held a short spear and a shield and wore chain armor.

I approached the soldiers, trying to catch my breath. "What's happening here?" I asked, my voice coming out more urgently than intended.

The soldier looked at me impassively. "Sorry, ma'am, no one in or out at this time."

I pointed towards my house. "Orcs attacked us and took my friend."

The soldier continued to look at me, unblinking. He even looked like he had straightened his back more. "That's why we can't let you in. The orcs could be right behind you."

I growled and flattened my ears. "They're not." As I stomped towards the metal gate, I flexed my claws. "My sister is tracking them right now. I need to get to Captain Aenwyn and launch the mission to hunt the orcs down."

The two guards exchanged glances. One of them shrugged. "Alright, since we haven't heard from the walls about anyone marching, get in here and we'll close the door behind you."

I growled again. *This is taking too long.* I raised my hands, letting the magic flow through me. Ice wrapped around the metal gates, growing thicker and thicker. I pushed my magic further, and with a loud crack and a bang, the gates swung open.

The two guards gaped at me, their eyes wide. "How—how did you do that?" one of them stammered.

"Out of my way, humans." I stepped through the open gates and took off running.

As I ran through the town, my magic crackled and chilled the surrounding air, leaving a trail of frost in my wake. It was keeping me from overheating from running so much. I needed to get to Captain Aenwyn and rally the troops. *I need to catch up with my sister. Nothing will stand in my way.*

One benefit of running through the town at night was that nobody else was in the streets to impede me. Almost nobody. One guard did get in my way.

"Easy there, lady. What's the rush? Are the orcs attacking?" The guardswoman looked towards the walls. "I haven't heard a horn. I didn't miss it, did I?"

I wanted to just run past her, but she stepped in front of me again. After huffing and rolling my eyes, I took this moment to catch my breath again. "I need to get to Captain Aenwyn's house and tell her to get The Maidens ready to follow my sister."

The woman blinked her green eyes a couple of times. "Okay, uh, proceed?" She stepped to the side while never taking her eyes off me. But as I took another step, she started talking again. "Do you know where you're going?"

I don't have time for this. I've been there once, and that's all I need.

As I ran towards the house, exhaustion weighed down on me. My legs ached, and my chest burned. But I couldn't slow down, not when Lucia was out there tracking the orcs who had taken Fina. I had to reach Captain Aenwyn and get the knights moving.

I pushed through the fatigue, gritting my teeth and ignoring the pounding in my head, until finally, my destination was in sight.

I slammed into the door, afraid that if I stopped running, I wouldn't start again. *Why does Captain Aenwyn have to live in the center of the city? Why couldn't she live closer to the gate? How does Lucia do this so much? She makes it look so easy, and she's so much faster than me, too.*

My hand slapped into the door repeatedly as I gasped for air. I hugged the door to stay upright. But there was no response, so I continued to pound on it. When I tried to focus on using my magic to freeze the door handle and force it open, I just couldn't do it. It felt like my magic kept slipping through my fingers.

"Captain!" My voice wheezed. "Help! Orcs attacked us and we need—"

There were footsteps on the other side of the door. *Finally!* The door opened just as I pushed off and held onto the frame for support.

"Lucia?" Captain Aenwyn swung the door wide and eyed me from top to bottom. "No. Lexia, what's wrong? What happened?"

Captain Aenwyn was in a tan nightgown that reached her feet. Her hair was a disheveled mess, and her eyes, while wide, clearly showed that she had been very much asleep until a few moments ago.

I took a deep breath, attempting to steady my breathing. "Orcs attacked Lucia, Mom, me... We killed them... Saw others attacked too..."

Captain Aenwyn held out her hand. "Come on, sit down, and slow down. Catch your breath."

I shook my head. "There's no time. Lucia is already following the orcs and we need to catch up with her."

The captain placed a finger on my forehead and pushed.

I fell backwards onto my butt. "Ow, what was that for?" I asked as I rubbed my sore bottom.

"You can barely stand. How do you think you can help your sister in the state you're in?" Aenwyn crossed her arms. "Besides, it will take some time to rally all the knights and get horses and supplies. So come in and sit down. I'll put some decent clothes on and spread the orders to mobilize. When I come back, you can tell me more about what happened. Okay?" She leaned forward and extended a hand to me.

I took it. "How long are we talking? We need to leave now. And horses?"

As I was pulled to my feet, the elf sighed. "Your sister is fast, and even with horses we'll have trouble catching up with her."

"Oh, I didn't think about that." *Right, humans are slow and weak. Elves aren't much better.*

The captain led me to a small table with a couple of chairs. I sat down in one of them. "Don't worry about it." Aenwyn gave me a wink. "You're not hired for your military strategy. Like your sister, your uses are more direct."

I crossed my arms as my tail lashed behind me. "Are you calling me stupid?"

The elf took a step back and glared at me. "No. I'm saying your ice magic and memorization are where your talents lie. You can't be the best at everything. You're still a kid by some standards." I was about to tell her I was not a kid, but she held out a hand. "I know that as a beastkin, you're different. That's why you're here now. You're not in charge, so don't act like you are."

I cringed. "I'm sorry, Captain Aenwyn. I'm worried about Lucia and Fina."

The captain nodded. "I understand. You and your sister are close. But you can't let that cloud your judgment. Now, let me get dressed and mobilize the knights. Sit and catch your breath."

Captain Aenwyn left the room, leaving me alone with my thoughts. I let out a sigh and leaned back in the chair, trying to calm myself down. I was exhausted, and I felt every muscle screaming at me. But I knew I'd let my emotions get the better of me again. *Lucia and I really are so much alike.*

I closed my eyes and took a few deep breaths, trying to clear my mind. I couldn't help but think about Lucia. *I hope she's okay and that we'll be able to catch up with her soon.*

Captain Aenwyn returned from what I could only guess was her bedroom and gave me a quick glance before walking out. As the door shut, I let my eyes close once more. But each moment left me feeling worse. There was a terrible itchiness in my hands and feet, but my pads had never itched before.

I stared at them, trying to figure out what I was feeling. *Lucia does something after she does a lot of hard exercises. She calls it stretching.* The movements my sister made whenever I watched her stretch played in my mind. I started with the simplest: touching my toes while keeping my legs straight.

As I continued with my stretches, I could feel the tension and pain in my muscles slightly ease. I took a deep breath and let it out slowly, trying to calm my nerves.

The sound of two galloping horses in the streets broke my quiet moment.

Captain Aenwyn reentered the room, fully dressed and ready for action. "Okay, the knights are rallying, and we'll be ready to go soon," she stated with a firm tone.

I stood up. "About time," I muttered under my breath.

The elf shot me a stern look. "Don't get ahead of yourself, Lexia. This is serious. I need you to tell me everything that's happened tonight."

I huffed and crossed my arms as I leaned back. My vision blurred slightly as my memories took over and reenacted themselves as if I were living them again. Every detail, every sight, sound, taste, smell, and touch flowed through my mind.

When my memories reached the gates, I let them drop. *She doesn't need to know from that point on.* I shook my head to clear the fogginess from my eyes.

When I could see clearly again, the captain was watching me closely. "After that, I made it here, and you know the rest," I said to let her know I was done.

"I'll never get used to that," she mumbled to herself while turning away. *Get used to what?* Before I could ask, she straightened her shoulders. "Alright, this is beyond weird."

"Why?"

The elf gave me a worried look. "Because the orcs, while never staying in one place for long, were never this close. And based on their movements previously, they should have been to the east. It's almost like you were targeted."

My ears perked up. "But they didn't have anyone in charge, and the orc didn't say anything about us specifically."

Captain Aenwyn started pacing. "I know. You didn't spare any details. But this whole situation just feels wrong. First these orcs, then we get news of the rider. Someone is quite the puppet master, and I can't help but feel like we're playing right into their plans."

"But we can't leave Lucia and Fina," I said in a far too whiny voice.

"And we won't." Aenwyn gave me a slight frown. "The orcs have likely taken more than just your friend. I just can't shake this feeling of everything being too coincidental."

"But that doesn't change the fact that my sister is likely in trouble." I pointed to the door. "We need to leave now."

The elf arched an eyebrow as she gave me a sidelong glance. "You aren't ready. Where are your supplies?"

"At home!" I stomped my foot. "We'll go by it when we leave. Mom already has my stuff packed for me."

There was another set of horse hooves striking the street outside. The elf turned to face the door and smiled. "That's our sign that everyone's gathering to leave."

There was a knock at the door just before the captain opened it. A thin woman who looked young for a human stood in the doorway with a sword on her hip and a kite shield on her back. Her chain armor wasn't doing her any favors to keep her stealthy.

"Everyone is assembling at the north gate like you ordered, Captain," the woman said.

"Thank you, Lindsey." Aenwyn stepped to the side and waved towards the door. "You'll get your wish. Come on, let's go."

I tilted my head back and shouted, "Finally!"

When I walked outside, I saw three horses. "Uh, what's the third horse doing here?" I asked as I pointed to the animal and turned to my captain.

"That's for you to ride."

I backed away from the beast. "I don't ride horses. That's not a good idea. What if it thinks I'm going to eat it?"

I felt a hand against my back. "Are you going to eat him?" Aenwyn asked.

After inspecting the stallion closer, I noticed he was quite large and there was plenty of meat on him. *It's been a while since I've had a good horse to eat.* I licked my lips. "It's tempting." The words slipped out unconsciously.

"Don't worry, we'll help you out." Lindsey grabbed my hand. "But a word of advice: don't bite him while he's running." She pulled me towards the large black horse. "He's trained, so you won't have to do much other than stay on."

My mouth went dry. "I don't want to. I'd rather run next to you guys."

Captain Aenwyn walked up to the horse and extended her hand. "You're not like your sister. These horses can outrun you. Also, you won't be able to run for as long as them. Just bear with it for this mission. You want to help your sister, right?"

"Y-yes."

"And how jealous would she be if you could do something that she can't?" A smirk grew on the elf's face. "You can be her knight in silver fur."

I couldn't think as Lindsey pulled me to the horse. He smelled like straw with a touch of sweat. As I stared at him, unable to move, the horse snorted and shook his head. His black mane flowed through the air and shone in the light of the moons.

This is for you, sis. You'll owe me a lot for this. "How do I do this?" I grabbed the saddle and looked at the stirrups. *My feet probably won't fit well in those.*

"Just lift your foot up like this." Lindsey grabbed my foot—I held back the desire to claw her spine out for touching my feet without asking—and lifted it into the stirrup. "Now, pull yourself up and swing your leg over the back and into the other stirrup."

I felt the leather strap sink in between my pads and my toes. *Yeah, Lucia, you're going to pay for this.* I grabbed the horn on the saddle and pulled myself up, but when I almost made it up and stuck my leg out to go over the horse's back, I started falling backwards. *No, no, no—*

Suddenly, there was a pair of hands on my butt.

"Up you go!"

Lindsey shoved me upwards, and I had enough momentum to get into the saddle. But when my leg went downwards, I didn't get my other foot into the stirrup like Lindsey instructed me. My weight shifted, and I started falling towards the other side of the horse. I shrieked and threw my arms out to prepare to catch myself. But one of my arms was pulled back.

"I gotcha." Lindsey pulled me back.

Captain Aenwyn came around to the other side of the horse and helped correct me in the saddle. She also helped put my foot in the stirrup, which again felt weird as it sat in between my toes.

After finally getting somewhat balanced in my seat, I dug my claws into the reins. My tail was held up as far as it could go before it hurt. *There's no place for my tail to go. Lucia, if the orcs don't kill you, I will. This is awful. The things I do for family.*

Both women were standing on either side of me with their arms up. "Are you set? Comfortable?" Aenwyn asked. "Like Lindsey said, just do your best to keep yourself upright and keep your movements subtle."

I flattened my ears and glared at her. "This isn't natural, just so you know." I nodded towards my tail. "This is as uncomfortable as it looks."

Lindsey chuckled. "I wouldn't understand. While my backend is healthily plump, I don't have the extra package you do."

Aenwyn hopped onto her horse with practiced ease. She guided the animal next to mine. "Just take it easy. The sooner we catch up to your sister, the sooner you can get off the horse. Let's hope that she doesn't lose their tracks."

I tightened my grip on the reins. "Lucia is the best hunter ever. There's no way she lost them."

14

LUCIA'S REVERSE RAID

I've totally lost them. Lexia can't learn about this.

I stared at the undisturbed ground. *This is impossible. One moment I see their tracks and smell their dirty scent, and then poof, it's all gone. How did they do that? Is that why nobody's been able to track them?*

A growl escaped my lips as I paced around. *I tracked them perfectly, but as soon as I reached this dirt path, everything just stopped. It's not like I'm in the wrong area.*

"I've searched everywhere around here. Nothing. How much time have I wasted? Their footsteps are right there." I pointed at the offending indents on the ground. "Some of them are only half a footprint too. It's like magic just buried everything."

I stopped moving.

"Of course, magic," I grumbled. "But who has magic that can do this? What kinda magic is it in the first place?" I ran my fingers through my hair and slammed my eyes shut. "Why does this have to be so hard?"

"Troubles, my pet?" a husky voice teased my ears.

Just my luck. I opened my eyes and turned to see a familiar red-skinned demoness floating lazily in the air. My magic surged through me as I coated my arms and claws with ice.

I bared my fangs. "What are you doing here?"

The former sin of lust, now Rider of Pain, smirked. "Just watching you ever so closely. Because you're going the wrong way." She pointed her tail towards the south. "The Rider of Death is that way."

A subtle scent of salt water wafted in my direction. I narrowed my eyes as I waited for her to make a mistake. "But the orcs who took my friend are in this direction."

The floating demon frowned. "Why are you letting yourself get distracted by something so trivial? Hurry up and take care of my problem."

A grin spread across my face. "I could end all your problems, right here, right now."

The succubus clapped her hands and, with a flap of her wings, floated up more. "You would?"

"Yes, come down here, and I'll take good care of you." *Come down here so I can rip you apart!*

She wagged her finger at me. "Ah, ah, ah. Those are the wrong emotions for that. And your tone is all wrong. You need to say it like this." The demoness folded her arms under her breasts and pushed them out more while leaning forwards. She batted her eyelashes while pouting. "Please, come here. I'll take *really* good care of you."

Her voice oozed with the lust she embodied. For a fleeting moment, I almost questioned why I was so hung up on being with just Victor.

Don't do it.

I shook my head and growled as my vision turned red.

"Aw, you almost fell for me," the demon said in an almost childish tone. "If you aren't going to be a good girl and do what I tell you to, I'll have to make you. I thought if I removed that silly girl you'd have one less distraction."

"You took Fina?" I lunged towards the demon, but couldn't catch her. She just flapped her wings and flew even higher. "I'll kill you!"

"Well, I didn't take her; I just nudged the orcs that were in the area to take a slight detour." She shrugged. "But... if you want her back so badly, let's make a deal. You help me kill the other riders, and I'll bring you back your precious little cat girl, alive and unharmed."

That would make things easier. But what else will she make me do? I already know what Daric would say. "No." My voice rumbled with a deep growl. "I'll save her on my own."

The demon rolled her eyes and sighed. "And how are you going to do that? You can't find their tracks, can you? What about their scent? Oh, that's right, that's gone too."

She's toying with me. Fine. Two can play that game. "What's your deal with me?" I dug my toe claws into the ground. "Are you so upset that I'm the one who got away? Did the spoiled little princess finally get denied a shiny new toy for the first time ever?"

The demon's eye twitched. "Your taunting is still as annoying as ever." Her voice was no longer sweet or lovely; it was lower. "Everyone has a price. And everyone has a sin."

I pointed a claw at the demoness. "Why do you need me to help you kill the other rider? Aren't you just as powerful as him?"

She clenched her fists, her claws digging into the palms of her hands. A few drops of blood dripped to the ground. "In theory, yes. Even a little more than him. There's just one tiny detail that makes all the difference in the world." She relaxed her hands, letting more blood dot the ground below her. "Experience. He's had hundreds of years of being a rider. I've had less than a season in this world. Pain's power is wildly different compared to mine, and learning to control it hasn't been easy. So, I'm keeping a slightly lower profile than usual."

I rolled my eyes. "And since the other Rider is already here on Centari, you can't stay hidden and practice. You need him dealt with before we deal with him without you, robbing you of your chance to steal his power too."

"Knowing what my little game is won't change the outcome." She paused and stared into space for a moment. "But if you want to still play hard to get? Fine." She waved her hand, and the tracks and scent of the orcs returned while the smell of salt water disappeared. "Go get your little cat friend. But we'll see who gets the last laugh."

I didn't waste any time. I took off in the direction of the orcs and

Fina's scent, using all of my senses to follow the trail. The demon's laughter followed me even though it quickly grew distant. My heart raced, the thoughts of what the orcs would do to my friend driving me ever onward.

As I ran, I couldn't help but think about the demoness and what she had said. *"Everyone has a price. And everyone has a sin."* *What's her angle? What does she want from me?* I knew better than to trust a demon, but I couldn't help but feel that there was more to this situation than what I could see.

But the sun was starting to set, and I was getting tired. I had spent the entire day running without stopping to eat. After taking a quick moment to stuff my face with half the jerky Mom gave me and closing my eyes for a few winks, I felt a bit more fresh.

How are the orcs still ahead of me? I thought my physical and recovery aptitudes would have allowed me to catch them by now. The demon didn't stop me for that long, did she?

The tracks were still visible, so I followed them until it looked like they were headed towards a small town. It looked like some more split off, but the majority headed there.

My geography knowledge wanted to tell me that there wasn't supposed to be a town in this direction. But I'd been wrong many times before. *And I don't have a map to prove anything one way or another. But since I can see it, I might as well check it out.*

The sun just ducked the horizon as I got close enough to make out some of the details of the village. But the closer I got, the more I could smell the orcs. *I finally caught up with them.*

As I approached the outskirts of the village, a sense of unease washed over me. The buildings were now nothing but charred remains. The straw thatched roofs lay in smoldering heaps on the ground. The smell of smoke still lingered heavily in the air. *Is this destruction recent?*

Throughout the open streets, I could see groups of orcs walking in tight circles, as if they were on patrol. I kept low to the ground, trying to remain unnoticed and creep closer.

As I got closer and ducked behind a building to hide, I noticed that the building wasn't just burned, but also ransacked. Everything was ruined. Nothing but gaping holes in the walls, damaged floors, and a collapsed straw roof remained.

When did this happen? Captain Aenwyn and Evalana didn't say anything about a town getting sacked, right? It doesn't matter. I just need to go in, get Fina, and get out. Simple.

I focused on my ears, trying to find any information I could. There were voices in the distance, but they were muffled. It sounded like someone was gagged and trying to scream.

I circled around the ruined village, looking for openings and trying to count how many orcs there were. But as I kept low and moved around, one by one, campfires were lit and illuminated the groups of orcs huddling around them.

The orcs stopped moving around in patrols and took up posts. *That makes things much easier for me. I just need to pick them off one by one. Also, I need to take the bodies some place where someone won't find them right away. The ruined buildings are nice to see through, so I can find all the orcs, but they won't hide bodies well.*

The more I circled around the town, the less the orcs moved and remained awake. Another detail stood out to me. There were a handful of buildings near the center that were in better shape than the rest. The orcs frequently entered and exited the smallest of the intact buildings.

When it looked like the orcs that were keeping watch were nodding off, I stepped up. *It's time to show you how a hunter eliminates her threats.*

An orc standing on the furthest outskirts of the ruins grunted as his eyes drooped periodically. I circled around to his left, nice and low, without making a sound thanks to my padded feet and hands. The orc didn't know I was next to him, and I held back my growl to favor stealth, then slammed my hand into his throat and pushed him against the wall he leaned on.

My prey flailed his arms around as I crushed his throat until the wall behind him crumbled and he fell through. The orc's head bounced off the ground with a crack and a spray of blood. He lay motionless as more blood pooled around his head. I clenched my jaw and listened for anyone who may have heard the wall collapsing.

I didn't hear anyone moving. The silence that hung over the night was delightful. I stepped over the orc and snapped his neck in one quick movement. *One down, twenty to go.*

I worked my way from the outside in. One by one, each orc's last sight was my face as I ripped their throat out, snapped their neck, or bit their spine. Eight orc bodies were hidden around the central buildings. *Things are going too smoothly. I don't see how I can isolate any more of them. But I've done too much to stop now.*

I looked around for any way I could get closer. There were three orcs sitting around a fire. Where the other nine were that I'd seen, I didn't know. No one went in or came out of the smallest building, but something about that building demanded my attention.

I looked for entrances to the other buildings and found some windows. Inside, several orcs were lying on piles of straw, sleeping. My claws extended as I very carefully crawled through the strongest window. I stepped up to my first defenseless victim.

Usually, when I stood over something sleeping peacefully, there was a small sense of guilt for what I was about to do. This time, I didn't feel that towards the orc. I stabbed my claws into his throat and covered his mouth. My claws raked through his flesh, opening a fatal wound where dark-red blood poured out.

The orc fought against me as he tried to remove my hand. I dug my claws into his jaw and cheeks to keep him from pulling my hand away, which was far more difficult than I thought it should have been.

I hoped that all of his rustling in the straw didn't wake the other three sleeping in the room. As more blood gushed from my victim's neck, his movements slowed gradually until they stopped completely. I relaxed as I removed my hand.

There was the sound of someone stirring in their straw bed behind me. I snapped my head around and saw one of the orcs holding his head as he looked around. Our eyes met. His look was full of confusion. Panicking, I created an ice spike and threw it at him, piercing his eye.

He covered his eye and bellowed in pain.

That wasn't the result I was hoping for. I sprinted and slammed a foot into his stomach. As the orc doubled over, I grabbed his back and head before biting down on the middle of his neck. His screams ended instantly.

The other two orcs' feet hit the ground with a thud, one on each side of me. They looked at me, unsure what to do.

I bolted towards the one on my right, the one furthest from the door, where more would certainly come from. My claws reached for his neck, but he lifted an arm in the way, and my claws left four deep gouges in his forearm.

The orc swung his wounded arm in a backhand for my face. I ducked and kicked his knee out. His leg went backwards, and he put his arms out to catch himself.

At this point, his partner moved towards me with a raised fist. I kicked back towards him when he got close enough. My toe claws left their mark and opened four lines of their own. His punch came up short as he stumbled back a step.

The orc I'd charged attempted to tackle my legs, so I jumped over. I came down on his back and stomped on his neck. A sickly snap, and his body went limp.

The final remaining orc growled as he threw his arm out wide and tried to tackle me. He learned from his buddy's mistake and aimed for my torso. I didn't get out of his reach, but I got my arms up high enough so he didn't trap them.

He started squeezing me and grinned. "You're mine now." His voice was just as grating and painful as every other orc's I had heard.

I could feel my ribs being crushed as my lungs lost air. I didn't bother responding with words. All I gave him was a growl before I dug my claws into his face. He let me go and covered the wound, blood pouring from between his fingers.

The doorway suddenly held another orc, a large ax in his hands. Before the orc could leave the doorway, I slashed the wounded orc's armpit. The sudden outpouring of blood told me I'd hit my mark. I then dug my claws into his chest and hooked them into his ribs.

The orc in the doorway lifted his ax as he charged me.

I spun around and threw the bleeding orc into the oncoming one. The ax slipped from the orc's grasp as he went backwards with the momentum of his friend. Another orc stepped into the doorway, a rusty sword in his grip, and stood over the two lying in a heap.

He turned his head and shouted, "Intruder!"

Great, now they all know I'm here. Do I run or fight them all in this room? I turned to look at the window I'd entered from. *No, I promised I would stay safe. It's time to go. I doubt they'd keep up with me. But now there are fewer of them.*

I jumped through the window and tucked into a roll before springing to my feet. The orc with the sword stood in the window, huffing and puffing through his clenched jaw.

An idea bubbled to the front of my mind. I held out my arms and sauntered backwards. "You want me? Come and get me." My voice was low as a rumble filled it. I turned and ran into the mix of buildings, waiting for them to follow.

After all, there are only eight, maybe nine, left.

15

ALL ORCS MUST DIE

I could hear the grunts and growls of the orcs behind me. I had just challenged one of them to chase me, and now I was doing my best to shake them off.

I ducked through a doorway and veered to the right, putting my back against a crumbling wall. I could hear the orcs getting closer, their heavy steps echoing through the night. But then the steps grew distant.

They lost me. Good, now I can get to work picking them off one by one again.

I spotted a window, and, without hesitation, I leaped through it, tucking and rolling as I hit the ground. I came up in a crouch, ready to keep moving. But I paused, listening for any signs of the orcs.

It wasn't long before an unknown voice boomed out, "What's going on here?" The new voice sounded unfamiliar from the rest, less distorted.

"It's a beast!" one of the orcs answered. "It attacked us."

"How? Where were the sentries?" the unfamiliar voice demanded.

"We don't know," the orc replied.

The leader-sounding orc's voice rose. "Where is everyone else?"

"I think it killed them," one orc answered with a shaky voice.

Given how horrible their voices naturally sounded, them sounding scared was even more off-putting.

"Fine, they were too weak anyway. Go, find this beast, and bring it to me." I could hear their footsteps begin moving again. "Travel in pairs," the leader ordered.

"Uh, who will go with you?"

"I want to see this beast and see how it can cause all this noise," the leader replied.

A knot formed in my stomach. *Does the leader want to face me alone? He knows I've killed most of his men, and he's still not fazed? That's not good. Well, it looks like I'm going to have to deal with the goons first. And now they're in pairs. Things just got a whole lot harder for me.*

Using only the moonlight, I stalked through the village, my senses on high alert. The orcs carried torches with them, broadcasting their locations to me.

That's both very helpful and extremely problematic. I really need to figure out how I got so scared of fire. It's starting to become a problem. Now, how do I take out them and their torches at the same time?

I stepped cautiously through the village, using the darkness to my advantage.

I spotted my first pair of orcs. Their backs were turned to me as they grunted between each other.

This is my chance. I crept closer, staying low to the ground. My heart pounded louder in my chest the closer I got to the orc carrying the torch.

Both orcs held clubs in their hands; the one without the torch just held a much larger club. The longer I looked at it, the more it looked like a tree branch than a proper weapon. I took a quick look at the area and saw that the other orc groups were getting farther away. As I walked downwind of the orcs, I could smell them and all of their filth and the burning torch, but also the subtle scent of alcohol.

While their heads moved on a swivel, they never once looked backwards. I grabbed a clay brick from one of the ruined buildings and prepared to throw it at the torch, hopefully dislodging it from his grip.

The brick hit its target, and the torch broke away. But it only dropped right in front of the orc.

Well, that was anti-climactic. The orcs looked at the fallen torch for a moment before turning towards each other, then finally turning to face me. *We're at the farthest edge of the town. Even if they alert the others, I have an escape route. Of course, after I deal with these two blockheads.*

As I predicted, the orc who held the torch turned his head and shouted, "Over here!"

The two charged me, the orc holding the tree branch leading the way. I lunged forward, tackling the closest orc once they came close enough so the fire wouldn't bother me. We rolled until he pinned me on my back with his weapon pressed against my chest. I brought my legs up and kicked him away. He flew into a wall and crashed through it, leaving his weapon in my hands.

The other orc turned to face me, and I sprang to my feet, dropped the tree branch, and delivered quick slashes with my claws. My attacks didn't strike anything vital and only opened minor wounds across his torso.

He swung his club high, aiming for my head. I easily ducked and slashed a deep gouge in his triceps, causing his arms to go limp.

The club hit the ground, and the orc roared as he threw a wild haymaker. I almost laughed as I leaned back to dodge the attack. But before I could step in for the kill, the other orc tackled me. My back exploded with pain as his shoulder drove me to the ground.

I barely caught myself enough so that my face didn't slam into the dirt. He pushed off me and lifted an arm to punch my face. I rolled over and watched his fist hammer into the ground, kicking up a small bit of dirt. I rolled back and bit down on his wrist.

How can their taste get any worse?

Immediately he pulled back, and I let him pull me to my knees. I bit down harder, feeling and hearing the bones cracking in the orc's arm. While he pulled, I slashed at his neck, but he put up his other arm, saving him from a far deadlier wound.

He roared as he held is free hand over his head to bring it down on me. I kicked his leading ankle, tripping him. As he fell, I pulled back so he didn't fall on me; instead, he landed on his partner. When the two orcs toppled together, the arm in my mouth snapped, and my teeth finally severed it.

I quickly got to my feet and spat the gross appendage out. The two orcs were figuring out whose limbs were whose, and I darted in and slashed the top orc's throat while he was busy pushing himself to his feet. As he gurgled his last breath, I moved to the other orc, who was busy trying to push his partner off him with only one hand.

He glared and snarled at me before I stomped on his head, crushing his brain. *Gross.* I flicked off parts of his brain and skull matter from my foot as best I could until I heard the sound of heavy footsteps running towards me. I took off and hid, but stayed close enough so I could hear them if they made any more plans.

"Two more down," the first orc that arrived said. "This beast is good."

"It's been picking us off one by one. Now two at a time. How is this possible?" the other orc that arrived asked as he kneeled next to the corpses.

More of the orcs arrived until seven orcs gathered based on the number of footsteps. I moved around to see if I was right. I found a small burned-out corner that gave me a sliver of the scene. Seven orcs stood over the bodies of my latest victims. Six of them were similarly built: tall, stocky, and carrying various clubs, axes, and swords.

One orc stood out from the others. He was slightly shorter, and his body leaner. All the other orcs I'd killed tonight had been bald, but this one had a strip of black hair, like a mohawk, that he had tied up in a ponytail. There still wasn't any hair on the sides, but that was the first time I could recall seeing an orc with hair. Also, his skin was a darker shade of green than the others.

"This beast is getting more and more interesting." I recognized the voice of the smaller orc. It was the voice I'd thought belonged to the leader.

That's the leader? He doesn't look that dangerous. The other orcs look worse than him. My instincts aren't acting up now that I can see him.

The leader kicked one of the bodies to flip it, then pointed. "You see this? These wounds are lethal. This beast is not an ordinary animal. It's thinking and attacking with purpose." He turned to his followers. "We are being hunted."

The other six exchanged glances and mutters.

"So, what do we do?"

The leader slapped his forehead and groaned. "Why do I have to do all the thinking around here?"

He walked up to the orc that asked and punched him right between the eyes. The punch was fast, and if I had blinked, I would have missed it. I clearly heard the crunch of bones as blood sprayed from the impact.

The orc's concave face stared blankly as he tilted backwards and hit the ground with a thud.

Okay, his danger rating just went way up. I don't know if I can slash my claws that quickly. Note to self: looks can be deceiving. A wave of guilt crept into the back of my mind. *That's something I should've been aware of. After all, Escaeris has the physical aptitude, and she doesn't look like she's that strong. You would think for being on my second life, I wouldn't be so shallow.*

"Now, any other stupid questions?" The leader eyed the other five, who all stood silently. "Good. Now, with that weakness culled, we can focus on taking care of our little problem."

Does that mean he killed his own man? For what, asking a question? Granted, he wasn't that bright, but you're a little short on numbers. You should use what you've got. Are you not taking me seriously? I'm a little hurt by that. Stupid orcs, you're going to be sorry.

"We need to stop playing its game and lure it into a trap." The leader started pacing in front of the others. "The beast likely followed that other beast that was here earlier. They tend to get attached and do stupid things." He pointed to another orc. "Go and grab one of the broods and bring her to a more open section. The rest of you, I want you to circle the area and stay hidden. When the beast shows up, surround it and kill it."

The orcs nodded and took off, the dark-green orc watching them before following at a much slower pace. He took one last look at the scene before resuming his stroll.

I leaned forward, eager to take him on now that he was alone, but my instincts shot me a warning. *So I am scared of him. It's no surprise after seeing what he did to the other orc. But there are several things I need to break down about what he just said. He talked about another beast. I assume he was talking about a beastkin. That has to mean Fina.*

My tail curled around my leg. *He talked about her in the past tense. That means she's not here. I guess I need to look for more tracks after I finish with these here. They have hostages or prisoners, by the sounds of things. I don't like the word "broods." I can't wait for Captain Aenwyn, and I can't leave things as they are. That leaves me with only one choice.*

I couldn't hold back the smirk at the situation. *Too bad for that orc. Traps only work if who you hope to trap doesn't know what's coming. Since I heard everything, that's going to make things much easier for me. If the orcs are going to hide, that means no torches. Thanks for making my job much easier.*

I stalked through the streets, watching their movements and keeping plenty of distance. They moved closer to the center of the town, near a well. Four of the orcs hid in the corners of ruined buildings. Two of them even went inside the ruined buildings. If my plan was going to work, I needed them not to see each other.

The orc leader headed off in a different direction than the others, but I made sure not to go in the same direction as him. *I want to leave him for last. I doubt the orcs will let me take him one-on-one. It feels like he'll require everything I have to beat.*

I crept behind the first of my victims as another orc pulled an obviously pregnant human woman behind him. My blood froze. Only dirt covered her bronze skin and black, mangled hair. She was covered in cuts and bruises all over her body. Her belly extended out, looking like she was into the second half of her pregnancy. None of her wounds looked dangerous, but the large amount of dried blood that I saw ignited a fire in me that I hadn't felt in years.

My vision shifted, and the only thing that existed was the five orcs. One thought controlled my next actions. *All orcs must die!*

16

WHY ALL ORCS MUST DIE

The orc closest to me suffered first. All ideas of stealth and patience were gone. I dug my claws into his spine and pulled. As he fell to the ground, I pounced on him. My claws ripped his torso open far beyond the point of killing him. His screams turned to wet gurgles as my claws tore through his lungs.

Heavy footsteps and shouts from the other orcs pulled my attention away from the bloody scraps below me. The first orc charged me with a club raised above his head. I darted to his side just after he swung the club in a powerful two-handed strike. Still crouching, I slashed at his hamstring. The orc reeled back and grabbed at the crippling wound.

I kicked at his other leg's knee, and the orc started toppling backwards. He tried to turn towards me as he fell. But as he did, I drove my claws into his gut through his fur clothing. My other hand dug into the space between his collarbone and neck.

Another orc shouted as he charged through a half-crumbled wall behind me.

I turned and threw the orc at the newcomer, who had a heavily rusted blade. The sword-wielding orc dropped his shoulder and, with one arm, lifted the orc up and over his head without breaking stride.

Ice slowly spread over my forearms as I sidestepped his stab.

After I dodged his first attack, the orc twisted the blade and swung it towards me. By that time, the ice around my arms had solidified enough to block the shoddy weapon. A few chips of ice went flying from the impact. There was more power to it than I'd thought there would be, and my arm bent and was forced into my chest. With my free hand, I slashed the orc's wrist. Before he could recoil out of my reach, I pushed his arm out wide and kicked him in the gut towards a corner.

He hit the ground, and his sword clattered as it skidded. As the orc tumbled backwards, he leaned into the roll and ended up on his hands and knees. He snarled at me as he pushed himself to his feet. Another orc followed behind the other two.

I created more ice to cover my torso before I lashed out at the orc I'd kicked. My claws slid into his throat as he wound up with a punch. Blood sprayed everywhere, and some even got into my eye as I ripped my claws through his neck.

The stinging in my eye was easy to ignore. I could only focus on killing the remaining orcs.

The one I had thrown earlier slowly got to his feet as another orc jumped over him. And behind him, I saw the last orc charging me.

I had to focus on the orc charging me since he had an ax in each hand. He pulled them both back to swing across his chest from right to left. I stepped into his attack and slammed my shoulder into the arm that crossed his chest. Then I grabbed his head from over my shoulder and pulled him over by it. Several popping sounds resounded in my ears as I slammed the orc to the ground. His axes went flying past and bounced on the ground.

Two orcs stood in the entrance they'd been entering from. One was uninjured and holding a larger sword with significantly less rust; the other was wounded and unarmed. The injured orc charged first with a haymaker. I ducked under the attack, but I didn't have time to counter because the sword came towards my head.

I had to turn and slide even lower to not get decapitated. As I felt the breeze of the passing sword, I pushed myself backwards to my feet. The blade came back towards me. At the same time, the orc moved to my other side to cut off my escape. I rushed the unarmed orc and stabbed my claws into his ribs again.

He threw a punch and hit me right in the jaw. My vision flickered for a moment as I tasted my blood. I growled and turned around with him still impaled on my claws. The armed orc thrust his blade at me. I moved the orc I'd impaled into the path of the weapon.

As the sword punctured through my meat shield, I had to move my hips so that I didn't get stabbed as well.

The blade got stuck as the orc tried to pull his weapon back. Before he could free it, I darted around and slashed at his throat. He let go of his sword and raised his arms to protect himself. My claws dug into his forearm, and I slashed at him with my other hand.

The orc pulled his arm down and reached for my throat with his free hand. Before he could get me, I bit down on his hand, severing three fingers. My free hand slashed into the back of his head, digging into the bone of his skull but doing little else.

The orc pulled his hand back and sprayed my face with more blood, then leaned forward to bite me. I pulled my claws free from his forearm and grabbed the sides of his head. With his head sandwiched between my hands, I pushed them together.

He grabbed my hands with his and tried to fight me, but he couldn't get a good grip with his missing fingers.

Slowly, I could feel my hands getting closer. The orc was strong. I could feel him resisting me, but I was still stronger. There were subtle cracks before everything just crunched and his face and head split open. My palms touched through the mess of bone, blood, and brain matter. I stepped back as I flicked the gore from my hands and watched the corpse fall into an unceremonious heap.

My vision slowly returned, and I was reminded I still had three orc fingers in my mouth. I spat them out.

I had to be wrong. Those were by far the worst-tasting things ever, of all time. I don't want to know where those have been. I gagged. *Now I'll need to wash my mouth out with soap. Yet another unappetizing prospect.*

I headed outside now, since all the orcs were dead, and saw the woman. She was on her knees, weeping. As I got closer to her, I could see they hadn't starved her, but her body looked weak, like she hadn't moved much in the past few years.

"Are you alright?" I asked. I kept my distance because I didn't know what state of mind she was in. And given how much blood was covering me, I didn't want to scare her more.

She looked up at me. Massive dark spots and heavy bags surrounded her bloodshot eyes, yet the blue in the sea of red looked at me almost hopefully.

She scrambled to her feet, her limbs barely holding her up. More tears flowed from her face as she attempted to head towards me. I didn't move; I just watched.

When she came close, I prepared to catch her. But she didn't run into my awaiting arms. No, she ran past me and into the building with the orc corpses.

What? Don't tell me she's sad that they're dead.

I followed. When I looked around for her, she held the rusted sword in her hands and aimed it at her stomach. My eyes went wide. I took a step towards her, but she drove the blade into her belly, screaming.

She kept screaming and stabbing. Stabbing and screaming. I froze. I couldn't move to stop her, and I couldn't look away. Everything went numb as I watched the woman brutally eviscerate herself until she couldn't move. Blood poured out of her, and I knew she was dead.

The sight of her body burned itself into my mind. I stumbled out, feeling lightheaded. It felt like I couldn't hear anything as I leaned against the wall. Bile crept up to the back of my throat.

She killed herself. She wanted to die so badly, she did that to herself. How? Why? I don't understand. She had a child.

Then the memory played in my head again, and again, and again. I vomited. Once I was reduced to retching my empty stomach, I slammed my eyes shut and grabbed my head.

Stop it; I don't want to see that again. It was bad enough the first time. I remembered the orcs and how they dragged her, and the leader said to grab a "brood" to use as bait. *She was pregnant with an orc's child. They raped her and impregnated her. How many times did they do that to her to drive her to that point?*

Then I was reminded of my first impressions of the world. I saw the cage the orcs had put me in after they'd tied me up.

I whispered, "I owe Captain Allen more than my life." *That could have been me if he hadn't saved me.*

My knees felt weak as I headed towards the smaller building. *She wasn't the only one. Now I have to save Fina. I won't let her suffer this fate.*

As I walked towards the building, I slowly started feeling better, but my anger grew. *How can such an evil race be allowed to live? Why haven't all the other kingdoms teamed up to kill them off and save this world from such a threat? They keep attacking everyone while nobody does anything about it.*

A growl rumbled from my throat as I stopped in front of the smallest building. *If I have to kill every orc myself, then so be it.*

I opened the door, and the sight that sprawled out before me left me feeling even more nauseated. Five women, all in different stages of pregnancy, were shackled to piles of straw. They were all thin, but not malnourished, and covered in blood, bruises, and minor cuts. As they all looked at me, I could see each one was empty inside. Their eyes were lifeless as they followed my movements.

A weak voice called out to me. "Kill us."

My heart hurt, and tears welled in my eyes. I walked into the room. The smell of feces and urine assaulted my nose. I closed my eyes and felt a familiar presence—my inner wolf.

I looked at her and saw the hurt in her eyes too. I then scanned the other four women. They had the same look in their eyes. One of them looked as distraught as the one did before she killed herself. Each one gave me a small nod, agreeing with the request. *They've given up.*

I can't do this. It's too much for me. If I don't do it, they'll do it themselves. And I can't just leave them like this. I'm not a monster. My inner wolf stepped up to me and nuzzled me in the chest. I ran a hand across her soft fur. There were no words, but I felt she would take care of things.

So I let go and let my inner wolf help the women find peace.

After a while, I felt myself being drawn back as my inner wolf told me she was done and wanted to be left alone to grieve for the women.

Thanks. After all these years, I've become more animalistic, while you've become more human. I could feel the smirk she gave me before she fell into the back of my mind.

I looked down and saw the blood on my hands. She at least sat me down by the entrance. After I stood up, I closed the door without looking. Using my claws, I wrote on the door, "Don't open. Just burn this building."

Hopefully, Captain Aenwyn will understand and fulfill this request.

As I stared at the building, a storm of emotions ran through my heart. But the sounds of boots stomping behind me disrupted everything. I turned my head and saw the orc leader standing in the center of the road behind me, holding two torches.

All orcs must die!

17

BLOODY BEATDOWN

The orc leader strode forward, holding the torches high. He was shorter than most of the orcs I'd killed tonight. His broad chest and toned arms were bare except for a few scraps of fur and hides draped over his shoulders. His legs were slightly larger than his arms and encased in rough, cured leather leggings that disappeared into rugged, knee-high boots. A bushy fur cloak hung from his shoulders.

"You see, little beast, I know your secret." The orc grinned. "You fear fire."

I stood frozen with fear as the orc leader approached me, my eyes glued to the torches. The flames danced in his eyes, illuminating the twisted joy on his face as he spoke.

"So, you're the one causing all this fuss?" he sneered. "A mere beast, challenging me."

I tried to lash out, to show him that I wasn't afraid, but the words caught in my throat. My pyrophobia had a grip on me, and no matter how much I tried to fight it, I couldn't bring myself to move.

"You should see the look on your face," he continued, his voice dripping with disdain. "So much for the great hunter, so much for the protector. You're nothing but a scared little girl."

His taunts only fueled my anger, but my fear was stronger. I couldn't move, I couldn't fight. All I could do was stand there, listening to his gloating. Even though we were at least an arc away, it felt like the flames flickered inches from my face.

He tossed one of the torches towards me. I flinched backwards from it. The orc laughed as he sauntered forward.

"Pathetic." His brow furrowed as he frowned. "And here I thought you might be a worthy brood mother for my spawn. But after seeing such a glaring weakness, you seem far less worthy. I should put you out of your misery."

You wanted me to have your children? The sides of my vision started bleeding red. A deep growl rumbled as I bared my fangs at the leader.

The orc rolled his shoulders. "You will be satisfied to know Asrok almost found you worthy of him."

I channeled my magic to create a small sphere of ice and launched it at Asrok's torch. The ice hit the flames, snuffing them out, and shattered the top of the torch.

Asrok looked at the broken torch and, for a moment, seemed surprised. But when he slowly turned his head and grinned, a shiver ran down my spine.

"You had my curiosity before." Asrok's grin grew wider. "Now you have my attention." He stomped a foot on the torch, the flame still burning on the ground. "Show me this strength that killed my entire tribe." He lifted his arms up in a defensive stance as he brushed off his cloak. "I'm going to enjoy breaking you and rebuilding my tribe, one truly worthy of my name."

With the fire gone, I charged him, my claws leading the way. He leaned back from my first strike, but my other hand came up and slashed four lines through his torso. But my claws didn't dig as deep as I was used to. His skin felt tougher than the other orcs'.

As I wondered why my claws didn't carve through his flesh as I expected, Asrok punched me right in the temple. I stumbled backwards, everything blurred. When my vision returned to normal, the orc kicked me right in the stomach. I went tumbling back.

There was a lot more strength behind his blows than I was ready for. He was as strong as the other orcs, but he moved so much faster. I growled to suppress the pain in my head, the ringing slowly subsiding. Baring my teeth, I charged again.

Asrok's hands seemed to move even faster. He punched into my ice armor on my chest. It cracked as I felt the impact. I slashed the inside bend of his elbow. He spun away after I drew blood to kick me in the side. While the strike cracked more of my armor, I caught his leg. He tried to pull it back, but I held on even tighter and slashed his knee with my free hand.

He tried to free himself by lifting his other leg and kicking me in the stomach. But his foot hit my armor and slid off harmlessly.

His assault wasn't done as he threw another fist towards my face, but I put up my ice-covered arm to block.

After the tingling in my bones stopped, I grinned at the orc, who was still in my grasp.

"My turn," I said in a low, threatening growl.

I placed my other hand under the leg I held to my side and heaved him over my head. His arms flailed as I threw him to the ground. Asrok caught himself mostly, but I slashed his hamstring and ruined his leg with my claws.

Asrok roared as he twisted and kicked me with his other leg. The blow hit me on the cheek, and I lost my grip on him. He twisted his body and stood up, even with his leg pouring blood. The snarl on his face tickled my instincts.

He's taking this more seriously. I lunged at him again. *It doesn't matter; he's going to die for his crimes!*

My claws reached for his head, but he leaned back enough so my claws raked four red lines from his shoulder to his nipple. I could feel my claws scrape against his ribs. Asrok flinched back for a moment before throwing punch after punch in a blinding display.

I tried to block his attacks, but after the first one made it through, I couldn't recover fast enough as three punches to my chest pushed me back with each blow until he ended the flurry with a roundhouse kick to my face. My world spun around me as I hit the ground.

Everything righted itself just in time for me to see his fist again drop down towards my head. I rolled out of the way. But he kept going. As he dropped his second fist, I rolled into it and pulled him to the ground with me. He fell on top of me, and I clawed at anything I could until he kicked me and pushed us apart.

We stood up and stared at each other for a moment. Blood poured from the myriad of wounds I'd given him, but I was feeling every bit of pain, too. The ice armor across my torso was shattered and no longer protected me. Our panting filled the air, neither one of us making the first move. Asrok put most of his weight on his good leg; there was still a ringing in my head.

The moment helped clear my head as I circled around the orc. He watched me, clearly ready to make a move once I got close. I reformed my ice armor and felt the last of my magic end. *It looks like I have to do this the hard way.*

I moved to engage again, but stopped short. Asrok's punch missed me. I took the chance to dive for his legs and put an end to his mobility.

My shoulder collided with his knee, bending it backward and causing the orc to scream in pain. He screamed until his back hit the ground, and he punched at me. His first punch hit me in the right eye, but my flinch caused his follow-up attacks to come up short.

I growled again and jumped on top of him, making sure to pin him as much as I could. My claws dug into his torso and arms as he kept his head and neck protected. But in between my strikes, he got his in too.

Punch after punch, his fist collided with my ice armor. Piece by piece, chunks fell off, and I could feel every hit. But each blow only fueled my rage even further, and I continued to slash his torso and arms, reaching for his throat.

He returned each of my strikes with a flurry of punches, and we went back and forth as I sat on top of him, raking claws and receiving punch after punch to my chest. Everything was a blur, as I could feel bones breaking and blood splattering everywhere. I couldn't see the orc below me, but I felt his punches as my claws continued to ravage him.

I could feel my consciousness fading, but I pushed onward. *All orcs must die!* My claws dug into flesh as if by instinct.

I lost my ability to feel, see, and hear. Only one thought kept me moving.

All orcs must die!

I lifted my arms, only to bring them down on the creature beneath me. I couldn't stop. *All orcs must die!*

Each moment stretched on. The edges of my vision darkened. *All orcs must...*

My body wanted to stop, but I wouldn't let myself. One more slash of my claws. *All orcs...*

One more slash. *All...*

The darkness finally swallowed me up.

INTERMISSION.

A CHAMPION FOR BALANCE

T he white marble demi-plane was far louder with the addition of the third being. The Judge had kept its attention on The Broker as he reviewed all the events of both the human boy and wolf girl. The Broker's methods were eccentric for a being as powerful as him. He'd even created a plush throne for himself to watch the proceedings from.

The Judge had never required a physical form to perform its duties and never understood The Broker's fascination with such frivolities. But as The Broker fell into another fit of laughter as they watched the wolf girl kill the orc, The Voice's violet sphere of light brightened just a bit. It had been shaking and flicking constantly, as it had many times while watching the wolf girl constantly put herself in such dangerous situations only to survive by some unquantifiable determination.

The Judge's own orange beam of light never wavered. "Broker, I would suggest you keep your presence under control."

The Broker placed a hand on his chest. "My sincere apologies. Powerful, primordial beings such as myself can't help it most of the time. As you yourself are aware, since we are in the same boat, so to speak. Our very existence can alter realities."

The Judge took The Broker's apology because he was right. But this was different. His presence had been slowly growing, deliberately.

The Judge knew The Broker was up to something. By the way his presence calculatingly grew, it could only mean that The Broker was testing his limits. The Judge had hardened the reality around him so that The Broker wouldn't be able to use his influence to read its mind.

The Broker twisted his head slightly from The Judge to The Voice. Despite a complete lack of facial features, everyone felt his grin. "And to our little one here, I will endeavor to ease their suffering in the presence of two such primordial beings."

Over most of his existence, The Broker hadn't been a problem. He had barely been available, despite his overwhelming power, so long as a deal was made. But recently, in the last few centuries, The Judge had received reports of his influence in far more places than reasonably expected.

Normally, such matters never concerned The Judge. But the others hadn't been seeking The Broker out. That could only mean he had been moving, but there was almost no proof that he had. Others had sent reports to everyone, warning against interacting with him.

But that was a problem for later.

"Such actions should be beneath you. However, I've already taken the subject's safety into consideration." The Judge enveloped The Voice in the same hardened reality that covered it. "My initial priority is to conduct a fair review."

However, the wolf girl had done something that The Judge didn't think she was capable of. It had been watching her grow up and face challenges throughout her second life. She had more than adapted to her new life. She'd embraced it. But as The Judge watched her kill the pregnant women, something seemed to click in its mind.

"Your fascination with the wolf girl is noted," The Judge said.

The Broker didn't shift his attention from the scene after it played out. "I'm interested in something interesting. Of all the times I've seen two souls fused like this, this is the first time it developed into such a smooth coexistence."

While The Judge usually refused to involve itself in any of the power shifts or plans of others so long as they didn't disrupt the balance or break the rules, the longing in The Broker's voice didn't sit well with it. The Judge wanted to state the wolf girl was off limits to The Broker, but that would break his impartial stance. It could not make the first move. And with several other problems arising throughout the multiverse, it needed a spare set of hands.

The thought, however fleeting, still crossed The Judge's mind. *Maybe I can use her as my champion.*

"It looks like your little heroine couldn't refuse killing some defenseless women." The Broker rolled out of his chair full of plush cushions and strolled towards The Voice.

"It's not like that." The Voice's volume barely registered even in the perfect space of the demi-plane.

"The wolf girl and human boy only have to do the task they were given," The Judge began. "Their other choices have little consequence if they do not pertain to the demon king's summoning. Besides, you are taking the action out of context. Refrain from doing so in the future."

The Broker twirled his gaudy walking stick. "True and fair enough. But how can you be certain that she'll even face off against the demon king when the time comes? She could, I don't know, run away or even join him." His laughter echoed off the marble stones as he threw back his featureless black face. "Now that would be a treat."

The violet sphere swayed. "No, that won't happen."

"I'm inclined to believe you, for now." The Broker spun on his heel and high-stepped back to his chair. "How much have you told them about what they really face?"

"Only the necessities." The Voice sounded more resolute in that moment than it had since The Broker had shown up.

The Broker jumped and plopped into his chair. He held onto the large diamond of his cane and pointed it at the violet sphere. "That's debatable. But, we won't have long before we know if he'll be released. After all, one of his little minions is really on the warpath right now."

The Judge stayed silent. It knew that the human boy wouldn't back down from fighting the demon king. Unfortunately, he also would be sorely inadequate to succeed alone. He never took his responsibility as seriously as he should've. He was too busy being a "hero" to be even half as capable as the wolf girl.

This entire review hung on her ability to stop the demon king. After all, it was certain the demon king would be released from his cell soon.

18

I WANT TO PLAY A GAME

As I slowly came to, a sharp pain shot through my chest. My body ached all over, and it felt like a stampede of horses had run me over. I tried to take a deep breath, but it felt like knives pierced my sides. I opened my eye, but the other one was swollen shut. The daylight was momentarily blinding. As I moved my hand to touch it, a searing pain shot through my ribs. At least six were broken. Cuts in my mouth made it hard to talk. I tried to remember what happened last night, but everything was a blur.

What happened? I tried to piece together the events. *I remember facing off against the orc leader. He was taunting me with the torches. There's this feeling of being so angry. But how did I end up here? Did I black out?*

My head was pounding, and I felt like I was on the brink of passing out again. I knew I didn't have time to relax. I looked around and saw that I was lying in the middle of a street, with the sun slowly rising in the sky. The orc leader's corpse was a shredded, bloody pulp. There was little left of him to recognize from the waist up.

Right, now I remember. So much for taking it easy. If there are more orcs like him, that might explain why they haven't been eradicated yet. But I can't let them continue to exist. And Fina needs my help. I can't let her stay their prisoner.

As I tried to stand up, a wave of dizziness washed over me. I was in no shape to fight or run. I needed food.

I shambled through the town, using walls to hold myself up. I could feel the weight of my injuries on my every step. Every breath I took was a struggle, and I couldn't help but berate myself for getting into this mess. My ribs felt like they were on fire, and every time I moved, I was reminded of the bruises that littered my body.

Focus, Lucia. You need to find supplies if you're going to make it through this. First things first, food.

After searching through several buildings, I finally stumbled upon a relatively large and less ruined structure. *Finally.*

A stockpile of food was all I could see when I entered the room, and a rush of relief washed over me. Dried meats, fruits, and nuts were all piled high, waiting for me to take what I needed. I tore into the meats, ravenous.

With my stomach finally full, I looked at the remains of the stock-piled resources. *I guess they had to feed the women something. After all, they needed them alive to give birth.* A sour taste filled my mouth. *Stop thinking about that.*

The pain in my chest reminded me of my pressing concern. I turned to my ribs, creating a makeshift brace with my ice magic to help stabilize them. *I just hope this will be enough to get me through the next few days. Fina needs my help.* I took a moment to restock my pack with as much dried meat as it could hold.

Slowly, I returned to my feet, headed to the edge of the ruined town, and looked for more tracks. I found the tracks that had led me here first, but I continued circling the outskirts and eventually found what I was looking for.

A wide collection of footprints with grooves in the ground from sleighs. *Gotcha. I'll save you, Fina, I promise.*

My pace was far slower than I would have liked. I couldn't run on all fours, and walking on two legs was painful enough as it was. But the images of the women chained in the small building pushed me forward. *I can't let Fina suffer that fate. I won't.*

The first day was slow and painful. I had to stop far sooner than I would have liked, but after sleeping for half the night, I could feel the improvement. Even though I still couldn't run on all fours, at least walking wasn't a constant flood of pain. I spent my ice magic maintaining the brace around my torso, preventing my ribs from moving around.

From what I could gather, I was losing ground on the orcs because I found evidence of where they had stopped for the night just after the sun rose on the second day. As I walked, my hunger seemed more demanding.

I'm beginning to think that Salien, Zenny's mother, is right. My recovery aptitude requires me to eat more when I'm injured.

I ate through all the food I'd collected from the orcs by the end of the second day. Based on the amount I grabbed compared to how much Mom thought would last me two days, there should have been enough for four days.

I need to recover as quickly as possible, so I can't be stingy with my food. But it looks like I'll need to hunt for something if I don't find anything tomorrow.

On the second night, I did something I hoped never to do again. I absorbed a portion of unfocused magic and held it in, despite all the training Mom drilled into me not to do that. But I was desperate to recover as quickly as possible. Everything was a blur as I eventually passed out and woke up the next morning.

The third day started with most of my injuries gone. Unfortunately, I was hungrier than I had been in the last two days. I made marks on the ground to lead me back to the tracks after I spent some time looking for something to hunt.

My head had started hurting from the lack of food when I found a small spring tucked away in a grove of trees. I fell to my knees as I arrived at the edge of the water. Several small fish swam innocently in the shallow water.

Nothing personal, guys, but a girl's got to eat. Plus, you look tasty.

I plucked three fish out of the water with relative ease. *I guess Gifford's fishing lessons have finally been useful.* After eating the fish, I took the time to clean off all the blood and dirt I had collected on my journey.

After grabbing another collection of fish and refilling my water-skin, I returned to the tracks I left and resumed following them. This time I could run on all fours, just not sprint as fast as I would have liked. My ribs were still tender.

I should be fine by tomorrow. Hopefully then I can really catch up.

I napped during the night, but I couldn't help but feel a little anxious about Fina. *I haven't caught the orcs even after three days. No, it's been five days. Stopping at that village cost me so much time. Was it worth it in the end, or did I let my impulsiveness get the better of me again? Should I have left those women to their fate? Was I supposed to just bypass it and hope Captain Aenwyn and the rest of the knights handled it?*

No. They suffered enough. Whatever hellish conditions that led to them asking for death and not to be saved couldn't be allowed to continue. I did the right thing, or at least I did what they asked, and that has to be good enough.

I started on the trail again, and I tried to keep my thoughts focused on the task at hand. However, they kept drawing me to the image of the woman who killed herself. *I killed the orcs, not to save her but because I hated what the orcs did to Fina and what they could do to her. Something about that sight should bother me, and it does, but not in the way I'd expect. For years now, I've only cared about those close to me. But seeing the orcs again has brought what I thought were long-buried memories back to the surface, along with what I see now could have been my fate if Allen hadn't saved me.*

My mood slowed me, but since my wounds were completely healed, I could run at my usual pace. As the day turned to afternoon, I noticed a grove of trees along the tracks' path. It looked like their travel slowed as they weaved through the trees, while I felt more at home.

"You're persistent, I'll give you that."

I stopped and looked upwards to the voice. The Rider of Pain was lounging on a large branch picking her fingernails as her tail swayed below her.

I took a deep breath. "Now what?"

She kept picking at her fingernails. "You're running out of time. The Rider of Death isn't slowing down and his army is growing. Your little stop in that village wasted so much time." She turned and grinned. "But you did surprise me with what you did to those women. I didn't think you would do something like that."

My neck twitched. "You've been watching me this entire time?"

The demoness turned and dangled her hooved feet as she balanced on the branch. "Of course. How else will I know when you give up and ask for help?" She pushed off and flapped her wings to hover in the air. "I'll give you another chance. You can have your furry friend right here, right now; no blood, no fighting, and no risk of dying. You just need to fight and weaken the Rider of Death for me so I can take his power."

I growled. "Are you telling me Fina is up ahead?"

"Potentially."

I started following the tracks again. "Then what do I need you for? If she's up ahead, I'll save her on my own."

"I'll have to add stubborn to the list too." I almost chuckled at the irritation in her voice as she hovered behind me. "One of these days you will do what I need. I can't understand why you're going through all this trouble for one girl when I need you to defend me and can stop thousands from dying."

I turned back. "She's my friend and I made a promise. You don't have to understand and I don't have to explain it to you." I shooed her away. "Now leave me alone. I'll never agree to a deal with you."

She gritted her teeth as she slowly turned transparent. "Remember, everyone has a price. You are no different. And I will find it."

Her voice gave way to the silence that hung in the small forest. *So much better. She calls me stubborn, yet she's just as bad. Although for her it's more of a personality thing as she can't control her desires. Either way, it's not my problem right now. Fina is ahead, and I need to save her.*

The woods eventually gave way to a clearing where a wooden fort stood surrounded by tree stumps. The walls were a head taller than me. On each of the four corners sat a square watchtower twice as tall as me, where an orc was clearly posted as a lookout. Each hard oak wall left one opening for entry. Small crowds of orcs were moving through the fort. I circled around, following the tree line, looking for openings or anything I could use. But the construction was strangely uniform.

I didn't know orcs could be so... disciplined. Did they build this or take it over?

Despite my scouting, I couldn't see any way I could sneak in. *I need to get in and save Fina. Maybe I'll try a different tactic. Let's see if I can take away their defensive advantage.*

I walked straight towards an opening. As I walked, I covered myself with my usual ice armor and made an ice shield for the inevitable arrows that would come my way.

Predictably, an orc in a watchtower shouted, "Incoming!"

He pulled back and fired an arrow. I raised my shield to block it. Another orc joined the first on the tower as I continued marching towards the opening.

"One beast," I heard an orc call out.

"You five, take care of it," another less distorted voice ordered.

Is that another leader? Why do they sound different?

More arrows headed towards me, but I sidestepped them as I watched five orcs heading towards the closest entrance. They filed out, each one armored in chainmail and wielding a sword. Their blades were shiny and looked well-maintained.

Uh, these orcs are nothing like the ones from before. It looks like their leader actually knows what he's doing. Well, at least they're taking the bait.

I let the orcs get another round of shots off before turning and running towards the trees. As I reached the treeline, I turned to make sure they followed, and the five orcs were running to catch up with me. To make sure I played the part, I slowed my pace so they would eventually catch me.

The orcs charged into the trees, hacking at any branches or brush that impeded them. I ducked around some trees as I moved around quietly. The orc's footsteps slowed as I undoubtedly escaped their sight. Stalking low through the brush, I watched them.

The more the orcs spread out from each other, the more excited I became. When the orcs were finally far enough apart, I crept behind one of them and slashed open his throat from behind and left before he hit the ground.

The other orcs turned to see their comrade bleeding out on the ground.

They didn't move closer together, so I circled around to their backs while they all swiveled their heads. Again, I took the opportunity and got behind an orc, then clamped my jaws on the back of his neck as I pounced. One orc started running towards me as I moved to hide behind a tree. The two others followed behind the first.

I tried to lose them, but somehow the one orc knew where I went every time. So I put a lot of distance between us and saw that they looked like they were giving up. *Good.* After they started heading back to where I'd killed the first two, I quickly and quietly caught up with them just before they reached the corpses.

The orc in the back suffered the same fate as the first two.

Now that the odds are nice and even—maybe even in my favor—it's time to end this little hunt.

I created a spiked ball of ice as the two orcs turned around. The farthest one received the ice in his eye. He stumbled backwards and bellowed, clutching at his face. The closer orc charged me with his sword above his head.

I met his charge, attempting to kill the first orc so that I wouldn't have to fight them both at the same time. He brought his sword down early. It was easy to sidestep, but he turned his blade and swung it towards me. I took my forearm, still covered in ice, and hammered it into the flat of the blade. Even though I could deflect the attack upwards, I still needed to duck under the sword as I stepped into his reach.

I kicked his leading leg to the side. As he fell forward, I stabbed him in the eyes with my claws.

The second orc had pulled the projectile from his eye, leaving a hole oozing blood from his empty socket. Either with misplaced bravery or plain stupidity, he charged me, his sword back and over his shoulder.

With my fingers still in the orc's head, I pulled him around and swung him like a weapon when the other orc started swinging his sword. He cut his buddy's legs off, which then hit him in the face. I pulled my claws from the orc's skull and charged while the only remaining orc shook his head, still disoriented after blood and boots hit him in the face.

I drove my claws into his unprotected neck and carved upward as I stepped past him. Blood shot from the wound as I headed back out of the forest towards the wooden fort.

When I walked into the clearing, I could see a strangely dressed orc standing with three others with bows in the closest corner. While the other orcs wore armor, he wore heavy robes and held a walking stick with both hands. I couldn't see his face, but by his body movements, I could tell he didn't expect to see me alone.

"You ten, get her." The robe-wearing orc, who I guessed was in charge, definitely sounded flustered.

Ten orcs came running out of the fort towards me.

That's it. Come to me. I want to play a game.

19

INTO THE FRYING PAN

Ten orcs took three times as long to separate and hunt down than the first five. By the end, I was soaked in orc blood and couldn't stand my own smell. My magic was almost depleted, but they were all dead. I distanced myself from the fort to look for a quiet spot to rest and recover my magic so I could clean myself off.

I probably should expect them to send another round of orcs to come find me after they realize that the last group isn't coming back.

I found a bundle of bushes large enough to cover me so I could take a quick nap. I used some magic to cover the rest of myself with ice so I wouldn't stink as bad. Taking a nap in a bush wasn't comfortable, and taking a nap while trying to make sure nothing snuck up on me made it even harder. Closing my eyes wasn't hard, but my hearing picked up every sound, and I had to judge if it was something I needed to concern myself with or not. I didn't actually take a nap; I more or less just rested my eyes and developed a small case of paranoia.

Is it paranoia if someone is really out to get me?

Despite my uneasy rest, I sat in the bush long enough for my magic to recover and the ice that was covering me to melt, soaking my fur and clothes. I used my magic to freeze the water, which soaked my fur, and pulled it off. I successfully cleaned off most of the blood from my earlier games with the orcs.

Right. I hope I don't have too many orcs left to kill. That fort didn't look that big, so there can't be a lot of orcs living there. On my way back to the fort, I looked around for tracks of other orcs who may have come out to find me. But it was clear they didn't, since I found all fifteen corpses with their weapons where I'd left them.

Okay, I would have guessed they'd at least have come for the weapons. Are they scared of me? Well, I did kill fifteen of them. If I knew a threat killed fifteen people, I probably wouldn't go into the woods either. These orcs are different from the others. They're maintaining a fort, not a ruined town. Their weapons are in better condition. And there's something about that one orc giving the orders that seems off.

I reached the edge of the forest and eyed the fort. *Maybe I'm overthinking it. Or not.*

I looked at the fort more closely; all four watchtowers were full of orcs. Each orc held a bow, and I could see quivers of arrows lining the tower walls.

Uh, this is bad.

The bad news continued to pile on as I saw that the wall was now surrounded by a moat of sharpened spears. They had also filled the open doorways with thick logs wrapped in metal bands. I walked around looking for an opening, but I didn't find one. I did, however, count another thirty-five orcs standing in the towers, and the orc leader was nowhere in sight.

Now what?

I tried to work through every plan I could, but I just kept running into the same problem: they looked like they didn't want to come out. *If there are thirty-five archers, and each archer has two quivers of a likely twenty-four arrows each, that's...* I grabbed my head as the numbers kept running away from me.

It doesn't matter, a lot. Lexia is going to kill me if she hears about what I'm about to do. No, I can't do it. I promised I would stay safe. But if Fina's in there, I have to save her. I had to sit down after getting lightheaded. My conflicting promises tore me apart inside.

I still don't know how far behind they are, but I know Fina is in that fort. At least according to the demon. But I can't save her if I'm out here.

I rubbed my eyes with my palms. *There's nothing left but to do this the hard way.* After rising to my feet, I created the largest shield of ice I could. It was a quarter of a sphere, and I held on to it with a handle, keeping it above and in front of me. *My only hope is that this ice is thick enough to stop arrows.*

I slowly marched towards the fort. The orcs in the nearest watchtower shouted and started shooting. I held my breath as the first salvo of arrows arced through the air and descended towards me. The first arrow bounced off, chipping just the smallest amount of ice away. Then the next arrow did the same. Soon, nine arrows were lying on the ground outside of my little protective ice bubble.

It worked?

Another volley of arrows sailed through the sky and replicated the results of the first one. Then eighteen became twenty-seven. Soon, I couldn't keep track of the number of arrows. My shield held up, but the damage was starting to show. *I have to get to that wall. If I can get in, I can use the buildings for cover. They'll have to come to me at that point.*

Before I could start my march for the walls, a huge boulder rose out from behind them, heading straight for me. *Oh come on!*

I moved to the side, keeping my shield up to block the next round of arrows. The boulder fell and struck where I had been standing. The rock was taller than me, and it hit the ground so hard that I could feel the earth shake.

Who threw that? Don't tell me that orc leader can use earth manipulation magic. Is there any other bad news I need to know about?

Another boulder flew out towards me. I moved to the side until I knew I was safe and resumed my march. *Kill the mage first. Then deal with everyone else.* Dodging boulders and the slow whittling of my shield made me question if I should continue. But after the fourth boulder missed me, I knew I was too close to run away safely.

As the arrows kept coming, one finally stuck into the handle of my ice shield. I winced. *It's not going to last much longer. I have to move now!*

I ran towards the wall, using the shield to block the arrows as best as I could. I could see the orcs starting to frenzy as they realized their arrows were digging deeper into the shield. They started shouting and pointing as I closed in.

As I approached, I could clearly see the moat of spears. It was wider than I'd anticipated, but there were gaps between them big enough for me to fit through.

More of the shield broke off, and an arrow almost hit me. *Now!* I threw the shield up and jumped over the moat. The orcs started leaning over the edges of the tower to shoot at me.

I dug my claws into the wood and pulled myself up and over the wall.

When I landed, I could hear more shouts and the whizzing of arrows that missed me. There was a building a short ways away with an open window. I sprinted on all fours and leaped for it. More arrows flew past me, and as I entered the window, a sharp pain shot through my tail and up my spine. I caught myself as I hit the ground, and I looked and saw an arrow sticking into my tail.

Ow! I grabbed the arrow and pulled it out, hoping it didn't do any permanent damage. I couldn't help but let out a low growl, and I shook my tail to ease the pain. *Whatever, it's just a scratch anyway. I can move it just fine.*

I quickly scanned the room. It was dark and empty, with only a few scattered crates and barrels along the walls. The sounds of shouting and clanging weapons came from outside, and I knew I had to find a way out of this building and find that mage.

I moved towards the door, my eyes scanning for any signs of danger. As I approached, I could hear the sound of footsteps getting louder. I quickly hid behind one of the crates and waited, my heart racing while the footsteps grew closer.

The door burst open and an orc walked in. It was a small one, probably half my height, but it was armed with a crude-looking spear and looked ready to fight. *Why is that orc so small?* I extended my claws, leaped out from behind the crate, and pounced on it, knocking it to the ground. It let out a high-pitched squeal when I pinned it with my claws.

I didn't hesitate to slam its face into the ground. There was a crunch as I stood up and quickly dragged the orc behind one of the crates, hoping it wouldn't be found anytime soon. *Hopefully they don't see the small puddle of blood either.*

I quickly moved towards a window and peered out, trying to get a sense of my surroundings. The buildings inside the fort were visible. *I have to keep going, but where? I didn't see that orc leader. Do I just wait here until they line up to take me on?*

My claws dug into the wooden frame as I prepared to launch myself out into the open air. *No, there's no telling what that mage is capable of. I need to deal with him, and then I can deal with the rest of the orcs. Dragging them through the fort at my leisure.*

The sounds stopped. I hesitated to jump out. *Something's really not right here.*

Then the chanting began. It began quietly, with one voice, until more voices joined in. It wasn't a word they were chanting, just a deep guttural sound.

"Rhag. Rhag. Rhag. Rhag."

They chanted incessantly. Each time they did, it got louder and louder. Soon, I couldn't hear anything. It was painful since their voices were so grating, but as the volume increased, so did the pain.

I covered my ears and gritted my teeth, trying to ignore it as much as possible. It was impossible. I let my vision shift into shades of red. It wasn't enough to let me ignore the vile chant. Soon my vision started shaking, and I dropped to my knees. I could feel my screams in my throat, but I couldn't hear them. I could only hear their chanting.

"Rhag. Rhag. Rhag. Rhag."

I curled up in a ball. I couldn't focus enough to use magic to cover my ears with ice. Then everything went quiet except for my whimpering.

"There you are." It sounded like the leader had heard me crying.

I shot up and looked around. There wasn't anybody in the room. *Which means they're waiting outside for me.*

I vaulted out the window. *If they're surrounding me, I need to move. Now.*

I was right. Just as I left the building, a cacophony of footsteps moved towards me. But when I looked around to see what I had jumped into, my instincts pulled me to look in a certain direction. There he was: the orc leader.

He was devoid of hair from the neck up. The orcs that I'd seen in the fort wore armor, but he didn't. He had bulky unornamented robes and held a thick walking stick in his right hand. His robes weren't clean, but they weren't damaged, either.

"Finally," he said as he tightened his grip on his staff. "You've been quite the troublemaker. Any particular reason for killing my troops? Why are you assaulting my fort?"

"Where is she?" The words flew out of my mouth. Nothing else existed but me and the orc.

"Who is 'she?'" The orc moved his staff into a defensive stance. "I have my share of broods. You're more than welcome to join them." A smile crept across his face.

Everything around me went from crimson to darker shades until everything was black except for the leader. I didn't bother responding.

All orcs must die!

20

TURNING TAIL

I ran on all fours and charged the robed orc.

He dragged the bottom tip of his staff through the dirt, across his body, and towards me. When he flicked the end up, a boulder flew towards me. I dove to the side, hugging a wall as it went by.

I saw his grin as he planted his staff on the ground. *So he threw the boulders. That makes this a two-for-one deal. I can take out their leader and the mage at the same time.*

The orc stabbed his staff into the ground again. Suddenly, the ground beneath my feet trembled, and a swarm of rocks rose up before they darted towards me. I hesitated for a moment as I looked for the safest path through them. I dove under them and slid to a stop. A few of the rocks had managed to pelt me. They stung, but they'd probably left nothing more than light bruises.

However, the orc didn't stop. He poked at the ground with the staff like it was a shovel and sent a rolling wave of dirt towards me. The ground heaved and buckled, but I propelled myself into the air and over the growing wave. When I landed, I stumbled as the earth continued to shake, but I whipped my tail around to keep my balance and spun around as another small boulder came my way.

The orc chuckled, making a low, menacing sound. He raised his staff again, and this time a pillar of rock shot up and towards me.

I gritted my teeth and braced myself to move out of the way at the last moment. I crouched low, then stepped to the side and sprinted towards him. The pillar of rock started bending and moving towards me. I stood up and cartwheeled over it just as it was about to hit me.

With a snarl, I kicked the rock, breaking the pillar in two. The orc howled as he clutched the side of his head with a hand after receiving the backlash. I couldn't help but smirk at him.

The rest of the pillar shattered into pieces as it hit the ground.

Unfortunately, the orc wasn't done yet. He glared at me as he shot out both his staff and his hand, making a gripping motion.

The ground beneath me turned to quicksand. Before I sunk into it too far, I leaped out and moved towards the orc mage.

But after I took one step, something latched onto my leg and tripped me. I looked back and saw a hand form out of the quicksand and start pulling me in. Reflexively, I dug my claws into the ground and pulled myself away. It didn't let go, and I knew I didn't have the time to get up or slash at it. I didn't have enough magic to disrupt him either. Frantically, I kept pulling myself forward. My powerful muscles kept fighting against his magic, and I could see the orc straining more and more as I got closer to him.

Finally, the magical hand shattered and I snapped forward into a roll, which took me the last distance to the orc's feet. He raised his staff to strike me, but I grabbed his leg and pulled first.

He hit the ground with a resounding thud. I pulled him towards me and grinned as I wrapped one arm around his neck and the other around the back of his head. Then, with a quick motion, I sliced his throat with my claws.

The orc thrashed and struggled, but I held on tight and started ripping open his chest. He tried to stop me by pulling at my arms and even trying to punch my face. None of it worked. I could see him weakening as blood poured from his neck and every new wound I gave him.

The orc went limp. I stepped back, staring at his unmoving body, panting and grinning. *Gotcha.*

As my vision started returning to normal, I could see I was surrounded. Eleven orcs lined up in a semi-circle and aimed their spears at me while they hid behind their shields. I did a quick look around and saw that one of the towers had a line of sight to me. But they didn't have their bows drawn. They weren't even looking at me.

That's when I heard the heaviest footsteps I'd ever heard. They sounded as heavy as the dire rhino I'd fought in the Wild Kingdom. My heart sank.

This isn't working out for me. Maybe I can intimidate them. I did just kill their leader.

"Who else wants a piece of me?" I shouted as I held up my claws, still dripping with the blood of their leader.

Two words boomed from outside the fort. "I do." They were low, but not harsh. It sounded like there was a perpetual rumble to it.

I turned to find the source of the voice, but all I saw was a closed gate. Then something hit the gate, and it exploded, sending shards of wood and metal flying in all directions.

As the dust settled, a figure emerged.

It was the largest orc I had ever seen, towering over me and radiating a sense of raw power. My instincts immediately sent me a warning about him.

He was taller than me, almost as tall as the wooden walls of the fort. His muscles rippled with even more muscles. He only wore a ripped pair of faded purple pants that were almost too small for his hulking frame.

"Huk. Huk. Huk. Huk."

The orcs all started chanting. Behind the massive orc was a small group of six more. None of them looked special. But what was behind them had my attention.

Fina!

Sitting in a cage, holding her knees to her chest as she curled her tail around her feet, Fina looked terrified. There were a few more cages, all with women in them. Seeing them there made me feel sick to my stomach, but remembering the sight of the other women in the hut fueled the fire of my rage.

"You, beastkin," the giant orc's voice boomed. "You killed Rhag. Surrender to me, and I will make you mine."

I turned to face him and bared my fangs. "Never." My voice was distorted by the growl that accompanied it.

"Good," he said, his eyes gleaming. "Huk strongest orc ever. I like it when they fight." The orc slammed his fists into his chest like he was a gorilla.

Did he just refer to himself in the third person? If I wasn't as angry as I was, I would've cringed.

I braced myself for an attack, but Huk just stood there, watching me with an amused look.

"Huk like beasts," he said. "They're strong, but Huk keeps breaking them. Huk will enjoy you until you break too."

I nearly vomited at his words. *You will not touch me or Fina.* "I'm going to enjoy killing you."

Huk laughed. "You can try," he said and motioned to the other orcs. "She's mine, do not touch."

The orcs moved out slightly, still surrounding me with their massive bodies, sharp spears, and shields. I wanted to lunge at Huk, but a nagging feeling pulsed in the back of my mind. *Great, he's even stronger than he looks. But I can't run away. I can't leave Fina to share those women's fate.*

A thunderous step snapped my attention back to Huk. He pulled his fist back and threw it at me with a shout. I darted around the orc and felt the ground shake as it shattered from the impact. I slashed my claws into his hamstrings, but my claws didn't dig deep into his skin.

The four thin red lines on his hamstring were barely a scratch.

Huk turned and swung the back of his hand at me. I leaned back and felt the wind blow past me as he missed.

He's strong, and he's tough. Does he have the physical and durable aptitudes? Can an orc have two aptitudes?

Every step the orc took sent tremors through the ground as he kept swinging his fists towards me. It wasn't hard to dodge his attacks. *He might have the physical aptitude, but it went all to his strength, and he didn't get any faster. It's almost like he's slower than a regular person.*

He swung his fist towards my head again, and I ducked under and stepped into his reach. I dug my claws into his abdomen, but they couldn't penetrate as deep as I liked. It was like trying to cut through a rock.

I left yet another mark, but I knew that unless I aimed for something soft, like his eyes, I wasn't going to cause any lasting damage. He was too tall for me to reach for his face normally. *I need to figure out a safe way to reach them.*

Huk leaned forward like he was trying to grab me. I dropped down and slid out from under him. Before he could see that I had escaped, I spun to my feet and toward his back. I kicked him in the knee, and it buckled slightly, but he didn't drop.

He moved to follow me, but I jumped on his back. My claws dug into his skin just enough to hold on. Huk stood up and arched his back as he howled. He twisted, reaching for me. I could shift my body so that I always stayed at his back out of his reach.

I slashed my claws at his back and hamstrings. All the wounds were superficial. *This will be a death by a thousand cuts, literally.*

The massive orc's grunting soon turned to growling and snarling as I kept moving. We kept our little dance going until, slowly, we got closer and closer to the wall of a building.

I wasn't in control of where we were going. Every movement I made was to keep away from the wild orc's arms, but I was running out of room to evade him.

His back was more red than green when my side hit the building. Huk grinned. He drew his fist back, and I dove into a slide between his legs.

As I turned onto my back, I saw Huk's hulking frame get larger. *He's going to sit on me?* I raised my legs, planted them on his buttocks, and pushed.

This is ridiculous. He weighs more than a bear!

Instead of pushing him away, I attempted to shift his weight and throw him over me. I did, somehow. My legs burned from the exertion as Huk's head slammed into the ground. Unfortunately, the rest of his body was still going to land on me. I pushed against him and twisted my body so that as he landed, it pushed me away from him.

I tried to roll to my feet before he could get up, but he grabbed my leg.

"Mine." Huk's eyes were bloodshot as he locked his gaze on me.

Oh, no.

I heard the snapping and crunching before I felt my leg break. There was nothing I could do but scream in pain as I dug my claws into his fingers. I couldn't pry him away from my leg.

It didn't matter after he threw me. I watched helplessly as I sailed through the air away from the colossal orc.

I didn't stop until another sharp pain exploded across my back. My head spun as my vision blurred, then went back to normal. I hit the ground in a heap, writhing in pain. A metallic, savory taste touched my tongue. It was a taste I experienced often, and I knew it all too well.

I coughed, and when my vision cleared enough for me to see, a small splatter of my blood stained the ground.

Every breath hurt, my head pounded, and my leg burned. *He only touched me once.* I felt the earth shake, and my rational mind retreated. Only the instinctual understanding of fear remained.

My broken leg dangled against the ground as I scrambled to my hands and feet. Somehow, I was next to the gate Huk had entered through. It was an exit, and I took it. I ran on my three functioning limbs. My shattered leg bounced against the ground with each step, but there wasn't any room for pain. Only fear.

"Stop her!" Huk bellowed, and I heard the myriad of footsteps from the orcs chasing after me.

My heart pounded in my chest as I sprinted towards the trees, sending more shots of pain through my back. I could hear Huk's laughter behind me, and it made my skin crawl.

"You can run, beast!" he shouted. "But I will catch you."

"Lucia?" Fina's voice shattered my heart.

I kept running, fueled by fear. I burst through the treeline and into the wilderness beyond, not stopping until I couldn't run any further. When I did, I couldn't hear the orcs anymore.

I collapsed onto the ground, my body shaking from exhaustion and pain. The memory of Fina's voice as I ran left me sobbing.

I failed you, Fina. I wasn't strong enough.

21

A HUNTED HUNTER

I kept sobbing until there were no more tears left. Eventually, I couldn't ignore my injuries. I looked at the most obvious one first: my broken leg.

Sniffling and wincing from the pain, I poked and felt around to assess the damage. From the near-blinding pain and how much everything was moving, my bones were likely broken in four places, maybe five.

A single break can be set, and I can throw a cast on it. But this many breaks? What can I do to make sure it heals correctly? Salien and Zenny never showed me what they do with such severe breaks. Do I try to remake my leg as best I can and wrap it in the hardest cast possible?

Without a better idea, I clenched my jaw and prepared for more pain. Moving the first bone into position nearly caused me to black out. The orcs were looking for me, and they would definitely have heard my screams. I created the beginning portion of my cast to hold the first bone in place. The cast was tight enough to feel like some of my blood was getting restricted. But I was afraid that if I didn't make it tight enough, the bones wouldn't set right. Then who knew what would happen?

I proceeded with the next piece of bone and followed the same process. One after another, I placed each bone in what I believed to be the correct spot. On the bright side, each piece after that was less painful. On the last one, I didn't scream. Although, that might have been partially because my voice was gone by that point. I had enough magic to create my cast and nothing else.

Panting, I leaned against a tree. My heavy breathing reminded me of another injury I was suffering from. As the pain in my now-cast-up leg subsided into a dull roar, my ribs were the next thing to look at.

I poked at them, and I didn't feel that any of them were broken. *Good, they might just be bruised.* Bruised ribs, while not dangerous, hurt plenty. The back of my head itched, but when I rubbed my hand through my hair, it felt like I had touched a scab. *Now I need to add a concussion to my list of injuries. He did that all with his bare hands and throwing me into a wall like I was nothing.*

I stood up and carefully broke off a large branch to use as a walking stick. After limping my way through the forest, I returned to the spot where I had left my pack of food and water. There wasn't any sign that the orcs were still looking for me. At least that's what I thought until I neared the edge of the forest to watch the fort.

Sixteen orcs spread out into four groups of four. Each was heading in a cardinal direction, one of which was where I was standing.

"Huk said to find her and bring her back," one of the orcs heading my way said.

"She killed Rhag and other orcs too," another responded.

"But she is wounded. Huk hurt her bad," a third orc added.

The final orc laughed. "Maybe we can have fun with her first. This should be easy. I saw her limping like a wounded beast."

I tightened my grip around the branch I was using to support myself. *You're lucky that orc did so much to me. Otherwise I would've turned you into fertilizer right here and now.*

Growling, I turned and headed away. I wasn't in any shape to fight. It would probably be at least a day or two, even with my recovery speed. *I just hope I'm not too late.*

Hiding in the forest wouldn't have done me much good since, by the sound of it, the orcs were being thorough in their search. Since they were moseying to check every bush, I could keep my distance. I headed south, since I knew that direction was the safest. I had killed the orcs that were living in that ruined town.

I kept walking for most of the day. It was tiring given all the effort I had to put into not stepping on my broken leg and not snapping the branch holding me up, while listening to all the things the orcs said they were going to do to me when they caught me.

They aren't taking this seriously enough. How do they think they're going to find me if they keep talking like that? I can hear them coming from dozens of arcs away.

But as their conversations continued, one orc's tone changed.

"She isn't in this direction," I heard an orc say.

Are they finally giving up?

"Nobody's blown their horns. She's still out here." *So, that's a no.*

"It's getting dark. Beasts are more dangerous in the dark."

"Are you scared? There are four of us and one of her."

"She killed the ones who followed her into the forest before you got here." *It looks like one of them is getting cold feet.*

"They were weak. I am stronger than them. Huk promised a reward for whoever caught her. So I will catch her."

"What if she killed the others, and she's now hunting us?"

"I've had enough of your weakness."

A squeal and the sound of something heavy hitting the ground caused me to turn around and investigate. I kept a low profile and saw that three orcs were standing, and one orc's headless corpse was pouring blood onto the ground.

Did he kill one of the other orcs?

One orc held up the severed head of the other. "Do either of you wish to retreat now?"

I swallowed as I watched the two just shrug and grab the dead orc's weapon.

"Good. Follow me." The orc threw the severed head into a bush and headed towards me, the other two following behind him.

While that improves my odds by a lot, it's still not enough. They still have weapons, and I can't dodge them effectively.

I resumed my retreat south until I found the exit to the woods just as the sun was touching the horizon. The orcs hadn't stopped searching for me. I looked around and didn't see anything to hide in outside of the forest. And if I left it, I knew they would spot me quickly. *Do I take my chances out there or in here?*

Unfortunately, I knew I had hesitated too long when I heard an orc call out, "There she is! Don't blow that horn. She's ours alone."

I guess they made the decision for me. Throwing the stick away, I dropped to all fours—actually, it was three since I still wouldn't let my broken leg touch the ground—and ran.

Their heavy footsteps thumped behind me as I limped out into the field. I ran, and they chased. But as I went, I looked for anything I could use to lose them.

Then I saw several small plumes of smoke in the general area of the ruined village.

Is that my chance? Did Captain Aenwyn catch up? I continued to limp away from the orcs, who were ever so slightly catching up to me.

I crested a small hill, and my heart soared.

Tents and small campfires were being tended to by knights. Other knights attached horses to posts and cared for them. But one individual stuck out against all the humans and elves.

"Lexia!" The shout hurt and wasn't as loud as I hoped for. My voice was still hoarse from when I tried to fix my shattered leg. But her head started swiveling.

"Lexia!" I shouted again, hoping it was enough for her to focus in my direction.

It was. Lexia turned and started running towards me. I didn't stop running, even as she called to me. "Lucia!"

"Orcs!" I shouted as I neared the base of the hill. I could hear the orcs cresting the top of the hill behind me.

Lexia slid to a stop. Her eyes turned from me towards the orcs. I could hear her growl as I saw her body glow with magic.

A wave of ice shot out from Lexia's hand, freezing the ground the orcs were running on and knocking them off their feet. They slid across the frozen grass, their weapons flying out of their hands.

One orc got up and charged her, but Lexia raised her arms. This time, the ice formed into sharp spikes that impaled the orc as he ran into them. He pitifully grabbed at the spikes and pushed himself off. A dozen holes in his chest began pouring blood. He was dead before he hit the ground.

The other two orcs retrieved their weapons and carefully walked off the patch of ice. Lexia created a spear of ice and launched it at the closet one. He tried to lift his sword to defend against it, but the spear moved under the blade, pierced through him, and kept going.

He grabbed at the hole in his stomach with one hand and stumbled towards my sister. The other orc shouted and charged Lexia, but her icy spear, still dripping with blood, turned midair and impaled the orc in the back.

He fell to his knees and looked at his two comrades. He lifted a horn off his belt and brought it to his lips.

He got a single brief note out before ice enveloped his head, horn, and hand. The orc dropped his weapon as he flailed his free hand at the ice.

Lexia's eyes locked on the last remaining orc. Her growl sounded feral as she bared her teeth and held out her hands.

The orc chipped away at the ice that was slowly suffocating him, but I watched as the ice around his head continued to grow. It was inevitable. He was going to die slowly. After a short while, the orc's body slowed down before he crumpled to the ground.

Lexia kept growling as she approached the three corpses. "You will not touch her!" Her scream filled the air as she created a pillar of ice and dropped it on one of the corpses.

Blood and flesh splattered everywhere. I couldn't take my eyes off my sister. *She's gone berserk.*

Lexia lifted the pillar and crushed the second corpse with a wild scream. She then crushed the final corpse into a smear on the ground.

She stopped glowing with magic as she stood among the carnage, panting. Her shoulders, ears, and tail all drooped.

"Lexia?" I called out carefully.

She snapped her head towards me. Her face was still full of fury. "And you!" She pointed a finger at me as she stomped towards me. "You promised you would stay safe. Why are you hurt?"

I flinched and sat on the ground, wrapping my tail around my legs. "I made a mistake. There was an orc who has Fina in a cage, and I wasn't strong enough to take him." Tears threatened to pour from my eyes.

Suddenly, Lexia was hugging me. "I'm sorry I yelled at you." She held me tightly and nuzzled her cheek into my shoulder. "You're safe now. I'm so glad you're safe. Now we can save Fina together." Her hugging hurt my ribs, but I put up with the pain for her sake.

I just sat in Lexia's arms. "That's not going to happen." Lexia leaned back and grabbed my shoulders. "I can't run. I can barely walk. How do you expect me to fight with my leg? The orc shattered it with his bare hands, just by grabbing it." I pointed to my cast.

Lexia looked at it then turned to me and growled. "Who did this to you?"

I grabbed her shirt and pulled her close. "Don't you dare!" I matched her growl. "You don't stand a chance, and all you'll do is get yourself killed, or worse."

Lexia growled for a moment, then relented. "What about Fina?" She lowered her head and slumped her shoulders.

"We need an army to save her," I said.

My sister grinned as she looked up. "It's a good thing we have one."

I heard footsteps behind me. When I turned to look, I saw Captain Aenwyn, Daric, and two other knights with them walking towards us.

Aenwyn looked at me. "You don't look so good. And I don't see your friend." She waved to the other knights with her. "Take her to Zenny. She'll get her fixed up." Then she turned back to me. "You can explain everything to me after you've been looked at."

I looked at my leg and wondered what Zenny could do to fix it. "How about I tell you on the way?" I gave Lexia a forced smile. "You can come too."

Lexia helped me to my feet and held me up. "You never get any lighter, do you?" she asked. The strain in her voice was obvious.

I growled at her. "I'm not fat; it's muscle."

"Whatever you say, sis."

22

CONFESSIONS

Lexia and another knight carried me to a tent and set me down on a cot. Zenny walked in with a scowl on her face.

"You never learn, do you?" she asked as she glared down at me.

I rolled my eyes. "You know, I'm not a masochist. All this pain isn't fun for me either."

"You two can go," Aenwyn whispered to the other knights. They headed out of the tent as the captain turned to Daric. "Do you want to go first, or shall we let her talk first?"

Daric crossed his arms. "I don't know. She looks really rough. But this is a big deal." There was a slight hesitation in his voice.

I twitched my ears. "What are you talking about?"

Zenny sat on the cot next to me, carefully avoiding my tail. She didn't look at me; instead, she stared at the ground. "We saw what you did. Lexia told us it had to be you."

What are they talking about? I looked around at everyone's faces. Lexia looked at me with hurt in her eyes. Daric and Aenwyn looked furious.

"Are you talking about what happened in the village?" I asked. "I was just so angry at what the orcs were doing, I had to kill them all."

Captain Aenwyn shook her head. "No, that's not it. Killing the orcs wasn't wrong. It's what you did after that upsets us."

I flattened my ears and looked at the ceiling of the tent. "Oh, that."

"Why? How could you do that?" Zenny grabbed my hand. "If that wasn't you, please say so."

"No, I did that." A mixture of pain and anger swirled in my chest. "I did it because they asked me to."

"That doesn't make it right." Daric stomped his foot on the ground. "We could've helped them."

"You weren't there. You didn't see the hurt in their eyes." I sat up enough to stare at Daric. "You didn't watch a woman drive a sword into her own gut and scream until she died because of what the orcs did to her. What I did was merciful. They asked me!"

Lexia stood in between Daric and me. "Stay away from my sister. Sometimes you have to give the wounded rest. Sometimes you can't save them, and your only action is to ease their passing. It was quick and painless. They didn't suffer."

"Everyone deserves a chance to live." Daric balled his fists and glared at Lexia.

"They didn't want to live anymore!" My shouting wasn't doing my voice any favors. "They were begging me to end their suffering. What was I supposed to do? Was I supposed to leave them there?"

"You could have freed them and given them food and water, then told them to wait for us," Daric said.

I growled. "If I had freed them, nothing would have changed. All of them would have found a weapon and killed themselves like the one woman did. And yes, she did kill herself. An orc didn't do that. How was I supposed to keep all those women from killing themselves, by keeping them tied up?"

Daric opened his mouth, but before he could say anything, Aenwyn placed a hand on his shoulder. "We can't change what happened." Daric stared at her with his mouth wide open. "We wanted to know why, and we got our answer." She turned her head towards me. "I'm disappointed that you couldn't find another way to resolve the situation, Lucia. I know you have a violent disposition, but to kill people so eagerly and willfully, that's disturbing."

I turned my head to look at Zenny and saw tears streaming down her face. "Honestly, I couldn't do it."

"What?" the four voices asked in unison.

"My inner wolf had to do it. I couldn't watch." I closed my eyes and silently thanked her for carrying that burden for me.

"Lucia, what wolf are you talking about?" Lexia's voice shook. "Sis, are you okay? You would tell me if there is something wrong, right?"

I sighed. *Well, that secret's out now.* "Well, as it happens, there's a wolf living inside me."

Daric tilted his head to one side. "You're just saying that because you're half wolf, right?"

I shook my head. "That's what I thought at first, too. But no, she's a part of me, and I'm a part of her. She has helped me understand my instincts. Personally, I think she's the manifestation of my instincts."

"Sis, you're scaring me." Lexia hugged her tail and took a step away from me.

I felt a wrenching in my heart. "Why? What's wrong, Lexia?"

"You aren't turning feral, are you?" Lexia's voice quivered. "Do you listen to the wolf? Does the wolf tell you to do things like killing those women?"

Aenwyn's head darted back and forth between Lexia and me. "What?"

My lips quivered as I held back tears. "No. It's nothing like that. She didn't tell me to. I asked her to. I couldn't handle seeing those women like that any longer. She did it. But since she is me, I did it too."

Daric clapped his hands. "I know what's going on here." Everyone turned to face him. "You have a split personality." He stood there with a giant grin on his face.

"How do you split a personality?" Zenny asked. "What are you talking about?"

Daric's grin grew wider. "I studied a bit about psychology in my past life." That earned him extra-hard stares from Aenwyn and Lexia.

"Basically, it happens when someone experiences extreme trauma and their mind can't take it. So a second personality is formed by their mind as a defense mechanism. It's a way to hide from the pain of said trauma." His face went blank for a moment. "I think."

I blinked several times as everyone stared at Daric in silence. "Uh, no." The words flew out of my mouth before I could fully digest what he'd said. Everyone's gaze turned to me. I slunk back onto the cot. "She's not like that. She can think and communicate like a person, except that she's a wolf and she can't actually talk. I can talk to her, and she understands me, but she responds with simple gestures and impressions of ideas."

Daric shook his head. "It looks like you're in denial." He straightened up. "It's going to feel like another person, but they are just a figment of your imagination. Have you experienced any trauma as a kid?"

I glared at him. "My first memories are of my village on fire and orcs tying me up and dropping me in a cage." Lexia flinched and looked away. "To say I've suffered trauma would be an understatement. Because it gets worse from there."

"I'm sorry," Lexia whispered.

Daric's chest inflated. "That only verifies my claim."

Aenwyn scratched the back of her head. "Where do you know all this from? Past lives? I don't understand what's going on here. How does this relate to Lucia killing those women?"

Daric turned to the elf and waved a hand towards me. "It has everything to do with it. You see, this isn't my first life. And my first life was in a world with far more advanced technology and sciences. One such science was the study of the mind. I had to take a class on it while I was in school. Most of it was boring, but some of it was interesting." He gave me a wink. "Lucia has a mental disorder and isn't fully to blame. If we can cure her, she'll be a better person. Who knows, maybe she won't be so violent or destructive."

"Cure me?" I could feel the desire to hurt him starting to grow. "There's nothing wrong with me."

"Yeah," Lexia joined in. "You make it sound like she's sick. But she's not." My sister glanced away for a moment.

At least I have one person on my side.

"Not yet," she whispered.

Yet?

Lexia straightened up. "Yes, she's easily angered, but that's normal for a primal like her." *Thanks, sis.*

"Daric, I know myself better than anyone else. My temper is a part of my instincts." I turned to Lexia. "And I heard that, sis. There's nothing wrong with me."

Zenny wiped away her tears and sat closer to me. "Lucia, I think Daric just wants to help."

"I know," I replied, trying to keep my voice steady. "But he's wrong. I don't have a split personality. The wolf inside me is not a figment of my imagination. She's real, and she's a part of me."

Aenwyn squinted her eyes. "But how can a wolf be a part of you?"

"It's hard to explain." I curled my tail around my waist. "But she's like an extension of my instincts. She kinda helps me tap into my primal instincts. That's the best way I can put it."

Lexia tucked her ears back. "That's still hard to believe. But sometimes she has mood swings, like she's two different beings in one body."

Daric scoffed. "See? That's exactly what I'm talking about. It's a classic symptom of a split personality."

I shook my head, holding back a growl. "That's not what's happening here. I'm not dissociating from reality. I'm fully aware of who I am and what's happening around me. The wolf is just a part of me, like an extra set of senses."

Zenny leaned forward, placing a hand on my shoulder. "Lucia, we believe you. And we know you're not crazy."

Zenny's smile helped calm me down. But Daric was still looking at me skeptically.

"Look, I don't care that you don't believe me," I said to him. Then I bared my fangs. "I'm not crazy. I don't need a cure because there's nothing wrong with me. And if you keep suggesting it, I will dislocate both your arms and tie them in a knot."

Daric threw his hands up in surrender. "Alright, alright. Fine, I won't push it any further. I can tell when I'm fighting a losing battle."

Finally.

Aenwyn cleared her throat, breaking the tension in the room. "So, there's another issue that could use some explanation." She pointed towards my ice-covered leg.

I looked around at everyone, feeling the weight of their gazes on me. "Right, that." I took a deep breath. "Please, don't get angry with me, sis. I know I messed up."

I could feel Lexia's stare the most. *I really don't want to make her upset. After all, I promised I would stay safe, and then I went and broke that promise like an idiot.*

"You all know about those orcs that were chasing me?" Everyone except Zenny nodded. She went a little pale. "Well, they have a fort nearby."

Aenwyn leaned forward, her eyes fixed on me. "A fort? How many orcs are stationed there?"

I sighed, already feeling tired from the conversation. "I didn't count them, but there were probably about forty."

Daric raised an eyebrow. "That's a lot of orcs. Did you get a chance to see how fortified their base is?"

I nodded. "Yeah, it's pretty well fortified. There's a wooden palisade surrounding the fort with four towers."

Zenny shuddered, then turned to Aenwyn. "There are forty-seven knights here. Do you think it's possible to just ignore them?"

I shook my head. "We can't. Fina's in there."

Lexia jumped. "We have to help her now!"

Aenwyn's glare calmed my sister's enthusiasm. "We will, but forty orcs aren't a joke. If we are to save your friend"—she turned to Daric—"and any others captured there, we need to handle this carefully."

"On the bright side, they don't have a mage anymore," I said.

Aenwyn's eyes narrowed. "What's this about an orc mage? How do you know they had a mage? And also, what happened to him?"

I shrugged. "Yeah, the mage was using earth manipulation magic to throw boulders at me."

Lexia's ears perked up. "Earth manipulation magic? Orcs can use magic?"

Daric nodded. "Yes. According to Midas, every race has the potential for magic. It's just elves and dwarves that always have it."

Aenwyn leaned back, crossed her arms, and held her chin. "Did the mage injure you?"

I scratched the back of my head. "No, it was a much larger and more dangerous orc." Zenny put her hand on my makeshift cast. "It was an orc who possibly has two aptitudes. If I had to guess, he has both the physical and durability aptitudes."

Zenny looked worried. "How did he break your leg?"

I flinched. "With one hand. He simply crushed it like this." I mimicked the motion.

Everyone flinched. Lexia growled. "I'll kill him."

I growled louder. "And how do you plan on doing that? My claws barely left a mark. His skin is extremely tough, and I doubt you can make ice sharp enough or hard enough to cut or pierce him. You can't make your ice as hard as mine."

"Did you try your magic?" Zenny asked softly.

I deflated. "No, it takes too long for me to do it in a fight. I'm better off using it for protection. Our only advantage is that he's slow. And I'm not talking about slow compared to me. He makes Zenny here look fast." I tried to give Zenny a playful smirk. "No offense, Zenny."

She shrugged. "I understand."

Captain Aenwyn snapped out of her recessed posture and placed a hand on Daric's shoulder. "You have the durability aptitude, correct?" Daric slowly nodded as he tensed up. "Are there any weaknesses you have?"

Daric swallowed hard. "Um." He glanced at me. I could smell him sweating. "Do you promise not to use what I'm about to tell you on me?"

I crossed my arms. "Don't give me a reason to, and I won't."

Daric sighed. "Fine." He shuffled his feet as he looked away. "My eyes are still very vulnerable. If you can figure out how, suffocation, extreme heat and cold, and probably electricity are effective options too."

Zenny hummed. "Electricity?"

Daric shrugged. "Lightning bolts from the sky would be the best thing you could understand."

Aenwyn pursed her lips. "I don't know of anyone here who can use such magic."

I shook my head. "Mom told me it's a very difficult variation of air manipulation magic mixed with fire manipulation. It requires a lot of preparation and concentration because she has to create a storm to do it." I chuckled. "She tried explaining that to me, and all I got was a headache."

"So suffocation and extreme heat and cold are our other options." Lexia stared at me. "I know he said the eyes were a weak spot, but that puts you too close to him." She pointed to my leg. "What's stopping him from doing worse next time?"

I flattened my ears. "You don't have to tell me," I whispered.

Aenwyn pointed to Lexia. "Your ice magic, is it strong enough?"

Daric shook his head. "Killing someone with pure cold would take a long time. I doubt you can make things cold enough, Lexia." He started pacing. "We have to kill him with fire."

"I'd rather you didn't use fire." My cheeks felt warm as Lexia gave me an apologetic smile.

Aenwyn cleared her throat. "You, young lady, are not coming with us. Your leg is broken, and you are in no shape to fight."

"About that." Zenny looked at the leg. "Can you remove your ice so I can get a better look at it?"

I pulled the cast apart and threw it on the ground to let it melt there instead. It had already left a wet spot on the cot. Daric looked at me more closely.

"How badly does it hurt?" Zenny held her hands just off my leg. "What do you think is the extent of the damage?"

I leaned back as the pain throbbed after I removed the cast. "On a scale of one to ten, with ten being the worst, I'd give it a solid seven and a half." I held up a hand. "Please don't touch it. It would hurt a lot more if you did. And I think there were five pieces I had to put together when I finally got away the first time."

Daric's eyes and mouth went wide. "Five pieces? And you put them back on your own?" I nodded. "How? Didn't that hurt?"

I snorted. "Absolutely. Let's say I'm more than acquainted with pain."

Daric pinched the bridge of his nose. "We'll likely need to give you surgery to put your bones back in order. You probably didn't put them back right." He looked like he had frozen for a moment. "Uh, I know there was a special metal they used for plates and screws, but I doubt you have anything we can use."

"Screws?" Lexia's scream hurt my ears. "In her leg?"

Daric flinched. "Really small ones." He held up his hand with his pointer finger and thumb at a short distance from one another. "They hold the bones together so they heal correctly."

"Is this another one of those things you know from your past life?" Zenny asked.

Daric nodded sheepishly as he kept an eye on my sister. Lexia stared him down with a look I was all too familiar with. *She wants to strangle him.*

"Daric, I suggest you leave," I said. "If you say one more word, Lexia might—no—*will* hurt you." It was hard to stay calm. I grabbed the sides of the cot to give myself something to focus on while blocking out the pain.

Daric turned his head to Lexia then back to Aenwyn.

"We'll talk a little more after we're done here," the elf said as she placed a hand on his shoulder and turned him to face the door. "Until then, I suggest you think about how to talk around Lexia."

Daric hunched his shoulders as he walked out of the tent.

"He's probably not wrong." I clenched my jaw. The pain in my leg was getting worse with each passing moment. "Zenny, I know you're not going to like this. And, sis, I'm going to need you to stay calm. Captain, I'm going to need someone to hold me down."

"Sis?"

"Lexia, I need you to stuff me with as much unfocused magic as you can." I closed my eyes, trying to keep my breathing calm. *If I can't stay calm, none of them will.* "Remember how I told you that I can use it to speed up my healing?"

"Yes."

"What do I have to do?" Zenny's voice shook.

"Zenny, I'm going to need you to cut my leg open to the bone and arrange the bones in their proper places." *I imagine there's going to be some explanations later, especially for my sister. I'm so not ready for this.*

"I see," Captain Aenwyn said. She then shook her head. "This is really reckless. And honestly, I don't know if I comprehend everything, but if you believe this will help you heal, I'll be back. Don't you dare start without me. If I don't like what's going on, I'll stop everything."

I could feel the bed beneath me snapping. "Oh, and bring the heaviest leather straps you can get and anything for me to grab with my hands."

"Sis?" Lexia's voice was quieter. "What's going on? Why are you saying these weird things? What if Daric is wrong?"

I heard Zenny get up and walk away saying, "Lexia, you need to trust your sister. I'm sure she'll explain it all to you afterwards. But right now, she's in a lot of pain."

Lexia sniffled. "Okay. Will you, sis?"

I didn't hear her walk next to me, but I felt her hand touch my shoulder as a rush of magic filled me. "I'll likely need you to remind me after this. But yes, I'll explain."

"You aren't allowed to leave this tent until I'm satisfied." Lexia's whisper was cold.

I didn't know which scared me more—the surgery I was about to have without anesthetics, or the conversation with my sister afterwards.

23

LEXIA'S WORRY

I sat on a nearby stool, watching Lucia on the cot in front of us. I did what she asked and filled her with unfocused magic. Zenny watched us with her hands in her lap as we waited for Captain Aenwyn to come back.

My sister started giggling.

"Are you feeling okay, sis?" I asked. *She talked about this. Unfocused magic makes her act strange.*

She giggled. "I feel funny, sis; it's like I'm floating."

I frowned. "Floating?" *She didn't say anything about feeling weird.*

Lucia's eyes glazed over. "Yeah. My arms and legs feel all tingly." She looked down at her tail. "And would you look at that? My tail's being bad again. It won't move."

My eyes went wide as I stood up and looked at Zenny. But before I could say anything, she shook her head. "It's alright. She gets like this when she absorbs unfocused magic. Her limbs go numb, she doesn't stop talking, she can't walk or stand up, and she giggles at everything."

As if to prove the point, my sister fell into another giggling fit. "Don't worry, sis. I'm gonna be just fine. Probably. I think. Maybe." She waved her arm, yet it seemed to be a pointless flounder instead of an ordered, calculated movement.

Anxiety flooded my chest, and there was a heavy, unsettling feeling in my gut. *This isn't like my sister. She's talking weird and acting childish.*

"What is the point of this?" I looked into my sister's half-opened eyes. "Why did you ask me to do this?"

"Haven't I done this for you before?" I shook my head. "Oh." My sister looked a little disappointed.

But as time passed, Lucia's condition only seemed to worsen. I watched her yawn. She never yawned.

"Sis, I'm so sleepy," she said, her words almost unintelligible.

I grabbed her hand. "No, Lucia. You can't fall asleep yet." I looked at Zenny, who wasn't reacting like she should. "Do something."

She shook her head. "Her falling asleep might make things easier. I'm sure you know this is all normal for someone who can use magic."

My heart dropped. *Right. I got carried away. She has a reaction to unfocused magic, just like me. But instead of her senses getting all mixed up, she acts like this and gets sleepy. That's not that bad.*

"She does wake up, right?" I watched as my sister's chest gently moved up and down with each slow breath.

Zenny chuckled. "She'll be better than ever when she wakes up. For some reason, this increases her recovery aptitude to an almost unheard-of level. My mom's been trying to research it, but she can't understand it."

She looked a little disappointed when she referenced her mother. Her mother, Salien, was Lucia's doctor while she was growing up.

"Wait, you were experimenting on my sister?"

Zenny jumped up and flinched. "Of course not!" Her eyes locked on me. "How could you say something like that? She's my friend. We could never hurt her."

I flattened my ears and sat back down on the stool. "Sorry. Sis says I jump to conclusions too often. I'm really sorry."

Zenny walked over and put a hand on my shoulder. "You care about her a lot." I nodded. "Good. She seems happy around you. I can see that your opinion really matters to her." Her voice felt different. It was like I was hearing it from Nora. A tear welled up in my eye.

I heard several footsteps heading into our tent before I saw

Captain Aenwyn and three other women with her. They were all the largest—and likely the strongest, besides Lucia—women in The Maidens.

I used my arm to wipe the tear that threatened to fall.

"She's sleeping?" The captain looked at my sister. "How? Wasn't she in extreme pain before we left?"

Zenny slumped her shoulders as she looked at the ceiling for a moment. "She's fine. It's something that happens when she is subjected to unfocused magic." Zenny turned and walked towards one of the knights, who was carrying several straps of thick leather.

Captain Aenwyn eyed Zenny for a moment and then shrugged. "I'll let you explain that to me later. But first, you three grab a limb and hold it down. Whoever grabs her broken leg grab her hips instead. Actually, never mind, I'll take that one."

The other knights watched Lucia like she was a dangerous animal. It was a look I'd seen far too often since coming to live with my sister. *Yes, she's dangerous. But only to those who deserve it. They don't have a reason to be scared of her.*

Regardless of their feelings towards my sister, they all followed the captain's orders. One woman placed a metal pot next to Zenny before grabbing Lucia's other leg.

Zenny approached my sister with a wooden box that had a knife resting on top. She set them down before grabbing a small stack of clean bandages. She placed those next to her stool too, then she sat down and picked up the knife.

I looked at Zenny's face. Any emotion she had was gone. The way she stared at the knife while she dipped it in the pot of water as a light touch of steam rolled off it unsettled me. It felt like a stone was growing in my stomach. And it only grew more as she cut the fur on Lucia's leg. The woman with the leather straps opened Lucia's mouth and nestled them between her teeth.

"Hang on to her," Zenny said.

The atmosphere in the tent change. Everyone tightened up as Zenny placed the blade against my sister's leg. She pressed in and drew the blade down, opening a red line.

Lucia immediately woke up, screaming. All the knights held her limbs as best they could. My sister started thrashing as her muffled screams grew. I rushed to her and grabbed her head from behind.

"It's okay; I'm here. You said this needed to happen." I held back tears as I cradled my sister. "Concentrate on my voice. I'm not going anywhere."

Her screaming died down for a moment, as did her struggling. Zenny had leaned back, holding the knife up. She shot me a glance; her face was impassive, but I could feel her expectant gaze. Every part of my mind said I needed to stop this. Lucia didn't deserve to suffer like this.

But this is her idea. She said that she needed this. This is for you, sis. I nodded, giving my permission to continue.

Zenny nodded back and returned to my sister's leg. I could feel Lucia tightening up. Zenny cut into my sister's leg again, causing Lucia to scream. It tugged at my heart. Guilt stabbed into my soul. *This is my fault. I should stop this. Lucia can't keep suffering like this. But this is for her well-being. She wants this.*

I wanted nothing more than to stop the procedure, but I also couldn't let myself do that. But since I couldn't, Lucia didn't stop screaming as Zenny continued cutting. I closed my eyes and flattened my ears. But I couldn't stop hearing her screams.

Tears fell from my eyes as I tried to close them harder. Lucia didn't struggle, but she kept screaming into the leather strips. Her anguished cries felt like burning knives in my ears. I had never felt such pain, but I also couldn't imagine the pain she felt at that moment either.

This is all my fault. I should've gone with her. Then maybe she wouldn't have gotten hurt. Maybe then Fina would be safe. Lucia doesn't deserve a sister like me. She deserves someone stronger. Someone who can keep up with her.

Lucia's screams hit an all-new high. Bile crept up in my throat as I sobbed. *I couldn't look after her. Again. Why can't I keep my sister safe? I'm the big sister. It's my duty to protect her.*

My sister's body started going limp. Her screams softened into sobbing whimpers. My tears didn't stop. They only intensified. I couldn't hold back anymore. The bile sitting in the back of my throat moved forward. I let go of Lucia's head with one hand and vomited on the ground. Everything burned, and some of it went up my nose. My gut pushed inward again as another round of vomit lurched from my mouth.

My vomiting ceased when Lucia put her head back down on the cot. Her breathing was ragged and her face was soaked with tears, but she was alive. When I looked at Zenny, I saw her jaw set and her eyes focused on the task at hand: stitching up the wound she had just made. Sweat poured from her brow and matted some of her hair. Her bloodstained hands worked with a surety I could appreciate.

Captain Aenwyn looked at me with an apologetic frown. She didn't say anything; she only turned her head and watched Zenny finish stitching Lucia's leg.

After Zenny finished, she grabbed several of the bandages and started wrapping Lucia's leg. She never lifted my sister's leg to pull the bandage through, instead shimmying it up her leg as she worked.

Aenwyn grabbed a piece of cloth, turned to me, and started wiping my face.

"Are you okay?" she whispered.

"No." It was the only word I could get out.

I grabbed the cloth and started cleaning my face of snot and some remnants of my vomit that clung to the fur around my mouth. I didn't bother with my eyes as tears kept streaming down, soaking my fur. Lucia's breathing looked like it was slowing down as the other women stood up. Each of them was breathing a little harder than Zenny.

After Zenny finished wrapping my sister's leg, she started washing her hands in the pot of water that she'd washed the knife in.

As we waited for Lucia to recover, Captain Aenwyn came to sit next to me. "I can see that you're struggling with something, Lexia," she said in a tender whisper. "What's going on in your head?"

I shook my head, not wanting to burden her with my guilt. "It's nothing. I'm just worried about Lucia."

Aenwyn placed a comforting hand on my shoulder. "It's okay to feel overwhelmed. What just happened wasn't easy to witness, especially for you as her sister."

"I just feel like I should have done more to protect her," I admitted, my voice cracking. "She's always been so reckless, and I've always been the one trying to rein her in. But this time I wasn't there, and she got hurt because of it."

Aenwyn squeezed my shoulder gently. "You can't control everything, Lexia. Lucia is a grown woman who can make her own decisions. You've been doing your best to keep her safe, but accidents happen. You can't blame yourself for things that are out of your control."

"I know," I said, wiping away a stray tear. "But it's hard not to feel responsible. She's my sister, and I love her."

Aenwyn nodded. "I understand. But you need to take care of yourself too. You can't let this guilt consume you. Remember that Lucia makes her own choices."

"I just wish she would let me protect her more." I stared at my sleeping sister. "She's so reckless and impulsive. It's who she is; I know that. But that doesn't make it hurt any less."

Aenwyn grabbed my chin and turned my head so I looked at her. "Then tell her."

"I have." My voice caught in my throat.

But she can never remember it in the heat of the moment.

"Then tell her again and again if she still doesn't hear you." Her voice was sharp. She let my chin go. "Then, if that isn't enough, show her how much it hurts. Lucia cares for you. She cares for a select few, but she cares so deeply for each one that it's hard for her to hold back."

I dropped my head and curled my tail around my waist. "I will."

"Good," Aenwyn said as she walked away. "Stay here with her until she wakes up. I have a siege to plan. One that's more difficult since the other companies didn' join us."

I snapped my head towards her. "And I'm going with you." The rumble of my voice filled the tent.

I had an orc to kill. He hurt my sister, and now he had to pay.

Aenwyn chuckled. "Of course. I'll come to get you when we're ready to attack. But until then, tell Lucia everything she needs to hear."

I calmed down once she walked out of the tent. Zenny quietly stood off to the side of the tent, her hands folded in front of her.

"I'll stay here with you." She grabbed her stool and moved it to sit next to me. "You aren't the only one who needs to talk to her."

"Do you feel the same way?" I couldn't help but ask.

"Sort of." Zenny looked like she was thinking. "I'm not angry like you; I'm more disappointed. She's still fifteen, so maybe she's not ready for all of this yet. Perhaps she should've waited a few more years."

I slumped my shoulders as I started brushing Lucia's hair with my fingers. *I wish she would give this lifestyle up completely. She should just live quietly with me, Gifford, and Victor. We don't have to be the ones to save the world.*

"Other people can save the world." The words slipped out of my mouth.

Zenny's eyes widened, and her body tensed up. "She told you about that?"

I glanced at her from the corner of my eye. "The demon king that's supposedly coming? Yeah, she did. But she didn't tell me how she and Mom know. She keeps changing the subject when I ask."

Zenny's face turned a little green. "That's..." She couldn't look at me as she hesitated. "It's not my place to tell."

A shiver ran down my spine. *She's keeping a secret from me. How could she? Why? I've told her everything.*

Zenny stood up. "I'm going to get some food. I'll be back with some for you and Lucia when she wakes up. No doubt she'll be hungry. She's always hungry."

I absentmindedly nodded. *Sis, what's so wrong that you can't tell me? I have to know.*

24

LUCIA'S EXPLANATION CHANGES NOTHING

I woke up to find Lexia sitting beside me, looking tense and worried. Her hands were tightly clasped in her lap, and she kept glancing at me as if she thought I'd do something unexpected.

"Hey, sis," I said. *Hopefully I didn't do anything too stupid last night.* "How long have I been out?"

"It's night," Lexia replied, her tone guarded.

I rolled back onto the cot. "So I didn't sleep through the night?"

"Yeah." Her tone felt like she wanted to say more.

I looked down at my bandage-wrapped leg. "How bad is it?"

"Zenny said that she needed to look at it once you were awake." She placed her hand on my shoulder. "I'll get her, but first, we need to talk."

I felt a heaviness in my gut. "About?"

Lexia closed her eyes. "You did say I might have to remind you." She took a deep breath. "You and Daric were talking about weird things earlier, and you had Zenny cut your leg open to move the bones. You said that you needed to have that done. Why? And why did you agree with Daric?"

The fog blocking my memory slowly faded as she spoke. "Right, that." *I wish she wanted to talk about what happened at the orc fort.*

"And Captain Aenwyn said you were to stay here and not join the fight for the fort." Lexia's eyes bored a hole in me as she stood up.

A whimper left my throat. "Why? What about Fina?"

"Because I'm afraid you'll do something reckless again," my sister blurted out while slamming her eyes shut. "Please, sis, let me take care of it for you. I'll bring her home."

"But—"

"I know you promised." Tears started pouring from Lexia's eyes as she interrupted me. "You can let me help you, can't you? I don't want to see you hurt anymore. I can't stand it. It hurts too much."

There were no words for me to say. They wouldn't have done my feelings justice. I sat up and grabbed my sister's hand. She sniffled as she opened her eyes and looked at my hand. I pulled her into a hug, which she returned.

"I'm sorry," I whispered. "Believe me when I say that those two words aren't enough. I just don't know what else to say."

"Does that mean you'll tell me?"

Her whisper set my heart racing.

She leaned back and looked me in the eye. "Will you tell me why you've been keeping secrets from me?"

Lexia's question hung heavily in the air. I knew what she was really asking, even if she couldn't bring herself to say the words.

Why did you ask that? I'll talk about anything with you, sis, anything but that. I can't tell you the truth. Not yet. Maybe not ever. What if you don't see me as your sister anymore? You're already suffering enough as it is. I shouldn't tell you.

"It's nothing you need to worry about," I said, trying to keep my voice light. "I'm hungry. How about some food?" I looked around the room for something to eat.

Lexia grabbed my head and turned it to face her.

"No," she said, gritting her teeth. "Don't. Not now. Why?" Her body relaxed as her lips quivered. "Why, sis?"

That three-letter word tore a hole in my heart more than I thought possible. *Why?*

"Because I'm afraid," I said. I slumped and looked away from her.

177

Her hands dropped to her sides, and she shifted to sit next to me. "Why? What's so scary that we can't face it together? We're sisters."

My heart raced even faster as tears welled up in my eyes. I choked back a whimper. "It's just—I don't know how to explain," I said finally. "It's not something I can easily put into words."

"What's wrong?" Lexia asked softly. "Please. Let me help. Don't shut me out."

I shook my head. My throat threatened to close up. "I can't. Not yet."

"Why not?"

"Because—because it's something that might change everything between us." I felt the tears prickle at the corners of my eyes, finally dropping down my cheeks. "And I'm scared of losing you."

Lexia hugged me. "You won't lose me. Nothing you can say will change anything between us. Whatever it is, you can tell me. If you don't want anyone else to know, I can respect that, and I won't tell a soul. Not even Gifford. Just tell me. I'm your sister."

I gently squeezed her back, feeling a small glimmer of hope. *But I still can't say it.*

I didn't know how long we sat there, holding onto each other. Time didn't matter at that moment. The only thing that mattered was the pain my sister was in because I couldn't tell her I was a reincarnated soul.

"It's too hard to say, sis." My tears kept flowing. "I'm not ready."

Lexia didn't let go. "Then I'll wait here until you are. We'll take as many tries as you need."

I sobbed into her shoulder, soaking her shirt and the fur underneath.

But at some point, I looked up and saw the pained yet patient look on Lexia's face, and I knew I couldn't keep my secret any longer.

"Lexia." My voice shook.

"What is it?" Her eyes lit up as she sat up a little straighter.

"I..." My throat felt tight, and I had to swallow before I could continue. "I'm different. I wasn't always Lucia."

Her face froze. "What does that mean?"

178

"I mean..." *How do I say this?* "This isn't my first life. I'm someone who lived before in another world. Just like Daric."

Lexia's eyes widened, and she pulled back slightly. "What... What are you talking about?"

"I'm talking about reincarnation." The words barely made it out of my mouth. Lexia gasped. "I know it sounds crazy, but it's true. I remember things from another life. Another world."

Lexia's face went through a range of emotions—shock, disbelief, anger—before settling on something I couldn't quite read.

"That's impossible," she said finally. "You're making this up. Why are you lying to me? I'm your sister. This isn't the time for another one of your jokes!" Tears drenched the fur on her cheeks as she yelled at me.

"I wish I were joking." I lowered my head. My claws dug into the edge of the cot. "But it's the truth. This is why I was scared to tell you. I was afraid you would run and not see me as your sister anymore. But I couldn't keep it from you any longer. Not after I saw how much it was hurting you."

"How is that even possible?" Lexia's voice was barely more than a whisper. "Reincarnation? That can't be real. You're Lucia. You've always been Lucia."

"This body has always been Lucia." I wanted to run and forget this conversation ever happened. But I could feel something—someone pushing me towards Lexia. "I'm afraid that the Lucia you knew died that day the orcs attacked. And..."

I'm just an imposter who took over. Somehow, those words never came out.

Lexia stood up and started walking around. "But you didn't die. You're here. You're real. That means my sister didn't die. Lucia didn't die." Her tone was shifting as her words came out faster. "Yes, the hit to your head must have done something."

Lexia turned to face me. Her eyes looked empty, like she wasn't looking at me, but through me.

I sighed. "You can't rationalize it."

"But... But you..." Lexia's words fought to all get out at once, and

179

her tongue tripped up as an absurd conglomerate of words vomited from her mouth. "Knows else who many does why others—"

Lexia stood, panting. She paused and took a deep breath as she collected herself.

"Mom? Does she know?" I answered her questions with a nod. "Zenny?" I nodded again. "How many others know? Captain Aenwyn?" I shook my head.

"I've tried to tell as few people as possible." I curled my tail around and hugged. "Normally it doesn't come up, and, honestly, I wish I could forget that I was reincarnated. Most of my memories from that life were taken away, and I've forgotten most of the rest."

Lexia stumbled back, as if someone had punched her gut. She eventually fell down and stared at me. Her unblinking eyes were too much for me to handle.

"I wish you hadn't made me tell you." I held my tail tighter. "I wish things could go back to the way they were. When we were happy together, you treated me like I was your sister, but now I've ruined it."

First, I couldn't save Fina. Now I've gone and destroyed my relationship with my sister. Why? Why did I have to be reincarnated? Wouldn't it have been better if I'd never had those memories to begin with?

The silence in the room kept burning at the heaviness I felt in my stomach. I turned away from Lexia. "If you don't want to see me again, I understand. I'm not the sister you wanted."

Before I could attempt to stand and try to leave, a pair of arms wrapped themselves around my chest.

"I said I wasn't going anywhere," Lexia said through the tears she poured on my shoulders. "And I meant that. It was stupid of me to say this would change nothing." There was a pause where I could feel the tension rising. "It changes everything between us."

I grabbed at Lexia's hands. *And that's why I shouldn't have told you.* "It's a stupid thing. Because of the last ten years, I feel like I'm more Lucia than whoever I was before. I don't even know my name from my previous life."

"And that's why you're my sister."

As she called me her sister again, the heaviness on my shoulders lifted.

I turned my head towards her. "Do you mean that? Am I still your sister?"

Lexia squeezed me tighter. "Of course. That will never change."

My pulse quickened. "But you said that everything between us changed."

She nuzzled my cheek with the top of her head. "Because we are now closer than ever. There are no more secrets between us."

"I... I don't know what to say."

"Then don't worry about it." Lexia let me go and sat next to me. "You're my sister. Do what you want to do. Say what you want to say. If you don't want to say anything, that's fine too."

The air in the tent felt lighter. It suddenly felt more open. I wasn't even aware that it had felt like the walls were closing in. It must have been so subtle, and now that it was gone, I could feel the difference.

I gave my sister a smile. "I'm sorry about all of this. Things shouldn't have gone this far, and it shouldn't have taken a situation like this for me to tell you. But I let my emotions control my actions again."

Lexia placed a hand on my shoulder. "And that's who you are. Am I upset you didn't tell me sooner?" She paused for dramatic effect. "Absolutely." Then she hugged me. "But I'm glad that you still told me. I can see how painful it was to. And I also realize my reaction didn't help the situation."

I hugged her back. "Does that mean you believe me?"

"Yes. Although, I still don't understand what it means, but I don't need to."

"You don't know how relieved I am to hear you say that," I responded, letting my eyes close, exhaustion creeping in.

Lexia broke the hug and smiled at me. "You know, there might be more of my old sister in you than you think."

It was my turn to be confused. "Huh?"

My sister giggled. "When you talked about how you have an inner wolf, maybe that's a piece of her still inside you."

"That almost makes sense." *How did she come up with that, and how have I never thought about that my entire life?*

She shrugged. "It's just a thought. And speaking of thoughts, how much of your being reincarnated is about this demon king? I heard you and Mom talking about it."

"Everything, unfortunately." I wiped the tears from my eyes. "This wasn't even the body I was supposed to be in." Lexia flinched. "But don't worry. I'm glad I have this body. I get to have the best mother and sister ever."

My sister relaxed. "I'm glad you're my sister, too."

My stomach growled. We giggled together. "It looks like I can't put this off any longer. There had better be some food around, or I'm eating one of the horses."

Lexia kept laughing. "Somehow, I doubt that's an exaggeration. I've seen you eat. But don't worry. Zenny left some food for you. And there should be plenty, even for your appetite."

25

ONE QUIET MOMENT

Lexia made me promise not to leave the bed until she came back with Zenny. *I feel fine, mostly. There's no pain anymore, but that doesn't mean anything with how broken my leg was.* I sat like a good little sister and ate the pile of jerky on my bed.

It wasn't long before Zenny and Lexia walked back into the tent. While the flap was open, I could see that it was nearly pitch black outside.

"I still can't get over the fact you can see in that kind of darkness," Zenny said as she walked into the tent, where a few candles, as far away from me as possible, illuminated the small space.

"I don't understand how you can live with such dull senses," Lexia quipped back. "How, as a race, have you survived?"

"Tools and technology." Zenny shrugged. "From what I understand."

I stared at the two, a piece of jerky inches from my mouth. "What kinda conversation are you two having?"

Lexia giggled. "Oh, I'm just teasing Zenny because she needed me to guide her here. Someone can't see in the dark." She nudged Zenny in the ribs.

Zenny rolled her eyes. "The moons aren't out. There are clouds covering them." She crossed her arms and glanced at me. "Is there going to be a storm heading our way?"

I shook my head. "There isn't one close enough for me to hear. But that doesn't mean that it won't rain. It hasn't rained for the last few days."

"Okay, I guess I'll look at your leg now." Zenny walked over and kneeled next to me. "First off, how does it feel? Is there any pain? Discomfort?"

I shook my head as I finished the last of the jerky. "There's no pain, but the wrapping is quite uncomfortable. If you made that any tighter, I'm afraid I'd lose feeling in my foot."

Zenny pulled a pair of scissors out of a pocket and started cutting the wrapping. "Good, then hopefully the bones are where they belong." She had to stop and stifle a yawn before finishing. "By the way, if we hadn't done what we did, your leg bones would've been slightly crooked. That probably would've hurt for the rest of your life."

A shiver ran down my spine. *Your bedside manner is usually better than this, Zenny.*

"Maybe next time don't tell her things like that," Lexia said softly from next to the entrance.

I eyed her. *How did she know?* "Are you thinking that I'm going to try and run away?"

My sister shook her head. "Nah. I just can't sit still right now."

I know that feeling. In fact, I'm kinda feeling that right now myself.

Zenny started poking my leg and pulling the fur apart, trying to look at my skin. "There's not even a scar," she whispered. "Mom would've loved to study you today. And she also would've yelled at you for an entire afternoon if she saw what you did to yourself."

Right, Mom. I flattened my ears. "Um, sis, don't tell Mom about this."

"Oh, no. She'll hear about this." Lexia wagged her finger at me. "You're in so much trouble for this. And I'm not just talking about the talk we had earlier."

"You told her?" Zenny asked without looking up from my leg as she pinched the sides.

"She made me," I grumbled.

Lexia started pacing around the tent. "So, what do you make of it, Zenny? When did you find out?"

Zenny stood up and shrugged. "I'll admit, it's hard to comprehend, but it seldom comes up. She's still Lucia. The same Lucia I've always known. It just makes it easier to trust her when she has one of her more unusual ideas." She offered me a hand. "Do you want to give it a shot? Standing up, I mean."

I exhaled a breath I didn't know I was holding. "You have no idea." I grabbed her hand and Zenny pulled hard, but I still had to stand up on my own for the most part. "It feels..."—I lifted my leg up and wiggled it around before setting it back down again—"weak."

I tried to balance only on the healing leg. It instantly gave out. Zenny and Lexia moved to catch me before I hit the ground.

"How much did you eat, sis?" Lexia asked with a pained groan.

"All of it." I got my feet under me again. "And I'm not fat."

Lexia and Zenny looked at each other before looking at me.

"Do you have any idea how much you weigh?" Zenny asked.

I shook my head. "No. People keep telling me I weigh a lot, but I have nothing to compare myself to."

A set of footsteps warned me that someone was coming only moments before a voice spoke. "Is everyone awake in there?"

"Yeah," I responded.

The tent flap opened and Captain Aenwyn walked in. "Good. Lexia, I hope you're ready. And Zenny, how's Lucia doing?"

Zenny frowned at me. "I think it would be better for her if she showed you."

"What's that supposed to mean?" I asked.

Zenny pointed with her thumb towards the elven captain. "Go and walk over to her while we watch."

She's up to something. Or she knows something and thinks I won't believe her. Fine, I'll play her little game.

I started walking towards Aenwyn and immediately felt the weakness in my leg causing me to limp severely. I turned and glared at Zenny after I stopped in front of the captain, who grimaced watching me.

"Happy?" My voice was harsher than I intended. I walked back to the cot I'd been using. As I walked, my limp improved slightly, but was still very obvious to everyone.

Lexia hummed. "It looks like you might be able to walk home after we come back. But you're staying here. No fighting for you."

I sat down and huffed. "You're not the doctor here."

Zenny leaned in my face and wagged a finger in front of my nose. "But I am. And I say you are to stay put."

Aenwyn groaned. "You are far too reckless for your own good. We're fighting orcs, and you want to go into battle severely handicapped? Not a chance."

Lexia sat next to me. "Sis, remember what I said? I want to help you. Let me carry this burden for you. You've done enough. You don't have to carry the weight of the world on your shoulders. Not everything is your responsibility alone."

I slumped. "Sorry. Just promise me you'll come back. You aren't the only one who can't stand seeing their sister hurt." I tried to give her a smile, but it felt far too forced.

The sides of Lexia's lips curled. "Of course. I will always come back to you. We'll never be apart for long again."

I wrapped an arm around her shoulders as she rested her cheek between my ears. "You're right. We're closer than ever." I glanced at Captain Aenwyn. "Does this mean you're all marching out right now?"

She nodded. "I've had a rotation of scouts watching the fort since you told me about it. They have just started settling down for the night. Their watch is likely at its weakest. Hopefully, we can use the element of surprise to take out as many as possible. And then the rest will be unprepared and inadequately armed."

"That's quite ruthless," I said with a slight grin. "Good, they deserve it."

Lexia stood up so quickly that I almost fell over. She gave me an odd smile, while her eyes looked a little glossed over. "Would killing the orcs make you happy?"

"After what I've seen of orcs, nothing would make me happier than seeing them all hunted down to extinction." I flexed my claws as I pretended to choke one.

Lexia turned and walked towards the door. "Then I guess I'll have to kill every orc in the world," she said in an upbeat tone.

What? She can't be serious, can she? She sounded like she was going to take a walk in the snow, which she enjoys almost as much as I do.

Aenwyn's jaw dropped as she watched my sister leave. "She's not serious, is she?" she asked absentmindedly. She stumbled out after her. "Lexia, stop. You're not seriously going to kill every orc, are you?"

"Why not?" I heard my sister respond from outside the tent. "They captured my friend, hurt my sister, and took her away from me when we were kids. My sister wants the orcs dead, and so do I. So I will kill them, all of them."

The bloodlust in my sister's voice sent a shiver down my spine. Not out of fear, but out of pride. *I didn't know she would go that far for me. Then I guess I'd better return the favor and devote myself to her just as much.*

"You can't possibly believe that you can do that." Aenwyn sounded like she was annoyed. "Better people have tried and failed. You can't possibly succeed where they haven't."

"I don't care," Lexia screamed. "They aren't me, and orcs will pay for the pain they have caused."

"You're not the only one the orcs have hurt. I know exactly what pain they can cause." Aenwyn's tone shifted. I straightened my back and almost saluted out of reflex. "I will not let you throw your life away like that. There is a reason none of the kingdoms have been able to wipe them out, even if we worked together. If you want to take your frustration and anger out on the orcs at the fort while we save your friend and any others held captive there, that's fine. But it can't go beyond that. You promised you wouldn't leave your sister behind, so don't go off on such a stupid quest leaving her here, alone, without you."

Lexia didn't reply. *Captain must have really struck a nerve using me against her like that. But how can all the kingdoms still not be enough to kill all the orcs? What does she know that she hasn't told us?*

"Are you going to stay put?" Zenny stood over me and crossed her arms after it sounded like my sister and captain were done shouting at each other.

I pouted. "Yes. But that doesn't mean I have to enjoy it."

Zenny's expression softened. "I know. But right now, you're vulnerable. Your sister was right. You've done a good job and more than enough. Let yourself heal. Fina will probably need you and your sister to help her when she comes back."

"I just wish she hadn't seen me running away," I said. "She sounded so hurt."

Zenny sat down and wrapped an arm around me. "But she wouldn't have wanted you to die to save her. You made the right decision to leave."

"But why does it feel so wrong?"

Zenny sighed. "I can't help you with that. You made your decisions in the moment. You did the best you could."

"Sometimes it feels like there are no good choices." I lifted my previously broken leg. "So, any idea why my leg feels so weak?"

My friend just shrugged. "Honestly? I've never done anything like this before. All I did is what you said I should do and improvised as best I could. Maybe you need to exercise it to rebuild your strength or give it more rest to heal the last bit." She put a hand on my thigh. "I know you heal quickly, especially with your little unfocused magic trick, but some things can't be rushed. Just do what feels right, as long as there's no pain. You should be good."

"Would you do me a favor, then?" I asked.

Zenny smiled. "Any time."

"Could you stay here for a while? I don't want to be alone right now." I hugged her close.

She hugged me back. "Sure."

26

LEXIA'S MISSION

I'm going to find the orc that attacked Lucia. And when I find him, I will make him pay. But I promised I'd follow Captain Aenwyn's orders. We snuck close to the fort and stopped at the edge of the trees. As we did, I could smell something in the air. It smells like it's going to rain.

The thought of revenge was at the forefront of my mind as I sat in the trees next to Captain Aenwyn. She ordered me to stay by her side so she could watch over me. Why doesn't she trust me? I just said that I want to kill all orcs. What's so wrong with that? The better question is, why doesn't she want to kill all orcs? They cause nothing but pain and suffering. They're evil and must be killed.

I felt a hand on my shoulder. "Stay with me," Captain Aenwyn whispered as she waved her arm forward.

I watched the other knights from The Maidens creep towards the fort. They moved quietly and stayed low.

"I know. When you give the signal, create a wall of ice for everyone to use as cover." I didn't bother to hide the growl in my voice. "After that, what happens?"

The captain didn't look at me. She kept watching the fort. "You will follow my orders as I give them. Depending on their reactions, I have different plans ready. If they fire back with arrows, I want you to make sure everyone is sufficiently covered. If there's magic involved, well, depending on what it is, you might have to figure out how to counter it as best you can. You're our most powerful mage right now."

I frowned. "Lucia said that she'd killed the mage already."

Captain Aenwyn placed a finger on her temple. "Think. What if another mage joined them? It would be better to have a plan for that and not use it than the other way around."

I flattened my ears as I lowered my head. "Oh. I didn't think about that."

Aenwyn placed a hand on my shoulder. "That's fine. But let's move up. Everyone is almost in position." She turned and glared at me. "Stick to the plan and follow my orders. Don't run off and do something you'll regret and you'll be back with your sister in a short time."

I know she's using my love for my sister to manipulate me. But I can't help but go along with it. There's nothing malicious about how she's manipulating me. She probably knows that I know she's doing it. But I can tell she cares about us. That makes it easier to follow her. The demon told me everyone has a price. It's true, and mine is Lucia.

It started drizzling as the captain stood up and shouted, "Now!"

I summoned my magic and created a pillar of ice in front of me and the captain. Then I poured more magic into pulling the water in the air to create a wall about fifty inches tall. Tall enough for everyone to stand and shoot their bows and crossbows before ducking behind.

The first volley of arrows and bolts hit the eight orcs in the four watchtowers. All of them went down; only three stood back up. Horns and shouts filled the air as I finished making the ice around one section of my allies.

I dropped to all fours and sprinted to the next group of knights as they reloaded their weapons. They fired just as I got there and before the orcs in the tower retaliated. I hurried and made a section of ice into a wall that matched the first one I had made. All the knights crouched down behind it as they reloaded once again. A couple of them even gave me a nod and a smile before I sprinted off for the third group of archers.

The rain started coming down harder. Large drops of water hammered into my fur and gambeson. As I ran, the ground softened. *I don't know if this is a good thing or not. It's making it very easy to use my magic, but I know all this water is going to soak into my fur and slow me down.*

I created a third wall of ice just as more orcs entered the watch-towers, bows at the ready. They released them as soon as they saw where we were.

I dove behind the wall of ice I'd made.

"Mage!" I heard an orc shout.

"Sorry, kid," an elven knight who took cover next to me said. Her name was Makaela, and she always seemed to have a smile on her face, even now. "It looks like they have a plan for you."

I heard another round of arrows chip into the ice. "I've got one more wall of ice to make. Eirina and the others need cover."

Makaela turned to the other four knights. "You heard her, ladies. Let's give her some covering fire." She turned back to me. "Go."

The five knights stood up and fired at the orcs in the tower. I sprinted towards the final group of knights. Two of them looked to be falling backwards as they fired their projectiles. The second pair of knights weren't shooting back, as one of them was being dragged by another knight. She was obviously wounded with two arrows protruding from her, one in her thigh and the other in her side just above the hip.

I reached out and created a short wall of ice just as another salvo of arrows streamed at the exposed knights. I blocked about half of them. Of the half that made it past my barrier, most hit the ground. One did not. It embedded itself in a human woman's neck as she pulled her comrade, who also now had an arrow poking out of her collarbone.

Alright, my job's done. I heard a couple more arrows get released. I looked at the tower and saw they were aiming at me. I ducked low and scurried closer to the walls, hearing the arrows land where I'd been standing moments before.

Pulling the water out of the ground and freezing it into an icy lance was easy; throwing the lance towards the orcs in the watchtower as they loaded their bows again was easy; hitting them wasn't. They dove below the ramparts, and my projectile flew over their heads.

My attack bought me enough time to run and hide behind my newest wall of ice with the other women. The knight with three arrows sticking out of her, whose name was Auicia, was alive, although she looked like she was in a lot of pain. The knight who'd taken the arrow to the neck, Hawyse, wasn't breathing, and it looked like blood had stopped pouring from her neck.

"Thanks for the cover. Uh, you're Lexia, right?" the knight who took cover next to me asked.

"Correct. The cover was Captain Aenwyn orders, Kaylein." I looked at the two knights on the ground.

Kaylein frowned. "One injured, one dead. I appreciate what you've done. Those orcs reacted quicker than we expected them to."

"Do you know the plan? What happens next?"

A pair of arrows hit the ice wall.

The other knight and I stood up and launched projectiles at the two orcs left in the watchtower. The knight's arrow hit the rampart, doing nothing. My icy spear, on the other hand, crashed into the wooden structure, because I knew they were going to hide again. It pierced halfway through. I heard a scream from an orc as splinters exploded from the impact.

The knight stood up with an arrow nocked and held it. "It depends on if another round of archers goes to the towers or if they open their doors. If they keep sending archers, we're supposed to take them down with our own ranged attacks until we're out of ammunition."

The orc stood up, but the moment he did, Kaylein released her arrow. The orc didn't react fast enough and took the arrow through his mouth. He grasped at it as he fell backwards.

"What if they come out of the fort?" I asked.

Both knights nocked another arrow but didn't pull them back. "Then we're supposed to fall back and regroup into a single unit."

Wow, she really did have plans for each situation. I guess she's earned her right to lead.

"There haven't been any signs of a mage, have there?" I watched the towers and saw that the other three were empty as well.

"Nah," Kaylein responded. "Head back to the captain. She'll tell you what you need to do now. All of us were ordered to tell you to return to her."

As I moved to leave, the other knight with us grabbed my shoulder. "If there are any more archers, you might want to make yourself a shield to protect yourself out there. We don't want any more deaths."

I arched an eyebrow. *Solidarity for someone you barely know. I didn't know humans or elves were capable of that.* "Thank you, Rozem."

The rain continued to get worse. The rain soaked my fur almost as bad as the ground. My feet squelched in the mud. *Ugh. Getting clean later is going to be a pain.*

Everything felt heavy as I ran and kept an eye on the fort. But just as I passed what I suspected was the entrance, the wood lifted and moved towards me. I paused and watched. The sounds of boots splashing through the mud and the grunting of the orcs left me conflicted. My first desire was to kill them, but my instincts told me to back off.

I followed my instincts, but not before freezing the ground in front of them. All the orcs slipped and fell, releasing the wooden piece of a wall they were using as cover.

Rozem and Kaylein dragged their wounded partner as they headed towards me.

"Thanks!" Rozem shouted. "Keep going."

I didn't do that for you, but sure.

I sprinted without waiting for them. Soon I was standing next to Aenwyn as she and four other knights fired arrows and bolts at the slipping and sliding orcs.

"That was a smart move," the captain said. "Can you do the same thing to those over there?"

I followed where she pointed and saw another group of orcs using the same tactic as the first. They looked like they were heading off one of the squads of knights as they were coming towards us. More orcs ran out from the fort entrances.

"There are more orcs here than we thought!" The panic in Aenwyn's voice was obvious. "We need to retreat!"

"No!" I growled. "We can't leave Fina. And I have to avenge my sister."

I didn't let the captain respond before I headed towards the orcs that were moving to cut off the other knights' retreat. I focused my magic and froze the ground around the orcs' feet. The knights kept running past me.

I extended an arm towards the second set of orcs charging me and released another blast of magic. The rain froze and turned into needles that flew towards the orcs. Most of the needles didn't cause much harm as they hit fur and hide armor. But the spell was enough to halt their charge as dozens of small red dots littered their faces and arms.

"All of you, help her!" I heard Aenwyn shout just before a volley of arrows joined my icy needles on the orcs without cover. Of the eight that had charged out, five lived through our assault.

Captain Aenwyn continued to order her knights behind me, but I was more concerned with the orcs that were freeing their feet. I created a ball of ice roughly thirty inches tall, which took more out of me than I would have liked, and pushed it towards the orcs.

As the sphere of ice rolled towards them, the sounds of bones snapping and screams from the orcs filled the air. After the ball passed the orcs, a grin spread across my face when I saw the disfigured and contorted corpses in the mud. Then I looked at the three remaining orcs, who simply watched the ball of ice crush the others. They turned to me and raised their weapons before resuming their charge.

I created a shard of ice and launched it before making a second one and taking a few steps back. The orc blocked the shard with his sword. But as the ice shattered, the shrapnel, some of which was quite large, peppered his body. His movements slowed drastically before he slumped to the ground.

I threw the second shard of ice. The orc attempted to move his club between him and my projectile, but it went through his club, his stomach, and stuck out of his back. The orc hit the ground with a satisfying plop in the mud. His partner was able to reach me before I could use my magic again.

He thrust his spear towards me. I threw my hips to the side, but the spear nicked me. I extended my claws and grabbed the spear's shaft as the orc pulled it back. I went with it, and the orc released it with his right hand and punched me in the face. My vision blurred as I stumbled backwards.

My vision corrected itself just before the orc stabbed at me again. I dove to the side and rolled away, this time uninjured. The orc growled and moved to follow me. I let out my own growl as I threw my arms up in the air and started freezing the orc's feet. He looked down, but I kept creating more ice. I froze all the water that was covering him. As more rain collided with the ice, I froze that too. Soon, the orc was nothing more than a statue of ice.

Mom's teachings on magic are way beyond anything the beastkin from the Wild Kingdom can dare to dream of. And with them, I have a way to help Lucia.

A loud, squelching sound caught my attention.

A massive green-skinned orc, with more muscles than would be considered healthy, grinned as he looked at me. "Ah, you came back. Good."

That has to be the orc that hurt my sister.

I bared my teeth. "You hurt my sister; now I'll kill you!"

The orc looked confused for a moment before that stupid grin returned to his face. "Two is always better than one. But Huk is always better than two."

He roared as he charged.

2 7

LEXIA'S VENGEANCE

A shiver ran down my spine as the orc charged towards me. He was even bigger than I had imagined, and his muscles bulged with every movement he made. My instincts demanded that I run. This was a fight I couldn't win. But a fire in the back of my mind wouldn't let me back down either.

I threw a spear of ice that shattered against his chest.

Huk stopped and grinned as he looked down at his uninjured chest. "A little beast thinks she can take on Huk? Huk likes little beasts. Huk especially liked the one with the fluffy tail."

The fire disappeared.

In its place was a raging volcano.

I sent a burst of icy wind towards him. All I accomplished was covering his skin with a shiny sheen of ice. It instantly shattered from his movements.

I tried again, this time aiming for his feet, but he simply sidestepped the attack.

Huk laughed. "Is that all you got, little beast? Huk has fought better than you! Huk will enjoy you too."

My tail stood upright as a snarl rumbled from my throat. *I will kill you!*

I threw an icy spear at Huk's knee, but he was too quick, jumping out of the way. My heart pounded as Huk charged towards me again. This time, I started running backwards.

Huk's fist came flying towards me. I quickly scrambled away and kept moving as his fist slammed into the ground. Mud erupted, coating his arms and face. I turned away to keep any from getting in my eyes.

As he wiped the mud from his eyes, I created a pillar of ice beneath the orc and slammed it up as hard as I could.

Huk grunted in pain and clutched his groin, but he quickly recovered and swung his other fist towards me. I ducked just in time, avoiding the attack and feeling the air rush over me.

Just one of those will kill me. I'll just have to kill him first. Just keep moving and find an opening. Lucia said that the orc might have the durability aptitude, and Daric, who has the same aptitude, said that his eyes are a weak spot.

I circled around Huk, hoping to find an opening, but he turned and slammed his fist into the ground again. I shoved a wave of magic into the mud and froze it. It was harder than manipulating regular ice, but I shaped it to wrap around the orc's hand and hold him to the ground.

With a roar, Huk lifted his arms and shattered the icy mud. I growled at my failure.

I tried to get some distance between us while using my ice magic to create a fog that would obscure Huk's vision. But Huk blindly bulldozed through it.

I couldn't help but growl even louder.

I heard more shouts and people running towards me. But the massive orc wouldn't give me the time to look at who it was. He threw another punch and forced me to keep stepping away from him. I created a spear and threw it at his leading leg. The weapon stabbed into his knee, but it didn't knock it out from under him like I had hoped.

As Huk kept advancing towards me, the spear fell out just from his movements. The only proof my attack had hit him was the small trickle of blood that was quickly washed away in the rain.

The frequency of the orc's attacks grew as he roared and sprayed spittle everywhere. I couldn't keep my distance anymore. My foot got caught in the mud, and I tripped. When I rolled over, Huk stood over me with a wide grin on his face. He reached for me. I couldn't focus on my magic to defend myself.

As his massive, round fingers nearly reached me, something stabbed into his fingernail. It was a spear. The fingernail popped off as Huk recoiled in more pain than I had been able to inflict with every attempt of my ice magic.

Captain Aenwyn stepped in front of me with a spear in her hands and another spear floating over her shoulder. I then realized how hard I was breathing as the knight tightened the grip on her weapon.

"Get up," the captain said as she lowered the butt of the spear towards me.

I grabbed it and was pulled to my feet just as the colossal orc roared and swiped his arms towards us. The spear pushed me back as Aenwyn ducked under and stabbed at the orc's face. Huk tilted his head, and the spear sliced his lip instead of going up his nose.

I let go of the spear so the captain could use it again as I threw another blast of ice magic at Huk's face, trying to freeze the water there. The orc flailed around, forcing Aenwyn to take a step back, but not before she stabbed at the spot my spear had struck before.

The wound opened up a bit more when Aenwyn retracted her spear. The weapon she was controlling with wood manipulation magic stabbed at the orc's hand as he pawed at the ice covering it. I then focused more on the rain hammering into the ice and freezing it as much as possible, building another layer of ice. Aenwyn struck the same spot on his knee again with perfect accuracy while using her spear to strike at the orc's hands to keep them from removing the ice from his head.

"Keep doing that!" Aenwyn shouted as she stabbed the knee a third time.

I could feel my magic running low. I didn't know exactly how much I had. Lucia was better at feeling how much she had than I was. But I knew I didn't have long left.

It doesn't matter. I will make it enough!

I raised my arms and stepped closer to the flailing orc. More ice built on the previous layers as the orc kept trying to remove it, but his mouth was open, and I knew it was full of ice too. Aenwyn's flying spear kept poking at the fingertips and under the fingernails and causing the orc to flinch away.

When Aenwyn stabbed her spear into his knee again, it went in much further than before. The leg buckled and snapped the knight captain's spear at the entry point. I kept creating more ice until it looked like the orc's movements were slowing down. He lifted his arms up and clenched his fists before punching each side of his head.

The ice shattered, and a wave of pain from the backlash caused me to stumble backwards. Huk kept kneeling and panting heavily, his eyes looking unfocused.

Aenwyn's spear floated from her hands, and she pulled back and threw the spear into the orc's eye.

He roared and rocked backwards as he clutched at the weapon in his eye. He started pulling the spear out. I could see Aenwyn struggling against the orc and pushing the spear back in.

"Oh no you don't!" I shouted. I created a large hammer head out of ice.

I slammed my creation into the butt of the spear and drove further in.

His body spasmed and went stiff.

"This is for threatening me!" I hammered the spear in further. "This is for Fina!" It was harder to hold the magic of my hammer together. I mustered every bit of anger and willpower and struck the back of the spear. "And this is for what you did to my sister!"

The hammer slammed into the spear one more time. This time, a shower of bone and blood exploded from the back of the orc's head, the tip of the spear poking out from the back.

My control over my magic dropped. I heard a faint buzzing in my head, and my limbs felt too heavy to move. Eventually, my legs collapsed under me. My knees sank into the mud as I looked around.

There were more knights surrounding the last of the orcs. Daric was even among them. I watched him deflect the blade of an orc before flipping his grip, drawing his sword across the orc's throat and nearly beheading it.

I guess he isn't all that useless after all.

Captain Aenwyn pulled her spear out of the orc's head as she knelt next to me. "Are you okay?"

"Yes, and no." My breathing was a mixture of wheezes and whistles. "I got him."

The elf looked at the lifeless orc. "Yeah, you did. We'll talk about this later." She wrapped her arm around me and lifted me to my feet. "You are so much lighter than your sister."

I giggled, which turned into a coughing fit. After I caught my breath, I could see that all the orcs were dead. "What now?"

"We tend to the wounded and find your friend and any other captives." Aenwyn turned me back towards where we started the siege. "Daric, I trust you can find the captives and bring them back to camp."

"I'm on it!" Daric shouted as he ran towards the fort.

Aenwyn turned towards another knight. "Makaela, make sure you take care of the wounded as quickly as possible." Makaela saluted before rushing off. "How about you, Lexia? Can you walk?"

I shook my head. "I don't think so. That was everything I had. My magic is exhausted."

Captain Aenwyn rolled her eyes. "You girls are perfect for each other. You two are equally reckless and get angry at each other for doing reckless things."

I growled at her as we headed for a fallen tree branch. "Don't tell me how to live my life."

Aenwyn sighed as she set me down on the branch. "I'm not. I'm just giving you something to think about while we get everything cleaned up here."

The rain helped clean the mud from my fur, but I didn't have the energy to get the rest out. *Lucia will be furious when she sees the condition my fur is in.* Then Aenwyn's words hit me. *She'll also be angry because I took on the big orc by myself. He could've, and maybe even would've, killed me, or worse. Maybe I should be a little more lenient with Lucia. She can't help it all the time.*

My breathing slowed down as I watched most of the knights enter the fort while the rest cared for the four wounded. I saw five other knights placed in a separate area. They weren't moving. Those who placed them there had grim looks on their faces. *They're dead. They died because we chased down these orcs. Is this why Captain Aenwyn doesn't believe that all the orcs can be killed? We attacked their fort. We had every advantage, and we killed more of them. We can kill the orcs so this never happens again.*

As I sat lost in my thoughts, Daric walking out of the fort caught my attention. I perked up my ears and saw a familiar girl curled up in his arms: Fina, her body battered and bruised. Daric continued to carry her towards me.

I tried to jump to my feet, but I stumbled to the ground since my legs didn't have the strength to hold me yet. Tears flowed from my eyes as Captain Aenwyn rushed over to me.

"Easy there," she said as she helped me sit back. "She's alive."

Daric didn't stop walking. "She needs medical treatment. I need to get her to Zenny as quickly as possible."

"I want to go with her," I said through my tears. "Help me, please."

"You can stay here, Captain." Another knight walked towards us. Rozem stood there and gave a slight bow. "I'll take her."

Aenwyn smiled as she stood up. "Alright." She looked down at me. "Go, be with your friend and your sister. The mission's complete. You can focus on recovering."

Rozem helped me to my feet and pulled my arm over her shoulders as she grabbed my waist. "Thanks for coming to save us. I know you were ordered to, but it still means a lot to see you put in the effort you did to help us."

A warm feeling trickled from my heart. "I... I don't know what to say. This is different from everything I know."

She smirked. "You could always just stick with 'you're welcome.' If it ain't broke, don't fix it."

I shook my head as we continued to follow Daric and Fina. "It doesn't feel right. I feel like I need to say something more meaningful."

"Why?" the woman asked.

"In the Wild Kingdom, it was always you surviving on your own power, but you always had to contribute to the pack. Here, everything I see revolves around money." *Why am I telling her all this? Why do I feel it's so easy to tell her all this?* More words just kept flowing without my consent. "I had to prove I was strong enough to survive, and only then would others help me when I asked. Even when I led a group to try to take down the Beast King, everyone had to contribute, or we would leave them behind. That was the standard I was held to."

"Wow." Rozem's voice reflected her surprise. "That's quite the info dump. It's hard to remember that you weren't raised here like your sister. I'm not saying our kingdom is perfect, but there are some things you could stand to learn from us." I was about to say something, but she spoke first. "On the other hand, we could stand to learn from you as well. Maybe the kingdoms being apart like they are isn't good for everyone."

"Are you suggesting that we have people leave their homes behind and move to a new kingdom surrounded by strangers who don't understand them?" I asked as we exited the woods. "That sounds stupid." *Maybe not so stupid. I did it for Lucia.*

Rozem rocked her head from side to side. "When you put it like that, yeah, it does. But like how a stagnant pond isn't safe to drink from, if people are too set in their ways, it can lead to problems in the future."

I didn't respond. *Something about that feels correct. But it also sounds like a dream where everyone can accept everyone. It's nothing more than wishful thinking.*

We walked in silence until we followed Daric to the medical tent where we'd left Lucia. He walked into the tent well before us, since I walked much slower than him. Before we entered, a deep growl almost sent me running. But I knew that growl. Lucia was livid and ready to attack at any moment.

"We need to get in there." I pointed to the tent.

Rozem shook her head. "Didn't you hear that? I'm not going in there."

I growled and threw her away. *So much for acceptance. Humans will be humans.* I stumbled through the entrance of the tent and fell to my hands and knees.

Lucia was standing over Fina, her claws and teeth bared at Daric. Daric lay on the ground with his hand over his bloody cheek. Zenny was holding Fina's head as she reached towards Lucia.

Lucia turned to me, and her expression shifted. Her face lightened up, and she ran over to me.

"You're safe," she whispered. She turned to Daric. "Out!"

2 8

THE RIGHT WORDS FOR LUCIA

L exia's fine. My sister looks exhausted, but I don't see any injuries. I turned to look at Daric. The edges of my vision were tinting red.

"What? Why would you do that, Lucia?" Daric asked, still holding the cheek I had slapped with my claws when I saw him holding Fina.

"Because you stink. It's really, really difficult for me not to rip your heart out right now." The growl in my voice rumbled through the small tent. "You are covered in orc blood, and right now Fina is covered in their scent too. I can't concentrate enough to separate your scents. I know orcs did this to her, and you aren't an orc, but you smell just like one right now."

Daric sat there, looking stupefied. "Is that really a thing?"

"Yes!" Lexia and I shouted at the same time.

"Daric, Lucia and Lexia have a stronger sense of smell." Zenny's voice was soft yet firm. "Please, I'll look at your face later, but right now you need to leave."

Daric shook his head and stood up. "Right. I'll be back after I clean up. We still need to talk about the others I saw. I won't let you do the same to them as you did to the ones in that village." He didn't wait for a response, and I wasn't going to give him one.

I gave Lexia a pat on the head. "You aren't hurt, are you?" *It's so much easier to think now that he's gone.*

Her tail wagged as she leaned into my hand. "No, I'm just magically and physically exhausted. But don't worry, I got him."

I frowned. *And she gives me a hard time for being reckless.* "We'll talk about that later." I turned back towards Fina as Zenny held her. "How is she?"

Zenny looked worried. "She's barely breathing. Bringing her here was probably the wrong decision." She placed her arms under Fina's shoulders. "Help me get her to the cot. We might as well get her off the ground."

I helped move Fina and gently placed her on the simple bed. Her eyes cracked open.

"Lucia?" Fina's voice was barely more than a whisper.

I grabbed Lexia and helped her over too. "Lexia's here too. We're going to take care of you."

"You're here," Fina said. She shut her eyes. "Not a dream. Not alone anymore."

Lexia nearly shouted as tears sprouted from her eyes. "We saved you. We would never leave you with them."

"We came as soon as we could," I added.

Zenny placed a hand on her head. "Shh. It's okay. You can rest now. It's safe." Fina seemed to relax more. Zenny turned to look at us. "I'll do everything I can to make her comfortable for now. But she might require a long time to recover. Can you help out, Lucia?"

"Yes, anything." I placed Lexia in a chair. "I'll help. Anything for Fina."

Zenny looked around. "If Daric and Lexia are back, that means the rest are on their way. I need you to set up the other cots for the rest of the wounded."

"Six," Lexia said flatly. "There were six wounded."

Zenny nodded towards the door. "Grab a couple extra just in case any of the other released prisoners need a bed too."

I went to work immediately. My leg was feeling better the more I walked on it. Which was okay since I had to look around to see where they had spare cots packed. Unfortunately, I only found three. *I guess they packed pretty light.*

As I was putting the cots together, some of the other knights came in to help after they brought in two women.

"I see you are on your feet and moving quite nicely already," a woman with disheveled, short black hair said. *I can't remember her name, but her smile is hard to forget.* "These two are the only ones who need extensive medical aid. The rest are just simple bandages and stitches. Others are taking care of that."

Zenny sighed as she inspected the first woman with three arrows in her. "Can you give me something for her to bite down on?" She held out her hand without looking away.

I grabbed a spare leg from one of the cots and placed it in her hand. Zenny put it in between the woman's teeth.

"Can you take the arrows out, Makaela? And Lucia, I need hot water and more bandages." The way Zenny barked out orders brought a smile to my face.

Watching Zenny work is a wonderful sight. She's good at her job. I left to see if anyone had hot water anywhere.

Throughout the night and almost into the morning, we cleaned, stitched, and bandaged wounds. There were two knights more wounded than the others. The one with three arrows in her had one of the arrows hit her collarbone and break it. None of the arrows hit anything vital; they just left her in a great deal of pain. Her greatest enemy was infection. The other woman had her arm broken and a cut across her eye. Sadly, her eye was damaged, and it was left blind.

At least the rain had mostly let up. It was barely more than a drizzle. I took my sister to a place where she could lie down and sleep while the other knights nursed their wounds. I dried her off as much as I could. She was thoroughly soaked, and her fur was a mess. Everyone looked tired, but there was a section in the camp where I was told not to go.

Daric needs to relax. I'm not going to kill the women they saved from the orcs. Oh, and speak of the devil. Daric strode up to me, not smelling like an orc and with a fresh set of clothes. The lines on his face weren't bleeding and looked like they would be gone by the morning.

"Are you free to talk?" he asked.

"You don't have to treat me like I'm going to kill everyone." I crossed my arms as he got closer. "I already told you why I did what I did earlier."

Daric pointed to the edge of the camp. "Maybe we should have this talk away from everyone else."

I looked around and saw everyone staring at me. "Fine."

I followed him to the edge of the camp, away from everyone who could hear us. *Lexia might be able to hear us, but she's sleeping hard right now.*

Daric kept his back to me as he started talking. "You asked me to be your moral compass, remember?"

I slumped my shoulders. "Yeah, I do."

He turned to me. I could see the hurt in his eyes. "And I'm telling you, what you did was wrong. I know you said they were asking you to, but there had to have been a better way. I'll even show you there's a better way with the women we rescued today." He lifted his arm towards the women, who were watched over by two knights as they slept. "They asked me if I would kill them. But I told them I would show them a better way."

I flattened my ears. "You do know most of them are probably pregnant, right?"

"So?" Daric waved his arm across his body. "That means they have more of a right to life than usual."

"That would be the case if they weren't pregnant with orcs," Aenwyn interrupted.

I raised an eyebrow and crossed my arms. "What is that supposed to mean? And why did you follow us out here?"

Aenwyn extended her hand. "You might want to sit down for this one." I looked at Daric, and he shrugged. After we sat down, Aenwyn sat down with us. "Have you noticed that every orc you've seen has been male?"

I looked up at the sky for a moment as I thought back on all my encounters with orcs. *I can't remember if I saw any female orcs ten years ago when they attacked my village, but it was a raiding party.* "Now that you say that, yeah."

I watched the captain's shoulders drop. "That's because there are no female orcs."

Daric shook his head. "That doesn't make sense. How are they still around? Why haven't they died off?"

It hit me. "Because they use women from other races to reproduce." The words that came out of my mouth almost didn't feel real.

"That's right." There was obvious pain in the captain's voice. "No matter what race an orc has sex with, the woman will always give birth to a male orc."

"That's impossible!" Daric shouted. "That's not how genetics work. Babies always take some traits from each of their parents. The woman always provides an X chromosome, and the man provides either an X or Y chromosome."

I growled at him. "When will it stick in your thick skull? That's how it is for humans. Look at me." I waved my hands at my fur-covered body. "I'm literally half wolf. That's impossible too, right? All the rules you know don't always apply here."

"You really are from other worlds, aren't you?" Aenwyn interrupted.

I waved my hand. "Technically, we're from the same world. He just remembers more than I do."

Daric buried his head in his hands. "Why does magic complicate things? It doesn't make sense."

I pointed a finger at the sky. "Since Fina was so close to her mating season, if they did... you know what"—I couldn't bring myself to say the words—"then would she have one orc or two, like is normal for a beastkin?"

Aenwyn licked her lips and swallowed. "She probably would have two."

I snapped my head back to Daric, who looked like he was sweating. I could tell it wasn't left over from the rain. "Did they?"

Daric rubbed his hands together and shifted around. "I... I don't know. It didn't look like it. From my view, it looked like they only beat her up. Did she still have on underwear?"

I buried my head in my hands. "I didn't look. And I didn't ask. No, it wasn't the right time to ask. She was just grateful to see us. So was I."

"Maybe they didn't, you know, rape her." Daric tried to have an upbeat tone, but it was obvious he was reaching for the good news.

Aenwyn shifted closer to me. "Just so you know, there are ways to deal with the child before it's born." She placed a hand on my shoulder. "If, and I do mean if, she were unfortunate and now carries orc children, there are herbs to end it."

I turned and stared at the elf. "Are you suggesting suicide?"

Aenwyn's eyes went wide. "No, no." She shook her head. "Just end the pregnancy. Sorry, that was the wrong word to use. I didn't mean to scare you like that."

"Is an abortion better?" Aenwyn and I turned and gawked at Daric and his question.

"You can't be serious, can you?" I asked.

Daric stood up. "Why does the child not get a chance to live? It hasn't done anything wrong yet."

I stood up and put my teeth inches from his face. "Because it's an orc! It's evil and needs to die."

Aenwyn jumped to her feet and tried to push us apart. I didn't move, and neither did Daric. "Calm down, both of you."

"We can raise them to be better," Daric responded, ignoring the captain's order. "Look at you. You are a beastkin raised by an elf. You're a bit wild, but you're better than your sister."

My vision snapped to red, and I shoved Aenwyn away as I grabbed Daric's throat. "I dare you to say that again." The rumble in my voice emphasized my threat. I bared my teeth in his face.

Daric grabbed at my hands but couldn't fight against my grip. He opened his mouth, but nothing came out as I lifted him off the ground. His struggling became more frantic as he kept trying to bat at my arms.

"Waterfalls!" Aenwyn's voice rang in my ears. I had to flatten them and ignore the ringing in them as I turned to face her.

She held a spear pointed it at me. "Put him down this instant. That's an order."

I growled and shoved the man to the ground. Daric gasped and coughed as he slowly rolled to his knees. "Leave my sister out of this. And if you compare her to an orc again, nobody will stop me from severing your head. I don't care about The Voice. It should've chosen someone better than a stupid idiot like you."

Daric looked up at me. There was a genuine hurt in his eyes.

"Daric, go." Aenwyn stepped in between us. "I understand your point and agree with you somewhat. But again, you need to learn that it's not what you're trying to say, it's about how you say it. I'll reason with her."

Daric looked like he was about to cry as he turned and ran back into the camp.

"You need to rein in that temper of yours." Aenwyn's glare didn't ease. "You need to stop jumping at any and every insult to you or your sister."

"I have a short temper, you know that." I stomped away as I flexed my claws. "It's not my fault."

"Yes, it is!" Aenwyn shouted. "Do you have any idea how upset Nora would be if she heard you talking like that? What if she saw what you just did?"

I instantly relaxed and whimpered. "It's just so hard. Being angry is easy."

Aenwyn stepped up behind me. "I can believe that." Her voice was soft, even motherly. "But anything worthwhile is never easy. Nora raised you to be better than this. It's understandable to get mad about what some people say, but don't use your fists; use your words."

My tail hung limp behind me. "But words never work. People talk, but nothing changes. My claws always get the job done, and they're never misunderstood."

"Then use the right words." Aenwyn turned me around. "Sure, words can be meaningless, but the right words can make a difference and move entire civilizations. The right words can change, or better yet, make history." She gave me a smile. "Now I know what you're going to say. We can help you. Your mother, Zenny, and me, if that's what you wish."

I pointed behind Aenwyn. "What about Daric?"

The captain threw her spear to the side. "This isn't about him. We're talking about you." She grabbed my chin and pulled my face down so I was looking at her. "Yes, I will have this same talk with him. I know you're young, and admittedly, I don't know what all this reincarnation stuff between the two of you means, but if this is too much for you, we can wait a few years until you've grown up more."

I turned my head and flattened my ears, curling my tail around me. "You're right. I'm still too childish. And trust me, this reincarnation thing isn't easy for me, either." I turned back to the captain and straightened myself before giving her a salute. "But I said I would be a knight to protect my friends and family, so I will do better."

Aenwyn smiled. "Your determination is something to be admired. Come on, let's get some sleep before the sun rises. We have to get back to Aquittemia as quickly as possible." She started walking back to the camp, and I followed. "I can see your leg's doing better. Can you hunt, or do you need a little more time? We're running low on food. This has gone on longer than we'd anticipated."

I grinned. "I think I'll be able to catch something for you all to eat for a day or two. There was a fishing spot some distance back."

29

THREE HEROES

I spent the night watching over Lexia. She didn't look very comfortable. *The ground is never comfortable.* But she looked so exhausted that it didn't matter.

A few of the other knights were setting up a pile of branches and digging a ditch around it. It was a funeral pyre. The somber looks on the knights as they worked were painful to see.

My tail flicked up and down beside me. *More pain caused by the orcs. And yet they are still allowed to live. Maybe I should ask Captain Aenwyn tomorrow while we head back. Do I talk to her before or after talking to my sister? Also, I need to talk to Fina. Ugh. And there's also the fact that I need to deal with Daric. I doubt he'll let what I did last night go.*

I watched as one of the knights started glowing with magic and walking around the funeral pyre. A few subtle wisps of smoke started as the wet wood dried out. I was glad they were far enough away that the flames wouldn't bother me if I didn't look at them.

Then guilt crept into the back of my mind. *They died to help me recover Fina from the orcs. And I wasn't there to help them. It's hard to let go of the responsibility. Lexia wanted me to trust her to bring Fina back. She did. I just can't help but believe that if I were there, there would have been fewer casualties and Lexia might not have been so worn out.*

I looked down at my claws and tail. *If we could change every if and but, I wouldn't be a wolf girl. It is what it is. I'm not a god, nor will I ever be. Even The Voice said it wasn't a god and it could manipulate my soul and memories.*

I closed my eyes and felt myself drifting until everything around me was a wide-open field of grass. A nudge on my back caused me to turn and face my inner wolf.

"Are you the original Lucia?" I asked her.

As she sat down, the air between us rippled, and shapes of ice appeared. They weren't just shapes; they were words.

We are Lucia.

I shook my head. "You are a piece of this girl's body—who this body was. I know you know the answer."

The ice shifted and created different words. **No memory. Only instinct.**

"This is a new trick for you. You didn't do this when we first met." I walked over and sat between her front paws. "You're growing."

Yes. I see your memories and know them.

"Soon you'll be able to talk." The wolf gave me a smile and a shrug. I couldn't help but giggle. "I guess I'm so protective because of you. How much is me and how much is you? But what will happen after this life is over?"

Do not fear death.

I frowned at the wolf as she curled around me, creating a fluffy couch for me to lean back on. "You just said that you've seen my memories. In them is The Voice, and why it sent me here. Don't deny that we both know that I didn't originally belong here."

Living is more important. Death comes when it does, not before.

I enjoyed the warm feeling of her fur almost swallowing me up. "Right. I have too many problems being alive right now." I looked up at the imaginary sun and then back to my inner wolf. "About what happened back at the village." The wolf's ears perked up and turned towards me. "Thank you, but how do you feel about it?"

The wolf turned her head and rested it on the ground. The ice shattered and formed again. **Hurts. You are honorable. Man is foolish and will only cause suffering.**

"You're talking about Daric, aren't you?" I started petting her in between her shoulder blades. There was an almost imperceptible feeling of contempt for weakness. "You feel it is a waste of time and resources to care for the sick and wounded." She didn't make any attempt to tell me I was right. I could feel it in the way her ears turned to the side and her eyes blinked. "I didn't let you kill them for that reason. It's because I couldn't bear to see them suffer any longer."

Honorable.

But what Captain Aenwyn said about my actions nagged at me. *I can't disappoint Mom.* "Let's make a deal." I stood up and walked to my wolf's head. "I need control. Please don't influence me when I talk to people. Let me handle that."

No cage. She growled and bared her teeth at me.

I placed my hand on her snout and gently rubbed it. "No. I promised, didn't I?" She relaxed. "How about you take me for a ride when I let you out to hunt? Does that sound like it would be fun?" She stood up and started panting and wagging her tail. "You can handle the hunts. Just take me along. They're fun for me too, you know."

My inner wolf pushed my hand away and licked my face in one fluid motion. I giggled as her tongue tickled my face. *Since I'm so bribable, it makes sense that she is too. She probably knows that I'm bribing her too. But just like me, she has no problem with it. She gets what she wants.*

"Okay, okay." I pushed her face down. "Just promise me you'll stay out of the way and not influence anything when I'm talking to people." There was a moment of hesitation in the wolf's eyes. "I'll take good care of our sister. Nobody will mess with her while I'm around." I gave her a toothy grin.

She pushed her snout into my arms and nuzzled me. I could sense a blissful feeling of contentment from her. I scratched behind her ear until I woke up.

I woke to find myself still next to my sleeping sister. It was still dark out, but I could see the sun's light blooming over the horizon. Lexia's breathing was shallow but rhythmic. Her ear twitched along with her fingertips.

I hope you're having a wonderful dream, sis.

I got up, trying not to wake Lexia, and walked around, looking for Daric's tent. The funeral pyre was burning out and barely more than a small campfire, but I still kept my distance as I looked for anyone who was up.

Since we both shared the recovery aptitude, he would likely be awake too, since we didn't need much sleep.

I heard pacing in one of the tents. The footsteps were accompanied by some muttering, but it was choppy, half-coherent words that didn't form a sentence.

I walked up to the tent and whispered, "Daric, is that you?"

"Go away, Lucia," he said.

I hesitated for a moment, wondering if I should just leave him alone. But I knew I couldn't let things stay like this between us.

"Daric, we need to talk," I said, trying to keep my voice calm.

There was a long silence before I finally opened the tent flap. Daric looked tired and scared, and it hurt to see him like that. He turned and pulled his sword from its scabbard and pointed it at me in one swift movement.

"Stay away from me." The sword wobbled with his words.

I deserve this. "Listen, I just want to talk." I put my hands up, but I could feel the touch of desire to rip the weapon from his hands. *Remember, let me handle this. I won't let him hurt us.*

"You don't talk. You just kill." Daric switched from a one-handed to a two-handed grip as if he were expecting me to charge. "That's all that you are. You're a killer."

"Yes, I am." Daric's jaw almost dropped as I admitted it to him. "It's all I've ever been good at. Killing. But look at me, what do you expect? Beastkin have a reputation for being aggressive, and it's well-earned. There's a reason for that. Have you ever wondered what it's

215

like to have animal instincts in your head all the time? You once asked me what it's like to be a beastkin, remember?"

Daric lowered his sword slightly. "You said that you don't remember what it's like to be human."

I lowered my hands. "Exactly. My senses are so sharp that I can smell what you ate from this distance. By the way, it was dried apples and bread." Daric almost looked like he was going to relax. "I see the world in a very different light than you. I experience everything differently. And that also comes with this desire—no, need—to defend those close to me. To fight anyone who can hurt me or those close to me." I placed my hands over my heart.

Daric lowered his sword to the ground. "But you said you would kill me."

I closed my eyes. "Yes, I did. But that was my inner wolf. She's why I'm so defensive and protective of my sister. Being called wild is a painful insult. Would you like it if I called you an ape?"

The man sighed and sat down on the ground, throwing his sword to the side. "No. But I'm sorry; Midas never really helped me develop any people skills. And when I was on Earth, I never had any friends either. When I was told I could be a hero, I guess I just... I wanted to be the perfect hero." Tears streamed down his face.

I kneeled next to him. "My mother told me this saying when I swore my oaths to The Maidens. 'There are three kinds of heroes. There are the heroes you want, the heroes you need, and the heroes that show up.'" Daric lifted his head to look at me. "Which do you think are the ones people remember?"

"What does that mean?" Daric asked as he wiped his eyes with his fists.

"You don't have to be perfect or the most ideal hero. If you show up and save the day, that's all people need you to do and be. Your actions make you a hero. Nothing else has to matter."

There was a pause as Daric glanced at the ground. "Does that mean you wanted to be a hero too?"

I shook my head. "I've never wanted to be a hero. People have called me that, and I tell them I'm not. It's not something that's important to me." *Not like it is to you.* "Keeping my family and friends safe is all I'm concerned about. If I have to save the world to do that, then so be it."

Daric hugged his legs to his chest and buried his face in his knees. "I haven't failed. Not yet."

"To be my hero, you need to stop me from losing control," I whispered. "I've made a deal with my inner wolf, but she's impulsive. It's just part of our nature. Of everyone I know, you and Mom are the only two who can stop me if I need to be stopped."

Daric shook his head. "I can't stop you. You're too strong. Now that you also know my weakness, I can't stop you. But what about Captain Aenwyn?"

"Captain Aenwyn runs an entire knight company. She doesn't have the time or freedom you do. Mom? She's not here right now." I placed a hand on his leg. He flinched away from me. "It has to be you. And you know my weakness too."

Daric looked up from his knees. "Fire." I nodded. "If I could use fire magic like Penny, then maybe this might work out, but I can't."

"I know you told me that you've had dozens of teachers try to teach you magic, but you've never been able to do it." I stood up and walked to the entrance of the tent. "Maybe you should let go of Earth and just believe. Let go, and maybe one day you'll be able to use the magic you were meant to."

"I'll think about it," Daric said as he returned his head to his knees.

That'll have to be enough.

I walked out and saw Captain Aenwyn with her arms crossed and staring at me.

"I don't see any blood," she said. "That's a good start, right?"

I rolled my eyes. "Yes." My exaggerated tone earned me a harsher glare from the captain. "We talked. And, well, you were right."

One eyebrow rose. "About?"

"Using the right words." I walked over to Aenwyn. "It also helped that my inner wolf and I had a little heart-to-heart, or heart-to-soul, chat."

Captain Aenwyn's muscles tensed up for just a moment, but then relaxed. "So what does that mean? What happens now?"

My stomach growled, and I placed a hand on it. "She's been a good girl and let me handle things. So I'll see about some breakfast for us and let her have some fun."

The captain didn't move or say anything as she watched me walk away. I stood at the edge of camp and could feel excitement building in me. *There are a couple of things I need you to remember. We need to bring back enough for everyone. So yes, have fun and get us something tasty, but we can't come back until we get something substantial.*

My tail wagged unconsciously as I relinquished control. I knew my inner wolf wouldn't see that as a problem, just an excuse to run and play more. Me? I just enjoyed the ride as I watched a master at work.

30

DISTRACTION

I couldn't help but notice Lexia squirming in her saddle. Everyone watched her struggle with the unnatural travel method.

"I hate riding horses," Lexia muttered under her breath, shooting a disgruntled glance at Zenny, who seemed to be thoroughly enjoying herself.

I slowed down to walk next to my sister and put a hand on her leg as she rode the impressive horse. "You can't find a place to put your tail, can you?"

She leaned forward a bit before curling her tail back around her waist. "No. Why do you two get to walk? I can keep up too."

I eyed my sister. "But can you walk for as long as us at this pace? To Fina and me, this is a light stroll. I know you. You would be tired well before lunch, and we have to get back as quickly as possible."

Lexia growled, and Fina flattened her ears. She was surprisingly spry for someone who'd been carried in unconscious the night before. She didn't actually beg, but I could tell by her body language that she really wanted to stretch her legs. *I guess being cooped up in that cage really got to her.*

Thinking about her in a cage sent another note of pain across my heart. "How are you feeling, Fina?"

Fina didn't answer right away, but her pace didn't slow either. "I..."

The hesitation didn't sit well with me or Lexia. "Sis, give her time," she whispered.

"No." Fina's voice was slightly hoarse. "Riding is wrong."

Lexia and I cocked our heads simultaneously. *I wasn't expecting that. Maybe deflecting for now will be good for her. Distractions are good, right?*

"Why is that?" Zenny asked.

"It is wrong to use other animals like that." Fina's pace quickened. "The horse helps you. But how do you help back?"

"She's right!" Lexia shouted as she hopped off the moving horse. Her dismount wasn't graceful, as her foot caught in the stirrup. She had to hop on one leg while the horse kept walking and she fought to free her other foot.

I rolled my eyes. *Really, sis?* With a quick movement, I was on the other side of the horse and scooping my sister up with one arm while carefully untangling her claws from the saddle.

"Come on, sis." I put her down.

Zenny frowned at my sister. "Riding isn't that bad. Besides, we lovingly care for these horses." She leaned forward and brushed her mount's mane. "Isn't that right, Buttercup?"

That caused Fina to turn her head. "Awful name."

"Please tell me you didn't name"—I looked under the horse to check—"her that."

Zenny frowned. "Of course not. Someone else did. But I think it's a lovely and cute name. Grimerakke are intelligent enough to learn their name. Sometimes they're smarter than a person."

As if to punctuate her point, Buttercup snorted and nodded her head. Lexia jogged next to me as I kept pace with the horse's long strides. Fina turned back around and slumped her shoulders.

Lexia's elbow tapped my ribs. "We should cheer her up," she whispered so quietly Fina might not have heard.

"What do you suggest?" I matched my sister's volume as I watched Fina.

"Take her for a hunt. She likes to help. Give her something to do," she hissed at me.

"Why me?" My volume caused one of Fina's ears to twitch towards us.

I flinched, but Fina didn't make any more movements to tell us she'd heard us.

Lexia pulled me back and stopped. "You're the alpha here. Now go." She didn't bother whispering that as she shoved me.

Her shove didn't really move me, but I got the message. *Right. Cheer up a friend. Just like I did when I visited her after our mating season was over.* Somehow, I missed the fact that I didn't refute Lexia calling me the alpha.

I took a deep breath and grabbed the reins of the horse Lexia was riding and held them out for her. She grabbed them with a sour look on her face. I then walked up behind Fina and placed a hand on her shoulder.

"Hey Fina, how about we go for a quick hunt, just you and me?" I put on a grin for her.

Fina perked her ears up at the suggestion. Her tail even lifted slightly. "We can?" she asked quietly.

I continued grinning at her. "Of course. Maybe there's something we can settle while we're out."

Fina flicked her tail. "What?"

"Who's faster, you or me?" I gave her a wink.

Fina shook her head. "You faster."

I frowned. "You aren't even going to try? Come on."

The lynxkin turned her head, wrapped her tail around her, and slowed down. "Don't want to."

Zenny, Lexia, and I all stopped next to her. The other knights in the company kept moving though. I rubbed my friend's back. "What do you feel like doing then?"

Fina just hugged herself. "Nothing."

"Do you want to talk, Fina?" Zenny asked from atop her horse.

She shook her head.

Ugh. She's shutting down. What did I do wrong? I continued to rub Fina's back. "Let's forget that race then. Let's just have some fun catching something."

The lynx turned and looked at me. She didn't say anything, but her eyes had a little more brightness in them. A slight nod was all I needed as I led her away from the other knights.

"Take it easy, Fina. If anything hurts or becomes uncomfortable, don't be afraid to stop and come back," Zenny called after us.

Fina stopped and turned around. "I will." She bowed and turned back to continue with me.

I leaned in close to her. "Lead the way."

We took off without telling anyone else. *I'm sure the captain might have a word with me about that later.* It took some time before we found any signs of tracks to follow. I let my inner wolf run, but I made sure she knew that this was more about Fina.

The two of us didn't share any words. We only wandered around the countryside until we found a patch of tall wild grass. We had been following the tracks of several ripclaws. I could tell Fina had never seen those kinds of tracks, and while I knew of them, I'd never had the chance to hunt one myself.

I pulled my inner wolf and Fina back. "Fina, we need to slow down." She blinked expectantly. "Ripclaws are pack hunters that live in tall grass areas like this."

Fina's tail went limp. "We leave?"

I shook my head. "We don't need to. Honestly, I've never tried one, and I'm really curious about how they taste." Fina's tail perked up. "But we need to be extra quiet. If we pounce first, the rest might run away."

A grin and a nod were all Fina responded with as she dropped to all fours and stalked into the grass. As we went through it, I couldn't help but admire her movements. She was silent and graceful, and if I hadn't been watching her, I would've easily lost her.

We followed the tracks for a while until we came across a clearing where a group of seven ripclaws were feeding on a carcass.

Each ripclaw tore into their dinner, which was unrecognizable at that point. With short, tawny brown fur over most of their bodies, you could see their sleek muscles flex with each movement. But as the fur spread to their legs, the fur shifted to scales that were a slightly darker color. There weren't paws at the ends of each of their four legs. No, there were reptilian claws, each long and black; they made ours look like toothpicks.

A ripclaw lifted its head as it scarfed down a chunk of flesh. The feline-shaped head with piercing yellow eyes and sharp teeth gleaming in the sunlight looked like it was staring right at us. Its small, rounded ears swiveled slightly. Then it sniffed the air. I knew we weren't going to be found since we were downwind, enjoying the wonderfully over-powering odor of blood mixed with their musky scent. But I lowered myself to the ground more. *Sometimes my silver fur makes things a bit more difficult.*

Fina and I remained crouched, observing them silently. My heart raced with excitement. I let my inner wolf out earlier, and I had to remind her to swallow the drool in my mouth. Fina's excitement was obvious by the way her tail twitched at the tip.

Suddenly, the ripclaw turned its head and called out. It let out a loud screech mixed with a growl. The rest of the pack snapped to attention and looked to our right. A few of them took off.

Fina and I sprang into action.

Fina bolted towards the slowest ripclaw. It didn't get a chance to defend itself as she slashed her claws across its back legs. Blood sprayed behind it as its limbs collapsed. Two of the ripclaws turned around as Fina's prey yowled in pain. They charged her, and I charged them.

I collided with the closest one and drove my claws into its ribs, crushing them. It didn't call for help as it died. Fina ran around her prey and slashed at it. She aimed her attack at its neck, but she slashed its shoulder as it leaned away. It tried to retaliate and swiped at her, but she was already far out of reach. The ripclaw tried to move, but its hind legs dragged on the ground.

The other charging ripclaw noticed me killing its packmate and turned on me. It dug its claws into the ground and pounced towards me. When it opened its mouth, I was greeted with an up-close look at its rows of tiny hooked teeth. My inner wolf pulled me closer to the ground so my shoulder would be below its jaw.

I drove my shoulder into its neck and forced the animal to catch itself on the ground instead of on me. Before the creature could get me, I bit it hard in the neck. The ripclaw raised its front legs to claw at me, but I violently pulled it forward and shook my head. A wet snap and a limp ripclaw were my reward.

With the creature still in my jaws, I turned to see how Fina was doing. She had clawed its face, and there was a stream of blood pouring from its closed eye. Fina ran towards it and feinted an attack. The ripclaw swiped with both of its front claws as it snarled and hissed. Before its legs could touch back down, Fina slashed the creature's neck.

She circled around it. My wolf grew angry as she saw how Fina was playing with her prey. *No, let her play. But stay close, just in case she gets hurt.* I could feel my inner wolf reluctantly relax.

Fina kept circling the ripclaw and watched as its movements grew heavier and slower. It wasn't long before she got behind it and pounced on its neck, driving her claws through the spine. The animal didn't get back up.

None of the other ripclaws returned. They must have gone looking for other food. Wordlessly, we collected our catch and headed away. I carried the three corpses as Fina followed me back to the knights.

As we were getting close, Fina tugged on one of the ripclaw bodies. I stopped and turned around to see a few tears clinging to the corners of her eyes.

"What's wrong, Fina?" I asked as I dropped the bodies. "Are you tired? Do you need to take a break?"

Fina sniffled. "Thank you." I was about to talk, but she jumped and wrapped her arms around me. I hesitated for a moment before hugging her back. "Can we talk?" Her whisper scared even my inner wolf.

I guided her to sit on the ground. She kept holding onto me. "Any time. Do you want to talk about what happened?"

The lynxkin wiped her face on my shirt. "Lentilee and Bosco? Are they fine?"

My mouth went dry. I flattened my ears and turned away. "They didn't make it."

Fina squeezed me harder while her tears began flowing again. "Orcs are bad," she chanted as she cried into my chest.

That was an understatement. As Fina's crying slowly grew quieter, I took a deep breath. "Fina, what did the orcs do to you?"

"They... They..." Her voice quivered. "They mated me."

I knew it was likely. I didn't want to believe it. Some part of me wished that it wasn't true. But hearing her say those three words wrenched my heart into a knot. Fina's crying resumed, even harder than before, and I joined her.

Now all I can hope for is that she isn't pregnant.

31

OUT OF TIME

As Fina and I cried over what had happened to her at the hands of the orcs, a soft chuckle from behind me snapped my instincts into gear. I turned to see the sin of lust floating next to a tree with a smirk on her face.

"What do we have here?" she said, eyeing us. "Aren't you two a lovely pair?"

Why now? Of all the times she could have shown up, this is the worst.

I gently released Fina and stood up, wiping my tears away. A growl rumbled from my throat. "What do you want?"

The sin of lust raised her hands in surrender as she laughed. "Relax, darling. I'm not here to hurt you. It would have been much easier while you were crying your little eyes out. No, your time's up."

I narrowed my eyes. "What?"

"The Rider of Death," the sin of lust replied. "He's almost at your precious home, and he's not alone. He brought an army of undead with him."

My heart sank. "How do you know? That can't be right."

The succubus just chuckled as she twirled a finger through her hair. "Let's just say I have my sources. But that's not important. What

226

is important is that you're out of time. So, are you going to accept my deal from earlier or not?"

I looked at the demon more closely. *She's gotten lazy. That's not the real her, just an illusion. There's no shadow.* "Why should I believe you? You've never shown any concern for our well-being before. Besides, what can you offer? Fina's right here."

The sin of lust shrugged. "So what if I don't care about anyone else but myself? I don't want to be caught by the Rider of Death. So take my warning or leave it. It's up to you." A wicked grin spread across her lips. "Besides, the truth is much more fun to play with than any petty lies."

True, she's never lied to me before.

"The rider will kill everyone in the city and raise their corpses to join his army. I can get you an audience with him alone. You won't have to fight his entire army to save the town." Her tail swayed behind her. *She thinks she's playing with her food.*

I grabbed my head and shouted, "No! I'll defend everyone without your help. There's still time to save them." I almost took off running.

The sin of lust smirked. "Remember, my pet, I'm the only one who can truly stop him. But if the Rider of Death gets what he wants, the demon king gets what he wants. And, well, let's just say nobody wants that."

My eyes widened at the mention of the demon king. "What does he want?"

The sin of lust shrugged. "That's not my business to tell, mostly because he hasn't told anyone the details. All I know is that you need to stop the Rider of Death now. It'll buy me time to find the power to stand up to him and overthrow his overgrown obsession."

With that, the sin of lust's illusion vanished, leaving us alone once again.

I turned to Fina, who just sat on the ground silently with a defeated look in her eyes. "Come on, we need to warn my sister and the rest of the knights." I helped Fina up and pulled her arm over my shoulder. "The Rider of Death is coming, and we need to be prepared."

"Why?" Fina sounded defeated too. "What are undead?"

"Honestly? They sound like bad news." *Maybe I shouldn't tell her what Mom taught me and Lexia about the undead. There's no reason to add more bad news to her already bad week.* "But we are going to stop the rider and his army." I put on a smile for her.

"We won't survive." Fina drooped her ears and dragged her feet.

I sighed. "Fina, you need to cheer up. I know for a fact that we will not only survive, but we will win. Do you want to know why I know that?" Fina turned her head slightly towards me. "Because my mom stopped an army of dwarves by herself once. She can handle the army of undead. But we'll also have our own army. This Rider of Death doesn't know what he's up against."

Fina's eyes lit up a bit. "Good." Her feet started moving again, this time without dragging them. Soon she pulled her arm back to her side and walked on under her own strength.

Good girl. I promise we'll make it through this together.

Fina followed me as I walked towards Captain Aenwyn. As we approached, I noticed someone on horseback I'd never seen before talking to the captain. Aenwyn nodded along to the stranger's words, her expression growing increasingly grim.

I waved my hand for Fina to slow down as we approached, trying not to interrupt the conversation. But as I got closer, I overheard the tail end of it. "All knight companies have been recalled back to the capitol," the stranger was saying.

Aenwyn nodded, looking even more troubled. "Thank you for letting me know. I'll make sure my company is ready to depart as soon as possible. You can head back with us."

The stranger nodded back, then nudged his horse towards the side before he dismounted. The horse looked tired and sweaty. *Who is he? All companies are recalled?*

I cleared my throat when we got close enough to the captain.

Aenwyn turned towards us with a stern expression. "What in the world were you two thinking, running off like that without telling anyone? You could have gotten hurt. Again!"

I opened my mouth to explain, but Fina beat me to it. "I wanted to," she said, her voice small. "Sorry."

Aenwyn softened slightly at Fina's words but still looked disapproving. "I understand, but next time, tell someone where you're going. And speaking of trouble, I have some bad news."

I know what you're going to say. "Let me guess, it has something to do with being recalled."

Aenwyn hesitated, then took a deep breath. "Your hearing is too sharp for your own good sometimes. But yes, all the local knight companies have been recalled back to Aquittemia," she said, echoing the stranger's words. "There are reports of a massive army of undead marching towards it."

I slammed my eyes shut. *Of course, she was telling the truth.* "Captain, I have something to tell you. The sin of lust warned me about the Rider of Death. She said he's after her, but she thinks I'm the only one strong enough to face him."

Aenwyn looked surprised. "The sin of lust?"

I nodded. "Yeah, the one I dealt with in the Wild Kingdom."

The captain's voice dropped. "What would she know about the Rider of Death?"

"I don't know, Captain," I admitted. "A lot more than she's letting on. But she seemed pretty convinced. And I believe her. We have to get home soon."

Aenwyn nodded slowly. "You're right. We can't afford to be caught off guard. I'll tell everyone to get moving. We're about four days away from Aquittemia." She rubbed her temples. "We're going to have to double-time it."

That means stopping only to sleep and rest the horses. Nobody's going to like hearing that.

The journey back to the capitol was a blur of motion and exhaustion. The knights pushed themselves and their horses to the limit, riding with almost no respite for two straight days. Fina and I ran beside the horses. It didn't take me very long to convince Lexia that she needed to get back on the horse. Some of the knights had to double up with the women that were rescued from the orcs.

At first, the terrain was rough and uneven, but as the first day went on, the landscape flattened out into sprawling fields of wildflowers. The scent of freshly turned earth mixed with the sweet aroma of wildflowers created a heady perfume that filled the air. Fina, Lexia, and I all had to either lead or be to the side of the cloud the horses kicked up, as it made it almost impossible to breathe.

As night fell, we made camp in a clearing by a small stream. Fina was still shaken by what had happened to her. But the urgency of the situation gave her something else to focus on. Daric and I took turns keeping watch while the others slept. The two of us pushed our recovery a little harder, as everyone slept only as long as the horses did. The knights didn't even change into their sleepwear.

I took the lead on the second day. My instincts kept an eye out as I focused on running. My inner wolf enjoyed the exercise, but even she understood that things weren't right. The knights rode in tight formation. I just needed to keep things at the proper pace for the horses so they didn't fall over from exhaustion.

By the end of the second day, everyone came to a stop as we saw the city walls in view. There was a collective sigh of relief that I could have sworn the horses joined in on. With home so close, Captain Aenwyn called off the double time and let everyone rest.

Since Lexia was still recovering her magic, I spent all of my magic creating water for the horses to drink, nearly to the point of fatiguing myself. Thankfully, there was another knight who could use water manipulation magic, and after I taught her how to make the water, she helped out where she could.

I stood on the edge of the collection of sleeping knights and horses, staring at the city. There were no suspicious fires, no lines at the gates, and no signs of a siege. *We made it in time.*

A shadow in the moonlight caught my eye. I looked up and saw the succubus again. She flapped her wings high in the sky. I was about to warn everyone about her until she pointed to the south. I turned and looked.

"Get up!" The words flew out of my mouth the moment I recognized what I was looking at.

Several of the surrounding knights jumped, releasing a cacophony of groans and questions.

"Get up," I repeated. "The city's about to be attacked."

Everyone jumped to their feet this time. All the knights scrambled next to me, and I pointed at the massive army heading towards the city.

Aenwyn stood next to me. "We're out of time." Her voice was barely a whisper, but a haunting giggle caused everyone to look around in a panic.

Why did she have to be right?

"Captain, we need to run. Now." I turned to look for Fina, Zenny, and my sister. "Everyone, if you want to live, make for the northern gate. Don't stop until you get there."

"Stop. They'll close the gates." Aenwyn held her arms out, causing everyone to flinch. "We need to retreat to Caska. There, we might be able to rally an army to challenge them."

I turned and growled at her. "No! This is my home, and my mom's here. I will not abandon her. If you won't help me, then I'll go by myself."

"Captain, we have to help." Daric's voice, somber as it was, joined in before the elf could respond to me. "We can't just leave the entire town to die while we run away. We can bolster the defenses."

The captain shook her head. "*If* you go there, you'll be surrounded and die. Is that what you want?"

Daric stood up straighter. "No, but it is the right thing to do. If I die, then so be it."

I rolled my eyes. "Shut up." Daric flinched as I turned back to Aenwyn. "No, I don't want to die. But I don't want my mother to die either. Zenny, Fina, Victor, Lexia, and even Gifford are all important to me. So I will fight to defend the city, and I will survive."

The elf captain slumped her shoulders and let out a heavy sigh. Everyone stared at her in silence. She stood up and looked tired. "If any of you want to run, now's the time to do it. I won't hold it against you. All I ask is that you take those women with you." She pointed to the women we rescued from the orcs.

Nobody said anything. Until a human woman, her arm in a sling, stepped up. "It's not that I want to run. But I'm afraid that, in my condition, I'll be of little help. I'll take them to Caska and warn them about what's happening here."

A smile crept across Aenwyn's face. "Thank you, Liliana."

Everyone quickly mounted up and headed for the gates. Lexia and Zenny gave me smiles. I turned to face the captain. "As for the gates, leave those to me. I'll get you in."

"Please." The one word from the captain felt heavier than ever before.

3 2

THE GATES

I dropped to all fours and left everyone behind. *I need to get that gate open before everyone gets there.*

As I ran, a putrid smell filled the air. The mass surrounding the city was a horror I wasn't prepared to witness. The shambling troops that made up the assaulting army wasn't a collection of trained soldiers. No, it was a random hodgepodge of walking corpses of different species with varying levels of decay and damage.

I recognized humans, elves, and animals. Swarming around were strange, short, green-skinned creatures with jagged teeth, long ears, and large yellow eyes barely covered in rags, exposing them all as female.

The walking dead moved towards me as I continued sprinting for the gate. Once I arrived, I stood up and pushed against the gate.

"Open up!" I shouted. "Let us in!"

"The undead are coming. We can't risk them getting in."

I took a step back to see who was refusing to open the door. It was a knight I wasn't familiar with. "And we're just expected to die out here?"

The guardsman leaned over the edge of the wall. "Why don't you just run? Save yourselves."

I pointed back to the horses carrying my friends, sister, and comrades. "Open the gates quickly, let us in, and close them afterwards. We're here to help. I'm not leaving my mother here. She needs to hear what I have to say."

The man extended an arm. "Tell me and then run away. I'll make sure your information gets to those in charge."

I groaned. *If you won't open the door, I'll open it myself.*

I channeled my magic and coated my claws with ice, extending them as I ran towards the wall.

"What? Are you insane?" the guard asked.

I ignored him as I jumped and made it halfway up the wall before driving my claws in between the stones. My toe claws scraped the stone as they found purchase. I scrambled up the wall, always keeping three points of contact with it.

"How are you doing that?" The panic in the guard's voice grew in intensity. "What am I supposed to do?" The other guards started murmuring incoherently amongst themselves. "You, go find a captain. They'll figure this out. I'm not paid enough for this."

I wanted to roll my eyes, but my mission was more important. I heaved myself up over the edge where a small squad of fifteen knights stood, their weapons at the ready.

"Out of my way!" The rumble in my voice encouraged the small crowd to split.

"What are you doing?" The man I was talking to earlier finally ran up to me.

I shoved him hard enough to make him lose his balance. He landed on his butt. "I'm opening the gate. If you try to stop me, I'll rip your arms off."

I didn't bother to listen to the response he sputtered. With a surge of magic, I strengthened the ice coating my claws and swiftly ran towards the inside of the wall. I dug my claws into the stone and began sliding down. But halfway down I lost my grip and I found myself free-falling. Just as I hit the ground, I tucked my legs in, rolled, and sprang to my feet.

Several guards and knights stared at me as I came to a stop. There was a slight tingle in my legs, but it wasn't anything I was concerned about. I bared my fangs at the crowd, which stood back and watched.

Useless, all of them. They're just going to stand there and watch me. Do they not care?

I removed the wooden beams, which usually required three or four people to move, from the gate. While I lifted them, more whispers started behind me. After throwing the two beams on each side of the gateway, I pulled the door open by myself.

"Stop her; the undead will get in!" I heard someone shout from behind me.

I looked and saw that the enemies surrounding the city were, in fact, undead. *Where did so many zombies come from? The Rider of Death created this entire army? Why? It wasn't just to kill the sin of lust, was it?*

Their silent march was slow, yet consistent. And I could see the problem. *The undead are going to reach the gate first. I need to buy time.*

Growling, I sprinted towards the closest undead, a cougar. It swiped at me with its claws, but I jumped and landed on its back. I rolled off it and slashed at another zombie with my ice-covered claws. The wound opened wide, but no blood exited it, and a fist from the zombie aimed for my head. I lifted an arm and blocked the feeble attack.

More undead reached for me, and animals opened their mouths to bite me. I had to jump and roll away before they surrounded me.

I took a second to focus. My vision slipped into its red hue, and I remembered the lesson Mom gave me for dealing with the undead. I could hear her words as if she were standing right behind me.

Remember, undead don't feel pain or bleed. If you don't attack the head or the neck, you're only wasting your time and energy. I hope that you never have to deal with a necromancer. Seeing the undead leaves a nasty impression that never goes away.

I took a quick look behind me and saw the knights and guards still cowering behind the gate, but at least they had their weapons drawn and stood in a tight formation. *It was worth a look.*

I took a deep breath as I waited for the first wave of undead to reach me, and I leaped forward, slashing through them with my claws. They were slow and clumsy, but their sheer number was a problem. My claws crushed skulls and severed spines easily. Every attack mattered, and I needed each one to be a kill to avoid getting surrounded.

Everything was a blur around me. I couldn't focus on any one thing for longer than a heartbeat. Some of the undead were faster and more agile than others, but I was still faster and stronger. What surprised me most was that some of the human and elf zombies carried weapons. Keeping my arms covered with ice acting as my primary defense only added to the hectic frenzy.

The bodies quickly started piling up around me, and the undead were climbing over each other to reach me. For every undead I killed, three would fill the space it created.

I blocked an undead's attack with my claws, then countered with a swift swipe that sent its head flying. Another undead charged towards me, but I sidestepped and stabbed my claws into its back, ripping its spine out. It crumpled to the ground, lifeless. My movements were slowing as I panted heavily.

The sound of hooves approaching broke the unending grumbles and shuffling of the surrounding zombies. *They're here.*

They charged towards the gate, and I had to fight even harder to keep the undead at bay.

I kicked one in the face, sending it reeling back with a collapsed skull, then lunged towards another. My claws met its head with a sickening crunch, and it collapsed to the ground. My heart dropped when I couldn't see the gate anymore.

They're relentless.

I slashed and clawed my way through them, pushing them back and buying time for The Maidens. Suddenly, I felt a sharp pain in my side. I glanced down and saw an undead's sword sticking out from just under my ribs. I gritted my teeth and pulled it out, freezing the wound shut with my ice magic.

I kept slashing at every zombie near me, but as a zombie wolverine bit my ankle, I could feel a sense of dread creeping in. After stomping on its head, I started clearing a path towards the gate. The Maidens were plowing through the undead.

I cut through another short green zombie, but when I took another step forward, I felt something jump on my shoulders. Something grabbed my head, and before I could reach up and pull off whatever grabbed me, it bit my ear. A scream burst out from me, and I grabbed whatever had bit me and threw it to the ground headfirst. The green-skinned zombie's head exploded as it did, but it took more than half my ear with it.

The knights continued to ride through the zombies into the gate, leaving me behind. *I've got to get back.*

A zombie rat climbed my leg and bit into my calf. More grabbed at me. I couldn't keep up anymore. I could feel the effects of all the small wounds piling up.

Somehow, more undead surrounded me than I thought possible. I stabbed my claws into the skull of a zombie, and my hand got stuck as a zombie grabbed my other arm and bit the ice covering it. A green-skinned zombie pounced towards my face.

I couldn't move my arms to catch it, and more pulled at my cloak and dragged me to the ground. Before the airborne zombie could reach me, a spear pierced both of its raised arms and skull at the same time. A sword cut the head off the one that was attempting to bite my arm.

More spears pierced the heads of the zombies that pulled at my cloak. Captain Aenwyn, Daric, and several other knights were using their spears to strike them. Lexia grabbed my arm and pulled me away from the horde.

The Maidens covered us as Lexia helped me limp back to the gate. Daric stood in front of all the spears, using wide, sweeping attacks to hack limbs from the zombies. Most of his attacks didn't kill, but they disabled them so they weren't a threat.

Daric walked backwards, keeping the knights' spears just close enough that he didn't have to defend his back. We reached the gate, and four knights broke off to prepare to shut it.

"Daric, get back, now!" Aenwyn shouted as she manipulated a

spear with her magic to stab a zombie in the head as she used the spear in her hands to kill another.

Daric didn't hesitate as he ducked under her spear and slid through the gate. The knights started closing the gate, and the captain continued to use her magic to ward off the undead as she entered, leaving the animated weapon behind. Other knights replaced the wooden barricades as soon as the gate slammed closed.

"Are you okay?" Lexia whispered as she set me against the wall.

I groaned. "No." My chest heaved with each labored breath, my body consumed by a growing, searing agony. "Everything hurts, and one of them bit part of my ear off."

My sister didn't bother hiding the pain in her face. "I'm sorry, but I can't use magic. If I could, I would've saved you. I failed you." She lowered her face and started crying.

I brushed my sister's hair, then lifted her chin. "Don't worry about it. I'll be fine. It'll probably grow back." It was hard to smile with the throbbing pain coming from my half-missing ear and my side.

Lexia sniffled. "It will? Are you sure?"

I kept smiling. "Yeah. I've had worse and completely recovered without a scar."

Lexia gave me a quick hug and turned away to wipe her face. I let myself relax and released the breath I'd been holding.

Please let my ear grow back. That's going to be really awkward if it doesn't. But I can't let her worry about me. This town is under siege from the Rider of Death with an army of undead. We have bigger problems.

"Hey, sis." Lexia's ears and tail perked up when I called her. She turned and looked at me expectantly. "Why don't you find Mom? We need to talk to her about everything."

Lexia placed her hand on my sealed stab wound. "Are you sure you'll be fine?"

I put my smile back on as I nodded to Zenny behind her. "I'm in good hands."

Fina and Zenny were running towards me past Captain Aenwyn, who was giving orders to the rest of The Maidens. I also saw Daric putting his sword back in its sheath as he strode towards me. Lexia smiled back and stood up. She took several steps backwards without looking away from me. I widened my smile.

"I'll be back with Mom." Lexia's words were quiet against the shouting headed our way.

33

LEXIA'S HOPE

Why does Lucia keep lying to me? I stared at my sister for a moment longer. *Does she not trust me? Is it because she's more than the sister I had?*

As Zenny ran by me, I placed my hand on her shoulder. "Please take care of her." My voice betrayed any attempt to hide my nervousness. *Regardless of her feelings towards me, my instincts are compelling me to care for her.*

The woman nodded and gave me a smile. "Don't worry, Lexia, I will." She gave my hand a gentle pat.

I flattened my ears and drooped my tail. *Maybe I'm overreacting.*

Another group of men nearly shoved me out of the way, and I almost tripped moving to avoid them. I'd not seen most of the men barreling through towards the gate and my sister, but I recognized one of them. It was the man Lucia called Allen—the one who saved her life all those years ago.

Zenny kneeled next to my sister before opening her bag of bandages. Her gambeson, as she called it, was riddled with cuts from both weapons and claws. But there was only one spot where it looked like she was injured through her cloth armor. Her legs, on the other hand, were covered with small bite marks and shallow cuts. Any one of them wasn't a danger, but the amount left me feeling queasy.

Allen stopped and looked around as Captain Aenwyn walked towards him. "I take it you're the cause of the commotion here."

"Yeah, you could say that. Although…" Aenwyn turned to look at my sister. "I'm more inclined to believe her scaling the wall and opening the gate had more to do with that."

Allen's head turned towards my sister before he looked up at the wall. "Why did she have to climb the wall? Didn't you let her in?"

A man who was watching from above jumped. His face turned a little pale. "I, uh, tried to tell her to run and save herself. The undead were coming, and I thought it was dangerous to open the gate and thought that she and the other knights were better off just running away, so they were safe."

Allen lowered his head to look at Lucia. "And why didn't you just stay away? Can't you see we're now surrounded?"

My sister's tail twitched. "My mom's here. So are Gifford and Victor, right?" Allen nodded. "We're here to help defend the city. I'm no expert on sieges, but more defenders should always be welcome, right?"

Right. Where's Gifford? I should ask Captain Allen if I can see him after I bring Mom here.

"You don't look to be in any shape to fight anytime soon," Allen said.

"She's already fought the undead," Daric interrupted. "Honestly, she made it much easier for us to make it through the gate without casualties. What she did was heroic." There was pain in his eyes.

"Besides, a little nap and most of these wounds will be gone." Lucia waved a hand that wasn't holding a bandage to her side.

"And your ear?" Allen's question somehow felt heavier.

Lucia lifted her hand to touch it, but stopped halfway as she looked at me. She turned her head and lowered her arm. "It still works. It's just a flesh wound."

Sis, if it really bothers you, tell me. I want to help you.

"She'll be taken to an infirmary. Is there one set up nearby?"

Aenwyn stepped between Allen and Lucia. "I imagine war conditions have been established."

Allen nodded. "Yes, and civilians have been armed and migrated to the center as much as possible. I'll send a runner to let them know your company is aiding with the defenses."

"Lexia can take care of that," Lucia said as she looked at me with sadness. "Please, go get Mom; I'll be fine."

Everyone turned to look at me.

A familiar sense of worry filled me as I shuffled a few steps back. *But you're not fine. I can see that. You keep deflecting, thinking that I'll forget, but I can't. You know that. Or do you do it because you need to deflect? If that's your wish, then I'll honor it.* I gave her a nod before turning around.

She turned to Allen. "I'm sure my sister misses Gifford. Could you send him here so they can at least see each other? It's been several weeks. And could you send Victor with him? I've kinda missed him too."

I stopped midstride. *Thank you for thinking about me.*

I wiped a tear as I ran into the streets.

I ran, looking for any sign of our mother. But the more I ran through the streets, the more I realized I had no idea where to start. *She's someone important. So where are the important people? Maybe I should ask someone?*

"Excuse me, have you seen an elven woman with long green hair, wears dresses, and is a powerful mage?" I asked the nearest pedestrian.

The man shook his head after the shock dissipated from his face.

My heart sank. I turned away and asked the next closest person. "You. Have you seen my mother? She's an elf."

The woman didn't flinch like the man. "You're going to need to be a bit more specific."

I growled. "Her name's Nora Stormleaf. She's seventy-seven inches tall. Her bust is forty-three inches, her hips are forty-two inches, and her waist is thirty-five inches."

The woman pursed her lips. "No, I'm afraid not. Although, with a title, she might be with the knights."

"Which knights? Aren't they all along the walls? It'll take me forever to search them." My tail flicked behind me.

The woman looked genuinely concerned. "You're going to need to ask a knight. I'm just part of the fire response teams."

I turned away and found the next closest person. He gave me less than the woman. I asked another person, and then another, then another, another. Face after face, man, woman, human, elf—nobody knew where my mother was.

How can everyone not know where Mom is? This is so frustrating! These humans are so stupid. I growled at someone who put their hand on my hip.

It was a little boy. He jumped back and started crying. He couldn't have been more than four years old. *No, humans age slower than beastkin. He might be six.*

"Sorry, I didn't mean to growl at you." I kneeled down and offered a hand to the boy. *I promised I would be nice to people for Lucia. This child didn't deserve my growl.* "It's just that I'm looking for my mother, and nobody can help me."

The boy's tears slowed down. A woman stepped next to him and pulled him behind her. "Stay away from my son."

I stood up and faced the human woman. "I said I was sorry. Nobody's been able to help me, and it's so frustrating."

The woman's hard face grew harder. "I've heard the stories. You beastkin growl at someone just before you beat them within an inch of their lives." She pushed her son back further. "He's a kid. Is beating up all the men no longer enough for you?"

Lucia, you've got quite the reputation. "That's my sister. And she only ever hurt someone when they deserved it." I leaned forward and flattened my ears. "Until now, I've never hurt a human, but if you keep slandering my sister, I'll make you the first."

"Stop, Mom." The boy pulled his mother's arm, increasing the distance between us. "She's just lost."

I turned to leave. *Don't hurt humans. Don't do anything that would upset Lucia. Maybe we should leave these humans and take Mom with us. The Wild Kingdom would welcome her, and we could be one big, happy family.*

"Wolf lady," the boy called out to me. I turned my head. "If you're looking for someone, go to the courthouse. My mom said that if things got dangerous, I should head there. Maybe she's waiting for you there."

My heart melted as the boy stood with his eyes wide, staring at me. *There's still hope for humans.* "Thanks."

I left the boy and headed towards the courthouse. It was as good a place to look as any. And the closer I got to the courthouse, the more people I saw. Many of them were guards, directing traffic and handing out small packages and sacks before telling people where to take them. It was loud, and the cacophony of voices was annoying, but I saw my destination.

Two knights flanked the doors to the courthouse. The etched emblem on their breastplate was one that neither Mom or Captain Aenwyn told me about. It was a thick, zig-zagging lightning bolt with a square bottom supported by a lion on each side.

One of the knights held out a hand. "Sorry, miss. No one's allowed inside."

I flattened my ears as I bared my teeth. "I'm looking for my mother."

The knights looked at each other. After a brief silence, the second knight turned and gave me an apologetic look. "Look, this is the acting headquarters. It's unlikely your mother is here. Ask around town. Somebody's bound to have seen her."

"My mother is Nora Stormleaf."

The knights' backs stiffened. "That changes things." The first knight placed a finger on his chin. "Wait a moment. Didn't I hear rumors years ago about a beastkin living in Aquittemia and that she was adopted by a hero of the most recent war with Brentiveil?" He squinted his eyes. "You're her, aren't you?"

I rolled my eyes. "That's my twin sister, Lucia." *Seriously, can't they tell us apart?* Both knights raised their eyebrows. "She adopted me recently."

"Be that as it is, we still can't permit you to go in." The second knight waved his arm to the side. "We can permit only knight captains and select individuals inside."

I started growling at them as my tail lashed behind me.

The knight raised his hand. "But that doesn't mean you can't stand here and wait for her if you think she'll be here. Nora is, after all, one of the individuals allowed inside."

I relaxed slightly, but my tail still whipped behind me. "So she's not here. Do you know where she went? My sister really wants to talk to her."

The two looked at each other and shrugged.

"Fine. I'll ask someone else." I moved to go through the door of the courthouse, but the two knights stepped together and blocked my way.

"We told you already. We can't let you in. I'm sorry." The barricade of metal and muscles just stood and stared at me.

I clenched my jaw and growled even louder. "Move. Now!"

The door opened behind the knights. "What's going on here?"

As the door opened more, I saw a human with shoulder-length golden waves flowing from his head. His beard matched his hair in color but was neatly trimmed and even fuller than his luxurious locks. Piercing green eyes snapped at me as he looked at me with curiosity. The man pushed both knights to the side, but they parted voluntarily once he placed a hand on their shoulders.

"Oh." He relaxed as he looked at me. "I should've known you would make this much noise. It's been a while, Lucia. You look, if you'll take this as the compliment that it is, quite beautiful. My sister's not here. She already fled to Caska."

I bared my teeth. "Wrong sister."

"Lexia?" I heard the familiar sound of my adoptive mother. I turned and saw her with her green hair tied into a flowing ponytail. "You're safe." She nearly ran me over when she wrapped her arms around me for a hug.

The man who mistook me for my sister squinted as he leaned forward. "Oh, so you're Lexia. My sister—who's Evalana, by the way —told me Lucia had a sister." He extended a hand before sweeping it to the side as he bowed. "My name is Aurtour, King of Rophmna. It's a pleasure to finally meet you."

"You don't look like a king." The words flew out of my mouth before I thought.

"Lexia!" Mom leaned back and nearly shouted in my face. She released me and turned to Aurtour. "I'm sorry about this. She's only dealt with Evalana, who doesn't bother telling everyone she's the princess of this kingdom."

"Don't I know it." Aurtour laughed as he waved his hand. "It's fine. It's the armor."

He wasn't wrong. Aurtour's plate armor covered his chest, shoulders, waist, forearms, and legs, while thick leather boots and gloves covered his hands and feet. In between the joints of his armor, I could see chain mail links. Oddly, there wasn't an emblem engraved on his chest plate like every other knight I'd seen.

"We're in the middle of a war right now." Aurtour's nonchalant tone didn't make his words seem any less impactful.

Mom stiffened as she snapped her head towards me. "Where's your sister? Did you get in before the undead got to the city? Do you know if the city's surrounded? I heard there was a commotion at the north gate, was that you?"

Mom's barrage of questions had me stepping back. "She's hurt, but she insists she's fine. Zenny's looking after her right now. She sent me to look for you because she wants to talk to you. Also the rest of The Maidens are here to help defend."

"Okay." Mom turned to the king. "I'm sorry, but I have to go right now."

"Go." Aurtour waved his hand. "Take care of your family. Just tell me if you know where this Rider of Death is. Did you learn anything while scouting at the south gate?"

"Unfortunately, no." She shook her head. "Anna couldn't sense him among all the undead."

The two knights who had been standing on each side of us, perfectly silent up until now, cleared their throats. "So, she's allowed to enter now, right?" one of them asked.

Aurtour frowned. "Of course, she and her sister are both allowed."

One knight scratched his chin. "Uh, what does she look like?"

I rolled my eyes. "Like me, except she's a primal beastkin with a smaller bust."

They stared at me blankly.

"Lucia's teeth are like a wolf's," Mom answered the unspoken question.

"How come they don't know what a primal beastkin is?" I asked Mom as we walked away.

Mom's eyes looked more tired now. "Because some people refuse to learn until they have to." Her face brightened up a bit, but the sag in her eyes was still there. "So, where's Lucia? Where did you enter from?"

We need to protect Mom. She doesn't look too good. "We came in through the north gate. Lucia fought the undead off to make sure we were clear to enter the city. That's how she got hurt."

Mom let out a sigh. "I was hoping you'd stay away once the undead started surrounding the city. And of all the times to be at the south gate, they didn't even sound the warning horns..." Her voice trailed off.

"What were you doing at the south gate?" I flicked my ears as I watched Mom's stare grow more distant.

"It was supposed to be a quick surveillance mission with Anna to look for signs of the rider." She turned and gave me obviously forced smile. "But you're safe, and here now. That's all that matters. You did well making it into the city with your sister."

"It all happened so fast." I extended my claws as I held up a hand. "I'm still magically fatigued. I wish I could've helped her more, but all I could do was carry her back after Aenwyn and Daric killed the zombies holding her down."

Mom placed a hand on my head and started gently massaging behind my ear. "You did exactly what you should have. Lucia is likely extremely grateful for the part you played. Never downplay your involvement, no matter how small it seems." I leaned into Mom's hand. "Even the smallest actions can make a difference, and sometimes they're the most important ones."

That's hard to believe. But you've rarely been wrong before, so I'll trust you. But...

"Does that include hiding the fact Lucia is a reincarnated soul?"

I saw Mom frown at my question. "So she finally told you." She headed towards the north. "It's true. She's not the first one I've come across."

"Does it change who she is? How many like her have you met? Why didn't you tell me? What does this all mean?" My questions flowed from me without so much as a pause for breath.

Mom gave me a smile. "Nothing about her changes. I've only met one other, so it's extremely rare, or other people are much better hiding it. Lucia also asked me not to tell you. She was afraid you would reject her. So have you?"

"I..." *Have I?* I paused for a moment. "No, I've still been calling her my sister. And she told me the same thing when I asked her why she didn't tell me sooner." I glanced at the ground, hoping it would miraculously provide some insight. "What now?"

She wrapped her arm around me. "Right now? How about we go see your sister? There's an army of undead surrounding the city and a powerful demon leading them." She then leaned closer to my ear and whispered, "Nothing has to be different if you don't want it to be. She still loves you and wants your love in return. But it's all your decision."

This must be why Lucia holds you so close to her heart, isn't it? You're so caring and motherly. I can feel it too. I promise, Mom, we'll take care of you. We'll get through this together. I wrapped my arm around her shoulders as I led her towards the north gate, my tail wagging the entire way. *Nothing has to change despite everything changing.*

34

LUCIA'S CALM BEFORE THE STORM

I sat on the makeshift infirmary bed, wincing as I shifted slightly to get more comfortable. *Lexia will find Mom. And with Mom we'll make it through this together, as a family.* The sharp pain in my head reminded me of the bite and made me more angry than anything. *Until my ear heals, people will be able to tell the difference between me and Lexia.*

While Zenny had patched me up, she continued fussing over even my minor wounds. I looked over at her as she worked, a worried expression etched on her face. I gave her a smile, and she shook her head before returning to work.

I glanced around the room, noticing Captain Aenwyn standing by the door, her arms crossed. Fina sat in a corner, her tail twitching back and forth. I could tell something agitated her. Daric leaned against the wall, looking lost in thought.

I couldn't sit still. My home was under attack, and I needed to defend it. But the pain in my side and the throbbing in my half-bitten ear reminded me that I needed not to be so reckless. *There are too many for me to take on alone.*

"Lucia, stay still." Zenny slapped my knee as she finished wrapping another bite wound on my leg.

"Ow." I grabbed my leg reflexively. "Sorry, I've still not gotten any better at sitting still."

Captain Aenwyn scoffed. "That's an understatement."

It was hard to listen to much of anything since my left ear sounded muted. But I managed to catch the sound of footsteps approaching the door before it burst open and Nora and Lexia rushed in. I sat up straighter, relieved to see them. My tail wagged as Nora rushed over to me, her face full of concern.

"Lucia, sweetie, are you alright?" she asked while reaching her hand towards my head.

I flinched away from her hand as it inched closer to my wounded ear. "I'm fine, Mom. It's just a flesh wound."

Lexia stomped over and glared at me. Her tail lashed back and forth while mine wrapped around me. *She's angry.*

"Stop that right now." Lexia's words caused me to flinch again. "Don't lie to us. Please don't lie to us." Her voice grew more tender with each word.

I snapped my head up and blinked at my sister. Mom even looked concerned. "What are you talking about?"

A tear formed in my sister's eye. "You're not fine. You're in pain. It's obvious you're hurt." Her lip started quivering. "This deflecting isn't healthy. Don't treat me like I can't help you. Let me help you."

I flattened my ears and perked them back up after the sting reminded me that one was still half-present. "I, ugh. Okay, fine. Yes, it hurts, but we're in a war. We don't have time to worry about my minor injuries. The undead can start attacking any moment now, and I have to help. I need to help."

My eyes caught Captain Aenwyn's smile. She met my gaze and gave me a reassuring nod.

I pushed off the bed and flexed my claws. "I'm going to help with the defense. You won't stop me."

Mom placed her hand on my shoulder. "Lucia, you're in no condition to fight."

"I can fight." I glared at her.

Mom looked at me for a moment, then sighed. "Alright, but I want you to stay close to me." Her tone left no room for argument.

I gave her a hug. "I have no problem with that."

The door opening took me by surprise. I was so lost in the moment that I wasn't paying attention to what was going on around me.

Two beastkin walked in. A large primal black bear beastkin, and a primal white-furred fox. Seeing Victor again sent my heart racing. My stomach felt a little weird as I resisted the urge to strip naked and shred his clothes.

Lexia sprinted and jumped on the foxkin. "My love, I've missed you." My sister and Gifford kissed.

Daric cleared his throat as he headed for the door. "I'm not needed here."

Aenwyn stepped between Victor and me before I said anything. "I take it Captain Allen has sent you with our orders."

Victor nodded. "You're to bolster the defense of the northern gate while The Brilliant Crusade is moved to the western gate."

Our captain nodded before turning to me. "Take your time and meet us at the gate when you've finished here." She stopped at the door. "But if you hear the horns, sprint to your posts. It means the undead are attacking."

We nodded.

Mom placed a hand on my shoulder as she walked to the door. "I'll wait for you two outside."

Zenny giggled as she waved goodbye before leaving. Daric didn't say a word as he walked out. His footsteps seemed to move even faster.

Soon it was just Lexia, Gifford, Victor, and me in the impromptu infirmary. My cheeks grew warmer as I looked at the large bearkin. My stomach also grew warmer. Except it wasn't my stomach; it felt lower.

Great, my mating instincts are kicking in. Now's not a good time. Maybe after we save the city, okay? The feeling didn't go away or lessen. I walked up to the bear, grabbed the fur on his chest, and pulled him close for a kiss.

The moment our lips touched, my instincts pushed even harder. I pushed Victor back just as he wrapped his arms around my shoulders. He looked baffled and a little hurt.

"That was my first kiss." My voice squeaked as my thoughts got cloudier.

"I, uh..." Victor stood motionless. It was clear he wanted to say something but didn't know what.

"She's probably dying to pin you down and mate you until she's satisfactorily pregnant." Lexia's crude statement made me blush even harder as my tail curled around my waist. "And as tempting as it is for me too, now's not a good time."

"Sis, I'm..." My vision blurred as everything tilted until it felt like my inner wolf took over. She growled at Victor and moved to pounce. "I can't hold back anymore." The words felt alien as they left my mouth, as it wasn't me who said them. I was trying to pull back the horny wolf inside me.

Victor grinned as he opened his arms.

Oh, you would like this, wouldn't you?

Just as I jumped, Lexia rammed her shoulder into my injured side and tackled me to the ground. We tumbled until I pinned my sister and growled at her.

She slapped me. "Wake up."

I growled again. "I want pups."

Lexia slapped me again, harder. "Wake up!" I didn't feel any bleeding from my cheeks. But my vision returned to normal, and my head cleared a bit. "Remember what you said."

I leaned back and sat on the ground, staring at my claws. "I can't have kids. Not yet. It's too dangerous if the demon king comes and I'm not able to fight because I'm pregnant. He's too close to being summoned. I'm sorry, Victor." I lifted my head to look at my sister. "Thanks, sis. You have no idea how badly I needed that."

She gave me a wry smile. "I figured it would be bad for you." She took a breath as she glanced at Victor, who looked concerned yet apologetic. "But I would never have guessed it would be that bad."

I stood up and helped my sister to her feet. "Again, I'm sorry. But if we make it out of this, we'll figure something out, Victor. But we still can't have kids."

Victor raised his arm with the silver armband, the one that matched mine. "When I said that I would wait however long it takes, I

THE BIG BAD WOLF BOOK 4

meant it. I will wait." His stoic expression melted almost immediately. "Although, seeing you that aggressive was quite... Uh, how do I put this?" He started fidgeting with his claws.

Gifford threw his arms out. "Please, don't. We know what you're talking about. Let's report to our posts before the girls decide that defending this city isn't a priority anymore."

Victor slumped his shoulders. "Alright. Let's go." He turned to me. "It was nice to see you again."

"Don't worry, we'll see each other again." I gave him a smile. *He's strong. He'll make it through this. Especially if he's with Captain Allen.*

We all walked out, and Mom extended a hand towards the north gate. "Are you girls ready to go?"

I nodded. "Yeah." *Lexia hit my injury when I sort of lost it there for a moment, but the pain is mostly gone already.*

"Do you girls remember what to do when fighting undead?" Mom asked as she walked with a daughter on each side.

"Go for the head. Anything else is pointless." Lexia bounced as she answered.

Mom had a somber look on her face. "Correct. I just wish you didn't need to use that information."

"Hey, Mom," I started. "You defeated an army once with your magic. Why don't you start with your lightning spell and defeat them again?"

Mom flinched. "Several reasons. The town I defended was smaller than this. Also, we were fighting dwarves, not undead. And I didn't defeat them by killing all of them, but by defeating their morale." Her eyes stared off into nothing. "Destroying the dwarves' siege weapons was my part of the plan. Without those, they had little else they could do to the walls. The undead won't stop until their master is dead. And if he has this many undead, I can't use too much magic too quickly."

I flattened my ears. "This won't end until the rider is dead?"

Mom nodded. "Correct. I don't know how much Captain Aenwyn taught you about siege battles, but this could take days." She rubbed both of our shoulders. "So if you have the moment to rest, take it. Our enemy won't need it."

"But, um, since I'm still fatigued, can you help me?" Lexia looked at Mom and gave her the puppy-dog eyes.

Mom rolled her eyes as she waved her hand over Lexia's claws. Ice condensed on them, covering her forearms and hands in ice while extending past her claws for another few inches.

I lifted my arms and mimicked the same magic. "Try to stay safe and not take on more than one. You're not as skilled in martial combat as me, so always fall back if you're getting outnumbered."

"Yeah, yeah, yeah," Lexia mocked as she took a few practice swipes.

I've tried to teach her a little about fighting without magic, but she surprisingly hasn't learned it as fast as she learns everything else. It's like she keeps trying to think about it rather than trust her instincts. Maybe this is one thing her memorization aptitude actually holds her back in.

We climbed the stairs to the top of the wall and joined Captain Aenwyn. The entirety of The Maidens were gathered along with Daric and Fina. Fina's ears, eyes, tail, and hands wouldn't stop moving. Other knight companies flanked us on each side. It looked like each company would be responsible for defending their section of the wall.

"What are you doing here?"

Daric drew his sword at my question. "Keeping an eye on you. You attract trouble frighteningly well. So I figured you'll need all the help you can get for this." He pointed to the horde of undead standing motionless below us. "Besides, the way they're just standing there is unnerving. They didn't hesitate to attack you when you opened the gate, but now? It's like they're waiting for something."

"So you know what's going on?" a voice asked from behind me.

I turned and saw Escaeris standing next to her twin sister, Elasha, both armed with a spear and shield.

I shrugged. "Kinda. It's complicated and would take a really long time to explain. Just know that there's a really powerful demon out there called the Rider of Death."

Daric turned with a flat expression on his face. "You see him, run."

Both elven women looked at each other and then back at us.

"We've got movement." The call came out just before horns blared from the other gates.

I looked to see the undead moving towards the walls. In their midst, wooden ladders appeared.

"Ladders!"

And so it begins.

35

HOLD THE WALLS

The undead placed their shoddy wooden ladders against the stone crenelations. "Fire mages, burn those ladders." Aenwyn's order rang throughout our company. "Nora, take the eastern side. The rest of you take the west."

Half a dozen knights, including Elasha, moved to the right side of the gatehouse. Mom tapped my shoulder and nodded back towards the inner city. *Yeah, I know. Turn around so I don't see and trigger my pyrophobia.*

I turned around and listened as best I could. My hearing on one side was still a little muffled. But I could hear the knights on one side of us lining up archers in front of the ladders and shooting the undead as they came up, and the other company used axes to cut the tops of the ladders off.

It helps to have the largest percentage of magic users compared to non-magic users in our company, even if we are one of the smaller ones.

Lexia tapped my arm with her ice-covered claws. "They're done."

I turned back around to see the smoke rising from the dozen ladders. Even though Lexia said they were done, I still kept my distance from the edge, just in case. *Now isn't the time to lose my head over seeing fire.*

"They're creating human ramps!" Aenwyn's voice made it sound like she was just as surprised as everyone else who heard her. She pointed to the edge of the wall. "Shield walls, now."

The knights followed her orders without hesitating. I again stood back. But I knew my part and waited for it. *Although, as unlikely as it is, I hope I don't have to. Because that would mean a shield wall was failing.*

It didn't take long for the undead to create their ramps, and my curiosity got the better of me. I moved to the edge of the wall and looked down. The zombies were interlocking their heads and shoulders as they created a pile that nearly reached the wall. There were two piles, one on each side of the gate, and they continued reaching towards the shield walls waiting for them. They climbed the three-hundred-inch wall, a full two arcs.

There are thousands of them. My mouth gaped as I looked at the swarming horde, which seemed to have only grown since I'd last seen it. *There have got to be thousands of them. No, tens of thousands if all the walls are surrounded by this many.* "Can we win?"

I started moving away until a hand touched my lower back. Daric's calm face seemed out of place, given our situation. "We're heroes, remember. We'll win. I promise."

I pushed him back and returned to my place next to Lexia. "Easy for you to say."

Mom was concentrating, and the glow of magic around her continued to grow. *Is she going to use her thunderstorm spell to call down lightning? Somehow that doesn't seem like it will be enough.*

I nudged Lexia. "We've got to protect Mom until her spell is done." She nodded. "I'll take the first shield wall that's breached. You take Daric and assist when the other one is breached. Okay?"

"Got it, sis." Lexia looked down at her claws before testing her dexterity.

I grabbed her wrist. "And, please, stay safe."

She grabbed my hand. "You too."

I couldn't help but smile at her. She returned it before we watched the other knights stab the zombies as they came up.

At first, they came up two at a time, and the knights could keep up. They even cycled the front line out with another row after a while. But as they kept killing the zombies, more came up at a time. Two became three, then five, then seven, and then twelve at a time. At that point, the knights struggled to keep up, and they didn't have the time to change the front line to let them recover. Fatigue was our greatest enemy.

Green-skinned zombies started jumping on the knights' shields before they could stab them in the head. One knight fell, then another, and soon it was a cascading effect.

"Lucia, west flank. Now! Deal with the goblin zombies." Aenwyn's orders were unnecessary, but now wasn't the time to be petty. "Back and regroup."

So those little green people were goblins. Wow, they're ugly. I was already sprinting towards the shield wall, which was barely holding together. Jumping over the knights and landing on a goblin's head, I crushed it. I suppressed the urge to kick off the brain matter that was wedged in between my toes and let my vision shift to red as I slashed at another zombie.

I whirled from kill to kill and kept moving forward. The knights had backed up a few steps to give me room, reorganize their formation, and pull the wounded out of the fighting.

As I kept killing zombie after zombie, the knights eventually resumed dealing the undead that were attempting to attack me from behind. Since I'd left my cloak with Zenny, there was less for the zombies to use against me. Unfortunately, one still grabbed my tail. I turned, cut its arm off at the elbow, and kicked its head so hard that it flew into another two zombies and carried them off the wall together.

"Daric, cover the east. Now!" Captain Aenwyn's shout managed to reach me in the middle of my melee. "Back and regroup."

As I killed yet another goblin zombie, something moved in the corner of my vision. I leaned back and saw a spear come from the zombie's ranks, nearly stabbing my head. I turned to see one of the three knights who had died standing and holding her shield up.

You have got to be kidding me. Most of her throat was missing, and it was a wonder the head was still connected. Another fallen knight joined the first, and then the third stood next to the other two. I was staring down a shield wall made by the undead.

"Incoming!" Mom's voice cut through the sounds of fighting.

I immediately turned and jumped over the living knights' shield wall as they hid their heads behind it. I hit the ground, covered my ears, and slammed my eyes shut. Several flashes of light still almost blinded me through my eyelids, and that was only a moment before the thunder battered my ears.

I wanted to run. My instincts told me to. But I couldn't. My heart threatened to run away after pounding its way out of my chest. Breathing became much harder as I curled up. A fluffy pair of arms pulled me along, and I went with them willingly. Hands pulled my own from my ears, and I opened my eyes to see Fina holding me.

"I help." Her voice washed over me and calmed my heart.

When am I going to get over the sound of thunder sending me into a panic just as bad as seeing fire?

I nodded. "You helped."

Zombies weren't climbing the wall and attacking the knights again. The Maidens resumed their formation and postings. A few of the knights grabbed the corpses of the undead and threw them back over the wall.

"Incoming." Mom pointed a finger towards the eastern section. Daric and Lexia squeezed through the other reformed shield wall just before the lightning struck.

I covered my ears and leaned into Fina as she wrapped her arms around me. Something about Fina holding me kept me from freaking out as much as before.

I recovered quickly and looked up to see a few dozen of the zombie corpses falling haphazardly. After the last body hit the ground, the knights resumed their shield walls, holding back the near-endless tide of undead. I patted Fina's shoulder and straightened out.

As I looked over the walls, hundreds of zombie corpses were burned, scattered, and still. The makeshift ramps of bodies were exploded, giving us and the neighboring companies some time to rest and clear the area.

Any other army would be calling for a retreat after that display.

I shot a glance at my mother, who glowed so brightly from the magic flowing through her I had to squint to look at her. "Why are you doing that already?"

Mom's magic aura lessened slightly. "Things are already looking bad. We can't keep fighting like this all night. We need to draw out the demon. I thought, maybe, if I presented myself as the most powerful person here, it would be drawn to me."

That makes sense.

"Anna is working with Folmas and summoning an angel at the south gate to seek the demon out." Mom looked around at the undead army.

"You may not need me to tell you this, but it looks like anyone who dies joins their army." Mom's head snapped towards me. "A few of the knights who were overwhelmed and died came back and attacked me just before you vaporized them with your lightning."

I noticed that a few of the knights who had backed off from the fighting were nursing injuries. Mom walked up and grabbed Fina. "Fina, dear, go help the injured to the infirmary and Zenny."

Fina nearly bounced as she took off for the closest knight. "Yes, I help."

I raised an eyebrow at my mother. She watched Fina take a wounded knight away. She didn't turn towards me as she answered a question I hadn't asked aloud yet. "Because if this doesn't work, we'll need to fall back as quickly as we can. If one gate is breached or any section of the wall falls, we have to defend the people in the streets. We won't have time to carry the wounded."

"So this is all just delaying the inevitable?" I whispered back.

She nodded. "Now, cover your ears. I'm going to try one more time with a few more bolts."

I clenched my jaw, covered my ears, and turned away.

"Incoming!"

That one word was all the warning anyone got before the sky sounded like it was torn apart. It felt like something exploded as I felt the impact of each bolt as they struck in rapid succession. I even saw the flashes of light through my eyelids.

My emotions started slipping, and the desire to run built. *Mom said she was done. There's no more. I'm fine. It's safe. I need to help defend the city. Think about waterfalls. Calm, steady waterfalls.*

As I took the time to gather myself, the undead had apparently resumed their assault. Despite losing hundreds, the horde wasn't slowing down. *All we did was buy time. There are just too many for her magic to make that large of an impact.*

"Nora, cover the east. Specialists, cover the west." Aenwyn's voice helped me to refocus. Specialist was the role she'd given to me, Lexia, and Daric. "Everyone else, reorganize."

I looked up and saw the knights' lines bowing against the endless onslaught. Daric gave me a nod as I stepped forward.

I know my role. Jump in the middle and cause enough chaos for Daric and Lexia to finish off the stragglers. Mom is the heavy hitter, and she's here mostly because her two adopted daughters are. The captain's constant orders and adjustments are our best chance to get out of this alive. If we can get out of this alive.

My vision flashed red again since the lightning had scared me. I jumped over the knights and started thrashing at anything that moved. This time, I wasn't worried about killing blows. If it moved, I cut it with my claws. There were too many zombies around for me to see anything long enough to distinguish any details. I could feel my inner wolf pushing me to move faster and faster. I wasn't thinking for a while. Every movement I made was out of reflex and instinct. All I could do was slash and hack, hoping that Lexia and Daric stayed away.

Limb after limb, I hacked at more limbs than I ever imagined, and there was still no end to them. My muscles started burning. It was getting harder to devote any thought to remembering to breathe. If I had time to think, it needed to be spent clawing at any zombie trying to stab, bite, claw, grab, or club me.

"Waterfalls!"

I didn't know who said it, or what, if anything, was said before, but my code word meant it was time for me to retreat. Just as I turned to run, two cones of water sprayed the zombies on each side of me. Lexia and Daric had already retreated. Two of our water mages soaked the zombies as Mom channeled magic and extended her arm when I reached the opening the knights made for me.

I felt a breeze blow past me, and I looked behind me. The water was frozen, and there stood a wall of ice with more than two dozen dismembered zombies frozen inside. When I turned to look at the other section, I saw another wall of ice, just like the one they just made.

"That'll buy us some time," Captain Aenwyn said as she placed a hand on my shoulder.

As her hand touched me, my legs nearly gave out, and I staggered backwards. "There's just so many." The words barely made it out between my gasps for air.

"You did good, Lucia." The captain's words almost caused my tail to start wagging. Unfortunately, standing up took whatever strength I had. She guided me towards my sister and Daric, who weren't doing much better than me. "Rest while you can. The other sections are holding for now."

I sat down next to my sister, who leaned on me as she looked more tired than Daric and me. *We have the recovery aptitude, so we'll be ready after a short break. Lexia's probably done for the rest of the night.*

"So, how'd I do?" *I might as well take her mind off all this fighting.*

Lexia scowled as she looked up before she closed her eyes. "You killed sixty-seven, wounded one hundred and twenty-two." Her voice was distant as she spoke.

"Oh yeah, how about me?" Daric leaned forward and held up a fist.

"You killed forty-four and wounded twelve," Lexia said without opening her eyes. "Please don't ask about me. I don't want to live through that for the fourth time."

Daric's jaw dropped. "What do you mean? I don't get it."

Lexia sighed as she leaned her head back. "Every time I recall a memory, I relive it. It feels like I experience the whole thing all over again and see every detail, feel every emotion, and feel every sensation."

I wrapped my arm around my sister and pulled her close. "Okay, I'm sorry. Why haven't you told me it's like that?"

She opened one eye and grinned. "You never asked." I chuckled.

She went back to relaxing. "But, seriously, it's hard to put into words, and nobody can believe it unless you have the memorization aptitude."

So it's like that for Zenny too. I'll need to make sure I remember that before I ask her to remember anything bad.

The zombies were pounding, clawing, or using whatever was in their hands to try to break the wall of ice my mother had made. It was holding, but chunks were flaking off. Fina returned, but there wasn't anyone wounded for her to take to the infirmary.

I looked at my sister and her still-closed eyes. I gave her a gentle shake. Her eyes fluttered open. "Hey, sis, why don't you head back? You've done enough." I started scratching her head.

Mom walked over and offered the two of us a hand. "Yes, you're no longer fit for combat."

Lexia grabbed both Mom's arms and stood up. "But everyone's still fighting. I have to help."

I stood up on my own. "No, sis. A dozen knights just from our company have been pulled away for injuries. Just like them, fighting in your condition will only make things worse." I waved Fina over. "Take her to the courthouse." Fina tilted her head. "Remember the building I told you where government stuff is done?" She nodded. "That place."

"Okay," Fina said as she lifted Lexia's limp arm over her shoulders. Lexia didn't resist, but I could see the disappointment in her eyes as she dragged her feet while she walked.

Sorry, sis. But this is for your own good.

I turned to see Daric standing, his sword resting on his shoulder. "Are you rested?"

Daric gave a half-smile. "I wish I could say yes, but even I can't recover that fast. But I can at least stand up again and run if I have to."

I closed my eyes and lowered my head. "Yeah, I know how you feel."

As I watched, Fina continued to carry Lexia down the stairs.

Mom placed a hand on my shoulder. "She'll be fine. But, you know, she's as stubborn as you sometimes."

I know.

Before I could say anything, a loud horn blared from the west. Everyone who could afford to look did, and saw the western gate explode.

"The west gate has fallen! Everyone retreat!" someone from a neighboring company shouted.

I looked at Mom. "Wasn't the west gate where The Brilliant Crusade was defending?"

The look of horror on her face as she tried to grab me was all the answer I needed. I pushed off her and sprinted towards the west gate, finding a reserve of energy I didn't know I had. The blare of horns sounding the retreat led the way.

Please be safe, Victor. Please be safe.

36

VICTOR OF THE WEST GATE

Victor stood behind the humans and elves as he watched the undead attempt to climb their ladders. Captain Allen had ordered half of the ladders destroyed earlier. The knights constantly rotated with each other to kill the zombies climbing up. The undead didn't rebuild their ladders or find alternative methods of scaling the walls. So long as the four ladders were intact, the undead swarmed to climb them.

Victor found the smell of the undead to be their most unappealing feature. Gifford's grimace showed his displeasure at it, too. But with how systematically they were killing the zombies, the situation didn't seem as tense as he thought a siege should feel. But since this was an unfamiliar experience, he thought it might be because he didn't understand the entire situation nearly as much as Lucia did. She made it seem like this whole siege meant the world was at stake.

Regardless of his mate's feelings about the situation, he continued executing zombie after zombie. Each time they crested the ladder, he slammed his claws on their heads.

He stared out at the legion of undead, and something caught his attention.

An odd movement of zombies waded through the mass of

walking corpses. Something didn't look right. The goblin zombies weren't walking. Instead, they were holding onto something—something massive.

"Captain, there's something out there." Victor pointed to the undulating mass of decaying green flesh. As the mysterious collection got closer, he felt a tingle in the back of his mind from his instincts.

Gifford stepped next to him. "You feel it too, don't you?" His voice barely reached his enhanced hearing. "It feels like a dire, doesn't it?"

Victor couldn't disagree. After feeling the presence of a true dire animal while he followed Lucia out of the Wild Kingdom, he couldn't forget the feeling, even if he wanted to.

"What is it? Can you tell?" Allen neared the edge of the wall and squinted as he leaned forward.

"It's a dire," Victor said solemnly.

Allen shook his head. "No, it's too large. I don't know of anything that can be that big."

"It is," Gifford said as he flattened his ears. "We can feel it. There's no doubt."

Allen swallowed hard. "Destroy the ladders!" He lifted his arm up, and without hesitation, the knights who could reach them ignited the ladders with torches. "All archers, fire on that mass of goblins moving towards the gate."

After he gave the order, knights armed with bows and crossbows lined the wall. The first volley rained down upon the undead zombies clinging to the dire animal, the arrows finding their marks and killing many of them. Corpses went limp and fell to the ground, revealing the matted black fur hidden beneath. The second volley purged most of the zombies from the creature's back and face.

Victor's eyes nearly bulged from their sockets when the face of a dire bear looked up at him.

The massive creature didn't bother avoiding the undead that it crushed under its gargantuan claws. Its movements were slow and lumbering, but each step it took left deep impressions and crushed zombies in its wake. The tallest of the surrounding zombies didn't come close to matching its size, even as it walked on all fours.

Its black fur was matted and tangled with dried blood, clumps of it torn out in patches to expose bone, muscle, and rotting flesh beneath. The stench of decay was overwhelming—a putrid mix of decomposing flesh and dirt that only grew stronger the closer it got.

The bones jutting out from the bear's back and shoulders like jagged spikes nearly stopped Victor's heart. Its sharp, ragged teeth, caked in gore and flecks of rotten flesh, almost halted his breathing. The bear's eyes, staring at him from empty, lifeless sockets, shook him to his core.

Victor raised his arm as he turned to run. The silver bracer on his wrist flashed in the torchlight, and the engraving caught his attention. It was a crude bird. The mark of his promise, which he made many years ago and again when he proposed to Lucia.

He didn't take another step. The dire bear reached the gate and raised a massive paw before slamming it into the gate. Everyone on the wall felt the impact.

All the knights froze as the bear reared up on its hind legs. At its full height, it stood almost as tall as the wall.

"Get back." Allen waved his arms away from the wall and gate. "We can't stop that thing. Everyone, retreat. The gate will be breached!"

Everyone turned and ran—everyone but one person. Victor stood still, staring at the engraving on his wrist. He lowered his arm as knights fled past him, some of them pulling at his other arm, Gifford included. He shrugged them off as he stepped towards the edge, just above the dire bear.

"What are you doing?" Gifford asked as he stepped behind him.

Victor turned and smiled. "I'm not running away this time. Lucia has suffered enough. It's my turn to carry the burden. She shouldn't have to feel any more pain."

Before Gifford could get a word out, Victor jumped.

Victor's heart pounded in his chest as he landed on the back of the undead dire bear. The beast rolled its head and tried to throw him off, but he dug his claws into its matted fur and held on for dear life. He had to kill it, and Captain Allen said the only way to kill the undead was to damage the brain or decapitate it.

As the dire bear reared up and twisted again, Victor knew he would never cut the beast's head off. That left one option.

As they struggled, Victor spotted an opportunity. The bear's ears were vulnerable, and if he could strike them just right, he could take the beast down.

He made his move, slashing at the bear's ears with his claws. The undead dire bear didn't howl in pain, but it still thrashed even harder, trying to dislodge him.

Victor held on tight and tried again. This time, the bear threw its shoulder into the ground, nearly dislodging him. His toe claws tore through the fur and flesh as his legs swung, and he held on with one hand. He was no longer clinging to the back of the bear's head, and he grabbed at anything to catch himself, which was the bridge of the bear's snout.

A soulless, bloated eye larger than his head was inches from his face.

There was never a better opportunity, even as the bear lifted a paw to slap him.

Victor struck out.

His hand sank into the jelly flesh of the decaying eye. The bear flinched and pulled his head to the side, causing the paw to land right behind Victor and crush another zombie.

The bear kept its head tilted as it ran forward. Victor reached further into the eye, but his arm hit something that felt like a bone. Panic started setting in as the gate came closer. As Victor tried to remove his arm, he felt a small opening. He reached for it, but only one finger entered.

The thundering steps of the bear didn't stop. Frantic, Victor swirled his arm until two fingers found the hole, then three fingers. Four fingers were all that could fit as his hand got stuck. The bear lurched just before a crushing force struck Victor in the back.

As Victor and the undead dire bear burst through the gate, an intense jolt of pain coursed through his body. The jarring impact left him disoriented and dazed. The feeling of his arm being driven deeper into the bear's eye caused a nauseating churn in his stomach.

Their tumbling continued, and Victor's injuries multiplied. His body slammed against sharp metal and splintered wood, sending waves of agony through his torso.

The bear stopped suddenly.

Victor, now dislodged, continued to fly until his head struck the ground with a sickening thud, causing his vision to swim with dark spots.

As the dust settled, Victor lay still, battered and broken. He felt a searing pain in his shoulder and little finger, and the weight of his injuries pressed down on him like a heavy blanket. Blood spilled out from more than a dozen deep wounds, yet even as he struggled to breathe, he had completed his goal, and that idea provided some solace in his misery.

Seeing the creature still in front of him, Victor clawed his way to his feet, his muscles burning with the effort. He swayed, his legs barely able to hold him up as his arm dangled lifelessly.

The bear didn't move. Its head rested between the breached doors, ironically keeping the opening too small for anything else to enter.

Victor collapsed onto the ground, resting in a growing pool of blood, and he gasped for breath. He had done it. He had killed the undead dire bear. One last thought went through his mind.

I did good, right, Lucia?

His eyes closed as he smiled, and his chest went still.

37

LUCIA'S BROKEN HEART

My run to the west gate wasn't long, and I could feel myself recovering as I went. *Is my recovery still improving?* Knights had gathered and formed a defensive line between the buildings. I didn't see anyone from The Brilliant Crusade. Civilians who couldn't fight but could help in other ways were being ushered towards the center of the town. Everyone else—guard, knight, man, woman, elf, and human—armed themselves with a weapon and set up to defend their homes.

But that wasn't my concern. There was only one thought in my head as I ran for the gate.

Victor, please be safe. I'm coming for you.

Eventually, I found my way to one of the largest streets that connected the west gate with the other three gates. Spanning the length of the street were knights from various companies, including The Brilliant Crusade. Captain Allen stared in the direction of the gate, and Gifford paced behind him. A shield wall of knights blocked my vision of the gate other than seeing the decaying corpse of a dire bear wedged into the opening.

But the one person I looked so desperately for I couldn't find.

Gifford lifted his head and looked at me. Tears were pooling in his eyes.

"Gifford." I sprinted and grabbed the foxkin. "Where's Victor?"

Gifford's lip quivered for a moment as his ears flattened. "I'm sorry."

I shook him. "Where's Victor?" My volume attracted Allen's attention.

"I'm sorry," Gifford repeated.

I pulled my sister's mate up to my face and growled, baring my fangs at him. "Where?"

"Lucia, calm down." Allen placed a hand on my shoulder. "It's not his fault."

I threw the sobbing beastkin to the side and grabbed the human captain. "What are you talking about? Where's my mate?"

"He jumped on top of the dire bear." Allen's voice grew solemn. "He stopped it by himself."

I turned towards the gate. *No, no, no.* "Victor!" The scream that left my mouth slightly parted the shield wall as everyone turned to look at me.

I pushed through the knights, knocking many of them over as tears welled up in my eyes. *Please, no.* A short distance from the undead corpse was a bear beastkin lying in a pool of blood, motionless. My heart jumped at the sight of Victor.

But my next step stumbled.

His chest isn't moving. "Victor? Are you okay?" I skidded to a stop.

My inner wolf pulled at me. I could feel her hurting. It wasn't a pain I'd felt from her before. My breathing stopped when I saw Victor's arm move. I started wagging my tail, but my inner wolf only howled in my head as she tried to pull me away.

Victor rolled over and lifted himself up with one arm; the other one swayed limply. "Victor, you're alive?" When he turned to look at me, his eyes weren't open. But once they opened, my heart twisted as my inner wolf howled even louder in my soul. "Victor, no. No!"

There was no holding back the tears anymore. Denying it was impossible. The two brown, beady eyes I thought were cute were gone, replaced by black, soulless pits. Victor's mouth hung as loosely as his mangled arm. There were dozens of deadly injuries across his body, yet none of them bled.

He's dead. But he can't be dead. I won't let him die. He can't die.

"You can't be dead, right, Victor?"

My question remained unanswered as he slowly shambled towards me. His legs barely held him up.

My knees gave up, and I fell to them.

"Drue, we need to deal with him." Allen's cold voice cut across my heart.

I shot to my feet and turned to swipe my claws. "You will not touch him!" My snarl and bared fangs elicited a startled jump from everyone.

Allen approached with his sword drawn. "Lucia, I'm sorry..."

"No." I swiped my claws and nearly opened four red lines on his face. "There's a way. There has to be. I need him. We can still save him."

Drue's scar-covered face twisted with regret. "Lucia, I know it's hard to accept."

"What do you know?" I shouted my question at the human. "Do you want me to kill your wife? Don't you dare touch my mate."

I could still hear Victor shuffling his feet behind me.

Allen lowered his sword. "Lucia, you're grieving. I understand that—"

"I am not." I stomped my foot on the ground. *You don't understand. None of you understand.*

Allen's knuckles turned white as they gripped his sword. "You are!" His voice lost all of its gentleness. "We are at war, and now isn't the time for this. We can't leave him like this. He'll hurt others. Is that what you want?"

"I..." I lowered my head. "No. But there's got to be a way to bring him back. There has to be magic that can do that, right?"

Allen shook his head. "No, that's necromancy. And this is what that magic looks like. It perverts life. That isn't living." Victor's steps stopped right behind me. "Lucia, look out!"

I turned and saw Victor raising his arm over his head. He brought it down towards me. My reflexes acted, and I caught his arm with one hand and held it back. Drue charged towards Victor, his sword leveled at my mate's head. I kicked Victor's chest and released his arm, forcing him away from Drue's attack.

With Victor safely sprawled out on the ground, I turned and grabbed Drue and threw him towards the other knights with one arm. "I said you can't touch him."

"Lucia, he's a zombie. It's not Victor, not really." Allen tried to run past me, his sword lifted to attack Victor as the bearkin tried to stand up.

"I. Don't." I grabbed Allen by the back of his breastplate and flipped him over my head as I threw him back. "Care."

Gifford stepped out from the crowd of knights that looked too scared to move. "Lucia, if you can't do this, let me take care of him for you. Go to Lexia and make sure she's safe."

"No." I let my arms and tail fall limp. "He's my mate. He's my responsibility."

Allen, who made it to a seated position with the assistance of another knight, paused. "Are you sure?"

Yes. I turned and watched Victor return to his feet. *I'm sorry, my love.* My inner wolf tried to push me out. She wanted to keep me from doing this. She didn't want me to carry the pain of killing Victor. I placed a hand on her snout in my mind. *It's okay. You don't have to this time. I can't run away. It won't make the pain go away.*

I stepped up to Victor, and he threw his arm out to stab my chest with his claws. With little effort, I grabbed his wrist and slammed his hand against his chest. "Forgive me, Victor."

Victor opened his mouth wider and leaned forward to bite me. With one arm, I pushed him back just far enough so he was unsuccessful. "This is my fault. If only I had been here to protect you."

The bearkin zombie kept trying to struggle against me. "I'm sorry." I raised my other arm and made sure the ice covering my claws was sharp with my magic. "I'm so sorry."

Tears flowed down my face as I inserted my claws into his eyes. There was no resistance as they slid in, and the zombie went limp. *Goodbye, my love. I failed, and you paid the price.*

I quickly pulled my claws out and caught Victor before he could fall to the ground. I wailed as I kneeled, gently putting my mate down.

A gentle pair of hands grabbed my shoulders and pulled me close. I turned and saw my mother's tears flowing down her delicate face. I hugged her close as I wept into her shoulder. Mom guided me to my feet and turned me away from the gate. One hand released me, and I felt a heat grow behind me.

First it was Evalana, then Silver, and now Victor. Evalana's alive, but she'll carry the scar of her missing arm for the rest of her life. I couldn't save the other two. I couldn't keep them safe.

Mom and I stood in front of the parting wall of knights when I heard metal groaning behind me. We turned and saw, past Victor's body, the dire bear being pulled backwards.

But a flood of zombies didn't run through the opening.

No, it was a single horseman on a huge black horse with black smoke billowing from its hooves. Atop the horse was a man in full plate armor. The black armor reflected the moonlight with an other-worldly sheen. But when I looked farther up, there was a critical part of anatomy missing: the head. In his hands was a weapon fashioned from a spine with a skull sitting on top that looked like it was vomiting up a wicked, bleached-white blade.

It's the Rider of Death.

LEXIA'S REFLECTION

As Fina and I reached the bottom of the stairs, she gave me a bright smile. *Lucia is still pushing me away. Is it because she doesn't think we're truly sisters?*

But my thoughts were cut short by the thunderous sounds of horns. I turned to Fina. "Those are to sound the retreat."

Fina's eyes went wide. "We go?"

I could still hear the fighting on the walls as shouts joined the blare of horns. *What do I do? Lucia will catch up.* I gave a nod to Fina, who helped me walk. My legs burned and felt weak at the same time. My arms weren't much better. *If only this happened tomorrow, I'd be safe enough to use my magic.*

"I'm sorry, Fina." I tried to put more effort into walking, but it was almost too much just to stay awake. "Thank you for helping."

Fina grinned again. "I help."

We hobbled through the streets. The fighting continued, and I could hear it slowly following us. As much as I wanted to, Lucia was right. I couldn't keep fighting. *Again, I'm a liability.*

"Fina, I know now's not the best time for this, but there's something I need to ask you." I pushed off her shoulder and used a nearby building to hold myself up. Fina flattened her ears as she looked at me. "There's something about Lucia—something she hasn't told you."

Fina stood there and tilted her head. "What? If she wanted, she would tell me."

I shook my head. *Sorry, sis, but Fina deserves to know the truth too. She's way too close to you not to know.* "What if I told you Lucia wasn't just my sister?"

"She is a good friend too." Fina walked over and rubbed my shoulder.

"No, that's not what I meant." I shook my head. "Lucia told me she forgot who I was because she's not really my sister. She's someone who took over her body after she died."

Fina paused. "I don't understand."

I slumped my shoulders. "Do you know what a soul is?" She nodded. "Well, apparently my sister was killed when orcs attacked my village more than ten years ago. But somehow, a new soul entered her body and revived her. It's hard to believe, I know."

Fina's voice quivered. "But she's Lucia, my friend."

"She's still your friend. Her actions haven't been any less genuine." I brushed Fina's cheek then wrapped her in a hug. "I want to believe her and trust her. It was easier knowing that she simply forgot because of her head injury."

"If she cares, she's still Lucia." The lynxkin wiped her face and glared at me. "Trust your sister."

"Right." My tail and ears drooped. "She still wants friends, a sister, a mother, and to save this world. If she wanted, she could have thrown all of that away, but she still hangs on to it more tightly than me. It means more to her because she's choosing us as her family, even if she's not really only my sister."

Fina pulled me towards the center of town. "You are Lexia, Lucia's sister, and she said to take you to safety."

I smiled. "Okay. But I'm slowly feeling better. The walking is helping."

I started walking under my own power, but a massive explosion sounded from the north gate. Both of us turned to see shards of wood and metal raining from the sky around the gate. *There's still a battle going on.*

Fina ushered me towards the city center, almost carrying me. The fighting grew even louder and followed us faster. I heard shouts of knights working together to form defensive lines and support failing ones. But that all went away with one word.

"Dire!"

My instincts tugged at me to run, despite my tired muscles. Fina's tail went rigid, and her eyes darted to where the voice called out. I turned to follow her look as she raised a hand and took a step backwards.

A shield wall of The Maidens was holding the street. They all braced as something large with short matte black fur charged them. Several of the knights gave up on holding the wall and dove out of the way. Others tried to do the same but didn't react fast enough and were caught on the dire boar's large tusks.

Its normally white tusks were splattered with blood, and one even impaled a knight in the leg, dragging her alongside as it ran towards me and Fina. Several spears jabbed into it as it ran past, but the other oncoming undead couldn't be ignored either.

Fina pushed me into an alley, but the creature had already stopped to turn around. It was as if it were on a mission to disrupt the knight's defensive lines for the other undead, like it was being controlled. *I don't know much about how the undead do things, but how can someone have such precise control of this much all at once? Controlling two separate objects beyond joining them together is ten times harder for me, and this city is surrounded by the undead. How powerful is this Rider of Death?*

I looked at my own blood-covered claws. *Should I help them? Lucia said I would be a hindrance, and some other knights also retreated. Do I owe them?*

Several of the knights broke off the defensive line and pushed the boar back. Captain Aenwyn and Elasha were two of the most prominent figures who fought the beast. Four other knights followed after them as the wall reformed, but the undead wave was almost too much for them.

I only work for The Maidens because of my sister. Then I saw one knight's chest get kicked in by the boar as it bucked. *But they were never mean, and they treated me with respect.*

I turned to Fina. "We have to help them."

Fina's eyes darted from the boar to the direction of the courthouse and back again. Her muscles tensed as she stood there, watching. Elasha threw a small gout of flame and burned a chunk of flesh from the boar's face, revealing the slightly scorched skull.

I grabbed Fina's shoulders. "You have to help. I'm not able to, but please, these people are friends also. They helped save you too."

Fina's eyes closed. There was a quiet rumble that steadily grew into a growl. Her eyes snapped open. "Stay."

Then she bolted off towards the undead dire.

One of the knights drove her sword at the beast's face, only to have it glance off a tusk that tore through her arm and sent her sprawling to the ground.

Fina ran up behind it and jumped on the creature as the captain used her magic to throw a spear at its eye, missing by a few inches. The boar bucked and ran into a building, sending chunks of brick and wood everywhere. The knight that was stuck to its tusk flew off and hit the ground with a heavy thud. Elasha ducked her head behind her shield.

My friend still hung on, though. Her claws raked down its spine, but they weren't digging deep enough or fast enough. The boar barreled through to the other side of the building.

This is my fault. I can't let her face that thing alone. There has to be something I can do.

I followed Aenwyn, Elasha, and the two knights. My muscles were moving surprisingly better than before. We walked out the other hole the creature made on the other side of the building. The boar was heading towards another group of knights who were surrounded by the undead.

The wave of zombies was funneling down the street until Elasha swept her hand in front of her and sent out a short wave of fire, burning and knocking down several zombies that hadn't been trampled by the dire boar.

Fina jumped off the boar as it bucked again, throwing several zombies in the air. She twisted and landed on the shoulders of a knight-turned-zombie, based on the hole in his chest. Before the undead could grab her, she pounced back on the dire boar.

The two knights finished off the zombies Elasha had knocked down. And Aenwyn's spear pierced three zombies in rapid succession as they made their way to the other knights. Fina dug her claws into the dire's shoulder and kicked out her legs before twisting and hammering her feet into the creature's front leg as it nearly reached the knight company's fortified circle.

She managed to disrupt its step enough to cause it to wobble. The boar's foot slipped, and it rolled over, crushing a dozen zombies before it stopped. Before it could roll over completely, Fina kicked off and hammered a zombie next to Elasha.

Elasha stabbed the zombie—which had instinctively caught Fina —in the head. She and Fina gave each other a quick nod before stepping back from the oncoming zombie horde. Then I heard some flapping behind and above me. I turned to see an angel, or at least an angelic individual. He had small white wings and wore a white robe. While he looked to be about fourteen or fifteen by human standards, he held a pair of subtly glowing silver short swords.

The angel dropped down and started slashing into the horde with astonishing coordination and speed. Each swipe of his blade cut through the zombies.

The dire boar stood up and turned towards the angel. It dragged its foot across the stone and charged.

The angel flapped his wings and lifted up and over the dire beast. He dropped down and slashed both swords down its hind legs, tripping it. As it slid forward, Fina shoved Elasha out of the way before jumping onto its back again.

Aenwyn stabbed at the dire beast's eye, but the creature moved its head enough so that the spear only left a gouge in its skull, never breaking through. Elasha rolled to her feet and lunged at the boar, digging her sword in just below its ear. The creature rolled over on top of her. She screamed as the bulk of the beast smothered her. Fina jumped off again in front of me.

As the boar stumbled to its feet, its back right leg hung limp as the angel went back to attacking the horde. "Kill the beast; I'll help the others," he said as he drove his sword into a zombie's sternum.

Elasha lay on the ground; her breaths were replaced by wet gurgling.

Her ribs were crushed.

The boar headed for Aenwyn, sweeping its tusks from side to side. The elven captain backpedaled but kept her spear leveled at its eyes. *She needs one good strike, but it isn't giving her the chance.*

Fina stepped away, but closer to the zombies. She kicked and shoved them away, just staying out of their grasp. More and more of the zombies were cut down, but there seemed to be no end to them. *I have to do something.*

The ground was soaked in blood. *Mom, please forgive me.*

As the boar kept up its assault against Captain Aenwyn, I let out the most challenging growl I could. But just before it stopped and turned its head toward me, I pulled whatever magic I had, froze the blood under its still-falling hoof, and pulled it into a rounded mound.

Its foot slipped out wide, causing it to land on its face.

Captain Aenwyn didn't hesitate. Her spear dove into the creature's eye.

It shook its head, snapping the tip of the spear off and forcing the elf to jump back. But she was already grinning as she held up her hand. Through all the thrashing, the spear tip was pressed further in by my captain's wood manipulation magic. In a few short moments, the creature lurched to a halt and fell to the ground. The two knights that had followed us had been keeping the bulk of the zombies from interfering with us, but they were sustaining small injuries that were building.

I leaned forward and caught myself on my knees. The knight company that had been surrounded had fought their way out of the writhing mass of undead and were quickly forming a line. Fina ran over to me and helped me up.

Aenwyn turned to us. "Help those two to an infirmary." She pointed to two knights who were bleeding heavily and barely standing as they limped out of the circle of knights.

"What about Elasha?" I looked down at the teal-haired elf.

Her breathing had stopped, and she had a look of terror frozen on her face. Blood pooled and spilled from her nose and mouth.

Aenwyn frowned and shook her head. "It's too late. Save who you can."

There was a twinge of pain in my bones, but I ran up and helped the smaller of the two knights who needed medical attention. Fina ran and helped the other. "I help," she whispered to the knight.

The fighting continued as Fina and I carried our charges to the nearest infirmary. A smile sprang onto my face when I saw Zenny. *Lucia will be glad to know she's safe.*

I turned to Fina as she helped the knight lie down on the bed, a couple of nurses hurrying over with rolls of bandages and stitching supplies. "Let's stay here. I'm too tired to keep moving. Besides, Lucia will be headed here after everything is done."

Fina nodded. "I help." She turned to leave.

I held out a hand to stop her, but she was already gone. *Ah, who am I to stop her? That's what she does. She helps because she's so good at it. Helping is the greatest thing she can do in the moment, because that's how she lives her life.*

A wider smile grew on my face. *That's why Lucia being another soul doesn't matter to her. Fina only cares about the choices someone makes in the moment. And Lucia has chosen to be her friend. She won't see Lucia as anyone but Lucia. Because she is Lucia, after all. She'll do the name proud. I'm proud to call her my sister.*

39

LUCIA'S FIGHT BETWEEN LIFE AND DEATH

My instincts told me to run, but I wanted to tear the demon apart. *It killed my mate and then made me kill him. There is no mercy, no forgiveness, and no hope for him.*

"This is something I wouldn't have expected to see." The rider's voice sounded like it echoed from inside its armor. "It seems all this world's defenders are gathering in one place for me."

"You do not belong here."

I turned to look at the sky, where I heard the voice. A being, much like the angel I'd seen with Anna when we fought the Rider of Pain, flew through the air on four pristine, white-feathered wings. Heavy plate armor with countless white-gold filigrees covered the top half of the angel, and a long, flowing white skirt covered it all the way to their feet. Their head was covered in a white hood with yellow-gold trimming, which covered most of the glowing yellow light emanating from within. They clutched a massive two-handed sword with an abnormally wide crossguard made of blue metal that almost seemed to pulse.

"The Archangel of Life." The echoing voice of the rider sounded almost amused. "Is your precious Seraph finally deciding to take this seriously?"

The angel hovered in the air, flapping their four wings. "I'm here at the behest of mortals who wish to preserve life." Their voice sounded like a choir of singers. The angel lifted and leveled their sword at the demon. "Your time here is up. Your wanton destruction of an entire race can no longer be overlooked. It's time to return to where you belong."

Death started laughing. "Make me." He didn't have a head, but I could feel him sneering at the divine being.

Mom gave me a gentle nudge towards the other knights. "Go, get out of here," she whispered.

I could see the zombies swarming the city walls. Most were making their way to the steps, while a few just dropped off the edge. When they landed, they made a sickening, bone-crunching sound as their legs collapsed and bent in unnatural ways. That didn't stop them though. They started crawling towards us.

Looking into the lifeless eyes of the zombies ignited a flame inside both my inner wolf and me. They were the same eyes Victor looked at me with just before I'd killed him.

My eyes narrowed on the Rider of Death. *It's all his fault.* His laughter rang tauntingly inside my head. *He killed Victor. He reanimated his body and forced me to kill him again.* A deep growl rumbled from my throat.

"Lucia, don't!" Mom reached for me.

Red lines filtered into my vision one at a time until everything was red. *The punishment is death!*

I slipped from my mother's grasp and dropped to all fours, charging the evil creature.

The archangel dropped from the sky, their blue sword leading the way. Death parried the attack as he sidestepped with his mount. The angel of life flapped its wings to float out of reach before the demon could counterattack.

Once I got close enough, I jumped and reached out with my claws, aiming for the horse's head. My claws dug in as I twisted so I could grab both sides of the mount's head and dig my claws behind its jaw bones. My feet touched the ground, and my back arched backwards as I saw the bone scythe dropping towards me. I pulled with my abs and arms to straighten, then continued to throw the horse into the wall by its face.

A loud crack rang in my ears as the horse and rider sailed over me and collided with the stone wall. The horse fell to the ground, limp, on top of its rider. Its neck shouldn't have bent at the angle it did.

The horse melted into a cloud of black smoke as Death rose to his feet in spectacular fashion. "Enough." He slammed the butt of his scythe on the ground. "I am Death. I am inevitable, and you will—"

I dove and grabbed his leg. After I pulled it out from under him, I threw him over my shoulder and slammed him into the ground on his back. There was no face to gauge his reaction.

To be safe, I lifted him by the leg again, over my head, and threw him to the ground again. Again, there was no reaction from the demon. So I did it again, and again. I threw him to the ground five more times, just for good measure.

The demon lay there. His armor didn't show any dents, and his weapon was still in his hand. Two small craters flanked me from where I'd repeatedly slammed him down.

I smirked. "I expected more out of you."

Death didn't move and didn't react for a few moments. "That would have been more impressive if I felt anything."

My eyes went wide. *Oh, come on.*

"But I won't be treated like some ragdoll to be thrown around so casually."

Fine, I just have to hit you harder. Let's see if you like kissing the walls.

I reached to grab his leg again, but I saw the scythe swinging towards me. I leaped backwards, and the demon got to his feet. As soon as he stood, a boulder slammed into him and pinned him to the wall.

"If you lay a finger on my daughter, your demon realm won't save you from me." Mom glowed, full of so much magic that her hair defied gravity.

The boulder moved as the Rider of Death pushed it away from him. He lifted his empty hand, and a cloud of black smoke spawned halfway between him and my mother. The horse I'd killed grew from the smoke and charged Mom. Before the horse could take its second step, a large blue two-handed sword severed its head, causing it to melt into the same cloud of smoke it'd spawned from.

"Everyone, hold the zombies off and protect the town." Allen's voice overpowered all the other sounds. "We'll deal with the demon. If we kill him, we just might end this nightmare."

I slashed my claws at the demon. He didn't bother defending my attack. It was easy to see why. My claws glanced off his armor without leaving a mark, and it looked like the tips of my ice claws had been blunted.

He swung his weapon at me. I twisted and leaned forward to let the blade harmlessly glide over me. But when I saw the blade in front of me, it seemed to shift until it wasn't a scythe anymore. The spine shrank as the skull tilted back until the blade pointed outward from the spine. The blade became wider and looked like a spearhead, only much longer and wider than usual.

The blade swung back towards me. I dropped lower and spun around, my leg extended. Death's legs went out from under him and he hit the ground with another heavy thump. Death's hand was swallowed by swirling shadows just before he punched towards me faster than I expected. I threw up an arm to keep it from hitting my chest.

My vision suddenly filled with feathered wings. I turned to see the Archangel of Life on the ground next to me, their wings blocking the Rider of Death's magic. "Careful, wolfkin. Like his undead servants, he does not feel pain or suffer injuries like you or I."

I watched one of the four wings wither and turn black. The feathers shriveled while the wing went limp. Soon it was nothing more than a husk that turned to dust.

When the angel stood up and faced the now-standing demon, they leveled their sword towards the demon's spear.

"It looks like death is still stronger than life." Death strode forward. He stabbed with his spear, and the angel parried, knocking the weapon up.

The angel flicked me to the side with one of their still-good wings as they slid the sword down the shaft of the demon's spear. Death retreated a step just before the blade got close to striking his armor.

285

He didn't care about my attacks. But the angel's weapon—he's afraid of it. Why?

I focused my magic, condensing my ice claws even further. They turned an opaque turquoise, their edges renewed. *If only I had more magic.*

The angel swept his sword from right to left, and the demon intercepted it with the haft of his weapon. Allen ran past me, sword and shield in hand. He rammed his shield into the demon's hand that was holding the spear. The top half of the spear tilted away, but the block held. A stone the size of my head flew between everyone and hit the bottom of the spear. This time, the spear slid, and the sword slipped past it. The blue blade left a white line as it cut through the demon's armor.

The Rider of Death's weapon grew even larger, and he swept it across his body, forcing everyone to step back.

As the demon took another step back, he placed a hand on the white mark the angel's sword had left. "Impossible."

"No, not impossible," Daric said as he walked out from behind the angel. "The word you're looking for is improbable." He held out a finger and wagged it at the headless demon.

The Rider of Death stomped his foot. "What are you talking about, you gnat? It's life's destiny to give way to death. All life ends with death."

"No." The Archangel of Life lowered their sword and lifted a hand. "It is true. All life gives way to death. But in death, life can be born anew." The angel turned its head towards me. "Do not fret or feel sorrow for your loss, little wolf. The bear made his choice, and his sacrifice was born of his love and respect for you."

I flexed my claws as the last reserves of my tears surfaced in my eyes. "You, shut up." The angel took a step back. "I don't care about that. He's dead, and it's my fault. I don't want his sacrifice. I want him here, alive."

The demon raised his weapon, and it shifted into a massive two-handed sword. Except it kept growing. There was no way a sword that large could ever be practical. It was longer than the angel was tall, and the angel was taller than me by a good ten inches.

The Rider of Death lifted the obscenely enormous weapon over his head with both hands. "Hold still, and you will see your precious beloved in the desolate abyss that is my domain." He dropped it towards me.

I jumped to the side well before it hit the ground and exploded in a dust cloud. "You killed him. For that crime alone, I sentence you to die. You're just another demon." I let out a deep growl as my vision darkened. "And demons can die."

I sprinted towards the demon before the dust settled. As he lifted the weapon, I could see it shrinking to something more reasonable. He swiped it towards me, but I jumped, grabbed his pauldron, and flipped over him. As my feet touched the ground, I pulled him up and over my head and threw him into the stone wall.

The stone cracked around him as he hit it, but he landed on his feet. He assumed a defensive posture with his sword out in front.

He turned the blade and swung it in an upward stroke. I twisted and slammed my claws into his wrist. The demon tried to cut off my hand with a draw cut. I pulled his hand so that his blade cut his arm. When his blade sliced through his armor and left another mark, black smoke leaked from the wound.

The rider pulled the blade back and thrust it towards me. I released his wrist, twisted, and drove my knee into the handle of the blade, knocking it wide. With my leg still raised, I kicked the breastplate, forcing my enemy into the wall again.

He bounced off it after breaking more stones.

He stumbled forward, and I raised my claws and stabbed into the wound the angel had left earlier. The demon backed away from me as he covered the wound with his hand.

He recoiled? I narrowed my eyes at him. "Your armor is just your shell. You're vulnerable without it, aren't you?" Then I looked at the largest wound he had—his very exposed neck.

The Rider of Death lifted his sword in his silent response.

A subtle clapping started above me. Soon it grew louder until I looked up to see the sin of lust in all her naked glory, sitting above the gate. Her hoofed feet swayed as she dangled them off the edge.

Could this get any worse?

"So, you aren't completely stupid after all." The succubus leaned forward and grinned. "Here I was thinking that you were going to rely on that stuffy archangel over there."

"Now you show yourself, abomination." The Rider of Death didn't turn away from me. It was hard to tell how he saw anything without a head.

The winged demon rolled her eyes as she pushed off the wall and flapped away just as a zombie reached for her. "Oh, please. After all I've done for the demon king, I broke one little rule I didn't know existed, and now I'm the most wanted demon of the demon realm." She fluttered above us without caring to look at us. "But I have to thank you. You've saved me a great deal of work by using that monstrosity of a dire beast to kill the poor wolf's mate. Now I don't have to use my hard-thought-out plan to make her attack you."

I'll still kill you one of these days. Just not right now. I'm a little overbooked today.

The demon pointed towards the flying demoness. "You are not the Rider of Pain you think you've become. You are an abomination that must be eradicated."

"It's time you returned to your realm, demon." The archangel flapped their remaining three wings and took to the air towards the succubus.

The Rider of Pain raised her hand. "Wait." The angel stopped and hovered. "Do I not get a chance to defend myself? You should be proud of me. I've never taken a life. In fact, all I've ever done is help promote life. And what I'm doing right now is preserving life. He wants to kill me. I don't want to die. I'm not the real threat. He is. His army is killing this city's army, slowly but surely. You need to deal with him. He's the greater threat to life here."

I could see the angel's wings almost hesitate as they gripped their sword tighter. "For now." He then looked down at the Rider of Death.

"If you're done ignoring me, here's a little taste of what a true rider is capable of—something you'll never become." The armored demon raised a free hand and pointed towards the succubus.

It started out as a whisper. Something that sounded out of place among the other sounds of fighting going on throughout the city. The flying demoness and angel both turned to look towards the forest to the west. It sounded like a bird flying really low, but the louder it got, the more I knew it wasn't just one bird. It quickly sounded like rushing waves of wings flapping.

There was terror on the demoness's face when she flicked her sights to the armored demon before looking at whatever was headed our way. Her body shimmered as she turned invisible.

"Your tricks won't work. I've marked you, and they will find you." The demon started laughing. His laughter continued to echo as the angel raised his blade. "Both of you."

I gasped as hundreds of black birds flew towards the angel. Then more birds flew towards them, and soon the moons were struggling to illuminate through what had to be thousands of wings flapping in the sky. The first bird flew towards the angel, but with a single swipe of their blade, they bisected the bird, and it hit the ground next to me. I looked down at the raven and then back up at the fowl swarm, just as they buried the angel in their endless tide.

"And now, where was I?" The demon lifted his sword, and it shifted again. This time, it was a smaller pair of blades held together by a single handle between them.

Before he could swing the weapon at me, I grabbed the handle between his hands. A sharp pain burned through my arm, and I flinched backwards. I had to take another step away as he swung his weapon at me.

Okay, that was weird. But whatever. Keep your toy; it won't help you.

I ducked and weaved around him. He tried to spin with my movements, but I kicked the back of his knee and grabbed his elbow with my hand. He tried to throw his other elbow at my face, but I caught that too.

I could see Mom glowing with magic, but I could tell she was waiting for me to provide her with an opening so she could safely strike. Allen and Daric stood near her and watched me.

"Aim for the neck!" I shouted. *It's time for you to shine, Mom.*

Daric lifted his arm and pointed at me. "Lucia!"

I heard something behind me and saw a cloud of smoke and the rear of a black horse materializing out of it. My eyes went wide as I saw it raise its hind legs. I twisted and placed the Rider of Death between the hooves and me just in time.

The hooves impacted the demon, and he slammed into me. We went flying together until we hit the ground with him on top of me. My head bounced as it hit the street.

Everything flashed white, then went black.

40

NORA'S EMOTIONAL INFERNO

Time slowed down for Nora as she watched her daughter fly backwards. She watched as Lucia hit the ground. Her heart stopped when she saw Lucia's head bounce as the demon landed on the poor wolf girl.

Nora had tried to throw a boulder at the horse before it could kick, but she wasn't fast enough. Her daughter's decision to place the demon between herself and the horse had probably saved her life. At least, she hoped it had saved her life.

The boulder crushed the nightmarish horse just before she ran to check on her daughter. She then threw another boulder to knock the demon back.

As Nora ran towards Lucia, a blue streak dropped in front of her. She skidded to a stop and saw the archangel's sword sticking straight out of the ground, the blade half-buried in the cobblestone street. Nora looked up to see what happened to its wielder. A massive black cloud of undead ravens slammed into the roof of a building, past the line where the knights and zombies fought. At the sound of the crash, Nora knew they had gone through the roof.

Allen and Daric ran past Nora towards the Rider of Death as he regained his orientation enough to stand up. The demon's chest plate now sported a heavy dent just above the waist. Allen pulled the sword out as he ran past, dropping his own sword and shield in favor of the divine weapon.

Daric led the charge with an overhead swing. The rider deflected the attack and lifted the back half of his twin-bladed sword. Daric pulled his sword back enough to cross the blade with the demon's. Allen led his charge with a thrust aimed at the dent in the demon's armor.

Nora dropped to her knees and cradled Lucia's head. Her fingers trembled as she touched the back of her skull. She felt a touch of wetness, and when she pulled her hand back, there was a smear of blood on her fingers.

Nora gasped as she placed her hand in front of her daughter's face. She let out a sigh of relief when she felt Lucia's breath and saw the subtle rise and fall of her chest.

"I've got you, sweetie." Nora brushed a hair from the unconscious girl's face.

Nora waved her hand and stood up. The road around Lucia shifted and created a tunnel over her, keeping her safely tucked away until the rider was dealt with.

Allen swung the two-handed sword to block the rapier the demon was using now. Daric's sword bounced off the demon's armor when he hit the pauldron. Allen succeeded in blocking the attack, but the demon's other hand was surrounded by swirling black mists.

Nora wrapped the demon's arm in hardened air and used her magic to pull it backwards. The mists flew from the Rider of Death's hand and harmlessly hit a stone wall.

Allen spun around and stabbed at the rider again. This time, he impaled the demon through the gut with the divine blade.

Daric took a step back as the demon lurched and leaned forward, as if to look at the weapon. Daric rested his blade on his shoulder. "Not so tough, are you?"

Nora felt her magic get broken and felt the backlash's searing pain just behind her eyes. The Rider of Death grabbed the weapon with his other hand before stabbing through Allen's neck with his sword.

Nora shrieked when she saw the look of horror on the human she'd once raised.

The rapier shifted until it was a scythe again. The demon pulled the weapon back, decapitating the knight captain.

Daric just stared as the demon pulled the blade from his stomach and threw it away from the fight. "You cannot kill Death. I am inevitable. Now it's your turn, you mouthy pest."

Nora wrapped the air around Daric and pulled him away from the demon as it slashed the weapon. The attack missed, and Daric tumbled backwards.

Seeing that the boy was safe enough, Nora released the magic holding him and started channeling fire in her hand as she stepped towards the demon. "I said that if you touched my daughter, I would kill you."

The Rider of Death straightened up. "Ah, you are not like the rest of these peons. There is power in you. Power to rival a rider." He extended a hand. "How about you become a rider? I can guarantee you will become the next Rider of Pain, not that abomination. Your power will grow beyond the limits you thought imaginable. Then you—"

A giant fireball engulfed the rider. Bright white flames roared, and just as quickly as they appeared, they disappeared. The rider remained where he stood, his armor holding a slight red tint above the normally black metal, seemingly unfazed.

"I'll take that as a no."

Nora didn't bother responding to the demon as she lifted her other arm, and a stream of water flew from it and doused the Rider of Death. The rider stumbled back a few steps. Steam radiated off his body, and the stones surrounding him looked wrong. They were all slightly deformed.

The demon raised his arm, but another brilliant flame swallowed him up. These flames lasted a little longer. Nora had seen her friends die before. She had seen a war where thousands died from her magic. Her heart broke when she'd learned a beastkin killed her niece. Witnessing her daughter's near death and a charge's beheading was too much for her to bear.

She stopped the raging inferno around the demon. His armor was even redder, and the surrounding stones were even more deformed. The scythe he held onto so desperately before lay on the ground, just out of his reach. Before the rider could take a step, she walked forward and created another large jet of water that exploded into steam once it touched the rider's armor.

"What are you doing?" Daric stepped next to the her. "Just burn him into nothing."

Sweat poured down Nora's face and soaked her shirt. The sweat also hid the tears pouring from her eyes. "It's not enough. My sister taught me that if you heat and cool metal quickly and repeatedly, it will make it brittle."

Nora could feel her magic depleting faster with each passing moment. She stopped the water, and the steam was quickly becoming a haze that obscured everything around the demon.

The rider's black armor still stuck out enough to make him easily visible. His back was against the town's stone outer wall. There were numerous tiny cracks all over the metal.

"One more." Nora's voice was as distant as her eyes as she poured the last of her magic into one final inferno to consume the Rider of Death.

Daric shielded his eyes as he felt the heat. Nora stepped closer. She couldn't feel the heat anymore. Her heart hurt too much for her to feel anything else. She stumbled as her grip on her magic faltered. The flames died out, leaving the headless demon leaning against the wall. His armor was glowing red, and the surrounding stones melted.

Nora straightened up and screamed a primal scream. All the pain of seeing her daughter hurt and Allen's death fueled her last pull of magic. A deep pain in her bones made it hard to keep her eyes open. But she did as she lifted both her arms and poured a final torrent of water to douse the rider.

The pain continued to build. Each moment was a tortuous experience that the elven mother had never felt before. She'd felt magical exhaustion before, but this was worse. She was beyond that, and she kept pouring more magic.

Without warning, her magic stopped. There was nothing left.

Her body gave out, and she fell to her knees. Her vision turned blurry, but before she could collapse to the ground completely, a pair of fur-covered arms grabbed her.

She looked up and saw the face of her daughter. It was hard to tell which one, since she couldn't see the details well.

"Don't worry, Mom," her daughter said. "I've got you."

Nora wanted to touch her daughter's cheek, but her body wouldn't move. It was getting harder to stay awake.

Her daughter looked up. "Gifford, take my mother back to Lexia."

Nora's eyes closed as she smiled. She couldn't have been more grateful that Lucia was such a resilient girl. She was fine, and that was all that mattered.

LUCIA'S DEATH TO THE DEATHLESS

"You alright?" Daric asked me.

I placed my mother in Gifford's arms and watched him carry her through the wall of knights. "My head's killing me. It's way too hot for me right now, and I have this seething desire to rip a certain demon to shreds."

Daric pursed his lips and nodded. "Good to know." He pointed to the wall of steam with his sword. "He's in there, by the way. Oh, and, uh, your mom, she's pretty cool."

I nodded and flexed my somehow-still-ice-covered claws. *Yeah, she is.*

I don't know how long my ice will last in the sweltering heat that's making my headache even worse. One of these days, I will stop hitting my head. There was an annoying ringing in my ears, but I could pick out the sounds of the metal-covered demon through the dull roar of combat around me.

After focusing on the location of the demon through the mist, I sprinted forward. Daric followed behind me. After just a few steps, I saw the demon holding himself up by clutching his scythe dearly. He looked like an old man who could barely stand and was using his walking staff as a lifeline, not a powerful demon who claimed to be unkillable.

Too bad for you. There's no mercy for what you've done. I pounced on the demon. He fell backwards, and when he hit the ground, there was a strange crack. I looked down and saw that his breastplate had an expansive web of cracks all over it.

The Rider of Death punched me in the side. I heard even more cracking as I tumbled, grabbing where he'd hit. Daric swung at the still-prone demon with an overhead swing. The rider blocked the attack with his scythe.

He blocked Daric's attack?

Daric stumbled backwards when the demon kicked him in the gut. The rider stood up, but I noticed his movements were much slower. My inner wolf spurred me on as my vision shifted to red. The demon barely got to his feet when I slammed my shoulder into his chest.

The breastplate shattered from the impact, and shards of metal shot out in every direction. Several pieces cut me, and a few embedded in my shoulder.

When the headless demon slammed into the stone wall again, his armor shattered more. I watched his armor fall off. But the sight beneath the armor almost had me vomiting.

The skin—I think it was skin—was charred black and red, blistered and oozing black pus from several open wounds.

"Wow, you're one ugly monster." Daric's comment earned a groan from me.

I charged and slashed with my claws. The rider swung his scythe to block me. My hand wrapped around the weapon. A burning sensation followed by a feeling of weakness forced me to involuntarily release the scythe. After I let go, the demon didn't pause. He swung at me.

I ducked the attack. Not wanting to test if just touching the weapon caused the pain, I grabbed his wrist and crushed the metal vambrace. With a pull, I yanked the demon closer and buried my claws where his heart should be. I missed and only punctured his lung.

I heard Daric's heavy footsteps behind me. "Stay back. You'll only get in the way." It took a growl to stop the human.

His fighting style is too focused on wide sweeping attacks. I don't want to be dodging both him and the demon.

The demon flicked his other hand out, and I heard the sounds of something moving behind me. *Fool me once, shame on you.* I turned and grabbed the horse's legs before it could kick, spun around, and used it as a club to smash its rider.

The rider slashed with his weapon, which was now a sword again. The horse split in two, and each half missed the rider.

I released the legs and flexed my claws. "You're going to die now."

The demon lowered his sword and charged me. I jumped back and waited for him to continue with his momentum and swing again before I dropped low and swiped at his legs. The demon jumped my kick, but I uppercut my claws, leaving four deep gouges through his torso before he touched the ground again.

The demon landed and pulled his sword across his body. I leaned back and kicked at him. My toe claws sliced open another set of wounds as I followed through with a cartwheel.

The rider stabbed at me with his sword, and I performed a round-house kick on his wrist, slicing it open and nearly cutting it to the bone. With his weapon knocked wide, I rushed in and slashed his chest open with three swipes of my claws.

Chunks of burned demon flesh hit the ground with a sickening squelch.

The demon punched me in the side of the head before I could cut him a fourth time. I stumbled back, then jumped away once I saw the sword moving. When I shook the dizziness off, I could see an exposed rib cage. *If you don't have a head, let's see how you do without a heart. If that doesn't work, I'll sever each of your limbs until you're nothing but a stump.*

The demon lunged at me again. I jumped over his head and brought my claws down on his back. He swung his arm to hit me with his elbow, but I ducked it. I spun him around, and when his wide-open rib cage was in front of me, I dug my claws through his heart and out the back. Bones snapped, and I held his heart in my hand.

I grinned as I crushed it.

The demon laughed. "Removing a heart is not enough to stop me."

"Fine." I pulled my arm back out. The hole in his chest oozed more of the disgusting blood. "The hard way it is."

I let out a growl as I grabbed his sword arm and kicked him in the waist, pulling his arm taut. The sounds of flesh stretching, bones dislocating, and muscles tearing were probably audible to Daric.

The Rider of Death punched me in the hip. I growled and clenched my jaw at the pain but pulled even harder. He punched me again. I closed my eyes and kept pulling.

I was tumbling backwards when all resistance disappeared. I opened my eyes and twisted to catch myself as I fell. The Rider of Death's arm—from the elbow down to his hand, still clutching his bone weapon—was in my grip.

I heard the sound of someone hitting the ground behind me. When I stood up and turned, the headless demon was trying to push himself up with only one arm. I looked at the severed limb in my hands and tossed it behind me.

A sultry voice purred above me, "Finally."

I looked up, only to be sprayed with water and knocked off my feet. When I could see again, I watched as the Rider of Pain held the Rider of Death with one hand buried into his chest, where I'd punctured through it, and the other holding his wrist.

A colossal wall of water held back an equally enormous wall of black carrion birds. The Rider of Death kicked and shouted incoherently as he squirmed in the other rider's grip.

The demoness twisted her hand and grinned. "You'll be a lovely addition to my collection."

Water dripped from me. I couldn't get the smell of salt out of my nose—a smell that was joined by the scent of ash.

Small white flakes started flying off the Rider of Death's extremities. The Rider of Pain started glowing as her arms darkened. Her hand grabbing the wrist grew. Her fingers elongated as they turned black and sharpened into points. I couldn't see where her fingers ended and where the claws began. Two points on her forehead started bleeding as a pair of thin white horns slowly curled upward.

The zombies dropped to the ground in a tidal wave, spreading from the two demons in the air. More of the Rider of Death scattered to the wind, then all of his arms and legs were gone.

"No!" The headless demon's torso squirmed as more of his body disintegrated in the Rider of Pain's grip.

The demoness threw her head back. "Oh, yes." Her horns grew longer and curled slightly backwards as her entire body got larger.

The remaining portion of the Rider of Death suddenly burst into white flakes and fluttered into the wind.

Daric stepped next to me, dripping wet too. *It looks like he received a slight soaking also.* But in his hand was the bone weapon the Rider of Death had used. It had returned to being a scythe. *How is he holding that thing? Is it because the Rider of Death is dead?*

"What was that?" Daric asked almost breathlessly.

"That, my dear pets, was lovely." The Rider of Pain turned her head and grinned at us. Her eyes had changed into solid black pools. "And I've got two others in mind. Now all I have to do is get them here before the demon king." She waved her hand and dispelled the wall of water that held back the undead birds. She gave me a wink. "So long. I'll be back."

She flapped her wings and lifted herself higher into the sky before flying off to the south.

Daric and I looked around to see that all the walking corpses were no longer standing. Allen's headless corpse caught my attention. *How many others didn't make it? Victor... Allen... who else?*

I heard a door open, and the Archangel of Life stepped out of a building. Blood covered their body. Their three remaining wings were broken, half-severed, and heavily gashed.

"That is a worrying outcome," the angel said as they limped towards us. "She got away and is more powerful. It is unfortunate, but I can't stay. I've caused my contractor enough suffering. Tell Folmas that I apologize for all the pain." A bright light enveloped the angel's body, then they exploded into tiny showers of sparks.

I turned to look at Daric. "I have so many questions right now."

Daric nodded. "You and me both."

My head started hurting again. "Where do we even start?" I looked at all the dead and wounded. "How do we handle this? What do we do?"

Daric hoisted the bone scythe on his shoulder. "Let's go find someone in charge. My cousin, the king, should give us some answers. I heard he's here."

My eyes darted around as I looked for Victor's body. Among all the fighting with the Rider of Death, I never saw it.

There was a glint on the side of the road. I looked and saw a silver bracer. When I picked it up, each beat of my heart ached. My heart grew emptier as I traced the crude drawing of a bird on the bracer.

I couldn't keep my head up anymore. "I should check on Lexia and Mom. And maybe do something for..." My voice caught in my throat.

Daric placed a hand on my shoulder. "I... I'm sorry."

I brushed his hand off. "Let's just go."

Daric's footsteps followed me through the streets as I heard cries from survivors, moans from the wounded, and the marching of other knights and guards.

Is there any recovering from this? What was the point of all this death? Why did the Rider of Death attack here specifically? Most importantly, are Mom and Lexia okay?

42

FRAGILE

As we walked through the streets towards the courthouse, I eyed Daric closely. The Rider of Death's weapon rested comfortably on his shoulder.

"Doesn't that hurt to hold?" I pointed to the weapon.

Daric held the weapon in front of him. "No. Should it?"

"When I touched it during the fight, I felt a jolt of pain. I couldn't hold on to it even if I'd wanted to." *Was that just part of the rider's magic?* I tentatively reached for the skeletal spine. I placed a finger on it and flinched back. "Ow! Yeah, it hurts."

Daric raised his eyebrows. "It doesn't hurt. The demon seemed to cut through anything with this. Bone isn't usually a suitable material for a weapon, but this feels harder than steel. Too bad it's not a sword. I never learned how to fight with a scythe like this."

The moment the words left his lips, the bones shifted. The blade grew and tilted upward as the spine shrank. Soon Daric stared at a bone sword of a similar shape and size as the one across his back.

"You were saying?" The words fell out of my mouth without a thought. "We saw it change as we fought. It can probably become any weapon you think of."

Daric giggled. "I have a magic sword. Awesome."

I had to roll my eyes and groan so I didn't break his arm. "It's obvious that the weapon is evil. The Rider of Death was evil."

Daric rested the blade on his shoulder. "Not so. A blade is nothing more than a tool. As long as it doesn't have sentience, I'll use this weapon to be the best hero this world has ever seen."

I growled. "I thought we agreed to keep the hero talk to a minimum."

"It's a magic weapon. Do you have any idea how expensive they are?" Daric held the weapon out as if to put it on display.

"Yeah, I do." I shook my head. "Mom told me once that a knight she knew spent fifteen years saving for a magic dagger."

"What did it do?"

"Never rusted or dulled." I shrugged. "Useful, but it seems like a lot of money for something that can be remedied by just caring for your equipment like you should."

Daric glared at me. "And what would you know about caring for a weapon? You don't use one, and you barely wear armor."

I flashed my teeth. "For the record, I take good care of my teeth and claws, thank you very much." I tugged at the collar of my gambeson. "Also, I wear this gambeson because my mother wants me to. You don't need armor if you don't get hit."

"Something you fail at." Daric's snide remark earned another growl from me. He held up his free hand between us. "I wasn't the one who got knocked unconscious during the fight."

"If I recall correctly, I was the one who did more fighting." I started stomping my feet. Which didn't do any good since they were still perfectly silent.

Daric gave me a worried look. "You told me to back off. Why did you think I would only get in the way?"

I slumped my shoulders. "Your weapon is too large for small swings. Dodging both you and the demon would've taken more effort for very little gain. Besides, if I want something done right, I'll do it myself."

"Dark." The man shuddered. "Anyway, with swords, like everything else, bigger is always better." His lips curled into a massive grin as he peeked at my chest.

I rolled my eyes as I walked faster. *Men.* "It's not the size that counts. It's how you use it." I froze. *Did I just say that out loud?*

When I turned around, Daric's grin stretched even further. "That's what she..." His grin and words died when I bared my fangs.

"Go on, say it." The rumble in my voice stopped his breathing. I crossed my arms and tapped my toe claws on the stone road. "I'm waiting."

"I..." Daric swallowed hard. His eyes darted around. "I don't think it's funny anymore."

"How does every man turn every conversation into a chance to gloat about his penis?" I pinched the bridge of my nose. "I mean it. Seriously. How? Women don't want to hear about that." Daric tilted his head. "After I turned thirteen and went into heat for the first time, I had an entire season of men trying to attract me. But your 'will you marry me?' still surpasses them all."

"Wow." Daric stood with his mouth gaping. "Well, I mean, how much experience do you actually have?"

"One, that's none of your business." I poked a claw at his chest. Daric stumbled back a couple of steps. "And two, beastkin pick one mate, and I've..." I looked down and realized I was still holding Victor's silver bracelet. The one etched with his crude, lovely drawing of a bird.

Tears started flowing from my eyes.

"Oh, no. No, no. I didn't mean to bring that up." Daric dropped his weapon and placed his hands on my shoulders. "I'm sorry. I didn't mean to..."

I shoved him into the nearest wall, then I cradled the bracelet as I fell to my knees. *He's gone.* "He's gone." My words echoed my thoughts as my heart burned. They fueled a wail that I couldn't hold back.

A pair of arms hugged me. A small yet firm shoulder caught my tears as I grabbed whoever it was. I don't know how long I cried before I could get ahold of myself. I wiped my face on the cloth covering the chain armor, too tired to cry anymore.

"Feel better?" The voice was smooth, almost melodic, and familiar.

I looked up at Escaeris and her blue eyes. Her teal hair was a horrible mess, and her face was covered in a lot of dirt. "Do you need help?"

I looked down at her now snot-and-tear-soaked shoulder. "No, I don't."

"To which one?"

"Both." I sat on the ground and let the bracelet drop from my fingers.

"That doesn't make sense." Escaeris sat next to me. "Could you at least tell me if you know if it's over? All the undead just stopped moving and fell over. Do you know what happened?"

I continued to stare blankly at the ground. "Yeah, it's over for now."

"For your safety, I wouldn't ask more than that." Daric's voice was hoarse as he coughed. "She's upset because someone very close to her died."

"Oh." To her credit, Escaeris didn't flinch. Instead, she wrapped an arm around me. "Do you need me to stay?"

"I'm done crying, if that's what you're asking." *There are no tears left.*

"It's not," Escaeris answered. "I want to know if you need me to stay with you. Do you need to talk with someone? Do you need anything?"

I shook my head. "No, I'll just... You know what? I don't know what to do."

"How about we start with introductions?" Daric stepped in front of Escaeris and extended a hand. "My name's Daric."

"Escaeris Teal Aqua. I've already met Lucia." She nodded towards me. "We're in the same knight company." She took Daric's hand and shook it.

"So, what were you doing before you found us?" Daric started looking around.

Escaeris bolted up. "Elasha." Her head darted from side to side. "I need to find my sister. We got separated when a dire boar zombie destroyed our shield wall. We had to fall back. I got lost. Have you seen her?"

"I don't think so." Daric picked up his new magical weapon. "How about Lucia and I help you find her?" He looked at me. "Come on. You need something to do." He held out a hand for me.

I ignored his help and stood up. "Sure, I'll help. It's not like I can think of anything else to do." The words felt empty, almost as empty as I was.

"No." Escaeris held up her hands. "You don't have to do that. Why don't you just go home and get some sleep? Uh, where's your home?"

Daric lowered her arms. "It's fine. She needs this. It'll give her something else to think about." He started off in another direction. "So, what does your sister look like?"

"They're twins," I mumbled.

"Oh, that'll make things easier." Daric almost sounded happy, even if he was forcing it. "Uh, her name was Elsa, right?"

"Elasha," Escaeris corrected as she followed Daric. "Her name's Elasha. Maybe if we check closer to the gate, we'll find her. But I don't know which way that is. I've always been kind of bad with directions."

"North's this way." I waved and led the way.

The two followed behind me for a bit before Escaeris started whispering to Daric. "Is this really a good idea? Maybe she should just call it a day. It's been a long day, for her especially."

"It's been a long day for me too." Daric didn't bother whispering. "But no, she needs a goal. Something to focus on." There was a slight pause. "She'll hear us anyway. So whispering is pointless."

"Oh, is her hearing that good?"

"Yes, it is," I called back.

Escaeris squeaked. "Okay, but why? What is the point?"

"Because I need to get her to her mother." Daric's tone turned somber. "I know it sounds like she's a spoiled mommy's girl, but it's not like that for her. In fact, I'm a bit jealous of her. She has one person in her life she can always go back to. Me? My father has his expectations of me, and he really isn't my father. I barely know my mother. The one person who took any interest in me has more or less let me figure things out on my own. Seeing her and her mother makes me wish I had someone like that in my life."

I... He can't be serious, can he? I turned around and saw Daric nearly on the verge of tears. He stopped walking. Escaeris also stopped in her tracks.

"Is that why you want to be a hero?" I walked up and wiped his eye. "You're just looking for someone to accept you?"

"You make it sound so shallow." Daric grabbed my hand. "No, I want to be a hero because it's the right thing to do. But I also want someone who cares for me. I've never had anyone fall in love with me, ever. I thought maybe I might have a chance now."

My heart ached again. This time it was a dull thrum. "Don't do that to yourself. You'll only be inviting more devastating pain later." I turned and walked away as Daric's jaw swung freely.

Whoever came up with the saying "'Tis better to have loved and lost than never to have loved at all" needs to have his heart ripped out of his chest.

"Don't say that." Escaeris ran up to me and put her hands up. "You're grieving. You don't mean that."

I shrugged and walked past her. "So what if I am?"

"Then you need to grieve," another voice called from our side. Captain Aenwyn strode towards us. A significant amount of blood covered her; some of it was hers. There was a heavy limp in her right leg. "Grieving is natural. You need to take care of yourself. We already had this talk."

"Daric's right, I need to be distracted." I turned away from everyone. "Please, don't make me feel. I don't want to. It hurts too much."

"Then you need to take a step back." Aenwyn's voice was soft. She limped over to me. "Come on, let's go see your friend. Can you help me? It seems my leg has received quite a nasty gash."

Escaeris scrambled next to the elven captain. "Captain, have you seen my sister?"

Aenwyn slowly closed her eyes as she exhaled even more slowly. "I'm sorry. The boar disrupted everything, and fighting it and the other zombies was too much."

Escaeris stumbled back. "No, no, no," she said as she shook her head.

"We lost many good knights, your sister included." The words sounded difficult for Aenwyn to say. "Too many were lost."

The death toll continues to climb.

Escaeris looked like she tried to hold back her tears, but it was a wasted effort. She started crying, and Daric dropped the bone sword again and grabbed the elf before she slumped to the ground. Captain Aenwyn looked exhausted and a bit detached from the situation. She walked up and placed her hand on Daric's shoulder as Escaeris wailed.

"You see that street over there?" She pointed, and Daric nodded. "Down that road one block and look south. Take her there when she's ready. Let her find closure." Daric nodded again. Aenwyn turned her attention to me. "I was serious. I need help. Do you want to help me get to an infirmary?"

I looked at Escaeris one more time and felt guilty. *She's on her own now. Her sister's gone, and I can't comfort her. I don't know how. I'm just as big a mess as she is.*

"Okay." *I need to get out of all this. I'm in no position to help those who've lost others.* "Can we try to find Fina, Lexia, and Mom too?"

Aenwyn looked like she was thinking something through. "Of course." She limped up to me. "And I want you to know that none of this is your fault. You did everything you could have."

"You don't know that." I scooped the elf captain into my arms, eliciting a slight shriek from her. "If I had been there, he would still be alive." *What if I had taken the demon's deal? Maybe none of this would've happened. What if...*

Aenwyn just held on to me and closed her eyes. "I'm too tired to have this debate with you again. Hopefully, your mother can talk some sense into you. Because it looks like you're not going to listen to me, no matter what I say. But believe me when I say I am sorry for your loss and truly wish you didn't have to suffer like this. I'm sure Victor was a great man."

How did she know Victor died? Actually, no. No more talking. And no more thinking. "Just shut up," I grumbled as I carried her towards the center of town.

"As you wish," Aenwyn said softly. "But one last thing. Lexia and

Fina were safe last I saw them. They were helping other knights to an infirmary. The closest one would be the best place to start looking."

"Thanks." *They're safe. That's good. But how did Aenwyn know they were helping knights? It's fine. So long as they didn't do any fighting. Helping others is fine. Hopefully fewer lives were lost because of them.*

I carried her through the streets, blocking out every sound and scent. My eyes were glued to the ground in front of me. Despite my efforts, thoughts would leak through my mind, but one kept returning more than the others. *What was the point of all this?*

The weight of Captain Aenwyn's limp form was heavier than I was expecting. The day's events were catching up with me. *It looks like I'm at my limit.* As we got to the center of town, more people came out of hiding and were moving around. Some assisted the wounded, some carried bodies out, and some carried supplies. One woman with her arms full of bandages caught my attention.

"Hey!" I called out. Several people around me stopped and looked, including the one I wanted to. I nodded at the woman I wanted to talk. "You, do you know where there are other beastkin at an infirmary?"

"The nearest infirmary is over there." The woman pointed behind her.

I shook my head. "But are there any beastkin there? I'm looking for my sister."

"Please, just humor her," Captain Aenwyn added. Her voice seemed quieter.

The woman's eyes shifted. "There is. A white fox beastkin and someone who looks a lot like you. That might be your sister."

I relaxed a bit, but when Aenwyn's weight shifted, I stiffened. "Good. And yeah, she's my sister."

The lady nodded, and I went to where she pointed. Following another couple of wounded knights, I found the infirmary and placed the captain on an empty bed.

A younger boy ran up to us. "How is she? Does she need immediate aid?" His face grimaced and turned a little green at the edges. "Is... Is all that blood hers?"

"No, not all of it," Aenwyn answered with her eyes closed. "But more than I'd like. I'm getting lightheaded."

The boy turned and cupped his hands around his mouth. I covered my ears. "Sharra! Blood loss and lightheadedness. Coherent."

A woman who looked like she should have great-grandchildren, and I assumed was likely Sharra, stood up and nodded. She pointed towards us and spoke to a man working beside her. "I'll finish up here. Go and get her wounds cleaned and stop the worst of the bleeding. Cauterize if you must."

I gave Aenwyn one last worried look. *It sounds like they have a system. But things are going to get worse for her before they get better. Hopefully she pulls through. I don't know how much more I can take.*

I looked around the building and saw some stairs with my sister standing at the base of them.

Lexia's eyes widened as she caught sight of me, and her mouth wordlessly opened and closed. "Lucia." After the initial shock wore off, she ran towards me, dodging all the people working. "What happened?"

My voice trembled as I caught her and embraced her. "Captain Aenwyn needed help. Where's Mom?"

Lexia lowered her head as she pulled me towards the stairs. *Please, no. Not her too.* Together, we weaved through the labyrinth of injured and working doctors. Lexia didn't say a word and barely picked up her feet. Her tail hardly moved as she kept leading me through the second-floor hall. Finally, Lexia guided me to a room with five other people in cots lining the walls and an extra empty bed.

Mom was lying on a cot, her breathing shallow.

My legs almost gave out on me as I stumbled towards my mother. Gifford was standing next to her bed. His eyes barely focused on any one thing.

I kneeled next to her and listened to her breathing. *She's breathing; that's good. That's really good.* I brushed a stray strand of her green hair to the side and saw sweat on her brow.

"What's wrong, Mom?" I whispered.

"Zenny said she's magically exhausted and somehow pushed past that." I could hear the pain in Lexia's voice. "Also, she has a fever and desperately needs to stay in bed until it breaks."

I snapped my head around. "Zenny, she's here? She's safe?"

Lexia walked over and hugged me. "She is, and she's safe. So are you. And don't worry, Evalana isn't in the city." I let myself melt into her arms. "I don't know what to say. Gifford told me what happened."

"No, Lexia, please; don't say anything," I whispered in her ear. *Hopefully, Daric can tell them what happened with the rider.* "Not now. I can't... I just can't. Sis, I'm so tired."

She shushed me and brushed a piece of my hair out of my face. "Then go to sleep. You've done more than enough. You don't owe these people any more. I'll take care of you now. Don't worry."

My vision blurred at the edges. I could have pushed her arms away from me, but I didn't want to. They felt warm. *I just want to let go. Maybe I should. There's nothing more I can do. While my body can keep going, I can't. Everyone else is here to take care of things. I should let them.*

I looked up as the black edges of my vision slowly grew. There were tears in my sister's eyes. Just before my vision went completely black, I mustered enough energy to smile for her.

I didn't get to see her reaction before I accepted the sweet oblivion and peace of sleep.

43

LEXIA'S CARE

Lucia looks so peaceful now that she's sleeping. I stared at my sister's sleeping face. The tears I'd held back flowed. *These people don't deserve your sacrifice.*

"Is she..." Gifford's voice shook.

I set my cheek on her forehead. I could feel her shallow breathing on my fur. "No, she's just sleeping."

Gifford crouched next to me and offered a hand. "Then maybe we should get her to bed. It'll take both of us to carry her like this." His voice was quiet in consideration of Lucia's needs.

I scowled. "She's not fat." I made sure to keep my volume low too.

Gifford chuckled. "It's all muscle, I know." He placed his arms under Lucia's. "Come on, love."

He's right. I can't keep her like this. She'd likely have a horrible kink in her tail when she wakes up.

Together, we lifted her up and carried her to the last remaining bed in the room. I went and found an extra blanket to place over her. The entire time we were moving her, she never stirred. *They really don't deserve her. Daric was right. She really is a hero at heart. I don't care if she doesn't see it that way.*

Gifford wrapped his arm around my waist and pulled me close as we watched my sister sleep. "How are you doing?" he whispered in my ear.

My stomach answered for me with a gentle growl. "It seems I can't ignore my hunger anymore. And we should tell Zenny that she's here and sleeping."

Gifford released me and moved to the door. "How about you talk to Zenny? I'll go and see if I can find us some food." He looked at the room full of people who were also recovering. A look of guilt spread across his face. "Maybe find food for everyone here. We should try to help everyone else too."

I also looked at each of the beds, especially the ones with my sister and adoptive mother. *Lucia's not the only one who's given herself to protecting this city. Others have given their lives too. Maybe I shouldn't be too hard on them, given the circumstances. But they can't ask her to give anymore. Not until I know she's ready. She's too young to have gone through so much pain, both physical and emotional.*

I nodded to my mate, and he left. *These humans better remember Victor. He gave his life to defend them. He died in a kingdom far from his home because he followed his love. I will make sure they remember him.*

I walked out of the room and down the stairs. I looked around and into the other rooms until I found Zenny. She was stitching someone's back with an expressionless look on her face. Sweat dripped from her eyebrow into her eye. She flinched and wiped it with her shoulder. Her hands were covered in blood, but even still, she held the needle and thread without trouble. I let the woman work and waited for her to finish.

Zenny tied off the thread and cut the excess before grabbing a bandage and turning to a small elf girl, likely eleven or twelve, to hand it to her. "Bandage him up tightly." Zenny stood up straight, placed her bloody hands on her apron, and let out a prolonged sigh. For a brief moment, I saw how tired she really was, before a smile spread across her lips and her eyes opened wide. *Others are giving all of themselves too.*

"Hello, Lexia. Need something?" Her voice was upbeat, as if she hadn't spent the entire night stitching, bandaging, cleaning, and doing whatever else she could for others' wounds.

I lowered my head, drooping my ears, and let my tail hang low and motionless behind me. The ache in my voice was palpable. "Lucia's here."

Zenny's calm happiness shattered into panic as she ran towards me. "Where? How bad is it?"

I caught her. "She's upstairs, sleeping." The human's body slumped. "But she's exhausted. And there was a wound on the back of her head. If you could, please check that out."

She didn't tell me she'd hit her head. She probably wouldn't tell me just to keep me from worrying about her. Too bad for you, Lucia. Your sister's going to make sure you receive nothing but the best treatment. You can thank me later. Because you know, you have the best sister in the world.

I quietly closed the door behind me as I followed Zenny into the room where Lucia slept. The last dim moonlight filtered through the window, casting a soft glow on my sister's face. *She's so strong and skilled, yet so vulnerable too. Sis, why can't you just take care of yourself? You can leave these humans anytime, but you don't. Why?*

Zenny's eyes narrowed as she observed Lucia's head. Her hands gently lifted Lucia's head, turning it enough to see the blood-soaked hair. She clicked her tongue. "That's a serious wound. She should have seen a doctor immediately."

I nodded, a frown pulling at my lips. "I know. But you know how stubborn Lucia is. She'll finish her job first before she even considers taking care of herself."

"It's what makes her special." Zenny smiled and reached for a clean cloth and some water from a nearby bucket. "Well, we can at least clean it up and bandage it properly now."

"She'll be sleeping for a while," I said as I brushed her cheek, feeling the warmth in her fur.

Together, we gently cleaned the wound. Zenny's skilled hands worked articulately, cleaning the blood and small pieces of debris from her hair. As we finished bandaging it, I couldn't help but smile. My sister's rhythmic breathing didn't change. The subtle rise and fall of her chest helped keep me calm. *She better not forget me this time.*

Zenny let out a chuckle. "Lucia sure is a heavy sleeper."

I laughed softly, making sure I didn't wake anyone up. "Oh, you have no idea. She doesn't sleep much, but when she does, it's impossible to wake her up sometimes. And don't get me started on getting her out of bed. That girl loves her cold ice bed. I kind of want one now too."

As we sat by Lucia's bedside, my laughter faded, and I flattened my ears as my head lowered. I leaned in closer to Zenny. "Gifford told me something... about Victor. He didn't make it, Zenny. He died, and Lucia killed his undead body. Victor was Lucia's mate."

Zenny's eyes widened, and her hand instinctively covered her mouth before she reached for me. "Oh, I'm so sorry. I can't even imagine what you must be feeling. And she..." She turned to Lucia.

Words didn't leave her lips for several breaths. "Lucia never told me she fell in love. She never told me a lot of things. Growing up, she liked to joke that she would never get married and have kids. She would tell me everything. Then it seemed like something happened, and she started avoiding me. If she loved this Victor enough to call him her mate... I know I saw the look in her eyes when she saw him when we first arrived back in town, but it's still a big step for her. And now that he's dead, she'll be devastated." Zenny squeezed my hand. "But you—you look just as bad as I imagine she'll feel. Are you alright?"

I nodded, a lump forming in my throat. "It hurts, Zenny. It hurts so much. Losing him hurts, but being unable to help Lucia hurts more. Seeing her in so much pain—nothing I feel compares to the pain she's in. The worst part is, she won't let anyone help her. She's shutting out the world. I don't want her to shut me out." I pulled my knees in and curled my tail over my feet.

Zenny grabbed my other hand and squeezed it. "You're not alone, Lexia. We know Lucia is beyond stubborn. We'll make her see that we can be just as stubborn." A smile crept on her face. "She'll just have to get used to seeing us more than ever. I won't let her out of my sight, and we definitely can't let her be alone for anything but sleep now."

My tail started wagging as I joined in on her infectious smile. "You agree? She'll try to run, but we'll chase her no matter where she goes."

Zenny helped me to my feet. "When she gets tired from running, we'll be there to pick her up."

Yes, we will. The more I see Zenny, the more I see why Lucia became good friends with her. Why did she avoid her? Maybe she was being immature again. It looks like the big sister has to show her little sister how to be mature.

As we made our way back downstairs, I could hear the sounds of people talking and moving more. Gifford approached us with some wrapped food, then resumed distributing rations to everyone in the infirmary. Zenny and I looked down together; our hands were still stained with the remnants of Lucia's blood. We washed up quickly before sitting for a moment and eating the sandwiches my mate gave us.

You know, this bread isn't all that great. It's so hard and thick. Meat is always nice, but this cheese is so weird.

After I finished eating, I glanced around at the people in the room, their exhaustion etched on their faces. *It would be wrong for me to do nothing. Gifford's helping, and he said we should help.* "Zenny, I want to help. I want to stay close and watch over Lucia. Can I help you?"

Zenny smiled warmly. It seemed less forced. "Of course, Lexia. Thank you. Having an extra pair of hands would be tremendously useful."

Gifford assisted with lifting the injured, carefully maneuvering them in and out of the beds. I watched him, impressed by his gentleness. *He's different too. Maybe this place has been growing on him. Is that the secret? These humans are selfish and slow to trust, but they're resilient, as evidenced by the way they band together in times of crisis. Even the beastkin back home could learn a thing or two.*

As Zenny worked on a patient, I stood by her side. My claws worked great to cut excess string and bandages. Whenever Zenny asked, I ran and grabbed supplies. The air was filled with a chorus of bustling activity as I saw a few younger kids scurrying around, eagerly helping. Their energy was contagious, and I couldn't help but admire the sense of community that surrounded me. A small smile tugged at the corners of my lips.

My vision slowly started blurring. Everyone was slowing down since no other people had been brought in for a while now. *It seems the worst has passed.*

I placed a hand on Zenny's shoulder. "I've gotta sit down."

My body was quickly giving up on me. The ride back, the fighting on the wall, helping Zenny with the wounded—it was becoming too much to stay awake. I'd seen several others stop working and walk out. Half the staff was still finishing up the final minor injuries.

Zenny turned and gave me a nod. "Yes, sit down. We don't want to add you to our list of patients. Your sister will never forgive me if you collapsed while helping me."

She blinked, but her eyes stayed shut for a few moments longer than they should have.

"Apparently I'm not the only one who's about to collapse." I nudged her with my elbow.

Zenny yawned. "Just one more," she replied, not bothering to hide her sleepiness.

"Kid, you don't have to prove anything." The man whose hand Zenny was putting in a splint placed his other hand over hers. "Look, this isn't life-threatening. You've been working all night, right? I know how you feel. So take your friend and get some sleep. I can finish this up from here."

Zenny let go. Her calm, determined look was gone. Nothing but relief and exhaustion remained. She grabbed my hand and wordlessly led me away, her eyes half-closed. Gifford turned to follow us.

I pointed to the stairs. "Go and make sure Lucia's safe. Then get some sleep yourself." While he did a better job of hiding it than most, I imagine he had to be just as tired as everyone else. Just as we made it to the door, a small crowd of people opened it and walked into the infirmary. I froze and watched as, one by one, the people walked up to a doctor, whom they gently relieved by taking over after asking at most a question or two. The new arrivals were awake and alert, as if they had spent the night sleeping.

I looked out the door and had to shield my eyes from the sun. Five more people walked through the door; I recognized three of them. Daric followed behind the man I had met just before the siege: Aurtour, King of Rophmna. His armor was covered in dents, dirt, and gore. And beside Daric walked another familiar face, one I hadn't seen since the start of the water season—Dinar. The elf had her hood pulled up to cover her bald head, while her gray eyes darted around like she was looking for someone. Her clothes were clean and pristine.

There was another elf next to Daric who looked like she'd spent the entire night crying. Her face was red, her eyes bloodshot, and she barely lifted her feet as she walked. I then saw how she clung to Daric's arm. She wore the armor of The Maidens, and after scanning through my memories, I knew the face belonged to Escaeris. Blood and dirt covered her as much as they did the king.

Another man, larger than both Aurtour and Daric, followed them. He was also bald, and he had several scars on his face, the most prominent one being the claw marks on the side of his head. *Gifford told me about Drue and how he's a friendly man.* He was probably the dirtiest of them all. The scars were difficult to see through the blood and dirt covering him.

Other than Escaeris, none of them looked like they were going to fall over at any moment.

Daric waved a hand at me. "Lexia, you're alright. Lucia will be happy to hear that. Have you seen her? Your sister, I mean."

"I have, and she's sleeping upstairs right now," I said as I turned to watch Gifford go up the stairs. "Why?"

Aurtour stepped forward. "I wish to talk to her."

My tail stuck straight out. I pushed Zenny back and growled. "You won't."

"Lexia, calm down." Dinar ran to stand between us and raised her arms. "He's the king."

I continued to growl and started flexing my claws. "I know, but I don't care. No one will disturb Lucia. Not while I'm alive."

"There's no need for such sentiments." Aurtour pulled Dinar back. "If you want us to wait for her to wake up, then we shall wait." I relaxed my claws, but my tail continued to lash behind me. "All I want to do is talk. I understand she's been through a lot."

I glared at him. "You don't understand. None of you humans do."

Zenny walked around and glared at me. "Then you should do a better job and make them understand. Teach them why. Tell them about her pain. This isn't the time to fight."

I flinched. *What?* "How can I tell them? They aren't beastkin; they don't know what it feels like."

Drue cleared his throat. "Um, while I hate to interrupt, it's been a very long night. Everyone is suffering." He motioned towards Escaeris. "Some more than others, but I think Lucia has the smart idea. Why don't we all just stop and rest? The doctors from Caska brought supplies with them. While they take care of things, let's get some sleep nearby. Then when Lucia wakes up, we can talk to her." Drue's deep yet softer voice drained all the tension from the room.

"Do you have a place you were going to sleep?" Aurtour extended a hand towards Zenny and me.

I looked at Zenny, and she gave me a nod. "We can trust him, Lexia. He won't do anything. Especially not since his sister is one of Lucia's friends."

I glared at Aurtour again. *I can't bring myself to trust you, but I trust Zenny. So if she says it's safe, I'll go.* I gave her a nod.

Zenny turned back to Aurtour and nodded to him. "We had a place, but if I know Lucia like I think I do, the first thing she'll do when she wakes up is check up on her mother and then look for Lexia. Having her close will guarantee she has a conversation with you."

Aurtour turned to look at Daric. Daric smiled. "Yeah, those two are quite close. It's almost terrifying what they'll do for one another."

The king nodded. "Okay, there's a company headquarters we've been given rooms to sleep in nearby."

"You better have a lot of food ready too." Everyone turned to look at me. "My sister has an appetite, and when she wakes up, food will help keep her calmer."

Aurtour laughed. "I think we can come up with some meat for her. Everyone else will just have to make do with a little less meat in their rations."

We walked out of the infirmary after leaving instructions for

Lucia on where to find me if she woke up before us. But the moment we walked into the street, I felt like someone was watching me.

"Well, well, well. Isn't my little pet taking care of her little sister?"

My blood froze at the sound of the velvety voice.

I snapped my head around and looked towards the roof of the infirmary. Sitting on the edge of the roof was the sin of lust. She looked very different from when I'd last seen her. Her skin was the wrong color. She had hooves, horns, and black claws. My instincts warned me to stay far away, and the memories of her inside my head only reinforced those feelings.

She leaned forward as she kicked her hooves from where they dangled. "You think you've won, and now it's time to rest, am I right?" Nobody answered. We just stared at her naked red skin. "It seems my plans are ruined, and I have to stop his plans first."

"What are you talking about, demon?" Aurtour's voice was loud and firm. The people in the street stopped and turned to watch the demon too.

The demoness smiled. "I want to wake up the wolf girl. But it seems someone put a rather strong sleep spell on her." She waved her hand in a circle as she shrugged. "Also, there might be this little thing about her wanting to rip me apart at the sight of me. She'll not listen to a word I say."

"What do you want with my sister?" I leaned forward and flexed my claws. "Why can't you just leave her alone? If you need to tell her something, tell me. I'll tell her."

"I'm not interested in you anymore, pet." The boredom in the demoness's voice was thick. "I'm out to bag something much larger and more powerful. But I need your sister, and therefore you, to make sure my plans go the way I want them to. But I've found a little meddler."

The succubus raised her other hand and held out a creature I'd never seen before. Dangling from her grasp was a snake that then shifted into the upper half of a woman. Scales covered her body from tail to head. The lower half of her snake body shimmered in a coat of emerald diamonds all along her back and sides. Contrasting the vivid scales, the underbelly of her serpentine half displayed a series of muted jade ones.

The portion of the creature that looked like a woman was, without a doubt, beautiful. Her skin, tinted a lush shade of green, possessed a mesmerizing texture that mimicked delicate scales. The creature's waist seamlessly transitioned from a snake to a tight stomach that gracefully curved into an enticing hourglass figure complemented by an ample and alluring bust.

Her face, almost rivaling the captivating beauty of Lust's, displayed sharp and defined features in contrast to Lust's soft and inviting curves. The same green, scale-like texture enveloped her face, emphasizing her features even more. A pair of plump, dark-green lips parted slightly, revealing four elongated fangs dripping with venom. But it was her eyes that held the most captivating allure—two glowing, narrow slits of emerald green, drawing all attention towards them. Despite the mesmerizing gaze, one could not help but notice the writhing mass of serpents composing her hair. Each snake, alive and livid, would extend to the middle of her back if they were to go limp. Instead, they snapped with an unsettling hostility towards the demon that held their mistress captive.

Even more surprising, she was only as long as Lust's torso. The fact that the demon was holding the little green monster by her tail showed who was in charge.

"You see, this little pest put the sleep spell on your dear, sweet sister, my pet." Lust dangled the snake woman for emphasis.

Despite the rough treatment, the scaled woman reached for the demoness with both her snake hair and hands. "You made me put that spell on everyone in that room, traitor." Venom spat from her lips as she spoke. I watched the green drops hit the ground and heard the slight sizzle of the stone.

"Your plans failed once. And now, I used your own plan against you." Envy's cocky tone didn't match her scowling face and spitting hair-snakes. "We all knew you lacked devotion once something new caught your eye, but treason is a whole new low. When the demon king gets here, I'll enjoy watching you suffer before he ends your pathetic little uprising."

We should back up a bit. I wasn't the only one who had that thought, as we all took a step back simultaneously.

Lust sighed. "There you go, ruining the surprise. If we keep ruining each other's fun, nobody will have any fun. So do me a favor and *shut up.*" She waved her hand. A sphere of water wrapped around the dangling woman's face. "No talking until I tell you to."

The snake woman tried to claw the bubble of water, but her hands couldn't enter it. She continued flailing, seemingly accomplishing nothing. But the fear of drowning wasn't in her eyes as she continued to glare at Lust.

Dinar placed a hand on my shoulder and gave me a nod as she stepped forward. "What are you planning? Am I right to assume that's the sin of envy? Why go through all this effort just to talk?"

The demoness eyed the elf. "Yes, I always have plans. And yes, Envy here, in all her minuscule glory, thought that she could beat me to the finish. She only has to create one more blood anchor to succeed. I need you to stop its creation."

The look on Lust's face made my heart race. *She's serious.*

"The Rider of Death's whole goal was to finish summoning the demon king. He headed for the largest cities one by one, leaving a trail of death and blood anchors on his way to kill me. I lured him here because I needed something to motivate the sleeping wolf girl. All this killing created more than enough blood to make the final blood anchor. Envy's little pet project snuck in with your relief efforts."

Aurtour turned to Drue. "Get every single knight that can stand to search for anyone who's doing anything demon-related. If they're acting suspiciously or have never been seen before, detain them. Go, now!" He shoved Drue and took off in the other direction.

The demoness pointed to the human king as he ran. "That's why." She returned her gaze to me. "So, pet, do you want to make a deal?"

"Don't," Daric said from behind me. "Remember what happened last time? Don't do that to Lucia."

I shook my head. *But Lucia.* Then I turned to face the demoness. A fire burned in my heart as I flexed my claws. "And what's stopping me from killing you and releasing my sister?"

The wicked smile she gave me as she leaned forward doused all my courage. She held a hand towards Envy. All the snakes bit into it. The demoness didn't even flinch as each snake head undoubtedly emptied every drop of venom they had into her. "Can you? I don't think so."

She pulled her hand back, and all the fangs from the snakes came with it. The medusa squirmed even more violently as she grabbed at the defanged snakes on her head. There was no doubt she was screaming in agony, but we couldn't hear anything.

"I am both the Rider of Pain and Death. Killing me is far beyond you. And if the demon king arrives, no one will be able to stop him." Lust flicked her wrist. The fangs clattered to the ground and blood trickled from her blackened hand and arm. "I need time, and your sister will give it to me. If you want to know where the blood anchor is being created and your sister to wake up from her slumber—which, by the way, will last years—then you will convince your sister to summon and weaken the other two riders for me."

I looked at everyone around me, each one in turn: Daric, Zenny, Dinar, and Escaeris. They each gave me a sad look. *What do I do? What can I do? I'm so sorry, sis. I failed to protect you, and now I have to make another deal with a demon just to save you again.*

"I don't want to." I couldn't look at the demoness anymore. A foul taste built up in the back of my throat. *I hate her. I hate her. She'll never leave us alone.* "Why can't you find someone else? Haven't we suffered enough?"

"Because your sister is one of a kind. Finding anyone even close to her capabilities is hard enough. This little snake found one, filled him with her venom, and controlled him. But even without her, he will still carry out his mission because he can't think of anything else anymore." Lust sighed. "Look, time is short. How about I sweeten the deal, hmm? You can keep your free will and I'll even let you accompany her. I'll mark you and know your exact location at all times. In return, you convince your sister to make a deal with me."

I clecnched my jaw and refused to answer her. *There's got to be another way.*

Lust rolled her eyes. "Look. I don't have a lot of time to deal with you. Last chance, if your sister agrees to help me, I'll even help your adoptive mother."

What? "My mother? What's wrong with her?" I stepped towards the door. "She's just in need of rest. She'll be fine, right?" I turned to Zenny.

Zenny clenched her jaw. "I don't know. I've never seen an elf magically exhaust themselves."

Escaeris gasped. "She didn't. She shouldn't have."

"What?" I grabbed the teal-haired elf. "What is it?"

"I'm sorry, but magically, exhaustion for an elf is often lethal." I turned to look at Dinar, whose apology was genuine. Tears started falling down her cheeks. "I was lucky when I magically exhausted myself earlier this year for your sister. I quickly recovered, so I wasn't in much danger."

Zenny sniffled. "Your mother pushed herself even beyond that."

My knees gave out. *No! Why? Why me? I can't do this. She's going to die. My sister will never wake up, and we're all going to die.* Tears streamed from my eyes as I stood up.

"Lexia, don't." Daric grabbed my shoulder before I turned around.

"You humans will never understand." I shoved him and stood up. Then I said the two words that would haunt me forever—again. "I accept."

"Good." The demoness snapped her fingers, and the water bubble popped, releasing Envy.

"No!" Envy screamed as she attempted to defend herself.

We watched the rider swipe her clawed hand and remove the medusa's head instantly. The head hit the ground and cracked and bounced twice before settling. The horror on her face was frozen.

Then the rest of her body hit the ground with a sickening crunch.

I looked up and saw the succubus floating in front of me with a hand outstretched, still dripping with Envy's blood. She was much taller than before. She towered over me. "Shall we, my pet?"

44

LUCIA'S BAD DECISIONS

I slowly opened my eyes. Everything blurred as my vision swayed. *Hopefully Lexia took some time to rest while I've been asleep. How long was I out this time?* The sun attempted to filter in through the shutters covering the window. *Was it a day? I was pretty exhausted.* One by one, each memory came back, starting out as fragments, but the holes quickly filled in. *I nearly died twice and faced a lot of danger on the wall.*

The memory of my claws as I dug them into Victor's brain haunted me the most. I looked down at my claws. The feeling of them inside his skull sent a shiver down my spine. It felt like his blood was still on my hands. I wanted to wipe it off, but there wasn't anything to wipe off. My hands felt disgusting, no matter how much I rubbed them on the sheet covering me. I rubbed as hard as I could, but my claws started shredding the cotton bedding.

I growled in frustration, but it quickly died and devolved into more sobbing. *Victor's gone. He's not coming back. I let myself have a mate, and this whole siege happened. Now he's dead, and there was nothing I could do to save him. Why am I so useless? I didn't kill the Rider of Death. Everything is his fault, and I couldn't make him pay. No, that sin of lust absorbed him. She got what she wanted in the end.*

I bundled the shredded bedding into a ball and buried my face in it before letting out a howl. *Why me? Why is this all happening to me? So what if I agreed to defend this world from the demon king? What does all this suffering have to do with that? Daric lived a nice, cozy, and cushy life. Why does it seem like everything good that happens to me always gets taken away? What's next? Something happens to Lexia? Something happens to Mom?*

When I thought about Mom, I remembered her condition the last time I saw her. A wave of dizziness hit me as I swung my head around to look for her.

She was still in the bed, covered in a similar sheet to the one I had ruthlessly shredded. Her body was terrifyingly still. I focused on my ears as I turned to get up.

The wave of dizziness washed over me again as I attempted to sit up. My muscles ached, but that was nothing compared to what my mother would likely feel when she woke up. *She's going to wake up, right? Right?*

I tumbled out of the bed, barely catching myself when my legs wouldn't hold me up. But I focused on my mother's still-sleeping form and demanded my body pull me closer. It didn't matter how much it didn't want to move. *I can rest once I know Mom's going to be okay. You're okay, Mom. I'll make it okay.*

Once I dragged my body across the room to my mother, my heart stopped, and it almost didn't start back up. Her breathing was barely audible, even with my sharp hearing. I put my nose on her forehead, and I could feel the heat and see the sweat soaking her face.

No. No, no, no! Why? She's just magically exhausted, right? Some rest is all she needs, right? Maybe if I give her my magic, she'll feel better.

I tenderly grabbed her head and placed my forehead against hers. After pulling all my magic to my head, I guided it into my mother.

There was no change.

More. She just needs more. Pulling every bit of magic I could find in my body, I shoved it into hers. I felt the emptiness of magic fatigue throughout my body. But it still wasn't enough to help my mother.

I did what I knew I shouldn't have done. I pulled for more magic.

There was nothing for me to grab at first, but I reached deeper. There, in the depths, I found a mere thread. I pulled it.

More followed the thread. My bones started aching; tiny, sharp jolts ran through the core of my body. Yet again, I pulled.

My muscles began to burn. The itching, burning pain was my body begging me to stop. I didn't listen. I kept pulling.

My eyes started watering and stinging. Shutting them didn't bring relief. Still, I couldn't stop. I pulled.

More magic trickled into my grasp. The world felt further away as a high-pitched ringing filled my ears.

It's still not enough. I need more. I pulled again.

My heart pounded against my ribs, each beat reverberating and pulsing with every bit of pain through my body. It left me gasping for air, rapidly suffocating me. But I ignored the strain. I kept pulling.

My head felt like it was being pulled apart in every direction. Agonizing pulses radiated through my skull and joined the cacophony of pain flooding through me. Still, I refused to yield. One more time, I pulled.

I focused on the magic I had collected. *All that, and I have less than what I started with.*

I gave it to my mother.

Please be enough.

I stared, watching her chest rise and fall ever so subtly. There was no change. *It's not enough. I'm not enough.* Tears soaked the fur on my face further as I slumped to the side of the bed and grabbed my mother's hand.

All my pain from my attempt to help my mother lessened, but it didn't go away. Instead, I couldn't concern myself with it. My mother was dying in front of me, and all I could do was watch. Anything else I felt was nothing compared to the sheer helplessness that almost made me miss the footsteps walking into the room.

I turned and saw Lexia. She looked like she hadn't slept. Her eyes were half-open, and her tail was stiff. *Was she worried about me the whole time?* Between me and her, Gifford lay on the ground, face-first, motionless. There was a slight puddle of drool under his slightly open mouth, and he had a peaceful look on his face. *Someone's having a good dream. But why is he sleeping on the floor like that? That can't be comfortable.*

"Gifford, no." Lexia dropped to her knees and held her mate's head. "Not you too."

When Lexia lifted Gifford's head, he squirmed. His eyes begrudgingly peered open. "Uh, what?" His ears and tail stuck straight up and out. "Wait. The demon?" He turned to Lexia. "There was a demon here. She was holding something strange, and..."

Lexia pulled his head to her chest. "I know," she whispered. "I know."

You know what? He said there was a demon here, and I slept through it? The demon had me perfectly defenseless, and she knows. "Lexia, what are you talking about?"

Lexia looked up at me, and the shock on her face made me jump. "Lucia! What—what happened to you?"

I raised an eyebrow. "What do you mean? And what do you mean, you know a demon was here?"

Zenny walked into the room, followed by Daric and Escaeris. They didn't look too rested, either. Daric kept staring at my sister. He looked angry. *No, not angry. Is he disappointed?* Dinar was the last one to enter and she looked around the room, giving extra attention to the others sleeping in the cots.

Zenny took one look at me and shrieked. "Lucia! What happened? Why is there so much blood?"

"Blood?" I looked down and didn't see any. My nose itched, so I brushed my forearm against it. When I looked at my arm, I saw a red trail on my fur. *I have a bloody nose?* I didn't get any more time to think when Zenny ran over and grabbed my head. She immediately started cleaning my face with the sheet that covered my mother. The blanket was slowly filling with red spots.

"There's blood around your nose, eyes, and ears." Zenny wiped my nose. "You need to tell me, what did you do?"

I turned to look at my mother. "She's not doing well. I wanted to help. So I tried to give her unfocused magic. But I don't have enough. So I grabbed as much as I could, and then I grabbed more. It hurt, but it still wasn't enough."

Lexia's jaw dropped. "You said you couldn't magically exhaust yourself."

Dinar shook her head. "She did more than that." She pointed to me. "You're lucky to be alive. When handling magic, if you feel pain, you must stop. No exceptions. You were literally tearing your body apart."

"I'd hate to agree with the bald one here, but you're no use to me dead," a pompous yet smooth voice added from just outside the door.

I know that voice.

To solidify my suspicions, the Rider of Pain walked through the door, her hooves clopping against the wood and her horns nearly scraping the ceiling.

A vicious growl escaped through my bared fangs. "You!"

I pushed Zenny away as my vision turned red, and I lunged forward. My mind wanted nothing more than to tear that demon apart. Unfortunately, my legs had other plans.

My face planted into the ground, causing more pain to wrack my body. It was hard to move beyond curling up in the fetal position. But I couldn't take my eyes off the succubus.

The demoness looked at me in awe. "What was that? Were you trying to attack me just now? Wow. That was pathetic."

The tone of her voice grated on my ears. I growled even louder, hoping to drown her voice out. My claws dug into the wood of the floor. But as I tried to drag myself towards her, all I did was make four gouges.

Lexia moved in front of me. "Lucia, you know I love you. You know I would do anything to protect and save you, don't you?"

I stopped growling. "Why are you saying that?" *More importantly* —"What did you do?"

Lust crossed her arms and tapped a clawed finger on her elbow. "I came here to solidify the deal your sister made. But after seeing you look so pathetic after seeing that bear die and now with your mother, I'm not sure I want to anymore. You're far too broken to be of any use now."

Broken? "I'll show you broken." As I tried to pull myself towards the mocking demon, my arms felt like they were going to give up. My vision turned a deeper shade of red as I resumed growling.

I wanted to kill her. My mind was made up, and nothing else mattered. But my body couldn't keep up. It couldn't do what I wanted.

Stop. It hurts, a small voice in the back of my mind wheezed. The words were mixed with a weak growl.

I closed my eyes, and I could feel my inner wolf huddling as far from the pain as she could.

I can't fight. I can't run. What can I do?

Sister. Sister can help. My inner wolf was speaking to me. It wasn't something I'd thought possible. But in my situation, it seemed low on my list of priorities.

Yeah, sis can help. I looked up at her, barely holding my body up. "Help me. Stop her."

Lexia looked away and flattened her ears. *Sis?* "I had to do it. There was no other way to save you."

"You're wrong." Daric's voice sounded more hoarse than usual. "There's always a way."

"But we don't have time." Lexia flinched forward. "And I won't lose her." She opened her eyes as she looked at me. "I can't—I won't lose you. Never again. Whatever it takes, I'll keep you safe."

"Even make another deal with a demon?" The venom in Daric's voice was thick.

Lexia curled her tail tightly around her waist as she flinched again. "Yes. If it means keeping her safe. Always."

Daric opened his mouth, but Dinar held up a finger and shook her head. "Not right now," she whispered.

The Rider of Pain rolled her eyes. "You almost aren't worth my time. I'm tempted to call the deal off." She waved her hand and turned to leave.

"Wait," Dinar called after the demoness. "You can help her, can't you?"

The rider stopped and glared at the elf. "Why should I? What would I gain?"

Dinar grinned. "Your lack of denial says you can." The demoness didn't say anything. "You're short on time. You need the creation of the blood anchor stopped. Why don't you stop the mage yourself?"

The demoness clenched her fists. Blood trickled from her fingers. "Because I don't actually know where he is." She spun around and huffed. "Happy? All I can tell you is an impression of a memory I pulled before I killed Envy. That was the last place she knew he was at."

"So tell us," Daric said as he stepped forward. "We don't want the demon king to be summoned just as much as you, maybe even more."

"I could search one tenth of this city in the time he would take to finish." Lust shook her head. "I need someone who knows this town. Maybe I should've use her mother's condition to leverage an advantage and make her do what I need."

"Wait. You can help Mom?" I felt hope for the first time today. "Can you really?"

The demoness rolled her eyes. "This patheticness is not a good look for you." She sighed. "Yes, I can. But your sister and I made a deal. It's time she held up her end."

I turned to look at Lexia. She nodded. "Don't be mad. She said you were placed under a powerful sleep spell, and if I wanted to save you and know where to go to stop the demon king from being summoned, I had to agree to let her know where we are at all times. Also, we have to help her."

"And you get to keep your free will. That was the deal." The Rider of Pain closed her eyes and paused. "I'll save your mother, and since I need you to be useful for now, I'll help you too. But just this once."

"How can you help her?" Escaeris, who seemed like she couldn't stand looking at the demoness, asked.

The demoness shrugged. "By feeding her magic, and a lot of it."

"I did that!" I shouted. "It wasn't enough."

The demon's tail flicked back and forth. "That's because your magic is quite weak. That elf's magic is extremely strong. Stronger than almost every other mortal's. And I'm guessing you didn't focus your magic, am I right?" I nodded slowly. "It requires a specific combination of magic and more than she can summon on her own. Now that I have the power of two riders, I have enough."

I eyed her. "Why haven't you done that already? What are you waiting for? My sister has already agreed."

Lust pointed at me. "You. I need you to agree to the bargain. Your sister can't accept a deal on your behalf. I killed Envy to wake you up. You can't very well agree to something while you're asleep, can you now?"

That makes sense. She tried to get me to work for her when I was trying to rescue Fina. Maybe I can get a little more.

"Do you remember what you offered me before? You said you won't bother this world if I help you." I watched the demoness twitch at my question. She scrunched her face. *Yes, she remembers.* "Add that to the terms, and I won't fight you anymore. As long as you hold up your end of the bargain."

Daric ran towards me. "You can't be serious. Why are you even considering this? She's evil. We should be killing her, not agreeing to work for her."

I eyed the human. "What's stopping you?"

Daric turned and eyed the rider. He gripped the bone sword tighter.

Lust laughed. "Boy, if you think that toy will allow you to even touch me, you're very, *very* wrong. I'd rather not waste my energy on you."

"If you kill him, I will end you." I infused a growl into my words. "I will make sure the demon king is summoned. I will help him hunt you down. I will enjoy watching you suffer. Then I'll kill him." Fear spread across the rider's face. I could even smell it from her. "And if you kill me, well, that's just more wasted time for you."

Daric started to pull his weapon in front of him.

"Don't Daric." Dinar grabbed his wrist. "Don't do that. If we fight now, the demon king will come, and we won't stop him. He *will* win."

Daric continued to glare at the demoness as he relaxed ever so slightly. "But why do we need her? We're the heroes. Heroes don't make deals with the devil."

Lust scoffed. "I'm a demon. Don't lump me in with those degenerates."

Daric's jaw dropped. "There's a difference?"

I sighed. "Daric, that's not important. But not everyone's able to sit on their moral ivory pillar. If she wants to use us, I say we use her back. She doesn't have any interest in our world, so I say the risk is worth it. Mom doesn't have the luxury of time." I looked at Lexia. "I can't lose her too. So if this deal saves her, then so be it." I raised my hand to my sister, but I couldn't reach her face. She grabbed my hand and held it to her chest. "Even though I don't like it, I'm not mad, sis. I know how you feel."

"I knew you would." Lexia brushed a piece of my hair from my eye. "Thank you."

I turned to the Rider of Pain and Death. "I accept the deal if you accept my terms."

The demoness grinned. "Good, then we can get moving." She walked up to me. "Oh, and you might feel a slight bit of discomfort."

She glowed with magic and focused it into a small ball. There was no visible aspect to it.

The magic felt odd as it hit me. There were no words to describe it. It didn't feel like any focused magic I knew.

Suddenly, there was an overwhelming pressure on my chest. It forced all the air out of my lungs. I tried to breathe, but I couldn't. My lungs couldn't expand. The pressure grew, and I thought my entire chest was going to collapse. But it looked like I was just sucking my stomach in and holding my breath after I exhaled.

The pain throughout the rest of my body disappeared, but I fell into my sister's arms as I writhed about, reaching for air.

Lexia panicked along with me as she tried to hold on to me.

Zenny slid next to me. "She's not breathing."

I slapped my hand on the ground and pointed to my face. My mouth was wide open, but I couldn't inhale. *She's supposed to help me, not kill me.*

Zenny gave me a curious look for a moment before she grabbed my head and placed her lips against mine.

I froze as Zenny kissed me. *What's she doing? This isn't the time to kiss me.* My vision blurred, and I could feel myself getting lightheaded.

Then I felt her breathe into me. My chest expanded a bit, but it collapsed the moment Zenny pulled away to take another breath. *Oh, she's not kissing me; she's forcing air into my lungs.* I tried to stop moving to make things easier for her.

She breathed another breath into my lungs, but the same thing happened. Though it didn't collapse completely this time.

I managed to pull a little air in once Zenny leaned back again. My breathing started off in very short, sharp gasps, but each one filled my lungs a little more than the last.

Zenny relaxed. "It worked."

Everyone watched me as I slowly started breathing on my own and got it under control.

Once I was sure I could speak, I looked at Zenny. "What was that?"

Zenny's eyes went wide. "Weren't you telling me to force a breath down your throat?"

I shook my head. "No. Why would I do that?"

"You weren't breathing." Zenny held out her arms. "I had to do something."

Lexia stood up and growled at the rider. "You said you would help her, not kill her."

The demoness walked towards the door. "I've helped you and your mother. Now let's go. We don't have time for this."

There was a tingle in my body as I could feel my magic again. *It looks like I need to hold up my end of the bargain.* I looked at Gifford. He stood next to the window; he was visibly shaking. *His instincts are telling him to run from the demon. I get it.* Mom was still motionless on the bed, but she was taking much deeper breaths.

"If something happens, get Mom out of town as quickly as you can. Got it?" I stood up, and my body felt better. I was a bit weak, but I could at least move freely. "Where are we going? What do we need to look for?"

Lust shrugged. "I don't know exactly. The last known place of Envy's pet was a fenced-in courtyard with a flower garden that's been neglected. It looked like it has lots of flowers, but now they're far too overgrown."

I narrowed my eyes at her. "Did you see any felonweed?"

Lust turned and glared at me. "Yes. Why?"

There was only one person who bothered to grow felonweed in this city.

My legs felt surprisingly stronger as I walked to the door. "I know where to go."

45

LEXIA'S PRESENCE

The furious look on my sister's face scared me. *Lucia, please calm down. You were dying just a few moments ago, and now you're running off.* I sighed as Lucia left me behind and stormed out of the room.

I nodded to Daric and Escaeris. "Keep up with her. Please, Dinar, you too." Dinar raised a hand towards me. I shook my head. "Don't worry about me. Keep my sister safe until I catch up."

Dinar looked at the others in the room, likely seeing what I had noticed. The other patients in the room were all dead. They weren't breathing or moving, and the commotion we'd made should have woken them if they were asleep.

Dinar had a sour look on her face as she pulled the hood of her cloak up. "I hope you two don't regret this."

So do I.

I turned to Zenny. "Go with Gifford if he leaves. Keep our mother safe."

Zenny looked at the occupied beds. "What about everyone else?"

"They're dead." Dinar pointed to the closest corpses. There were two puncture wounds on their necks with a small trail of black blood coming from them. "The demon bit them. Her venom is likely more lethal than ever now." The elf's voice couldn't hide the pain she was undoubtedly feeling. "If you have to help everyone, start leaving now. Take whoever will go." Dinar left.

"You want me to start an evacuation?" Zenny's eyes glistened. "Do you think Lucia is going to fail?"

I grabbed her shoulders. "Did you see her? Do you know what she did to herself? I'm preparing for the worst. Lucia is distracted right now. But if things go wrong, she'll need you and Mom safe and alive."

Zenny swallowed hard. "She needs me? But others need me too."

I let her go as Gifford wrapped his arms around my shoulders. He said, "Please. She just cares about her sister. She's worried, tired, and this situation is a lot. What I think she means is that the others here need doctors. But Lucia needs her friend."

There's that spark of brilliance I love.

"That's you," I said. Zenny wrapped her arms around herself. "Lucia lost her mate. If she loses another so close to her so soon afterwards, I'm afraid there won't be much left of my sister to save."

"Okay." Zenny's voice was soft, yet I knew without a doubt she would do what was best for Lucia. "I'll go with Gifford, and we'll get Nora out of town. Find us at your home."

I nodded and gave my love a tight hug. He returned it and gently rubbed my back. "Stay safe. You're more important to Lucia than the rest of us."

"I know," I whispered before turning to leave.

I was tired. I wanted to curl up and sleep in Gifford's arms. Unfortunately, there was no time to rest. When I exited the building, which nobody made any indication that the Rider of Pain and Death had just strolled through, Dinar stood with her arms crossed as she stared towards the northeast.

The elf turned and walked towards me. "Lucia said they were headed to the orphanage she grew up in. She said you'd know where to go."

I nodded. "She took me there once. The lady running the place, Melody, was sweet."

Dinar waved her hand in the direction she was looking earlier. "Lead, and I'll follow."

We took off and tried to catch up. Lucia would likely still arrive before us, but I dropped to all fours and sprinted as much as I could. Dinar surprised me—she was able to keep up. It looked like the wind was at her back. *But there was no wind today. It must be magic.*

Elves always glowed with a subtle hint of magic in their bodies, but I was never as sensitive to seeing magic as Lucia was. If Dinar was using magic, I could only guess.

As we ran through the streets, I saw knights going from door to door, knocking, talking, or entering if no one answered. Most only gave me a single look before resuming their task.

I know where to go, but if I tell them, they'll see the demon, and we'll have to say we made a deal with her. That will cause problems for Lucia. So they can't help us. We have to do this on our own. Besides, they'll only slow us down.

But two faces I saw running towards us as I turned on the larger road were two faces I wanted to see. Anna waved her arms, and Fina sped up to stop in front of us.

I almost tackled the lynx woman when I saw her. "You're safe, thank goodness."

"Something wrong?" Fina ended our hug and pushed me to arm's length.

"Yeah, someone's creating a blood anchor." Dinar came to a stop next to us. "Lucia and Daric are already heading to the location."

Anna finally caught up and leaned forward, placing her hands on her knees as she panted. "How does she know where?" *She really needs to exercise more. I've had to just so I can somewhat keep up with Lucia.*

Anna's breathing had a slight wheeze to it as she took a deep breath and started composing herself. "Something bad is happening in this direction. It feels like a blood anchor, but not quite."

"Anna, I'm going to need you to stay calm." Dinar raised a hand, ready to stop the half-elf. "Lucia and Lexia made a deal with the sin of lust, who's calling herself the Rider of Pain and Death now. In return for saving Lucia and Nora's lives, they have to help the demon. That includes stopping the creation of the blood anchor. Lucia thinks it's being created at the orphanage."

Anna stopped breathing for a moment as her eyes blinked slowly.

"We don't have time." I pushed Fina forward and started heading towards the orphanage.

Anna and Dinar followed behind. More people turned to look at us as we ran through the street. Some of the knights even started following us. *Please don't cause problems for Lucia.*

We made it to the orphanage with a small company following us. Daric stood in front of Lucia while Escaeris held my sister back from entering the building.

"Lucia, we need to wait for your sister and Dinar. What if this is a trap?" Escaeris shoved Lucia backwards. *How is she strong enough to do that?*

"I don't hear anyone." Lucia dug her toe claws into the ground. "That can't be good. There should be the sound of someone in there. Melody could be in trouble."

Daric grimaced. "As much as I don't want to agree, we need Dinar's expertise. What if there are hostages? We need to save them."

My sister growled. "If we take too long, there won't be any hostages to save." She flicked an ear towards us, then turned her head. "Good. It doesn't matter. Here they... are?" Her eyes went wide and her jaw hung slightly ajar. She lifted her arm and pointed behind me and past Dinar and Anna. "Sis, who are they? Why are they following you?"

Fina and I stopped next to her. While Fina looked like she could run for another half a day, I couldn't. My joints, muscles, and heart would give up before then. I panted as I waved my hand. "Don't know. Don't care." I looked around for the demoness. "Where is she?"

I heard the demoness scream and turned to see her pound her fist against a wall. "What did that dwarf do? It's just a stupid wall." She punched again. This time her fist distorted, and I heard the crunch of the bones breaking. She let out another frustrated scream as she turned and walked towards us. "I can't get in. Get in there before he finishes. He's almost done."

"You weren't joking," Anna whispered as she and everyone else saw the demoness flap her wings and float to a nearby building's roof to sit down.

Dinar sighed. "Unfortunately not." She walked up to Daric. "Were you waiting for us?"

Daric nodded. "Yeah. This looks like it could be a trap. The rider can't enter the building. She keeps mentioning a dwarf. It sounds like he knew she was coming and set up defenses against her."

"Demon!" one of the knights following us shouted, and pointed at the rider.

She turned her head and arched an eyebrow before rolling her eyes. "Ugh. Pests."

The demoness waved her hand, and a ball of black smoke covered it and flew off towards the center of the group of knights that had followed us. Those who had shields raised them. The others took cover with a fellow knight who could grant it.

The ball of smoke grew as it approached the knights. I was too frozen in fear at the sight of the magic to move. My instincts told me to run. Eventually, I slowly started walking backwards for a couple of steps before the knights were engulfed in the thick fog.

The haunting stillness that enveloped the knights in the mist was abruptly shattered by a choir of piercing screams. Just as the screams began, the cloud quickly dispersed, revealing the knights.

Daric ran towards them, but Dinar grabbed the back of his gambeson by the neck.

I gasped as I saw the knights' skin darken and become leathery. Their faces became gaunt, their eyes sunken, and the rest of their bodies shriveled.

The screams died quickly as each body shriveled impossibly thin and stopped moving. Daric wrestled free from Dinar's grasp and kneeled next to the closest knight. He placed a hand on their face.

He looked at the demoness responsible. "You mummified them." He sounded like he didn't believe the words he was saying.

The demoness seemed nonchalant, even amused, by the man's shaking hand as he gripped his unique weapon tighter. "I don't know what you're talking about. But you're wasting time. All they would have been was a distraction, and we can't have any more distractions." She pointed to the orphanage. "Now get in there and stop him from finishing the blood anchor."

Dinar grabbed Daric and pulled him to his feet. "Do you really want to fight her now?" she hissed. "You think you can stop her after a display like that?"

Daric just gritted his teeth so hard that I thought heard something crack. The screams had drawn a crowd. They all started pointing at us and the demoness.

"Sis, let's go." Lucia grabbed me and pulled me into the building. I was lucky I didn't trip on the steps with how hard she was pulling.

The door didn't even slow my sister down. She barreled through without hesitating. Daric, Anna, Fina, Escaeris, and Dinar followed us. After we entered the main hall, there wasn't anyone or anything moving. My fur stood up on end as my tail flicked back and forth.

"Okay. Stop!" Anna held out her hands just as she entered the building.

Lucia and I watched the woman pant for a moment. "What? Is there something wrong?" My sister sounded genuinely concerned.

"Dinar said you made a deal with that monster." Anna pointed out the door. Her face was flushed, and both Lucia and I tilted our ears back from the volume. "She just killed those knights, and... and she smiled. Why? How could you make a deal with her?"

Lucia growled and walked up to the woman. She leaned forward and bared her teeth inches from Anna's eyes. "I had no choice."

The flat tone of my sister's voice left an ache in my heart. *It's not like she wanted to.* The words wouldn't leave my lips as I shook.

Anna flinched.

Daric pulled her back and challenged my sister's glare. "We'll talk about this later." He turned back to Anna. "Right now, let's concentrate on the blood anchor."

Escaeris's eyes looked distant as she leaned against a wall. "I can't take this anymore. It's too much." She slid down the wall and hugged her knees to her chest.

Dinar ran up to the distraught elf and slapped her. "Not now." Escaeris held a hand to the cheek that Dinar had slapped. "Get ahold of yourself. You are a knight. If you're going to break, do it after the mission is over. Not before." She pulled a dagger from her sleeve and held it by the blade as she handed it to Escaeris. "After this is over, you can cry all you want. I'll even cry with you if that'll help."

Escaeris grabbed the weapon with one hand and accepted Dinar's still-offered hand. "Thank you," she whispered.

Lucia shook her head. "What now? I don't think they're in the courtyard, even though that's what the demoness said she saw. If they were there, she wouldn't have to worry about getting inside."

"Do we split up?" I asked.

Daric stomped his foot. "No."

I glared at him. "Why?"

Daric pointed at Lucia and me. "Because you two can't be trusted anymore. If another demon shows up, what's stopping them from making a deal with you? How do we know you won't just work for them?"

Lucia flexed her claws and nearly pounced on the man. "I. Had. No. Choice." Each word forced its way between her fangs.

"In here."

The tension in the room snapped when a voice came from behind the double doors, where Lucia had shown me the classroom. Daric held up his weapon as he approached the door. His body went stiff at whatever he saw.

The weapon clattered against the floor when he dropped it.

Lucia walked over and threw open the second door. "No." Her voice was barely audible. As soon as the door opened, the unmistakable scent of blood flooded my nose. It overwhelmed my other senses for a moment as I saw why.

All of us gasped at the horrid sight in the room. Melody, the kind human woman I had met only once and a few days before we went into our mating season, was lying in the middle of a four-ring spiral of strange symbols. Two puncture wounds on her sides looked like something had stabbed through her torso. The blood that had poured from the gaping holes was rapidly drying.

The symbols were written in one continuous stream of Melody's blood.

But that wasn't the worst part of the sight we saw.

Six children were lined up along the wall. All dead. Their throats were slit, but there was no blood around their bodies, meaning they were moved there after they were murdered.

Our eyes fell on the one living individual in the room.

In a simple brown robe sat a balding dwarf. He was only about forty inches tall, but his shoulders measured the same. He stood up from kneeling in front of the odd spiral painted on the ground to turn and face us. He barely had any stubble on his very square chin. The tips of his thick fingers were dark red from the dried blood. His eyes were bloodshot, and his cheeks were bright pink.

Has he been crying?

"I'm sorry, but you're too late." His voice sounded devoid of all emotion except one: regret. The pain in his voice almost had me feeling sorry for him. "If you believe that I should die for my crimes, I will say that it is the least I deserve. But know that this is for the good of the world. I didn't want—"

Lucia didn't let him finish. She pounced on him and drove her claws right through his chest and out the back. Blood sprayed from the wound and his mouth as he coughed. The dwarf grabbed my sister's arm. Lucia grabbed his hand and bit it off.

More blood gurgled from his mouth.

My sister's eyes were focused as she growled and snarled. *Sis?* I barely recognized her as she started tearing open his chest. Bones and organs flew through the air as my sister shredded the dwarf in a primal display I didn't know she was capable of. I don't know when the dwarf died, but he was undoubtedly dead before Lucia slammed his head on the ground and crushed it.

I slowly walked towards her, my hand held out. "Lucia? It—it's over."

Daric grabbed my arm and pulled me back. "Don't. She might have the frenzy again."

I pushed him away. "That's impossible. She was cured." I strode towards my sister as she stared at the morbid display. "Lucia, are you okay? It's me, your sister."

She turned to me, blood covering her face and the dwarf's arm still in her jaws.

I flinched, but I stepped closer. *No, she needs me. She can't go feral. She's too strong for that.*

"Come here, sis." I held my arms out. "Your big sister will take care of you."

Lucia looked down at the arm in her mouth and, with a look of horror, released it. She stumbled back from the gory mess she had created. Her foot slipped as she retreated. Lucia let out a yelp as she landed on her tail. She scrambled away from the corpses and into my arms and held me tightly—too tightly. I could feel my breath being squeezed out of me.

But I held her and rubbed her back.

My sister held me even tighter. I patted her head and scratched right behind her ear as my vision went blurry. She melted around me, letting me breathe again. Then I noticed the wetness on my shoulder and the faint sobs coming from her.

"Shh." I kept petting her. "You're safe. Your big sister's got you."

"He said we were too late," Anna whispered. I turned to see her pale face as she stared at the spiral. "We are too late."

I turned to look, and the symbols were glowing with magic. *Oh, no.*

"Everyone, out!" Dinar shoved Escaeris and Anna towards the door. "Now!"

Daric stood motionless as he stared at me and Lucia. Dinar grabbed him and pushed him, breaking his wide-eyed, blank stare. She even grabbed the sword, but let it go and screamed.

"What?" Dinar stared at the weapon. "Where did you get that?"

Daric looked at the weapon and picked it up. "The Rider of Death," he said emotionlessly. "Get out of here. I'll cover your escape."

Daric held the sword with both hands as he watched the spiral glow with more than just magic. The glyphs were glowing red, and the space between the symbols turned red. It looked like the floor started moving, swirling even. A black spot swallowed Melody's body and then spread towards the edge of the spiral.

A low, deep growl shook the building. "Finally."

Lucia stopped crying and looked at the scene behind her. A single talon exited the portal. It was as long as I was tall. Fear gripped me when a second matching talon joined the first. They seemed to pull the portal open wider.

I pulled Lucia towards the door. Dinar and Daric weren't far behind us as the two talons turned into six and the portal nearly swallowed the entire room. When we left the orphanage, there was no sign of the Rider of Pain and Death. *At least she's gone.*

The building shook as we heard a loud crash from inside. "Really?" It was the deep, growling voice again. It sounded frustrated. "Of all the places in this pathetic world to break my seal, they do it here?"

Lucia, Daric, and I all exchanged glances before watching the orphanage explode into debris.

Out of the building came a creature almost as large as the building. It looked like a giant lizard covered in jet-black scales with two colossal wings on its back. Each wing held the massive talons I had watched widen the portal.

The black scales shimmered in the sunlight. I could see the muscles beneath shift and bulge. Two horns stretched backwards from his triangular, ridged head. When the creature grinned, he exposed the rows of vicious-looking teeth inside his mouth. Each leg ended in a clawed foot that crushed what remained of the orphanage underneath. His spike-covered tail was the same length as his body. Then he opened his eyes, revealing two glowing purple orbs radiating magic.

That's the demon king?

He raised his two massive wings and flapped them down. More debris flew everywhere.

A large beam of wood came towards us, and Lucia threw me into the air, away from and over the projectile as she ducked under it. I watched as a piece of the brick wall struck her afterwards.

She hit the wall of the building across the street and fell limp.

"No!" I screamed.

When I landed, I scrambled to check up on her. She moved, but it was obvious she was in a lot of pain, her arm held uncharacteristically to her side. My sister hissed as she threw her head back and closed her eyes. "Don't worry about me. I'll be fine."

"Lucia's hurt; we have to run." I turned to see Escaeris lifting some debris that had trapped Dinar.

Dinar stood up, but there was a heavy limp on her left leg. She nodded. "Right, then run."

The demon king took a deep breath as he hovered in the air. When he opened his mouth, a stream of flame engulfed a nearby building.

Lucia saw the flames, scrambled away from me, and limped down the street. I looked back and saw Daric hand something to Dinar as Escaeris picked her up and carried her. He whispered something to her, but I didn't catch it.

"Go. I'll buy you time to get to safety," he said.

Dinar stared at him for a moment. "What are you talking about? What are you doing?"

Daric turned and stared at the demon king. "Being a hero."

NEWSLETTER SIGNUP

Do you want more? More is coming. If you want updates about this series and possibly more, please consider joining my newsletter here:

subscribepage.io/13PBC

I will keep you posted on my progress on future books and projects.

If you don't mind doing some alpha reading, come find me on Royal Road:

https://www.royalroad.com/profile/241783/fictions

Whatever you choose, I hope that you find it in your heart to leave a review on whatever platform you purchased this book from. Authors —including me—love to receive feedback. There is something about algorithms, but that is just a bonus.

It doesn't have to be complicated. Just say what you liked, what you didn't like, and/or your favorite scene or character(s). Or you could simply just hit the rating button. One click and you're done.

www.ingramcontent.com/pod-product-compliance
Lightning Source LLC
Chambersburg PA
CBHW060226030726
47499CB00004B/1203